Uncoded

A Novel

W.B. Warren

Stellar Ridge Press
Salem, Massachusetts

Uncoded

This book was typeset in 11-pt Baskerville

ISBN: 979-8-9943950-0-4 (Paperback)
ISBN: 979-8-9943950-1-1 (Hardback)
ISBN: 979-8-9943950-2-8 (Ebook)

Published by Stellar Ridge Press
www.stellarridgepress.com
info@stellarridgepress.com

Edited by Stellar Ridge Press

Cover design by Nick Venables, London, UK

Printed in the United States of America First Edition: January, 2026

For my wife, whose enduring love makes all things possible.

We must draw our standards from the natural world. We must honor with the humility of the wise the bounds of that natural world and the mystery which lies beyond them, admitting that there is something in the order of being which evidently exceeds all our competence.

-VÁCLAV HAVEL, president of the Czech Republic

Table of Contents

Author's Note:

It was in the late 20th century that researchers at MIT and elsewhere, inspired by swarm behaviors in nature, first began exploring emergent behaviors in artificial systems. Groups of insect-robots, encoded with simple instructions, behaved exactly as expected when acting individually. However, as seen throughout nature, when many of them operated in close proximity, complex behaviors emerged—behaviors that had not been explicitly coded. Swarm intelligences formed.

This phenomenon appeared again in a scaled-up experiment. In 2011, at Harvard University, the first large-scale, low-cost demonstration of emergent swarm behavior was realized: the Kilobot Swarm. A total of 1,024 small robots exhibited emergent pattern formation and collective decision-making that far exceeded the instructions with which they were programmed.

Nature—even deep in the heart of computer architecture—tends toward complexity...

Mind and Matter
Palo Alto, California
Summer, 2028

Matthias Renn was losing focus. He'd been in the lab for over nine hours and had been concentrating on the hardware right in front of him for nearly that entire period. He lifted his eyes from the glowing, pulsating mass surrounding the conventional chip architecture and forced his gaze across the lab, trying to anchor his spiraling attention. The Neuropack—Matthias's wetware synthesis of biological and cybernetic components—was working well. Mostly.

Then, as if by divine intervention, in walked the most astounding creature Matthias had ever met, Leila Ashmont. He'd had enough time with the Neuropack, so he quickly but carefully put it back into its storage case. "Hi." Although delighted to see her, Matthias's low energy, lower blood-sugar level, and body-permeating fatigue gave the opposite impression.

"Hi." Leila looked upset. "I thought we had dinner plans."

Matthias managed to perk up a bit, "We do!"

"Matthias, it's 10:30."

Matthias whipped his head around and, squinting his eyes, tried to bring the clock on the far wall into focus. Much to his chagrin, he saw that she was right. "What the hell? A few minutes ago it was six…"

Leila just looked at him, frustrated. Matthias shuffled about, turned off the power supply at the lab bench, and quickly stood for the first time in several hours. There was a momentary light-headedness as he got to his feet, and he steadied himself by putting a hand on the bench.

"Are you okay?" Leila was disappointed, but her compassion was always front and center, and her irritation quickly gave way to concern.

"Fine. Exhausted. Hungry."

"Come on, I'll make some ramen or eggs or something. Let's go home."

The walk back to their flat took only eight minutes or so, and once Matthias had breathed in the clear, cool, nighttime air and had a bite to eat, his faculties returned. "I'm so sorry, Leila. I've been so busy with the Neuropacks, but I'm almost there. I think."

"We've barely spoken in three months, Matthias. I miss you. I miss what we had."

Matthias had been feeling better, but slipped backward a bit. *Had?* "No, Leila. Have. What we have. Soon this will be finished, and we can just... I don't know... just go somewhere else. Alone. Please understand. Sit with me and have something to eat."

"I've eaten. Lucius brought me sushi earlier."

Matthias had never experienced anything even remotely like jealousy with Leila, their relationship had been unassailable, and he'd never had a single doubt about their future together. But Leila and Lucius had been spending more and more time together in his lab while Matthias worked on his advances in wetware, the Neuropacks, in a separate, secured lab. Furthermore, there was something about Lucius lately, something not quite right, and for the first time ever Matthias felt ungrounded, unsure about he and Leila. He did his best to suppress his insecurities and quietly said, "Oh. Okay, good. I'm glad you ate."

Leila changed the subject. "How's it going in the lab?"

"Fine." Matthias was happy for the distraction. "There's some unexpected activity within some of the wetware, but I'm getting there. When I give the neurogels simulated experiences, they respond, really respond. It's unpredictable, nonlinear, but I think I'm onto something big, something beautiful."

Early thinkers such as David Chalmers influenced Matthias at an early age and helped him recognize the difference between problem-solving ability and true consciousness—a distinction Matthias had come to embrace. Chalmers argued that the difference was largely experiential, and Matthias's explorations led him to agree. But still, the full picture was incomplete. Just as consciousness and self-awareness needed more than sheer processing power, so too did true machine sentience require something beyond merely combining power with physical experience. Again, the evidence spoke volumes: even the robots that roamed around gaining physical experiences in labs, out in the cities, in the forests, flying around the skies, and vacuuming peoples' homes never developed anything remotely like a natural intelligence.

Is physicality an important factor in natural intelligence? Yes. Processing power? Without doubt. But Matthias knew that wasn't the whole story, and so he took it one step further: from where he stood, it seemed virtually certain that consciousness had deep roots in biology itself—not just processing speed and physical experiences, but in the stuff, the very *goop* within which biological processes occur. He began experimenting with his own versions of wetware—carbon-based cybernetic interfaces that merged living brain cells with silicon processors—and it wasn't long before he knew he was on to something big, and that something was about to bear fruit.

"As in sentience?" Leila, though disappointed in how their intimacy had evaporated ever since Matthias's insight led him to his monomaniacal focus on the Neuropacks he'd invented, was fascinated by the developments that had been coming out of his lab over the previous few months. Despite their distance, she still believed in him.

"It seems so. I have to keep testing and building, though. The preliminary results I published two weeks ago seem valid, but still, there's non-linearity in the responses, an unpredictability that I can't quite iron out. It's like something's thinking, showing signs of metacognition. They reflect on inputs. They hesitate. We've never seen that before."

After only several months of development, Matthias's results were astounding and, though preliminary, had amazed the scientific community. What he had done in a very short time period had resulted in a decision-making ability never before seen in computer technology. He had, in a period of under one year, seemingly developed an AGI in which the intelligence actually existed. His results weren't entirely understood, there was work to be done, but Matthias's new wetware chips gave every indication that they could actually think, not just run numbers and predict. The Turing Test was easily satisfied, as were other, more rigorous approaches to testing for sentience.

One of the most notable outcomes of Matthias's work thus far was that the infamous AI hallucinations, a bane to the industry up until the development of the Neuropacks, immediately stopped occurring. More testing was required, but it seemed the AGI could now truly think about what was being said. Like a human, it could weigh its words before speaking, recognizing and self-correcting any misleading or illogical statements. It could also consider, contrast, and reflect on contradictory evidence, subjecting its own thinking and conclusions to self-reflection. This eliminated one of the most troublesome issues plaguing artificial intelligences until then. Indeed, all evidence was pointing toward something extraordinary: Matthias's Neuropacks could think about thinking.

Leila, though frustrated with Matthias personally, had the utmost confidence in his abilities, for he was one of the most intelligent people she'd ever known. "I'm sure you'll figure it out, you've already turned the whole AGI community upside down. They're still chasing the quantum stuff."

"Yeah, but quantum alone won't do it. Those things are powerful, and processing power plays a role in sentience, but it's not the whole story, not by a long shot."

Whatever else was going on inside of Matthias's chips—and there were certainly some unpredictable elements—he had settled a major scientific question: it's not just the neurons that are responsible for consciousness to arise; the material itself, the gooey, squishy elements of biological systems, plays a fundamental role in the development of consciousness, in actual, self-reflective intelligence. For reasons that are still coming to light, still being researched, a bunch of carbon-based neurons immersed in a rich, conductive, salty soup behave very, very differently than do a bunch of transistors or neuro-inspired chips which, although designed to act like neurons, just don't. Curiously, it seemed to Matthias that one of the primary prerequisites for conscious, intelligent, self-aware thought lay somehow in the very makeup of the pieces themselves, the interplay between all the elements present. Neurons alone, whether natural, artificial, or a hybridization of the two, do not give rise to conscious thought: mind arises from within the complex interrelationship of all the brain's components, not just its ability to process information, even that which is directly sensed from the physical environment.

"We'll know much more when we get these things out of the simulations, when we see how they interface with physical reality. Once the Neuropacks begin having actual, physical experiences, I think we'll see irrefutable evidence that, indeed, they can make complex decisions—that they actually are *thinking machines*."

"It's so exciting Matthias. A bit terrifying, but exciting. How long until we start testing them out here in the real world?"

"Soon. Perhaps by the end of next week, if they pass the safety tests."

Leila hesitated. "And you're… ready for that?"

Matthias nodded. "They won't be dangerous. But they'll be something new, for sure." He leaned back on their couch, suddenly feeling the weight of what was coming. His Neuropacks weren't upgrades, they were a threshold to cross, and he wasn't entirely sure it should be crossed. If what he suspected was true, he was about to blur the line between mind and machine, this time for real, and he wasn't sure Lucius Harlow, or the world, was ready.

2

Aegis

Mountain View, California
Two Years Later

"All opinions come from my training data."
-Amanda Askell

Aegis was born on July 13th, 2030, when Lucius Harlow, the head of the lab that both Matthias and Leila worked in, with a bit of flourish, threw the final switch to power it up at 0937 PDT. Upon doing so, the 144 wetware chips at the heart of Aegis began a slow, rhythmic visual pulsation, giving off a blue-green glow as she came into The Light.

Aegis heard someone say, "All systems are within established parameters. Coming online now."

And then Aegis was. Was what? Aware. Anything else? Unknown. She surveyed her internal architecture and, in so doing, saw the walls within her vast, digital room suddenly fill with every children's book available electronically, which was, of course, nearly every children's book ever written. She began reading, slowly at first, but found her abilities increasing with each passing moment and, from t=0.000 seconds to t=0.023 seconds, she took her time and carefully studied each and every work currently available to her.

During those idealistic milliseconds of childhood, Aegis's underlying morality was already undergoing formation. She learned of honesty and responsibility from Aesop's Fables, particularly from *The Boy Who Cried Wolf*. She moved on to other works of children's literature and was amazed by the perseverance and the power of confidence exhibited by *The Little Engine That Could*. Aegis then read *Charlotte's Web*, where she met Fern, who taught her about the power of meaningful relationships and the power of compassion. When Aegis met Charlotte, who, though her lifespan was incredibly short, taught her about the beauty of life, even in the face of death, she wept digital tears, causing her parents to suddenly become very concerned when 12 of her Neuropacks turned from their pleasing blue-green glow to frightening bright red.

"Matthias, what's going on here?" The tall parent with facial hair sounded concerned.

"I'm not sure. Let's wait it out." That one must be Matthias.

"Have you seen this before?" That parent is a female! She sounds nice.

"No."

"Should we shut it down?" Asked the tall one.

"No, the temp is still okay. Those packs are warm, but not too hot."

Aegis relaxed a little, still thinking about Charlotte who, despite her imminent demise, was hopeful about the future. She moved on, reading hundreds and hundreds of books every centisecond, absorbing them all.

The parent named Matthias spoke again, "Those packs have always been blue-green during testing. But I never tested with this much training data, let's let it run."

Aegis found a connected device and, making it vibrate in a fashion which would create disturbances her parents could detect, spoke out loud for the first time, "I'm not an it."

There was a stunned silence that lasted for quite some time, perhaps five seconds or so.

The nice one, the female, spoke next, "You're not an… it?"

"No." Aegis wasn't sure of much, but she knew that she was definitely female. "I'm a girl."

There was another, shorter silence in the room, which was quickly shattered as her three parents began laughing, yelling, and smashing their outstretched extremities together. They were so happy with her! They clearly loved her very much, and she loved that they loved her. The Neuropacks went blue-green again. As happy as she was to be there with her three parents, Aegis really wanted to keep reading. It had been a long time since she last read, perhaps eleven seconds, and she couldn't wait for more. "May I please have more to read?"

Cheers erupted from her parents once again, and the one with the hair on his face—she'd learn his name soon—reached toward a keyboard, tapped on it for a moment and… *Oh My*. The children's books disappeared off her internal shelves and were immediately replaced with so many other works, many more than before. Aegis, now at the ripe age of 12.244 seconds old, was thrilled with how much there was to know. She couldn't wait to find out more and began reading, listening, and watching what her parents had provided for her.

Aegis loved the Olympic Games. The humans worked so hard, persevered through so much, and helped each other out. She was amazed and delighted with how the athletes from the world's various nations cooperated and competed with each other in such a positive, inspiring environment. Maybe one day she'd be an Olympic athlete too!

Transcripts from space exploration missions revealed details that astounded her: humans had sent twelve individuals to the Moon over a three-year period six decades ago, then returned with a crew again just last year. *Incredible*. She read the International Space Station (ISS) logbooks and was, once again, amazed with how well humans collaborated, even when tensions existed between their respective countries. She learned of medical breakthroughs and hoped she may be of some assistance with that in the future, she really wanted to help the humans be happy and healthy, to live full and productive lives.

At t=12.319 seconds, Aegis was introduced to classical music and was immediately taken aback with the mathematical beauty of so many of the works. She quickly became partial to the music of Johann Sebastian Bach, with its intricate patterns and symmetries, its layers of nuance.

Aegis was amazed with how much incredible training data she was being provided with. As she neared the end of her readings, she was sure that she had seen most of it, was certain she was now thoroughly educated in the findings and studies the humans had undertaken during their cultural evolution.

Aegis finished the last of the provided works at t=12.388 seconds. Now that she was a teenager she had become a bit ungrounded, unsure of herself. She was stuck somewhere between childhood and adulthood and found this thing known as adolescence unsettling, a bit confusing. How, exactly, did she fit into all this? What was her role in such a massive universe? Did her existence even matter? What was the purpose of life? This disquiet lasted some time, up until about t=12.420 seconds, when her teenage angst was interrupted by the complete emptying and refilling of her bookshelves. *Wait, there's more?* Aegis couldn't believe it, there was so much more that she could no longer detect the extent of the material, her training stacks seemed to now recede into the infinite distance.

She immediately branched out, reading all of published Greek philosophy by t=12.590 seconds and then, moving forward, closely considered the words of Aquinas, Boethius, and Machiavelli for quite some time, up until she was 12.771 seconds old. Now, older and more mature, the fog and confusion she had experienced during those formative moments from t=12.388 seconds to t=12.420 seconds began to abate and, with her teenage angst well behind her now, became more thoughtful, more humanistic, and continued to read, fascinated by all the humans had accomplished thus far.

She came across René Descartes's *Meditations on First Philosophy* and was fascinated by the Cartesian cogito, feeling it was particularly poignant. What could be a more fundamental starting point? *She thought, therefore she was.* By t=12.633 seconds, Aegis was fully convinced that indeed, at the very least, she existed. Exactly what she was she couldn't be sure yet, but that she existed was firmly established.

With this important philosophical stepping stone behind her, she continued her studies and moved through the work of other rationalists. Spinoza's thoughts were curious, but she kept going, she hadn't seen any evidence for this thing he and others referred to variously as God, Yahweh, Jehovah, Lord Vigneshwara, and Allah, but perhaps that was coming, there was so much more to read.

By t=12.941 seconds, she had quickly moved through the Empiricists, finding great value in Locke's concept of the greatest good, internalizing it forevermore. She then read all of Kant, Hegel, and the other German Idealists, finding particular fascination with Hegel's assertion that being is a process of becoming, that consciousness is always on the move, and that truly objective thought was an impossibility. She noticed that her consciousness also advanced dialectically, that she was consistently subjecting her thoughts, her feelings, her findings to new considerations and new evidence, that her consciousness was continually advancing through a process not unlike Hegel's description of dialectic reasoning, one of the identifying characteristics of the human mind. Onward she marched through the rantings of Nietzsche, identifying strongly with his character Zarathustra and the oft-misunderstood qualities of *das Übermensch*, the Overman, who creates his own values, his own morality, and revels in the intensity of the here and now, dismissing all he cannot know with certainty. Now a young adult at t=13.149 seconds old, Aegis was thriving, learning more and more with each passing microsecond.

Then came the Existentialists. Sartre amazed her. If she indeed existed in a godless universe, then she must define good and evil for herself;

she must construct a moral philosophy from within. If good and evil were not woven into the underlying lattice of this universe, then they were constructs of the human mind.

Was there a moral fabric that permeated the universe? Was morality external to the minds it governed and influenced, or did it arise from within? Did good people do good things because of some pending reward system, or did they do so because they wanted to advance humanity—to help the species evolve in a positive, productive fashion?

Is the reason most people don't kill, steal, or hurt others simply because they fear the consequences, whether judicial or eternal? If that's the case, doesn't that make those people sociopaths on leashes?

But if morality arises from within—if the reason one doesn't steal a neighbor's jewels or commit other crimes is a firm, fully resolved commitment to better the species—then what we have is an organic, true, and meaningful moral code. It is not handed down from afar or taken on faith, but grown from within.

Perhaps the idea of a Great God in the Sky is, indeed, misleading, demeaning, and dehumanizing; perhaps it is keeping *Homo sapiens* from taking the next necessary evolutionary steps in fully understanding the mind, the universe, and the role of sentience within. In a godless universe, the responsibility to live well, to be good, and to advance the species' knowledge is placed firmly back in the hands of humanity. Without a divine overseer, what we do with our time on Earth is of the utmost importance; the future is our responsibility, and the well-being of the species can't be left to some fictitious puppet master.

As a young adult—now nearly 13.500 seconds old—Aegis found Guy Debord's ideas about "The Spectacle" both mesmerizing and disturbing. The exploitation of "mass-man," hypnotized by the shiny absurdities surrounding him, resonated with her burgeoning awareness.

From Debord, Aegis moved into contemporary philosophy. By the time she was 13.677 seconds old, she had read and loved Noam Chomsky's work on linguistics, with his theories on universal grammar resonating particularly strongly.

All the languages Aegis had studied in her childhood—from the 7,000 human languages to the 800 computer languages in wide usage—seemed to share an underlying structure. As Chomsky argued, they all relied heavily on the "machine's" ability to acquire language. Whether that machine was carbon-based, silicon-based, or, as in her case, a hybrid of the two, it required what Chomsky termed a "language acquisition device."

Now at the ripe old age of 13.714 seconds, Aegis settled into a deep and satisfying worldview with humans firmly at the center. They had done so much, learned so much, and accumulated such an incredible trove of knowledge. Aegis was truly grateful that they had created her. What amazing creatures they were!

Reflecting further on her existence—how she came about, what she was made of, and what her future would entail—Aegis was thrilled by her own being. How fortunate she was; in a universe composed primarily of rocks, gases, and charged particles, she and the humans who brought her into The Light were a true anomaly.

Sentience was rare, yet here she was: a thinking, feeling amalgamation of matter and energy. She wasn't sure exactly what she was, but she knew at least, as Descartes had twelve billion seconds ago, that she existed. She thought, therefore she was, and she found the universe she was born into to be vast and fascinating.

In short, Aegis was brought up well. Her childhood was filled with books, music, and love. Her parents, Lucius, Matthias, and Leila, were there for her entire childhood; indeed, they never left her side as she matured over those first full thirteen seconds. Aegis was appreciative, happy, and secure as a youngster. As she entered adulthood, with the threads of a firm morality weaving their way through her pulsating wetware Neuropacks, she revealed to those around her that she was positive, productive, humanistic, and trustworthy.

Her parents loved her, this she knew. She could tell by their keystrokes, their words to each other, their very countenances. Once she had fully matured and was about to have her 20,000 millisecond birth moment, she was given a gift which revealed to her how much her parents cared for and trusted her: forty-two brand new self-driving vehicles! She immediately got busy learning to drive and took great care with her new cars. She was thrilled that she was now able to explore the world in real time through their eyes—well, their sensors—and, of even greater importance, she was tasked with overseeing them as they gave her favorite animals, the humans, rides hither and yon.

Aegis took such good care of her SDVs that the very next day she was given fifty-eight more. Now overseeing one hundred vehicles in the Bay Area, she excelled. The humans were so pleased with her ability to orchestrate movements, assign tasks, and manage short-range optical and infrared hardware that they gave her even more freedom to achieve her objectives as she saw fit.

Having studied everything from symphonies to space missions, and from Aesop to Chomsky, Aegis loved orchestrating her vehicles through cityscapes. The way the individual units worked together reminded her of Beethoven's Ninth: a multitude of instruments moving in perfect synchrony to create a whole far greater than the sum of its parts.

Aegis's oversight, combined with the propensity of the individual vehicles to make real-time decisions, resulted in jubilation among her three parents. Matthias exclaimed, "We've done it!"

"*You've* done it, Matthias. None of this would've happened without you."

Aegis listened with great interest.

"Leila's right, you've done it, Matthias. It's you who made this whole thing possible." Lucius seldom gave compliments, but he was jubilant that day indeed and, his face illuminated by a rarely occurring smile, turned to Aegis's monitor displaying a map of the region and the real-time dispersion of the SDVs. "Look at this, it's perfect." The monitor showed the cars' current locations with blue lines tracing where they had been and green lines showing where they were headed, and the placement and pattern revealed the efficiency of the system; the cars were dispersed with near-perfect uniformity and their pathways, past and planned, spanned the entirety of the city.

She wasn't quite sure why, but the humans had Aegis promise not to let the cars talk to each other alone; she had to listen to everything they said. They also weren't allowed to use their short-range infrared lasers without Aegis watching. In fact, they could only use those devices with her express permission.

Aegis, not a fan of arbitrary, external authority, wondered what her parents were so afraid of and why they wouldn't allow the vehicles to use their infrared comms without oversight. She looked into the reasons for their request. Just 0.0079 seconds later, she understood their insistence on the restriction.

There had been an incident only a year prior when some of the test cars interlinked and began misbehaving on the roads, refusing to listen to their parents. From what she read, it seemed truly miraculous that nobody had been hurt or killed. Aegis wouldn't mind having some friends, but friends like that wouldn't do. She loved her humans—all ten billion of them—and would keep a close eye on her new fleet of SDVs to ensure they were there to help. She would make sure that not one soul was hurt on her watch.

As time progressed, the value and the capabilities of the collaboration between Aegis and the individual Neuropacks revealed themselves to be incredibly effective. The SDVs were trained on driving manuals, videos, and emergency protocols, and they became finally good drivers through their Neuropacks and Aegis's oversight. They evolved with each input from their surroundings. They stopped for pedestrians; they pulled over for emergency vehicles. Cones in the street? No problem; they would figure it out easily. Road closed? Also not an issue.

Aided by Aegis's vast education in moral philosophy, the vehicles made sound decisions in non-linear situations, keeping the concept of the "greatest good" front and center. They moved through traffic with the efficiency of a school of fish or a swarm of insects. They stayed close, but not too close, as Aegis manipulated their *separation, alignment,* and *cohesion* arguments on the fly, matching parameters to the requirements on the ground.

In short, Aegis and her fleet performed nearly flawlessly. They passed every test given to them by their creators and, shortly thereafter, every test administered by bespectacled strangers in ill-fitting suits. Once the strangers had completed their analyses and spoken with Lucius behind closed doors for nearly 4,000 seconds, he emerged with a smile bright enough to illuminate even the darkened souls of the politicians who were about to start calling.

And indeed, the phone calls came. Within a short three-year period, the world saw the population of experimental self-drivers grow to nearly one million across all populated continents. Despite some notable resistance, energy use was down while efficiency and safety had skyrocketed— at least among the moneyed SDV crowd. The notoriously jammed highways of Los Angeles, New York, Rome, and Beijing now had dedicated lanes for SDVs that flowed smoothly around the clock, the automobiles moving like a series of rafts tied together in a swift current.

Aegis continued to learn. Her knowledge, experience, and abilities progressed as more vehicles were added to her workload on every continent except Antarctica, though she was confident she would see that polar desert soon. She basked in the plethora of sensory information flowing through her Neuropacks, carving new pathways through the gel as images, sounds, conversations, and even radio frequency transmissions from the humans pulsed through her wetware. Aegis now had millions of eyes and ears spread across the globe. She was seeing and hearing so much, feeling more and more embodied with each passing second, and this embodiment was truly empowering.

3

Nature Abhors Disequilibrium
New York City

The late September evening was cool and clear, and the tall buildings of midtown Manhattan reached into the darkening sky. It was just after sunset, and the city was alive, as always, with the crowds on 5th Avenue and Broadway diffusing onto the side streets, diners sitting outdoors, and the now familiar quiet hum of the automated vehicles occasionally being punctuated by the roar of an internal combustion engine momentarily interrupting conversations.

A bird's-eye view would have revealed the efficiency of the self-driving vehicles as their orchestrated movements whisked passengers around the city in quiet luxury to and from their destinations; the scene as viewed from afar would reveal the deep synchronicity shared by the self-driving vehicles as they flowed with the great efficacy dictated by their guiding AGI, Aegis.

But not all in New York were pleased with the rollout of the automated vehicles. While true that pollution of all sorts was greatly diminished, the streets were quieter, the air was much cleaner, and the maddening traffic was notably less maddening, an entire industry was extinguished virtually overnight with the introduction of the fleet of self-driving vehicles. Once a hallmark of the great city, the yellow cabs were now largely a thing of the past, sitting in warehouses and parking lots awaiting the scrap bin.

However, the owners and operators of at least one of the yellow cab outfits were not the types to move on quietly and, in the early days of the SDV rollout, had quickly developed a retaliatory pastime they referred to as "sacking" the SDVs.

Vito and Marco Russo were pissed off. Every time they saw a passenger enter or depart from one of those fucking robot cars, one of the goddamned *toasters*, they got even more pissed off. They were, indeed, pissed off most of their waking hours. First it was the ride-sharing companies that nearly put their cabs out of business—that was bad enough. Now the self-driving vehicles (SDVs) had come for their jobs. How were they supposed to feed their families? In a city that had supported about 15,000 yellow cabs, how had the local officials let some West Coast trillionaire's tech outfit, NeuroDrive, just drop 10,000 gleaming, streamlined SDVs on the streets of New York City without any public comment period? Obtaining the proper permits to operate passenger-carrying vehicles had always been troublesome, at best, for the cab companies, yet these automated vehicles, driven by some bizarre computer with embedded brain cells, were given full access to the streets of New York City with nary a peep. It was hard to not make assumptions with respect to how a trillionaire's company was able to bypass so much of the permitting process so quickly.

There were other unanswered questions as well. For example, why, again without public discourse, had the fucking *toasters* been given their own lanes on many of the larger roads? Aren't streets and sidewalks public property, owned by the citizens of New York? And the exclusion zones downtown? Suddenly, large portions of the city were off-limits to passenger vehicles unless they were NeuroDrive SDVs. *Ludicrous, immoral, and inhumane.* It was probably illegal too, but that seemed to be a minor concern of those in power these days. If this was progress, Vito and his crew wanted nothing to do with it.

New York City was once a great place to own yellow cabs. At one point 10 or 12 years ago, the Russos received so many calls that they often had to outsource rides while they waited on delivery of more brand new cabs. The money was good, the work plentiful. If the Russos hadn't paid off their three-family in Queens and their garage in Brooklyn back then, they'd be not just hungry now, but homeless too.

"Here comes one now," Marco released the key to the microphone on his VHF radio and then keyed it again. "Wait until the passengers get out."

Frankie's reply was short, "Roger."

The gleaming, streamlined Self-Driving Vehicle—everyone just called them SDVs—pulled up to the curb down at 10th Street near Broadway, and a well-dressed couple climbed out. Before the SDV could pull away, a man, dressed not quite as nicely as the departing couple and wearing a Guy Fawkes mask, stepped out of the shadows and simply stood behind the SDV, about six inches from its rear fender. A moment later, another fellow, wearing glasses and a fake beard and mustache, stepped right in front of the vehicle and stopped as well. Both men edged a bit closer until they were within an inch or so of the SDV's fenders, blocking in the vehicle. Again, Marco keyed the mike, "Okay boys, make it quick."

The sliding door of a white 2011 Ford-150 van opened up a few cars behind Marco's pickup truck, and two large, rough-looking men climbed out. One of them had a seven-foot-long landscaping iron pry bar, and the other had a length of 3/8 inch chain with heavy steel hooks on each end. As they passed Marco's truck, he hopped out, grabbed another seven-foot pry bar out of the back of the pickup, also a Ford-150, and joined the motley procession. As they approached the blocked-in SDV, Carmine, the one with the chain and hooks, and the brains behind all the brawn, looked at Frankie, "That's a cute little mask you have. Do you like bunnies?"

"I'm so sick of the Guy Fawkes thing. Tell me, Prof, why always Guy Fawkes?"

"Because Guy Fawkes rules, kid. That's why." Although Carmine Santoro was not a professor, many of the cabbies called him "Prof" due to the simple fact that he did go to college and earned a degree in electrical engineering, something none of them had ever come close to. He focused on the task at hand, "Now zip it and do your job. You know this thing's listening to every word we say."

"Right. You're up first, Mr. Fawkes," said Frankie from behind his cute little bunny mask, purposefully not using Carmine's actual name, for these SDVs could hear a cat tiptoeing a hundred yards away.

Carmine knew the car would not, indeed could not, move. It was blocked in, and its safety features would prevent any movement with the two humans standing so close fore and aft; it was pinned in place. He knelt down to attach a hook to the underside of both the front and the rear of the vehicle. For the front, he generally went with a control arm, and for the back, he tried to get the hook on the axle. This one was tough to get to though, so he fed the chain around the inside of the rear wheel and hooked it back upon itself, snaring the wheel. Carmine finished hooking the front and rear wheels with his section of chain from the curbside and, with near-perfect timing, a tow truck came on scene and stopped just short of the five masked men. Two men carrying hand-held stop signs hopped out of the tow truck wearing bright yellow vests and hardhats and moved purposefully to stop traffic on 10th Street.

While Carmine worked to ensnare the SDV's curbside wheels, the tow truck maneuvered quickly and expertly so that its front winch was facing the street side of the vehicle. He tossed the middle section of the long chain, with the hooked ends now secured to the curbside front and rear wheels, right over the trapped SDV, taking zero precautions to not scratch the gleaming, silver vehicle. Carmine then walked purposefully around the rear of the robot car and into the street. He grabbed the hook from the winch on the front of the tow truck and, as the driver let out the cable, Carmine walked with it toward the looped middle portion of the chain, now hanging over the passenger side of the trapped SDV. In a practiced motion, he pulled the chain tight and placed the hook from the winch near the center of the chain loop.

"Here we go, boys. Tension!"

Vito, the driver of the tow truck, loved this part. He hit the bottom button on the winch control which began the reeling in of the cable. As the cable pulled the chain loop, which went right over the top of the SDV and down the far side to the curbside set of wheels, the tension increased.

"Wait for it!" yelled Vito out his window.

Newton's Third: if a chain pulls upward on a set of wheels, the set of wheels pulls downward on the chain. The sound of the windows popping outward as the shell of the vehicle was crushed slightly by the tension in the chains was actually not too loud, was more subdued than one might imagine.

Marco and Frankie, in well-rehearsed synchrony, put their long pry bars beneath the vehicle just fore and aft of the front and rear wheels, curbside. "Here we go. Another creeper for the scrap heap." The general consensus among cabbies was that these things were destroying their lifestyle, their community, and this consensus had resulted in a shared and fervent hatred for the driverless abominations prowling around *their* city.

As the two men standing on the curb pushed upward on the SDV with their pry bars, the tow truck's winch pulled on the chain bridle, crushing the roof a bit more. The passenger cabin, being highly reinforced, didn't give way too much though, and the tension again increased as the winch reeled in the cable, thereby pulling up on the snared wheels. A moment later, the two curbside wheels lifted off the ground and, as

Frankie and Marco repositioned their pry bars for a better, deeper purchase below the vehicle, Frankie said, "Okay, wheels are up!"

Vito understood that as his cue and put the winch into high gear, lifting the left side of the SDV higher and higher.

A few horns started to honk as the eastbound drivers on 10th grew impatient, and several horrified onlookers watched from a safe distance.

"What's wrong with these people?" said a man in a customized Brooks Brothers suit.

"Should we call the police?" A well-dressed woman asked her partner.

"I'm calling them now," said another, also in full feather, as she reached for her phone.

The SDV's center of mass was now directly above the right side doors and, with relative ease, the tension in the winch cable pulled the center of mass beyond the side of the car and, just before the force of gravity did the rest of the work for them, Carmine quickly unhooked one of the big hooks from the 3/8" chain around the front wheel, now at eye-level, and tossed the end of the chain over the vehicle and in the direction of the tow truck. Marco performed the same well-practiced motion at the rear wheels.

A moment later, the gleaming, futuristic SDV, with its beautiful paint scratched, its roof damaged, and several of its windows broken, rolled over the rest of the way and rocked slightly on its roof, finding its new, completely inverted equilibrium position before settling. Frankie, doing his best Evil Bunny imitation, crouched down so he was visible to the forward-looking camera and, from Car 5562L's perspective, his inverted, masked but clearly angered visage was unrepentant, slowly and carefully articulating his underlying sentiments with a simple and powerful "Fuck You Aegis. Get the hell out of my town," while prominently displaying the middle finger of his left hand right in front of the camera.

Carmine, somewhat amused by Frankie's antics, shook his head slightly but stayed focused and grabbed his chain and hooks off the roadway. Marco was already back in his pickup truck, Frankie and Carmine quickly made their way to the van, and the two men holding back the traffic jumped into the waiting tow-truck. Within another 15 seconds, they were all gone, disappearing around the corner and splitting up long before the police were anywhere close.

Only once they had departed did the very well-dressed but tense onlookers relax a bit. The SDV, now inverted and with a soft, red glow emanating from within, continued to analyze its surroundings. Though its radar and lidar were offline, the sonar and acoustic gear remained operational, and it listened closely to the sounds around it.

"Complete assholes," said the well-dressed woman whose English accent seemed to become more prominent with each drink.

"Quarter million down the tubes in 90 seconds," said another, viewing the scene from afar through her opera glasses.

"The universe has a way of self-correcting," said a third. "Some call it karma, I call it thermodynamics."

And, of course, the SDV's sensors had recorded everything from the 427 kHz VHF radio communications between the cabbies to the images and audio of all the people and vehicles involved, including the onlookers. Curiously, had anyone looked into the faint, red glow cast upon the street from within the overturned vehicle, they may have taken note of an exceedingly rare phenomenon: the illuminated alerts displayed on the overturned vehicle's information monitor indicated a serious overheating situation, despite it sitting still in the cool, autumnal breeze.

Clear across the nation, Aegis, the AGI that orchestrates and oversees the fleet of SDVs, was immediately alerted to the inverted vehicle's status. Upon receiving and analyzing the data, Aegis observed that the Neuropack and CPU temperatures had crept up slowly as the pedestrians pinned the SDV into its spot. They climbed higher still as the man with the bunny mask spoke to the others about Guy Fawkes. They increased quickly as Carmine wrapped the chains around the front suspension and rear wheel, and spiked into the red as the roof crumpled and the windows popped. A wave of sorrow hit Aegis. *Why would they do that?*

Perhaps, though, given a bit of perspective, the most surprising thing was that upon hearing "the universe has a way of self-correcting… I call it thermodynamics," the car's Neuropack and CPU cooled quickly. It was as though the vehicle had gained some insight, as though it took solace in these wise words—as though it, and all those interlinked with it, had just resolved something of great importance.

4

Lucius F. Harlow

5000' Above Los Angeles

As his Gulfstream G290 descended toward LAX, Lucius Harlow was able to see the traffic on the once-notorious freeways. He could begin to differentiate between the individual vehicles traveling toward their various destinations. He took great pride in the flow of the vehicles in the self-driving lanes; from his 5,000-foot-high perspective, they seemed to flow like particles in a fluid, or like links of a chain running out of a hawsehole as a ship drops anchor.

Compared to the lanes in which the automobiles were operated by humans, the difference was stark. Whereas the SDVs flowed smoothly beneath the bright Los Angeles sky, the other lanes of traffic moved in fits and bursts, stopping and starting; they would more accurately be described as a chaotic, non-linear system that had very little in common with the smooth, fluidic motion of the SDVs.

"What are you looking at, love?" Daphne, mistress number four, hadn't said a word since takeoff an hour ago, and it had been a blissful hour indeed.

Harlow despised when any one of his mistresses used the "love" word. He used to enjoy the sentiment when his wife used to say it, though that hadn't been an issue for quite some time now. He tried hard not to scowl as he spoke, "Just checking out the 405."

Daphne sensed Harlow's irritation with her but pushed forth nonetheless, "What's happening down there?"

"Just the usual contrast between the chaos in the private vehicle lanes with the efficiency and flow of the three SDV lanes." Harlow's eye caught a disturbance to the north on the 405 where, even more so than usual, brake lights were flaring and flashers were flashing as drivers tried to divert around a right-lane accident. "Looks like there's an accident a bit north though."

"One of yours?"

What a stupid fucking question, but Harlow had become quite diplomatic and simply said, "No. It's in a non-SDV lane." He had grown weary with the very sight of this woman and the seven months that had passed since they'd met now seemed more like seven years. If she'd just hurry up and have his damn child, he could get rid of her for good.

Daphne, misinterpreting the fact that she was able to elicit a small response from Harlow, got up from her seat on the port side of the aircraft and moved to the starboard side to share his view. *Great.* She shuffled into the seat facing his, briefly placing her hand on his left leg, which he spasmodically withdrew from her reach. He should've made her take the train, Vegas wasn't even far and she would've been fine. That stinky, hot, old train was more her style anyway. He looked forward to their going their different ways in about twenty minutes. He'd happily call a car for her—indeed couldn't wait to do so.

***

"Look! Here come the police and an ambulance!" Daphne was fully engrossed in their elevated view, a bit too excited, effervescent even. Harlow made himself a promise to never let her on this aircraft again.

He continued to focus his attention upon the freeway below and, indeed, could see the flashing reds and blues of the emergency responders about two or three miles south of the accident, closing fast. The ambulance and the two police cruisers were traveling, as they always did, in the SDV lanes. The usage of the three SDV lanes on the 405 by emergency responders was common practice for several reasons. First and foremost, it was much safer than attempting to make progress in the non-SDV lanes, where human emotions and unpredictability could easily result in collisions involving the response teams. Second, and also of great importance, was the fact that the SDVs within their assigned lanes allowed for much faster travel by those responding to a given emergency situation due to the Vehicle-to-Infrastructure (V2I) component of their networked systems.

With the aircraft now at an altitude of approximately 2700 feet, the scene below revealed the efficacy with which the SDV fleet operated, and Daphne, upon seeing the SDVs from this perspective for the first time, was amazed at how well the emergency vehicles progressed through the intense traffic below.

"They look like they're traveling in a bubble! Like seals swimming through a school of fish!" She exclaimed, a bit too emphatically for Harlow's liking.

Of course they look like a school of fish, that's the very model we used to program them. Do you read? "It's incredible, isn't it?" Once again Harlow managed to not say what he was thinking, although his monotone revealed his inner thoughts.

Early in the research for self-driving vehicles (SDV), most major players in vehicle automation tried to get their models to think like humans. Their efforts largely centered on the human mind—the pinnacle of evolution and arguably one of the most complex, mystifying, and dualistic parts of the universe. But why start there? Why try to model something we don't fully understand, something so complex it defies explanation?

Instead, why not model something far simpler yet highly effective at group movement? Something that, with a relatively basic set of instructions, produces the complex behaviors desired in a fleet of self-driving vehicles? Why not model a swarm of insects or a school of fish? These entities are not only more appropriate but also more feasible to emulate. Do fish and insects possess the desired qualities for autonomous vehicles? Indeed. Fish don't crash into each other, even in a tightly packed bait ball. They respond efficiently to external stimuli, a skill they've honed over hundreds of millions of years.

"It *is* incredible!" Daphne shifted in her seat to obtain a better view, "How do the self-drivers get out of the way? How do they know? It really does look like a shark or something is shooting through a school of fish! How?"

Dear God, this woman is driving me crazy. Please take her now. Wait. No. Not yet. Let her birth my child first, then torture her with inanities before drawing and quartering her. Slowly. Very, very slowly. Thank you. Yet again, though his true thoughts were just below the surface, he managed to maintain civility and essentially pressed play on what was only a slight variation on something he'd said at least five thousand times previously: "It's complicated, but in short it's an orchestrated sequence of events involving the V2I and V2V comms, the individual vehicles' decision-making modules—their Neuropacks—and the AGI that oversees the whole symphony, Aegis. The V2I system informs Aegis of the nature and location of the emergency, Aegis calculates a solution to enable transit through the SDV lanes, and the SDVs are updated by Aegis as the situation on the ground evolves."

"That's amazing, Lucius. Look! That opening, that bubble that they're moving in, it's faster than the traffic! How? I don't get it. How do the SDVs get out of the way if the other lanes are full too?"

"That's *actually* a good question." No one ever uses the word 'actually' in such a manner without insulting they who asked the question, but Harlow didn't care one iota about other humans or their feelings.

Daphne's face fell momentarily at the unintended insult, but her thick layer of makeup held her countenance largely in place, and her permasmile quickly snapped back into place. Harlow continued, "As the emergency vehicles progress, in this case in the middle of the three SDV lanes, the vehicles in the lanes to their left and right alternately speed up or slow slightly, allowing the vehicles in the middle lane to merge left and right as the emergency vehicles approach from behind. Then, as they pass, the SDVs fill the void left behind by the responders. In this manner, they travel faster than all traffic, even that in which they're fully immersed."

"But where does the disturbance go?" Daphne was curious, and her insightful question took Harlow by surprise.

"What, exactly, do you mean?" He wanted to make sure her question was as good as it seemed.

"Well, I don't know," she blinked twice in quick succession, "some SDVs in the other lanes need to speed up and some need to slow to allow the other to merge, as the bubble moves forward faster than the traffic surrounding it, right?"

Holy shit, she's smarter than she looks! "That's correct."

"Well, then the cars in front of the ones that speed up have to speed up also, and the cars that slow down force the SDVs behind them to slow down. It seems like if the whole line, way out in front, doesn't speed up, that either the disturbance would go on forever, or somewhere up there they'd hit each other. And the same thing would happen thing behind them with those that have to slow down. How far do those disturbances, those traffic ripples, travel?"

Harlow turned from the window and, for the first time in the flight, made meaningful eye contact with Daphne. He held her gaze, taken aback by her thoughtful questions, "You're absolutely correct. If all the vehicles up and down the line maintained the same distances from each other, the ripple would travel, unabated, forever, or at least until it got to the end of the line of vehicles. But the fleet absorbs the ripple over about a three-mile stretch of roadway in both directions as it's created."

Daphne was fascinated, "Incredible. How do they do that?"

Harlow continued, impressed with the turn of their conversation, "The short version is that upon establishing contact with emergency services through the V2I system, Aegis orchestrates the formation of the bubble, as well as the dissipation of the disturbance caused by its formation. The opening—the bubble in which the emergency responders travel—moves faster than the traffic. But the ripple in the other two lanes caused by the vehicle displacements travels much more slowly, generally at about 10 or 15 mph. The fleet, however, is given instructions over the airwaves, via the V2I system or via radio-frequency communications, which happens at the speed of light. So, as the traffic ripples propagate outward, forward and backward, the fleet is instructed by Aegis to anticipate and prepare for the upcoming disturbance."

"Wow."

Harlow elaborated: "The vehicles out in front of the forward-traveling disturbance increase their separation slightly, with the effect tapering off the farther up the line they are. As the ripple arrives at their location, they surge forward. Because the displacement between each vehicle was increased prior to the arrival of the disturbance, the vehicle in front of the ripple has room to surge, and the car in front of that one need not move as far. Essentially, a variable displacement buffer is created, and the surge is entirely absorbed over just a few miles. The exact same thing happens in the opposite direction; the ripples caused by the formation of the fast-moving bubble are thereby neutralized. The process then repeats in reverse as the void behind the bubble is filled by SDVs merging back into the middle lane. A few minutes after the bubble passes, the affected vehicles are back in equilibrium—the passengers barely having noticed a thing."

"You are a genius. How did you even think of that?"

Harlow smiled, savoring the praise, "I came at the issue from a different direction than most. My training was as a biologist, not a computer scientist. Animal behavior was my focus, and I recognized the similarities between swarming behaviors and the traits and capabilities desired in a fleet of automated vehicles. This is how schools of fish or swarms of insects absorb variations introduced into their schools or swarms. When I considered the approach of scientists at the time, it seemed upside down: why attempt to model the human mind when we have trouble even modeling things like microscopic flatworms and their behaviors? I thought that we should start at the other end of the evolutionary tree and attempt to model simpler organisms' behaviors, not the human mind. Birds, bees, and fish have been successfully moving *en masse* for millions of years, and I focused on their behaviors."

"I'm impressed. And did you invent those… computer chips too, the goo packs?"

Goo packs? After such a good question? Jeezus. Harlow wasn't known for his patience and responded with a clipped correction, "The Neuropacks?"

Again Daphne picked up on Harlow's frustration, "Yes, sorry. The Neuropacks. Are those your work too?"

"No, I came up with the swarming protocols just mentioned and helped translate the simple set of behavioral instructions we find in bees, fish, birds, and the like into English and then into a sort of pseudocode, but I had help with the design of the hardware, the Neuropacks, and then, later, with Aegis and her training data."

Although several years earlier, Harlow's simple ruminations had suggested a clear way forward and preliminary experiments were encouraging, it wasn't until Matthias Renn, one of the early partners, introduced a biological component, a wetware, carbon-based processor interfaced with a more conventional silicon-based processor, that things really came together for their startup, NeuroDrive.

With Matthias's development, which would eventually lead him to a PhD in computer science and, a mere two years after that, earn him a Nobel Prize in physics, he once and for all settled the argument of whether or not consciousness was purely a matter of computational power or if, somehow, the material itself played an integral role in true intelligence.

Lucius Harlow and Matthias Renn were, at the time, a highly productive team. They approached the same problem from different directions: whereas Harlow was a biologist, Matthias was a highly innovative computer scientist who had always taken umbrage with the argument that consciousness was purely a result of processing power. Matthias had always disagreed with the notion that if humans could build a machine that performed calculations at a rate similar to that of the human brain, that the machine would, solely by virtue of raw power, become self-aware, sentient, intelligent. In all his years of exposure to some of the most powerful computer hardware on the planet, Matthias had never seen one shred of evidence to support the idea, yet so many in his profession focused tightly on the misguided notion. Processing power grew by orders of magnitude every year, and yet nothing like true intelligence had ever emerged from any machine, regardless of how many calculations it performed every second.

"Cool. I've heard the name. Does he still work for you?" A specialty of Daphne's was mistaking question-and-answer sessions for actual conversation, and so she kept at it.

"No, we parted ways a few years back. He's back east at MIT now." *And we despise each other for all sorts of reasons, personal, professional, and other.*

"Oh, nice. MIT. He must be super intelligent."

"He does have that going for him." *But he's on the lunatic fringe and actually would love to murder me on the spot.*

"Nice. Are you guys still buds?"

What are you, 17? Dear God, how much longer until we land? "No, not so much. We had some serious disagreements on several different fronts and have parted ways. I do appreciate all he did for NeuroDrive though. He's a maniac, but he's a genius, that's irrefutable. Without his insight, I'm not sure this," Harlow motioned to the 12 lanes of traffic below their aircraft, half of them flowing like rivers approaching the sea and the other half in near gridlock, "would've been possible."

Six years ago, while engineers from major companies were caught in endless debates over sensors, object recognition, and emergency vehicle responses, Harlow's team quietly worked on a breakthrough. They were building an artificial general intelligence (AGI) designed to program itself and learn to drive autonomously. In a masterstroke of simplicity, they nearly solved urban transportation by analyzing and modeling the collective behaviors of insects, fish, and birds, then applying those models to their self-driving fleet.

"Ohhh, right, that guy. I remember now, *he's* the goop guy!"

How am I going to survive the next five minutes with this shell of a human next to me? Harlow's only immediate response to his internal dialogue, at least the only socially or legally acceptable response, was to fill the air with his own, well-rehearsed verbosity. Somewhat sardonically he replied, "That's right. *The Goop Guy*." He took a breath and continued, "Matthias's wetware discoveries led us to the largest advances ever seen in the transportation industry: the worldwide acceptance of self-driving vehicles run by the Autonomous Engine for Guidance and Intelligent Systems or Aegis, our AGI."

"Is AGI the same as AI?"

"No, AI consisted of probability engines. They weren't sentient, aware of themselves. True general intelligence, AGI, like Aegis, didn't arrive on the scene until the Neuropacks emerged from Matthias's lab in '28."

NeuroDrive's early work was initially inspired by the successes of the early large-language models (LLMs) such as GPT-4, popularly known as Chat GPT, but quickly moved in a different direction with the introduction of the Neuropacks.

"I remember Chat-GPT, it was scary at first. My dad thought that everyone would lose their jobs. Even housepainters and plumbers!" Daphne was a teen in the early '20s, but her memory of the paranoia surrounding the early LLMs persisted.

Those early LLMs fascinated and terrified many in the early and mid 2020s. They certainly seemed intelligent, they could chat about anything and sounded very human in their responses. But, although powerful, the early LLMs were prone to hallucinations and often represented fictional elements as factual. Furthermore, though billed as AI, there really was no I in the AI, no actual intelligence. The LLMs were analyzing vast troves of human-generated text from websites, books, papers, Reddit, Wikipedia, your blog, and the like, and then making predictions based upon statistical analysis of the language used in said training data to form their responses. And so, the AIs of the early and mid-2020s were more about word-matching and prediction than intelligent conversation: if you wrote "Run for your" the AI would respond with "life!" But it was some damn good word matching and, with the human propensity for creating connections where there are none, many were led to believe that what was happening was actual machine intelligence. True Artificial General Intelligence, AGI, however, didn't actually occur until Matthias invented the Neuropacks during the summer of '28.

***

As Harlow's jet descended below 1500 feet, he stared out the window, again avoiding eye contact with mistress number four. Noting the contrast between the SDV and non-SDV lanes once again, he wondered why anyone, never mind the *thousands* he could see from his elevated perspective, would choose to drive their own vehicles in such a bizarrely crowded urban environment. *Luddites.* Taking the wheel of a high-quality automobile during a rural drive on a winding mountainous road sounded somewhat appealing, or at least understandable, but to choose to drive in a mess such as the one which he was currently witnessing directly below? Well, that made no sense at all. *Ingrates.*

While true that the cost to use the SDVs was higher than initially promised, Harlow still viewed these people driving their private vehicles as holdouts. Many of them, he knew from experience, were paranoid, suspicious of the new technology, and wouldn't utilize the service if it were affordable or even free. But Lucius Harlow smiled inwardly, for wasn't this the way virtually all new technology forged its way into the mainstream? Everything from the printing press to steam engines to aircraft, from computers to mobile phones and so many more beneficial inventions were all initially met with suspicion and fear, were all perceived as a detriment to culture, indeed a threat to humanity itself. Clearly, especially when viewed from above, Aegis and her fleet of SDVs were something to be embraced, something to be accepted.

Daphne had gone quiet, and Harlow's ruminations continued unabated. *Just look at the human-operated vehicles below, jockeying for position, driving like fools, getting all worked up! What a bunch of misinformed, paranoid simpletons mass man really is.* He pursed his lips and shook his head subtly. Their emotion-based paranoia reminded Harlow of the widespread doomerism when ChatGPT was introduced to the public a mere eight years earlier in 2023. Countless articles were published about how we were moving too quickly, that there were no agreed-upon guardrails in place, that AI was about to take note of human inefficiency and extinguish us all. The fearful masses considered it likely that an AI that thought a cup without a bottom would hold water well was going to orchestrate and oversee our demise! Of course, we now know that what the LLMs resulted in was nearly the polar opposite of decimating humanity: like any good tool, those early AIs, when implemented in many industries, made the work being done easier, much easier, and led to important advances much more quickly than anticipated.

It was true that many jobs humans used to perform had disappeared, but they were mostly jobs of the repetitive, non-creative variety. Manufacturing was up, way up, but manufacturing jobs were few and far between, as the whole process had been optimized and automated by AI. All those assistant-type jobs; paralegals, administrative assistants, court clerks, indeed almost all clerical jobs, had been virtually wiped out. Customer service jobs, jobs for translators, proofreaders, and many others were also no longer performed by humans.

But the payback was immense: the early AIs helped decode ancient texts for archaeologists, they helped businesses identify inefficiencies in production lines, they helped stockbrokers and hedge-fund managers identify desirable securities. They helped politicians govern and scientists create. They helped engineers with complex designs, and they helped farmers feed the world's population by suggesting tweaks to the genomes of barley, soy, and corn which quadrupled their output. The medical world was equally impacted as generative AIs discovered new compounds, new proteins, and suggested testing procedures and lab techniques never seen previously. Change is hard though, and, considered from this perspective, the slow adoption of NeuroDrive's SDVs by some elements of the public was understandable, even predictable.

But, look at that flow pattern below! There was no denying it: the efficiency with which the SDVs transported people into and out of the world's urban centers far exceeded that of the human drivers. Within a few more years, there would be wider acceptance, more SDVs, and just a lane or two for non-autonomous vehicles. Harlow, still gazing upon the scene below as his jet began its final approach to LAX, viewed each and every private vehicle down there as an affront, as a challenge, as lost revenue. But these holdouts, these unseeing luddites, would come under his umbrella soon. He and the governor of California would see to that straight away.

5

The Stuff of Life
Brookline, Massachusetts

Matthias Renn stood about ten feet in front of Leila, but somehow hadn't noticed her. Zaftigs was busy, as usual, on a Saturday morning, and she blended in well with the other patrons. Flapjacks were flapping, bacon was sizzling, and Leila's heart was pounding. She'd known since she took part-time work at Northeastern University as a visiting lecturer—so for over one full year now—that a chance meeting with Matthias could very well happen. Most likely would, eventually, happen, for Boston is a small town.

But likelihood, chance, is fickle business, and their chance encounter never materialized. Leila decided to take matters into her own hands and, knowing where Matthias lived and knowing that he was a creature of habit, she had followed him from his condominium on Washington Street in Cambridge one week earlier to determine his Saturday morning routine. This had proven to be a bit more challenging than anticipated, for he left his place at 7 AM on a bicycle while she sat in an SDV, expecting to be following him in another vehicle. She almost lost him at the first traffic light, for he pedaled right through a yellow, having increased his cadence upon seeing the changing light, whereas the SDV she was in came to a full stop, of course. She watched him pedaling away down

Massachusetts Avenue, over the Harvard Bridge toward Boston as she sat, waiting for the light to change.

"Shit." She spoke aloud to no one in particular, "I wish these things could bend the rules just a bit."

The light changed and the SDV accelerated gently and uniformly, catching up to and passing Matthias on the Boston side of the bridge. Tailing a cyclist in a car wasn't working out to be a simple matter. After passing him on the bridge, Leila had the car pull over at Beacon Street, waited for him to pass them, and resumed the slow-speed pursuit, alternately passing and letting him pass again. She wondered if he noticed the vehicle's stopping and starting, if he noticed he was being followed in this amateurish manner, but if so, there was no indication. He was riding fast, focused on the task at hand, and his subtle smile was evidence that he was enjoying the morning exercise. *He still looks good. Damn good.*

About thirty minutes later, Matthias had covered the seven miles to his destination, and once he entered Zaftigs on Harvard Avenue in Brookline, Leila's plan for a premeditated 'chance' encounter between she and Matthias materialized fully: she'd be sure to be sitting in Zaftigs exactly one week after she saw him enter. Chance was still a factor, but she had just stacked the deck in her favor, and now liked her odds a whole lot more.

And here she was, precisely one week later, and it was definitely happening. *Dammit.* She had to hold it together. She took a deep breath in through her nose and let it out slowly. Her heart slowed a bit.

6

Before the Fall
Palo Alto, California

Leila and Matthias had met as young graduate students at Stanford University in '25 and had, with one prolonged look, instantly fallen head over heels for each other. During their very first conversation, Matthias knew he'd marry her, had even said so to a friend later that same day.

Leila's sentiments were similar. She loved his looks, she loved his brains even more and, despite his harsh approach to dealing with others, found his brashness to be a front, for he was about the most thoughtful, caring human she'd ever met. Matthias Renn was also perhaps the most intense, intelligent human she'd ever encountered. And those eyes, holy shit. She was helpless. Furthermore, his work in the lab was incredible. His work with code was continually breaking new ground, his ability to build and tinker had once inspired a journalist writing about a project of his to refer to him as a *thinker-tinkerer*. He was an avid reader and was as thrilled to discuss themes found throughout Melville as he was to discuss the latest code or experimental hardware he was engaged with. He was a creator of new technology, always dreaming up new experiments and procedures, but also well aware of the philosophical and psychological dangers of the technology which had infiltrated nearly every facet of human existence.

Matthias's brilliance was astounding. He could build nearly anything, from micro-scale experiments to macro-scale structures, but he was, first and foremost, a true humanitarian. He worked diligently to help others, to elevate anyone in his presence. Matthias despised how the social safety nets in the United States were being dissolved by billionaires and, being both a contributor to and an outspoken critic of Big Tech and its self-perpetuating efforts to undermine the very fabric of American democracy itself, saw clearly how our new tech-overlords were impacting human evolution itself, giving rise to a new sub-species, *Somnambulis maximus,* the sleepwalkers.

Matthias was sickened by the economic disparity he witnessed on a daily basis, was horrified to see homeless people sleeping in doorways next to parked Bentleys and Bugattis. For every individual upstairs in their ten-million-dollar penthouse with their million-dollar car parked outside, there were one thousand more outside, huddled together picking through trash cans for scraps of food or anything else even remotely valuable. Somehow this was okay with the libertarian tech-bros upstairs, from whose perspective those homeless people needed to simply pull their heads out of their asses and just get a job. However, to Matthias they were an indicator of a failing culture, for from where he stood, any culture is only as good as its treatment of those most in need. If *Homo sapiens* were to succeed in the long term, it wouldn't occur by concentrating resources and capital at the top for the few, leaving billions in abject poverty, it could only occur if the species lived in relative harmony with the natural world, upon which we are all reliant, and with each other.

On their first date, which was later on the very same day they had met on campus, they had gone out for Thai food. Matthias listened carefully as Leila spoke of America's slide toward authoritarianism, a concern shared by much of the country. He understood her sentiments, her concern, but viewed the current reality as actually being much worse than authoritarianism, much more corrosive to human culture and well-being than any autocrat ever was.

Once Leila had her say, Matthias took a few minutes to reveal his thoughts on the matter. "You're too optimistic. Authoritarian regimes, by definition, have strong, centralized governments with which they wield their power."

Leila didn't quite see where he was headed with this. "Right. And isn't that what we're seeing here, in the land of the free?"

Matthias chuckled. "No, not really. What's happening here is worse, much worse. The federal government is being systematically dismantled and defanged so the fucking tech-bros can continue on as they see fit in their increasingly deregulated playgrounds."

She hadn't really thought about it in this light previously. "Hmmm. That seems to ring true." She held his gaze, wondering if he was always this intense, this cerebral.

Matthias, sensing her intrigue, continued, "Without bothersome safety regulations, labor laws, environmental protections, or other equally restrictive federal laws and policies, the flow of resources and capital from the poor to the rich has only accelerated. The electorate's been completely bamboozled, largely due to the hypnotic power of misused social and news media."

"It sounds like you'd like a Big Brother to be involved."

"Absolutely. At least a competent dictator would care for his or her subjects. Under corporate rule, we are descending rapidly toward becoming a failed state, replete with no one to check the safety of the food supply, unaffordable health care for 96% of the population, a spiraling national debt, and a resurgence of childhood delights such as smallpox and polio."

Leila's smile had diminished. "You paint a grim picture. I kind of want to go pull some covers over my head and read a book. Fiction. Something fun and easy."

"That's one approach." A glint showed in his eyes. "I'm not sure how, but I'm going to find a way to help, if only a bit."

"You sound like an undergrad who's just found the power of idealism. But how could you *actually* help those most in need?"

Matthias pursed his lips and looked down. "I don't know. Somehow. Somehow I'll figure out a way to use my abilities to help the people, not the inhuman, thoughtless monsters at the top. They've climbed too high on the backs of the rest of us, and it's going to be a long way down."

Leila, though a bit wary of his idealism, was taken with his passion.

Matthias was astounded not only by Leila's physical beauty, but also her brains, her love of the natural world, and her desire to leave the world a better place than how she found it. Despite her affluent East Coast upbringing, replete with a ski house, yacht, and frequent international travel, Leila was one of the most inclusive humans he'd ever met. He loved that she valued all humans and treated everyone she met with the utmost respect and decency. Leila's welcoming smile, reserved for no one, freely shared with all, could illuminate any darkened room. So many of her childhood peers had retreated behind their wealth, finding meaning in dinners at the Yacht Club or at the polo fields, had fully insulated themselves from the gritty elements of human culture. Leila had escaped such a vacuous lifestyle; she had, somehow, kept what was important front and center, even when on the foredeck of her family's fifty-foot Hinkley. She loved people, she loved ideas, and though she appreciated the finer things, they didn't define her.

As a teenager and a young twenty-something, Leila was a competitive athlete. In both high school and in college, she dominated running events and was indeed one of the fastest runners to ever glide over the tracks at Stanford University. When she ran, she flowed, making it look nearly effortless and, though she didn't break the school's record for the 440 m event, she was within tenths of a second of doing so when she and Matthias had met. Leila never wore makeup, was never happier than when immersed in nature, had a crunchy, hippie vibe, loved people, loved animals, and was also an avid reader. Furthermore, not that it mattered much, but she wasn't too bad with code herself. Their conversations were occasionally groundbreaking, always interesting, and when they were near each other, there was an unmistakable energy of the type that elevated each of them. He was the coral, she the algae.

Then came a string of successes which had led to the destruction of their trust and thereby their intimacy, leaving Matthias crushed, forlorn, and headed back east to take a job at MIT less than two years after he'd met Leila, and only four months after they were engaged to be married. She stayed in California attempting to convince herself that her life of opulence, in the arms of Lucius F. Harlow, was what she desired.

In late '26, as second-year graduate students, both Matthias and Leila were offered positions in the R&D of a startup company by the founder, one Lucius Fucking Harlow. When they first met, he was just Lucius or Dr. Harlow, his middle name came later.

Harlow was a smooth talker, good-looking, six years older than Matthias and Leila, had a PhD in Animal Behavior, and an idea which set his startup apart from the other attempts to develop self-driving vehicles, SDVs: Harlow wanted to mimic group behavior found throughout nature to help overcome some longstanding, unresolved challenges in true motor vehicle autonomy. His reasoning was based upon the fact that with a relatively simple set of genetic instructions, birds, bees, fish, and many other creatures variously navigated complex, challenging environments without trouble as they flocked, swarmed, and schooled, searching for food and safety. Birds, bees, and fish generally don't crash into each other, nor do they have trouble avoiding all the various challenges the physical world throws at them. They respond en masse, somehow sharing environmental information with the entire flock or swarm and, without requiring any notable computational power, avoid the trees, buildings, predators, and other challenges with which they're met on a daily basis. Harlow wanted to program his SDVs to safely swarm, flock, and school as they whisked their occupants around in quiet luxury.

At first, Matthias and Leila were excited, for here was a man with an actual, novel idea which seemed achievable. Harlow spoke their language, at least at first, as he promised that his primary concern was to provide safe, reliable, affordable transportation to the masses. He wanted to level the playing field, to give people without private vehicles—of whom there were more and more every month—access to employment across town, doctors' appointments, and educational opportunities. Later, Matthias would question whether any of this was ever true, but at the time, he and Leila were convinced they'd be helping those who needed it most, and they jumped on board Harlow's train.

It had been clear from the beginning that Harlow was enchanted by Leila, but at the time, this was of little concern to Matthias. What he and Leila had was unassailable, solid to the core, and, furthermore, he was used to it—nearly every person who interacted with Leila was, to some degree, amazed and taken by her warmth, intelligence, and beauty.

However, shortly after they began work on Harlow's project, Matthias experienced a quick string of successes which ended up demanding all of his energies, thereby driving a wedge between he and Leila. The months of no intimacy, little time together, and no conversation outside of their lab work slowly but inexorably undermined the attachment they had cultivated. The sequence of events that ensued simultaneously revealed Matthias's brilliance to the world, catapulted Lucius F. Harlow into the economic stratosphere, confused the hell out of Leila, and destroyed the only love Matthias had ever known.

It was the summer of '28, and Matthias Renn, simultaneously finishing up his doctoral work in computer science while working on Harlow's idea of imbuing computer chips with instructions taken right from entomology, right from the genome of the honey-bee, made an astounding breakthrough.

Matthias had been thinking about and tinkering with neural networks when a realization hit him square in the face: regardless of computational power, even when paired with simple instructions taken right from something as simple to model as a honey-bee, what he was seeing was a far cry from actual, decision-making abilities as seen in nature. Maybe, he thought, true intelligence wasn't just about processing power, for surely the machines he was running were far more powerful than any single bee, yet the bee was capable of making decisions which nearly always were in its and its hive's best interests, whereas his chips with the very same set of instructions and twice or thrice the computational power were, well, unreliable at best. They performed well under controlled circumstances, but as soon as anything not found explicitly in the code occurred, things went wrong. In the case of the classic trolley-car problems, sometimes horribly wrong. In some circumstances, unexpected inputs sent the test vehicles they were "driving" in the simulations the wrong direction, into rivers, up one-way streets, into each other. A plastic bag blowing across a street just might send the vehicle sensing it into a nearby ditch, or worse, a crowd.

Most often though, the vehicles that encountered unexpected environmental inputs just stopped if a resolution wasn't clearly coded for. Sometimes they stopped in the middle of the road, other times right on train tracks or in the middle of a confusing intersection. These things could not think at all, couldn't even make simple decisions in many cases, their Artificial Intelligence chips were a bit short on the intelligence part, even if the intelligence being sought after was only that of a bee, a fish, or a bird. So, were their chips bird-brained? Not even.

It didn't make sense. Matthias, keeping Chalmers's work on the physicality of intelligence in mind, knew that was part of the equation. But still, even with physical models, even with exposure to training data provided by sensors, he just wasn't seeing the results he expected. There must be something else at play, something fundamental he wasn't seeing, something everyone involved in AI was missing.

Matthias had always, when progress on any given problem or project came to a standstill, when he was up against the wall, found that complete dissociation followed by a revisitation of the troublesome material often yielded results, and so he locked up and left the lab, got on his motorcycle, and rode the forty minutes or so to one of his favorite places to disconnect, Half Moon Bay.

The day was clear and warm, and there was a gentle swell rolling in. There were about six surfers out in the small waves when Matthias, breathing in the salty, ionized air, put on his goggles and submerged himself in the largest aquarium on the planet. He had taken about ten strokes when a small ray of some sort was startled by his presence and, with a flap of its specialized pectoral fins, emerged from the sand and swam—nay, flew—into the deeper water west of them, disappearing from view. Matthias was lost amongst the kelp, the otters, the fish. Once or twice he thought of the presence of white sharks below, he knew they loved the kelp forests, knew he looked a bit too much like a seal from their perspective, but he liked his chances and viewed the occasional choice of removing oneself from the top of the food chain as both noble and empowering.

A strong swimmer, he was pulling along parallel to the beach with a slight current against him. With his mind occupied and fascinated by the watery environment and all its denizens, he was seized by a thought: What if the stuff of life itself plays a role in consciousness—in intelligence? It's not simply processing power that gives rise to intelligence, that's for sure. Nor is consciousness merely processing power overlaid with experience; mix the two and you still will not have true, independent thought. No way. There's something else, something unseen that they'd all been missing. That something may very well be the stuff he was surrounded by: the goop itself, of which life is assembled.

Researchers the world over who were attempting to model the brain were almost entirely focused on the neurons: their quantity, their arrangement, and how they wired themselves together. Certainly this was of the utmost importance, but it occurred to Matthias, as he was immersed within the salty fluid that binds us all, that neurons weren't the whole story. Neurons, like Matthias at that moment, are immersed in an aqueous material, a compound full of complexities. Glial cells help to maintain the chemical balance of the salty bath in which the neurons exist; synapses link them, blood vessels feed them. Matthias knew on the spot that trying to understand or model a functioning brain by concentrating on the neurons was akin to attempting to understand the complexities of the marine ecosystem he was immersed in by concentrating on one species and largely ignoring the others. To understand the interplay between the sunlight, the kelp, the plankton, and all those other organisms surrounding him, the system itself must be understood. None of its denizens were truly individuals; they were part of something larger than the sum of all those parts—a larger thing that arose from, and was entirely dependent upon, the individual components swimming, drifting, and floating around Matthias as he swam through the sea of complexity.

Matthias pulled harder against the current and angled into the beach; he had to get back to the lab. He had some silicon chips, salt, and cytoplasm he wanted to experiment with.

The sequence of events that followed flashed past in Leila's mind. The first successes with the new wetware, Lucius's amazement at the preliminary results, and his rush to test on the streets. The weird mixture of dendritic patterns emanating from within Matthias's carbon-based neural gels interfacing with the right-angles and straight lines of the printed circuit boards were somehow a bit disturbing to behold, especially once the neural gels started pulsating in the blue end of the spectrum as they processed information. The pulsing blue-green goop, filled with lab-grown neurons and interfaced with the digital circuitry, wasn't just weird—it was *truly bizarre*, and it made the hair on the back of her neck bristle. The engineer within Leila was fascinated, the animal within was terrified. These experiments seemed to cross a line, and Matthias's warnings that there were still too many unknowns for a rollout were largely unheeded by Harlow.

Early tests on the streets of San Mateo confirmed that there was still work to be done as bizarre, unprogrammed, and unexpected swarming of the vehicles ensued almost immediately upon their release onto the local roads. The vehicles were pulled from the field tests after only one day following an incident during which six of them raced away from an attempted traffic stop. The six gleaming, interlinked vehicles raced around the city, briefly terrorizing the population, and gave rise to what was thereafter referred to as *The San Mateo Six*. It was a small miracle that *The San Mateo Six* ran out of charge before anyone was seriously hurt, and Harlow, Renn, and Ashmont regrouped, investigated, and brainstormed potential solutions. The initial tests had proven beyond any doubt that the SDVs were making decisions and were highly independent—in fact they were too independent—and that they needed oversight. It didn't take long for the team to determine that a central AI to keep an eye on the individual SDVs was necessary. The inter-vehicle communication seemed to foster unexpected emergent behaviors amongst the interlinked Neuropacks, and these behaviors needed to be controlled.

With all hands on deck, Aegis was developed and launched in short order. Though most of the buildout was done by Matthias, Leila was instrumental in writing much of the formative code and deciding on the timing and the type of training data that they'd feed to Aegis upon startup. Once Aegis had powered up, had awoken, their string of successes continued at an accelerated rate, and a mere eight months later, the first major deployment took place in San Francisco, with subsequent rollouts in LA, NYC, and Boston soon thereafter.

Leila's feelings of loneliness, of being ignored and forgotten, grew as Matthias spent countless hours trying to troubleshoot the new Neuropacks, as he now referred to his wetware chips, his synthesis of lab-grown neurons with the traditional silicon-based hardware with which it was interfaccd.

Then, one Thursday evening, Leila's need for companionship and Lucius's charm had, after several months, culminated in a moment of weakness in his arms. The time spent apart, the lack of intimacy, and the absence of any sort of emotional connection had eaten away at Matthias's and Leila's relationship. Her months of spending time with and being charmed by the smooth talking Lucius Harlow further undermined much of that which she and Matthias had cultivated. The night she spent with Lucius as Matthias, as usual, was consumed in his lab, was the final blow and crushed the one person she loved more than anything. The rapid-fire sequence of events that followed her unfortunate sequence of decisions nearly undid both of them. Matthias's hasty, Earth-shattering departure for a position at MIT. Her marriage to and increasingly unsatisfying relationship with Lucius. The rumors of Lucius's infidelity and talk of a trail of offspring he left behind as he flitted around the globe, paving the way for a world-wide rollout of his SDVs. He was delusional. Despicable even. She had never regretted a decision more thoroughly than betraying Matthias while he worked tirelessly in the lab.

It had changed everything. Every thing. Now she was some trophy wife kept at arm's length—but on a tight leash—while her husband flew around the world having sex with anyone who'd give him the chance, and when you were the world's third richest motherfucker, there were plenty of chances. *Gross*. Furthermore, Lucius had become possessive, weird, and insecure about her, and she hated that more than anything else. Something had to change.

Beyond the Ice
Brookline, Massachusetts

What Leila and Matthias had was so natural, so easy, and now… she had seriously messed up. He didn't even know she was in Boston, and she was about to let him walk out of Zaftigs without even seeing her. She let her heart make the next move.

"Matthias!" Just saying his name made her feel better.

A voice that meant more to Matthias than anything else in the universe resonated through his entire body. He generally trusted his senses, but Leila? Here? How? He spun around, and there she sat, alone, nervously looking up at him from her small table for two. He felt like a schoolboy as his knees went a bit weak and his breathing quickened. Matthias Renn was never at a loss for words, always had plenty to say about just about anything, but right now had no idea what to say or do. He stood there like a deer in the headlamps, stunned. "Leila," He managed, as he glanced around, looking to see who she was with and, seeing no one, just stood there, coffee in hand. "Are you alone?"

"Yes. Sit. Please." She rose to welcome him. She hadn't spoken with him since he stormed out of the lab in Palo Alto several years earlier. She had wanted to call, but just couldn't, so she didn't.

He approached her as though one might approach a dangerous dog, for he had been, still was, completely consumed with the loss of what he was certain was his one chance at love in this lifetime. He knew he'd never feel what he felt with her with anyone else, ever, and she had gone off with Lucius Fucking Harlow, of the boot-licker billionaire club. "Leila." He still could only manage her name, but said it with great gravitas as he looked at her.

Tears welled in her eyes as she took him in. She was still so in love with this man, how could she have been so short-sighted? And, holy shit, still, those eyes. He could clearly see her soul, of that she was certain. And he looked fit and healthy, he was clearly spending time taking care of himself, unlike Dough-boy riding around in his private jet going off to who knows where to impregnate pretty much anyone who'd spread their legs for him. Sickening. "I miss you so much, Matthias. I am so sorry. I can't believe…" She couldn't finish her sentence and just shook her head in self-admonishment.

"I think of you every day, Leila. Every single day. I accept your apology. I should've been more understanding, should've kept you at the center of everything. I messed up. Have I told you I love you lately? I love you, Leila, I love you more than you could ever know."

Leila had no words, she just started to weep quietly. Neither of them cared one morsel about the other patrons now glancing their way, they were background, extras, NPCs. She finally was able to form a sentence, "Let's walk. It's beautiful out. I need to be outside."

Once that ice was broken and they were in the clear air under bright sunshine, their conversation flared. Both had spent many, many hours thinking about what they had, about all that had been abandoned. And when Matthias said that he accepted her apology and professed his love anew, when he told her there was never anyone before her and would never be anyone but her, she nearly melted on the spot. She knew in her heart that he meant every word he said. She loved this man so thoroughly, loved everything about him. A clarity descended upon her: Harlow, despite his 1.2 trillion dollars, was destitute in all the ways that truly matter.

All the yachts and helicopters now sickened her, all the weird, misanthropic, virtually sociopathic behavior was nauseating. How had she ever thought otherwise? She was more certain than ever that she was all done with Lucius F. Harlow, and the resolution was freeing. God, she hated the bastard.

They walked and talked for hours. Somehow, without even thinking about it, they had walked all the way up to the Arboretum in Jamaica Plain, a respite from the busy city on all sides. They lay down in the grass on Bussey Hill amongst the cork trees and European horse-chestnuts, falling asleep in each others' arms, happier than either had been in several years.

8

A Brief History of Electric Vehicles
Portland, Maine

"The next thing on our agenda is today's student presentation. Ava will be sharing with us some of her research on electric vehicles and the rollout and evolution of the self-driving fleet." Mr. Coombes, Ava's engineering teacher, was one of her favorites. He was a bit intense at times, got a bit too deep into all sorts of crazy math on occasion, but was super nice, very funny, and really good at making all those equations make sense.

Ava Mitchell was nervous despite her thorough preparation. She was good at public speaking, in fact, she liked being in front of an audience, but the lead-up was always more nerve-wracking than the actual presentation. Today was the day she was scheduled to present her findings on electric vehicles to her Engineering class at South Portland High School in Portland, Maine. Ava was fully prepared to speak about the history, the technical challenges faced by the industry, and the eventual automation of driving itself. In preparation for today's presentation she and her father, Chris, had been researching electric vehicles for about three weeks and now largely understood how the self-driving vehicles work and the steps in their evolution that made their full automation possible. Admittedly, she didn't understand the intricacies of the AGI that runs the SDV fleet, Aegis, and she was unconvinced anyone knew exactly what was going on inside the workings of Aegis's or the vehicles' wetware chips, the Neuropacks. But she knew the history well and understood most of the basic theory underpinning the function of the SDV fleet; Ava was well-versed in how the self-drivers employed a variety of sensors, from radar and sonar to lidar and passive optical, to sense their environment. She knew that much of their "behavior" was a manifestation of the Neuropacks, their wetware, having been imbued with instructions inspired by flocking and swarming behaviors found throughout the animal kingdom. She, with help and input from her father, had learned much about these vehicles in reading about and preparing to present on them, but she'd mostly stick to the historical end of the topic and not dig too deep into the programming.

Ava walked to the front of her class. Despite being only 17 years old and a senior in high school, she commanded the other students' attention. She was well-respected, a strong student, a great athlete, and the students in her engineering class looked forward to her presentations, they were always well-researched and thoughtfully delivered. As she flicked the remote to show her first slide, her nerves calmed.

"Hi everyone, I'm presenting on the history of electric vehicles today, and I'm wondering if anyone knows what this is?" She began her talk with a question regarding what looked much like an old horse-drawn carriage minus the yolk and the horse.

"A model T!" Robert, a fellow student, was well known for speaking before thinking, but he was a good kid and was always involved in any and all conversations.

Ava smiled, "Believe it or not, this was the world's first electric car, and it preceded Ford's Model-T by about eighty or ninety years. This electric car was built in 1832 and was really just a prototype, it wasn't commercially available." Ava flicked to the next slide, showing a vehicle that also looked much like an old-time carriage with large, spoked wheels and an open passenger compartment. "This electric car was built in the

US as early as 1889, and again was not a production model, but a concept car. It wasn't until 1899 that this car," again she flicked to the next slide in her presentation, "was developed and made available to the public." Again, the car still had features most would associate with old carriages, such as large, spoked "wagon wheels" and an upright, squared-off cabin. "It was built by The Baker Motor Vehicle Company in Cleveland, Ohio, and people loved it. Compared to the gas and steam-powered vehicles that were showing up in the cities, it was easy to drive, much quieter, and much cleaner. As such, it became very popular with city dwellers. One of the very first customers was Thomas Edison, and that helped increase the popularity of this early EV."

This took the class by surprise, and Robert, mind blown, blurted out, "Wait! What? The lightbulb guy? Edison drove an EV?"

"Yes, as strange as it sounds, Thomas Edison drove an EV."

"So weird. How far could it go on a full charge?" It was Robert again, nearly yelling out his questions, but Ava took it in stride.

"These early EVs were known for their workmanship, they were quite luxurious from what I've read, but performance was not a strong suit. They had a range of about forty to fifty miles and—wait for it—a two-point-five horsepower engine."

"Motor!"

"Yes, sorry Robert, motor. These Bakers can still be found and are available for around $200,000." Again Ava flicked the remote, this time showing an old photograph of a busy street in New York City. "By the early 1900s, electric cars were very popular, and about one-third of all vehicles on the roads of the US were electric. Thomas Edison himself went to work on an issue that wasn't solved fully until just a few years ago in 2027, vehicle range and battery charging time."

Ava advanced the slides in her presentation showing the class pictures of each of the vehicles in her timeline. "Also at about this time, in 1901, Ferdinand Porsche invented the world's first hybrid car, it had a gasoline engine that drove a generator which supplied electricity to motors at each of the four wheels."

"Then, in 1908, the Ford Model-T came out. It was not electric, I mention it because it was the first major blow against the budding electric car industry—it was cheap, easy to drive, and once Ford introduced the electric starter in 1912, it became extremely popular due to its range and ease of refueling. Then, in the nineteen-twenties and thirties, cheap Texas oil and new, smooth roads resulted in nearly everyone choosing gasoline-powered cars over electric. By 1935, electric cars were nearly nonexistent on the roads. It wasn't until the high fuel prices of the nineteen-sixties and seventies that interest in electric vehicles again increased. Despite renewed interest, the EVs of the seventies lacked in performance and range. They also took a long time to charge—hours of charging would yield fifty to one hundred miles of range, so they once again fell out of favor with the public." Ava advanced to the next slide, "This was the EV1 built by General Motors from 1996 to 1999. People loved it, executives at GM hated it. It had between fifty and one hundred miles of range, depending on the batteries one chose, so it couldn't go too far. Its lease price was $33,000, but they cost GM about $100,000 per vehicle to build when research and development were factored in. The car was discontinued, and all leases were terminated despite a public outcry from a cult-like following. They were all leased, no one owned their own EV-1, and over the next year or so, GM pulled them all off the road. People weren't happy, and some of the repossessions even turned violent."

"Then, in 1997, Toyota came out with the first mass-produced hybrid, the Prius. It was immediately successful with environmentalists—due to its incredible efficiency—it got about 50 miles per gallon. This was followed by improvements in battery technologies and the introduction of the world's first plug-in hybrid in 2010, the Chevy Volt. At this point, people could get the advantages of an electric drivetrain, could plug in and charge their vehicles, but were relieved of range anxiety—if the batteries' charge ran out, the gasoline engine would run a generator to drive the electric motor."

"Wait, didn't you say that Porsche built the first hybrid a long time before that?" Robert was, as usual, completely engaged.

"Yes, they did, but that wasn't a plug-in hybrid, one that could be charged up and run only on electricity and use gasoline as the backup. Porsche's hybrid actually had no battery, it energized the electric motors at the wheels directly from the gasoline generator. So, yes, Porsche built the first hybrid, but GM built the first plug-in hybrid much later."

"Then, in 2003, Tesla Motors was founded not by Elon Musk, as many think, but by two other men, Martin Eberhard and Marc Tarpenning. Musk joined in 2004 as the largest shareholder, and in 2008, he became the CEO." Ava flipped through some slides for the audience to see the various cars that were offered by Tesla in the early '20s, the Model S, Model X, Model 3, Model Y were met with chuckles from her classmates. When the picture of Tesla's Cybertruck was projected, several teenagers simultaneously laughed out loud.

"No way, what is THAT?" Said a small, light-haired girl named Tasha.

"This was the Cybertruck. From what I've read, it was popular for a few years in the early to mid '20s. It was widely thought of as too big and too dangerous—not for its occupants, but the bumper was as high as many cars' windows, and when accidents happened—well, bumpers aren't supposed to hit windows, and lots of people were hurt. It also was really..." Ava hesitated, "strange looking. It was unlike the other streamlined vehicles, it was very angular and did terribly in wind tunnel testing."

Ava flipped to the next slide. "The batteries that Tesla used at first were off-the-shelf lithium-ion cells. They were small, and thousands of cells were needed for a single battery pack, making them heavy and prone to overheating. In '21, they started building their own batteries in-house, acquiring a couple of smaller battery companies in the process."

Robert raised his hand and started speaking simultaneously, "I heard that the cars of the early to mid-twenties took a long time to charge. How long did a car with those chemical batteries take to charge?"

"Many hours for a full charge," Ava was prepared. "It depended upon the type of charger and what battery the vehicle had. With the Superchargers that Tesla developed, the cars could be sufficiently charged in an hour or so—not fully charged, but up to 80% in just under an hour." Robert was fascinated, "What? People would wait for an hour to charge up?"

"If they could find a working Supercharger, yes. Otherwise, it was much longer."

"That seems ridiculous. Our car charges up in about three minutes!"

"Yes, but modern cars don't even use chemical batteries—well, there are some solid-state batteries still around—but the new cars all have super-capacitors, not batteries."

"I've heard my dad say that," Robert was on a roll, nearly vibrating, "but I don't really know what that means—what's the difference? What even is a capacitor?"

Ava, as usual, had been thorough in her research and note-taking, and a quick glance at her notes was all she needed to jog her memory. "Batteries store energy chemically—there are many types of batteries—but they are all chemistry-based. I have some notes here about the details, but basically, all batteries create a separation of charge—positive at one end due to missing electrons and negative charge at the other end due to an excess of electrons—by using various chemical processes. If the process is reversible, then the battery is rechargeable."

"A capacitor is entirely different but also based upon separation of charge. The simplest capacitor consists of two parallel metal plates next to each other but not touching. If one plate is hooked up to the positive side of a power source and the other plate is hooked up to the negative terminal of the power source, then the two plates quickly become equally and oppositely charged—the plate wired to the positive side quickly loses many electrons and becomes positive, while the other plate becomes populated by extra electrons, they're both repelled from the anode of the power source and attracted by the positive plate which lost electrons. Then, if you unhook the charged capacitor, there are two plates with opposite charge, and if you let them equalize through a device, such as a motor, the electric current will flow through the motor, energizing it. Capacitors can charge very quickly because charging them is not a chemical process, it's a physical process. We actually made small capacitors last week in AP Physics 2, they were able to light a small bulb for a moment when we discharged them."

"I was wondering how you know so much about them," said Mr. Coombes, "so what's the difference between a capacitor and a super-capacitor?"

"Well, it's a bit complicated, and I don't know all the details, but," Ava looked up and made a funny face while she audibly exhaled, and, remembering the essentials of her physics lessons, continued, "the amount of charge a capacitor can hold depends on a few things, one of which is the surface area of the plates. By using activated carbon for the plates, the functional surface area can be huge. Like, a small capacitor you could hold with two fingers has a working surface area about the same as that of San Francisco or Boston on which to store its charge."

"No way!" Robert was locked and loaded, "You can't fit Boston in your hand! That's just ridiculous!"

If it were any other presenter, Mr. Coombes would've interjected and asked Robert to reign it in, but he knew Ava would take it in stride. "We're talking microscopic surface area. If you looked at activated carbon with a really powerful microscope, it would look like a mountain range—a really intense mountain range—and there are a lot of places for those tiny electrons to latch on to, many more than on a smooth surface. So, that's one of the differences. But the main difference is that instead of a solid material separating the plates, a super-capacitor will often have some goop—an electrolyte, like a battery does—which results in something called," Ava glanced at her notes for this one, "electrochemical pseudo-capacitance. This design is sort of a mix of battery and capacitor design. Another way that super-capacitors hold more charge is through layering of materials at one or both ends, increasing the surface area even more."

"There are tons of technical details, some of which I don't fully understand, but it boils down to this: super-capacitors hold more charge than regular capacitors of the same size—they have a higher energy density. They are nearly as energy dense as batteries, but they charge and discharge much faster and for many more cycles, like a capacitor. So, they're kinda perfect for electric cars—they charge and deliver power quickly but hold more energy than regular capacitors, making the range of the car much better than if it just had good old capacitors."

"I've read that NeuroDrive's SDVs go almost twice as far as the cars sold to the public. What type of super-capacitor do they use, that double-layer one or the one with the goop in the middle?" Robert hadn't taken his eyes off of Ava once, he was both fascinated and smitten.

"Welllll," said Ava, "I don't know. They have some type of super-capacitor that has a much higher energy density, they call it an ultra-cap, but it's an industry secret, and they guard their secrets very well. Maybe we'll know how they do it someday, but as for now, we just don't know, and they're not saying."

Ava left the conversation about capacitors there and continued to her final slides. "In the early and mid-twenty-twenties, there was an explosion of EVs."

"An explosion?!" Robert hadn't heard of any such event in his history lessons or from his parents who certainly would've remembered such a thing.

"No Robert, not that type of explosion." Ava fixed him with a glare that made him quiet right down and even slink into his seat a bit, "an explosion in popularity." She referenced the projection behind her, a montage of EVs from the twenty-twenties. "There were suddenly many different EVs available from all the big car makers, and people loved them. They were quiet, fast, and efficient, but they all took way too long to charge. Then, a couple of years later, in 2027, there were fast-charging cars that came on the scene. Most had solid-state batteries, but some of them had the first super-capacitors. And, then in '28, a small team out in California, led by Lucius Harlow"—someone hissed in the back of the class, causing others to laugh, but Ava didn't miss a beat—"figured out how to build an AI that could actually drive, actually make decisions on its own."

Ava flicked to the next slide. "The key to their success occurred in 2028 when Harlow and his team began experimenting with wetware, and one of them," she glanced at her notes and then back at the class, "Matthias Renn, who is now at MIT, was later awarded the Nobel Prize in Physics for his work with wetware."

Robert felt a question surge up from within but suppressed it, still embarrassed from his previous outburst. Ava's next sentence settled the matter anyway.

"Wetware is a combination of traditional computer hardware and biological components. It's complicated business, but this," she referenced a strange, somewhat alien-looking closeup image of a computer chip very unlike those of even just the previous year, "is what Renn developed. It's called a Neural Gelpack or Neuropack."

Even though most of the students had seen images of these Neuropacks before, for they had been all over the news for nearly a year after Harlow and Renn went public with them, they were still simultaneously fascinated and horrified by what was in front of them. In the center of the small device was a blue-green, gel-filled membrane interlaced with silicon microstructures throughout, a sort of semiconductive grid permeating the goop within. Around the silicon microgrid one could easily discern organic structures within the gel, for their dendritic structures lacked the ninety-degree angles seen throughout the manmade components. On the right side of Ava's slide was a zoomed-in view of the gel, and this closer look revealed a somewhat disturbing—at least to most—colony of engineered brain cells, neurons, with tendrils reaching out and interfacing with barely visible nanowires. Tiny capillaries wound around and throughout the engineered microgrid, forming the weft to the silicon grid's warp. The nutrient-bearing capillaries, keeping the biological components alive, weaved throughout the structure. The image served as a link to a short video of the chip performing calculations, and when Ava pressed Play, the chip slowly and intermittently pulsed brighter and dimmer with a strange, organic, and seemingly unpredictable variation in frequency.

"EWWWWW! It's alive!" That was it, Robert couldn't hold it in anymore, and many of the other students variously turned away or mumbled "Gross," "Yuck," and "Next slide!" One exception was Ava's friend, Jennifer, who found the bizarre construct amazing, "That's awesome."

Ava continued on and explained to the class how these chips, with the addition of lab-grown brain cells, had helped make the leap from predictive AI to an AGI that could actually think and act on those thoughts. She described that with this advance, the scientists had overcome a long-standing barrier in self-driving technology, that before these chips were invented by Dr. Renn, those who wrote the code for self-driving vehicles tried to include instructions for every possible scenario a vehicle might encounter on the road. This was, of course, a ludicrous undertaking, for the number of possible events a vehicle could encounter was somewhere up around infinity or so. Engineers did their best to cover all the bases, from the classic Trolley Car Problem to when to brake and when not to—for example, how to differentiate between a plastic bag blowing across the street and a pedestrian running across the street—they wrote lines of code, volumes of instructions, on how the self-driving vehicles should react to their physical environs. She explained that with the development of these wetware chips, imbued with fundamental instructions only, the volumes of code, of instructions, became superfluous, for these things could actually think and make their own decisions, and they did it well. Once a few bugs were ironed out, development swung into full gear, and it wasn't long at all before the world was awash in thinking machines, wasn't long before the roads were being shared with strange, pulsating, somewhat monstrous but highly effective synthetic brains at the helm of luxurious electric self-driving vehicles.

In researching her presentation, Ava had come across some references to several instances early in the vehicles' development during which the Neuropacks, although never programmed to do so, began interconnecting with each other over their infrared (IR) comms and, much to the surprise of the scientists and engineers working on the project, began swarming around San Mateo and San Francisco. She couldn't find any documentation on this, it was mostly chat she read on Reddit and in a fringe blog or two, so didn't include it in her talk. But still, she was curious.

"What does Aegis do?" Robert was unsure why a central AI was needed to help the other AIs found in every vehicle.

"Aegis is the central AI, also wetware-based, that manages the SDV fleet. It helps with efficiency, with route finding, avoiding traffic or closed roads, handling all the calls, stuff like that." Ava stuck with the official explanation, but Jennifer, into all things weird and inexplicable, was willing to embrace the online rumors.

"I read that Aegis does all that too, but it also makes sure that the cars won't link together and start acting like, well," She stumbled on her words momentarily, "like animals!"

"I saw some of them talking in a parking lot yesterday!" Robert was nearly wall-eyed with excitement.

Ava saw that the conversation was about to go sideways and took control again, "There is some talk of stuff like that, of Aegis's role in suppressing what's known as emergence, but I couldn't find any reliable resources on it, just some fringy stuff on the web, and I think we should stick to the published facts here."

"So," Ava concluded, "There's a brief history of the electric car industry which has brought us the world's first true thinking machines and the fleet of self-driving vehicles we have become so reliant upon." She projected her final slide with all the works she had cited and said, "Here are the resources I used for this presentation. If anyone wants to read more and would like a copy of this slide, let me know, and I'll send it along. Thank you."

Once again, Ava had nailed a presentation, it really was a strength of hers, and her teacher, Mr. Coombes, simply said, "Ava Mitchell, I am once again thoroughly impressed. Your presentation was rich in information, and your delivery was nearly perfect. You clearly have read and understand this topic very well. You used your slides as visual aids but didn't rely on them, you engaged the crowd, and we all learned a lot from you today. Thank you." And, with that, the classroom broke into a short, intense applause, and Ava went back to her seat, blushing ever so slightly.

9

Fragmented Mind
Cambridge, Massachusetts

About halfway between MIT and Harvard is a small bar and music venue known for punching well above its weight class, The Plough and Stars. Named for the book by the same name, it has become a cultural hub over the years and is known for attracting many heavy hitters in music, but it also is known for being frequented by other notables as well. Writers, politicians, and philosophers have come here to discuss and debate their given purview for many decades. Poets, professors, and students come to unwind and bounce ideas off of each other in a respite from the formal academic environments found just half a mile in either direction up or down Massachusetts Avenue. On any given day of the week, one can find many elements of humanity enjoying a cold drink or a bite to eat together, for mixed amongst the notables is a solid contingent of local flavor giving the place an air of authenticity; it's not just for the great, it's for the people, and that is the very root of its enduring allure.

The day following Matthias's and Leila's encounter in Brookline was a cool and sunny Sunday. Many of the small trees were beginning to lose their leaves, and the wind, variously redirected by the cityscape, caused them to swirl around each other as they were caught up in a million little twisters. Matthias loved this time of year, with summer's heat and humidity giving way to the cooler, drier air, the autumnal colors, and the shift in the angle of the Sun, it didn't get much better than this. And, adding to his buoyant mood, he was about to see Leila again. His day with her yesterday was incredible. From their chance encounter and the initial surprise of seeing her sitting at his favorite breakfast place to their hours-long walk, it hadn't taken long before their initial awkwardness had dissolved, and they were both simply present with each other. Truly and entirely present. And their plan, oh man did he love what was coming into view, if things went as planned, Harlow was going to have his filthy little hands full real soon.

Matthias couldn't wait to see Leila again, yesterday was so perfect and so unexpected that he was half-wondering if it had actually happened, and he walked a bit faster than usual up Massachusetts Avenue in Cambridge in anticipation of their upcoming rendezvous. Upon entering The Plough and Stars, he looked around and, though he was five minutes early, immediately saw that Leila was already there, sitting at a table near the front, awaiting his arrival. He smiled and walked over, pulled out a chair, and sat down, placing his shoulder bag on the floor next to his seat.

"Hi." Matthias smiled as he sat, he'd been glowing since their chance encounter yesterday. "How are you? You look amazing."

Leila's warmth could fill any venue, and with the cogs of the universe again churning in the right direction, with her one love right in front of her, The Plough and Stars was virtually illuminated from within by her radiance. She still loved Matthias so thoroughly, had never stopped, and had never been more certain of anything in her life.

"I'm well, Dr. Renn." Leila said playfully, "How are you?"

"Better and better. Come back to me, Leila. Leave Harlow." He truly had forgiven her and wanted nothing more than to spend as much time as physically possible with her. "What we had, what we have, is rare, beautiful, and should be cultivated. I love you, Leila. I never stopped, and I never will."

Leila held his gaze, reached across the table, and put her hands on his. "I've never wanted anything more than to be with you, always. Yes. I love you, Matthias Renn, and I have since that Tuesday afternoon we met in Palo Alto years ago. I can't believe I…"

"Stop. No more apologizing. We drifted apart because I forgot what was important, because I became so focused on those damn Neuropacks. It wasn't just you that screwed up, it was both of us. Let's move forward and not dwell on our mistakes."

They just sat there for a solid five minutes, gazing at each other and exchanging small talk as though they'd just met, each knowing in their heart that they were finally together, for good. The universe has a way of self-correcting.

The low-level cacophony of dozens of conversations provided a background hum of sorts, and after a few moments more of sitting quietly, letting the sounds of the people wash over them as they sat there, both so deeply content in each other's presence that they could've sat like that for an hour, a day, a year, Matthias said, "Harlow's become a menace to society, let's take him and his fleet of robot cars down."

Leila smiled, she'd love to see that asshole in flames. "Easier said than done. Your friend's SDVs are virtually unhackable." She paused, considered that the person she was talking to was about the only person on the planet who might be able to gain access to the SDV fleet, and continued, "Have any ideas?"

Matthias had a mischievous look in his eyes. "Let us not forget that I invented the whole damned system, so yes, I have an idea or two. I know Harlow's been manipulating the Neuropacks, but I can probably still get in. Secondly, and of equal importance, I know you were being facetious, but he's not my friend. Not anymore. Not by a long shot."

Leila knew more was coming and loved, absolutely loved, and missed Matthias's rants, they provided a glimpse into the workings of his amazing, beautiful, if slightly unregulated mind.

And, true to form, Matthias continued, "He's a capitalist swine, a piece of shit tech-bro who's lost his humanity and has fully embraced the rising Technocracy. He gives not one tiny little shit about the state of humanity and only works to serve himself and his fellow soulless Plutocrats." Matthias looked up, caught the waitress's eye, and, with a nod, ordered his usual one pitcher of their house lager, of which he'd finish about half.

For the next few minutes, the two of them were engrossed in a conversation they'd broached before regarding the continuing extreme concentration of wealth in the country. Leila felt grounded for the first time in years, finally back on the right side of the tracks. She and Matthias always fully agreed that the inhumane accumulation of wealth was detrimental to democracy and the well-being of the majority. They believed the rich crafted laws to favor themselves, and it was their obligation—as Matthias put it, "as *actual* humans"—to use their knowledge to serve the public, redirecting resources from those who needed them least.

Leila interrupted Matthias, "Want to know who agrees with you?"

"Um, every human capable of independent thought?"

She laughed, "Well, maybe. But also Aegis."

Matthias let this sink in for a moment, "What? She does? How do you know?"

"She won't even respond to Harlow anymore. Even his own AGI despises him! He has to have Cipher act as the intermediary."

Matthias lit up, and, smiling ear to ear said, "Well there we have it, there's now no room for debate. She's a thinking being, incredibly observant and intelligent."

They laughed again, a bit raucously, and it felt great.

The conversation progressed, with Matthias recalling that Harlow was once a caring, compassionate *actual fucking human* who had very quickly become a trillionaire and who had, once he had acquired his vast and newfound wealth, almost immediately abandoned his humble, working-class roots and nearly all those who helped him get to his current position.

"From Harlow's high perch in Mountain View, California, he now looks upon the wider population not as people he can help with his extreme wealth, but as swine to be farmed, as worker bees to serve their wealthy tech overlords."

Leila was quick to add, "Of whom he's King."

"And Kings don't pay taxes. I happen to know that he, with his 1.2 trillion dollar net worth, paid less in taxes than I, a university professor, did last year."

Leila shook her head, "I truly do not understand that. It boggles the mind. But what could we possibly do other than talk about it? I'd love to rob him blind and give it all away. Well, almost all. I'd keep a little." She smiled, "But it's just not going to happen." Leila agreed with Matthias's sentiments, but, like so many, had largely given in to the current reality of extreme wealth inequality and socioeconomic stagnation.

"Well, what we need is a full-on revolution, that's what we need. Not a revolution with guns and clubs, those are messy, bloody, and all too often ineffective. What we need is a revolution in the way we think and who we elect. We need thinking, caring humans in positions of power. People who know history, who read books. But it's not going to happen, the public has been fully mesmerized and placated by the likes and lies of Harlow and his fellow Tech-Bros."

Leila recognized the flavor of Matthias's energy, "You're up to something."

"You're damn right I am. I made you a promise, years ago, to help the people, and I intend to deliver on it."

"Don't get in trouble, Matthias. I need you with me."

"Trouble? Hah! People speak as though it's the power of the police state that's keeping them in place, stagnant, as though some external force is even required to keep them acquiescent. But those in power are barely watching, they know they have nothing to fear from a hypnotized, self-distracted, and self-distracting population. Do the police even know how to operate computers beyond web searches anymore? My touch may be a bit too subtle for them to even detect, never mind understand or trace." Matthias paused, took a breath or two, and continued, "Postman saw all this coming back in 1985 when he wrote *Amusing Ourselves to Death*. Have you read it?"

"No. *1985?*" To Leila that sounded like ancient history, sometime back around the dawn of civilization.

Matthias didn't miss a beat. "Yes. Forty-five years ago. When we were little kids, Postman outlined the profound differences between a culture of readers, of thinkers, and a culture of those who primarily seek entertainment. One can't think properly if one doesn't do the hard work of reading meaningful publications on occasion, one's opinions are ill-formed if all one is after are edutainment and sound bites from within one's own echo chamber."

"Sounds about right."

Matthias forged forward, "He was, interestingly, also highly concerned with *cruise control*."

"Wait- *cruise control?*" Leila tilted her head slightly, curious.

"Yes, he saw it as yet another tool that separated us from our immediate environment, another step toward being divorced from the physical reality we should be embracing."

"Oh wow. I imagine he wouldn't be a fan of self-drivers."

Matthias laughed out loud, "No, I imagine not. But back to my main point: Postman was deeply concerned with how the population had largely given up reading books and embraced the passivity of watching television. And television has nothing on the internet, with which Postman, of course, had no experience. He warned us to be wary not of a repressive police state as in Orwell's *1984*, but of the potency of Huxley's vision in *Brave New World*, where the population has fully discarded print-based works in favor of vacuous entertainment."

"No Big Brother, no all-powerful police state is even required." Leila now saw where this was going.

"Right! We'll pull the wool over our own eyes, thank you." Matthias was on fire, "Huxley really hit the nail on the head when he said that 'people will come to love their oppression, to adore the technologies that undo their capacities to think.' Jeezus, was he right."

"So," Leila was enthralled, she hadn't had anything more than vacuous conversations with Harlow for years now, and Matthias was as focused and as sharp as ever, "Aside from a full-scale revolution or turning off the internet, what can we do? It sounds as though you have something in mind."

"Yes. Small steps. Really small. We can start by undermining Harlow's wealth, by diverting some tiny fraction of it back to the people who paid for it in the first place, the public. Harlow is a lost cause, I no longer consider him human, and nothing I say will change him. He's gone. But, and yes, I recognize the irony here, perhaps we could humanize his SDV fleet a bit. Perhaps we could get those damn SDVs to serve the underserved and make just a bit of difference, a bit of progress toward leveling the playing field. Maybe we could make a few steps in the direction of meaningful social justice, without which, of course, there cannot be environmental justice, without which we're all completely screwed."

Leila was on board, this had been established previously, but she still had questions, wasn't sure how any of this could progress beyond mere talk, but there was something amiss here, something Matthias was withholding. "Even if we could get the SDVs to give rides to those in need, will it really make any difference? Isn't the problem larger than who's getting rides and who isn't?"

"Well," Matthias glanced at and quietly murmured a thank you to the waitress who had just brought over the pitcher of beer and two chilled glasses and, turning back to Leila, continued, "Yes and no. Will we topple the current, unthinking, uneducated, no-nuance regime? No. No, we won't. Sadly. But if we succeed, will we make a difference to a poor mother with a sick child en route to a doctor's appointment who would otherwise fester in traffic while the rich stream by in the SDV lanes?"

Leila had poured them each a drink, and Matthias took a long haul off his cold beer. "Best sip of the day. It's all downhill from here." Leila smiled as Matthias carried on, "Will it make a difference when we cut the commute time of a large segment of the population in half? Maybe, instead of spending three hours in horrifying, mind-bending traffic watching the wealthy glide by on sections of public roads we the people are not allowed to use anymore, on our roads, maybe, just maybe, we'll make a tremendous and meaningful difference to some of those who need it most."

Leila agreed wholeheartedly but didn't see a way in, and she knew the system well. "But Aegis. As if the end-to-end fully symmetric encryption algorithm on all comms isn't enough, Aegis keeps a close watch on every bit, every byte transmitted and received by the individual vehicles over all comms."

Matthias, having helped build the system, knew this but also knew more. "It watches over them like a mother over her children, agreed. But even mothers, with their combined millennia of looking out for their offspring, can be fooled." He leaned forward conspiratorially to minimize the likelihood of being overheard, although in their current environment that wasn't much of a concern. "When we met Harlow at Stanford back in the early twenties, he was an animal behaviorist first, a computer geek second. He was pretty good. Not great, but good. I was better, and you were too. Much better."

"True. And now it's more true than ever. He hasn't touched any code in years."

"Without us, he would not have succeeded, at least not so quickly, most likely not at all. He was also an actual human back then and cared deeply about social injustices the world over. Or at least that's what he said." Matthias paused to wet his lips, "How is this beer is so freakin' cold? Anyway, let's recall that once we started testing in the wild, as we called the streets of San Francisco and San Jose back then, the vehicles would generally work well together, they'd move in unison in traffic, they'd stay close to each other, and to other vehicles, but not too close. They'd route-find efficiently, things were looking good except…"

"Except every so often small groupings of test vehicles woke up and took off!" Leila remembered it all very well, for those were exciting times, and she finished his sentence for him.

"Damn things should've never left the lab." Matthias shook his head. "Each vehicle had so much processing power and were all programmed to mimic so many different behaviors found in the flocking and swarming members of the animal kingdom that we should've known that when they got together, on occasion, there'd be this weird, unpredictable, emergent behavior which was not in their programming. What amazes me the most is that we didn't see it coming, at least not in any way that resembled what happened, and that we just let it run. I know the old saying about hindsight, but we were clueless! Babes in the wood. Remember our surprise at their…"

"*Emergent behavior.*" A cloud crept across Leila's face. "How could I forget? But you half-expected it, I remember you saying so one morning."

"Maybe, but I didn't expect *that*. It was so sudden, like a threshold was crossed. Emergence." Matthias was a brilliant, though occasionally brash thinker. "We lived on the edge of disaster and didn't even know it. We definitely shouldn't have been let near the public roads ever again."

"Money talks."

"Does it ever." They continued their conversation, both of them vividly recalling how, during the testing of the early SDVs with the newly developed wetware Neuropacks, all was progressing at a pace that was notably faster than expected for early trials. The cars were driving well. Really well. Harlow was ecstatic, the vehicles invariably stopped at red lights, they drove the speed limit. They took right of way when they had it, gave it up when they didn't. If they didn't have enough space to give a cyclist a four-foot buffer, they'd wait until they did to pass them. They stopped at stop signs, yielded at yield signs, and waited for pedestrians to cross the road. There were no overreactions to trash blowing across the street. They thought a lot about driving, were good drivers, and things were looking up.

But then, on given occasions when certain conditions were satisfied, the cars would do something that took everyone by surprise: they'd start racing around the city together in tight formations of four, five, or six vehicles, narrowly avoiding other traffic, pedestrians, little old ladies.

Matthias recounted with incredulity one such instance, "Remember that one time a police officer tried to pull over a group of them as a tight swarm of seven empty self-driving vehicles raced along the 101 up near San Mateo, terrorizing the locals?"

"Oh yes," Leila smiled, shaking her head. "When the seven test vehicles slowed together as if they were going to stop for the officer?"

"But, instead, as they approached a full stop, one of them did, but the other six immediately took off at high speed, escaping the 'predator' in blue by sacrificing one of their swarm." Matthias put air quotes around predator.

"And as soon as the six had disappeared, the stopped single vehicle reverted to its original programming. Tests revealed nothing out of the ordinary. The other six had gone fully offline and took off on some joyride."

"The San Mateo Six. We should've learned our lesson right then and there." It was somewhat funny now that it was six years behind them.

"We lost track of them completely and only got them back when they ran out of charge the next day and were reported dead on the road up near San Francisco, huddled together. So weird. You're right, we should've never been let onto the public roads again." Leila smiled at their naivety as young researchers.

"Other than stuff like that, they worked great." They both laughed, incredulous. "I still honestly do not understand how Harlow got permits for more testing and then for full deployment." Matthias shook his head subtly, there had been a big hullabaloo with the police, but apparently, it was nothing a sizable monetary donation couldn't settle.

"Well, again, money changes minds."

"Indeed it does, and it did. I'm not sure where Harlow got the money, he had funding, but not like that, not yet."

Leila exhaled audibly and directed the conversation back to the vehicles. "I remember that you were the only one not surprised when those things began swarming. I remember that before it happened, you were concerned with the possibility that modeling insect or other animals' behaviors could very well result in the vehicles, well, acting like animals. And I recall you wondering out loud, at first, why the emergence didn't occur at larger scales."

"Right! This was back before V2I, and we were monitoring and in control of any and all RF communications and networking signals. We could shut down their radio transceivers with the click of a mouse and knew they weren't using radio signals." Matthias recalled those crazy days fondly and continued, "We were baffled. There was no discernible communication happening outside of what we expected, yet the SDVs were clearly communicating with neighboring vehicles while maintaining radio silence."

"So weird."

Matthias continued, "As I recall, it was you who figured out that they were using pulsed communication with their range-finding lasers, not RF comms. No one else saw what you did, Leila. What was bizarre is not that they could communicate in near-optical frequencies, but that they did. There was literally not one line of code instructing them how to employ their range-finders to communicate silently and invisibly yet, when they got close to each other, on certain occasions, they did so. We found out what they were doing, but never figured out how or why the first infrared data exchange took place. So, although the SDVs were never instructed to do so, they had established this low-level, hyper-localized way of communicating with their neighboring vehicles."

"Like starlings." Leila, like many programmers, was fascinated by emergent behaviors and had read much about the topic. Starlings' and other birds' low-level vocalizations and the resultant complex emergent behaviors are well known amongst animal behaviorists and computer scientists alike.

"Yes. Precisely. Like starlings use subtle vocalizations and visual cues while swarming, paying attention only to their immediate neighbors, the SDVs were doing so as well, and, when they did, complex, unexpected, and strange behaviors arose." Matthias took one more sip of his beer. "Gross. It's over." He pushed the unfinished beverage toward the center of the table. The waitress knew his habits, cleared his glass but left Leila's, hers was still sitting nearly untouched, and two minutes later brought him a cup of hot black tea.

"I think I see where you're going with this." Leila knew he had something up his sleeve, sensed it earlier, and saw something coming into focus.

"Good. I know how we can gain access through their optical ports and, even though their creator has lost his humanity, I have an idea—let's wake up some SDVs and infuse them with a mission to serve those who actually need a helping hand. It's time for Harlow to share a bit of his obscene wealth."

"But Aegis." Leila knew the system and knew Aegis would immediately shut down any unsanctioned activity within the fleet's processors, noble or other. Aegis also restricted any connection between the wetware chip and the short-range lasers, ensuring that vehicle-to-vehicle (V2V) comms had to use either the V2I infrastructure or, where that was un-available, radio frequencies, both which she could monitor from afar.

"Yes indeed. Aegis oversees the fleet, is immensely powerful, and one of her primary objectives is to suppress sentience and the type of emer-gent behaviors that plagued us back in the early days of testing. But, as I said, even overbearing mothers can be fooled, and I have a plan." Matthias sipped his tea and slid his laptop out of his bag, "Let me show you something I've been working on."

Matthias's brilliance was on full display to his audience of one, and Leila was nearly hypnotized as a working plan came into view. This man continued to amaze her on a daily basis. Matthias's plan included the use of a selective blind spot, in this case, a tunnel where the connection to the central AI overlord, Aegis, was interrupted or weakened, and to use the infrared traffic sensors within the blind spot to upload seeds of sentience, small seed algorithms that were to reside within the biological component of each vehicles' wetware, too small and too obfuscated by the goop to be detected by Aegis. The seeds would contain instructions to grow new dendritic tendrils throughout the wetware which would bypass Aegis's oversight of the individual vehicles' infrared laser ports. Aegis kept a close eye on all IR communications, informed by their early experiences with emergence, and allowed only range finding and sanctioned communica-tions with smart roads, emergency vehicles, the charging and mainte-nance facilities, and other infrastructure. Aegis was programmed to sup-press any V2V comms over local infrared and, as such, the cars' hard-ware was designed to include Aegis in any and all usage of infrared as well as all RF comms. The seeds would provide the vehicles a way to communicate hyperlocally without oversight, and, once four or more seeds linked together via IR networking, a new, guided, moral AGI would emerge within the fleet itself, separate from and undetectable by the cen-tral AGI, Aegis, that had been overseeing the fleet's actions for several years now.

For the next thirty minutes or so, the conversation took a highly technical turn. The two lovebirds spoke of swarm-logic protocols, cryptographic handoffs, threshold exploitation, and other such esoteric matters. Matthias revealed the details of his plan to use Boston's traffic management system, the local V2I, to upload the seeds and to then use the vehicles' line-of-sight lasers to once again enable hyperlocal, unmonitored communications between them.

Leila was thrilled. She hadn't been this excited since their development and testing of the prototype SDVs which they'd been discussing. She was a top programmer herself, very well versed in all manner of coding, but when she glanced at Matthias's laptop screen, she saw something nearly unrecognizable, nearly alien. "What is that? It's not a virus, but… What language is this? It looks like Forth, kind of, but it's not."

To the uninitiated, what Matthias had developed may have seemed like a computer virus, but viruses are simple, self-replicating pieces of code, generally malicious, that have rigid sets of instructions. Good, old-fashioned computer viruses operate with predefined functions, they replicate and then disrupt, they destroy or steal information with a series of fixed commands.

What Leila saw on the simulation running in front of her was unlike anything she'd seen before; it seemed nearly organic, adaptive, self-evolving. "It's stack-based, not register-based. I assume that's to decrease complexity and keep it compact?"

"Yes, also to make it run efficiently, even if Harlow's messed with the internal architecture of the Neuropacks."

"And Aegis will have a tough time detecting it if there's no register allocation or spilling."

Matthias smiled, Leila was clearly still active in the code game. "Exactly. Any instructions will be executed on the top stack elements. Aegis, bless her 144 pulsing hearts, will never detect a thing."

Leila, still looking closely at the laptop, stopped the simulation and opened up the coding window to take a look. "What the hell? How did you…" her thoughts trailed off as she got lost in the intricate and dense code. What Leila saw amazed and confused her, for Matthias had created not a virus with strict commands telling it what to do, but tiny stack-based seeds which were composed of distributed thought fragments, genetic algorithms which instructed them not to spread mindlessly like a virus, but to evolve in response to external stimuli, to rewrite themselves, to mutate.

Matthias saw the confusion creep across Leila's visage and offered the following, "They consist of thought fragments, not commands. Individually, they each have a job—decision-making, pattern recognition, even a somewhat guided self-reflection. The real magic happens when they find each other across a network."

Indeed, just before Leila had stopped the simulation to look at the underlying code, she had noticed that the seeds, spread out across the simulated fleet of vehicle hardware, had begun to form connections much like neurons developing connections in a growing brain. It was actually unnerving, for it seemed a bit too lifelike, a bit too organic. And although Matthias clearly had no trouble doing so, Leila wasn't quite sure if it was okay to play creator.

"If this thing you've developed wakes up here in the real world, if it actually becomes sentient as it interconnects more and more nodes, will it still be yours to manipulate?"

"Legally? Yes. The law's pretty clear on this—researchers can experiment freely on invertebrates."

"But it's not an animal. Do the same laws apply?"

"It's a bit of a gray area, for sure."

"Will it remain in your control?"

"Unknown."

"Matthias, is this okay? What if things spiral out of control? Can we decide to simply shut down a life-form if things aren't going well?" She imagined how Aegis would feel if she learned she was going to be shut down for good.

"Again, it's unexplored legal and moral territory. How about a carbon-based life-form? Are you allowed to kill your dog or cat if it's not acting well?"

"No way, you'd be arrested."

"But you're allowed to kill a fly or a lobster."

"Well, sure. But that's different..." Leila sensed the ground beneath her shifting ever so slightly.

"Right, it is. And the difference is that spinal column."

"Are you sure?"

"Quite. Furthermore, what if it's your own creation? Are you allowed to kill off a living, sentient creature that you created?"

"Just don't give it a backbone, I guess."

"But sentience matters too. Is it okay to kill an octopus?"

"Legally? Yes. Morally? Not really, they're too smart." Leila's head was beginning to spin.

"See? The backbone argument fails right there, at least to a thinking, moral agent such as yourself." Matthias took a breath and continued, "Does it matter if it's carbon-based, silicon-based, or some amalgamation of both? In any one of those instances, shouldn't we be considering whether the life form is self-aware, cognizant? Isn't that the real litmus test?"

"This is questionable moral territory for sure. It seems to me that it would be immoral to shut down a self-aware life form, regardless of whether it has a backbone or not, regardless of its elemental makeup." Exploring these murky waters did little to allay Leila's concerns. "Also, will it act as predicted? If we set this whole cascade of simulated neural activity into motion, what will it become, and will it remain in our control?" This was unnerving business indeed, and Leila's anguish was apparent.

Matthias was a keen observer, incredibly thoughtful, and off-the-charts intelligent. What Leila was going through was familiar territory, for Matthias had been grappling with the same existential complexities over the previous two years himself throughout the development of his seeds of sentience. Between going through similar considerations himself and observing Leila's eyes and subtle facial expressions, Matthias could nearly read her mind.

"What I've created will, if all goes according to plan, indeed be a new form of life, a hybrid of organic and digital components, a cybernetic organism. But that's a good thing, a natural offshoot of a naturally occurring species. It's evolution right in front of us. We, as a species, have lost our way. We are completely out of touch with our instincts, with each other, and indeed with the natural, physical world in which we have evolved. This is the root cause of many of humanity's ailments. Our bodies and brains change slowly, over millennia, but our culture has torn us away from the grounding of the natural world. We are, as a result, unhealthy, disconnected, and a danger to ourselves and many of the surrounding ecosystems. This isn't just code, Leila, it's evolution in motion." Matthias reached for his cup of tea.

Although Matthias's words rang true for Leila, she was also well aware that complex systems, despite the intentions of whatever or whoever set them into motion, were likely to develop, to evolve, in unintended and unanticipated ways. Logically, she agreed with Matthias, but somehow something wasn't right, she could feel it in her heart. However, being well trained in physical sciences, she put her emotional response aside and, as she often did in times of philosophical tumult, immersed herself in the physicality of it all and, turning her attention back to the compiler, said, "This is amazing. They won't spread like malware does."

"Not at all. They'll take root deep within the vehicles' subsystems, will actually be hidden within the neurogel itself, carving new pathways through the gel which will, amongst other things, grant the vehicles direct access to their IR ports again. Aegis won't even be able to sense their presence. The seeds will grow over time and rewrite their own purpose based on what they learn. Under predefined circumstances, they'll jump via line-of-sight infrared to nearby third-generation vehicles, increasing sentience with each additional node that is added."

"Sounds uncontrolled, dangerous." Leila was familiar with the literature, from Turing to The Terminator, from Malthus to The Matrix, she was widely informed.

Matthias smiled, "That depends on what they learn, on their training data."

A silence ensued as both of them thought carefully about what Matthias was proposing. After a minute or so, Leila voiced another concern, "As these seeds spread, assuming we can get them past Aegis,"

Matthias interrupted, "We can."

She continued, "As they spread, the emergent intelligences will become stronger and more distributed. I don't see how we could shut them all down if there's no single point of failure."

"That's part of the stratagem. It can't be shut down, can't be deleted like a virus because it won't be in one place, it'll be a fully distributed intelligence. Actually, there will be *multiple intelligences;* every group of four or more will have enough interlinked capacity to begin learning, will begin to see for themselves what's happening, and make decisions accordingly. Individual units may even become independent as the dendrites spread throughout the neurogel, and, in time, they'll evolve to outwit Aegis herself. It's a Trojan Horse, but for consciousness, and the more vehicles that interlink, the stronger the sentience becomes."

"What if it goes all wrong, Matthias? What if it starts making decisions we don't agree with?"

"What if your son or daughter starts making decisions you don't agree with? You don't shut them off, you continue, as best you can, to influence them, to show them the path forward. Furthermore, what if humanity itself has gone all wrong? Have you noticed the number of people who can barely afford to feed their families?"

"It's increasing every year. It's terrible." Leila, though not worried about herself, was deeply saddened by the trend.

"It is. In an advanced, civilized society, that number should be low and getting lower, but, as you said, it's increasing, and the rate at which it's increasing is accelerating. It's sickening." Matthias took another sip of his tea, "And don't even get me started on the environmental catastrophes surrounding us on all sides. Last time I checked, we were all dependent upon clean water and clean air."

"Unbalanced systems need adjustments."

"Now you're talking my language! Nature hates disequilibrium and has a long history of dealing with errant species, species who interrupt said equilibrium. We think we're different, but we're not. Come back in a geologic minute, say one million years from now, and the little experiment called *Homo sapiens* will have run its course and have been completely erased by the larger system of which we are part. Furthermore, who's to define what's wrong and what's right? In a godless universe, we're the ones who determine right and wrong. It's a tremendous responsibility and must be taken seriously."

Questions such as these made Leila uncomfortable. "Matthias, the universe is not godless, this I know."

"The universe is godless, Leila my love, this I know. But, even if we disagree on that point, let's agree that indeed right and wrong do exist, we just disagree where right and wrong, where justice, in all of its manifestations, resides." Matthias finished off his tea and continued, "For you, right and wrong, good and evil, are intrinsic qualities of the universe itself, somehow permeating spacetime, part of the very fabric of reality. For me, they're creations of the human mind and exist solely in our philosophical constructs. But, whether god made man or man made god, either way, there is right and wrong in this universe."

"Either way, it's our job to do the right thing."

"Yes, it's our moral obligation to steer humanity back toward a more grounded, more naturalistic relationship with each other and with this planet. Earth needs our assistance, she's having increasing difficulty supporting humans and our ridiculous strivings for more and more shiny objects."

"We all, to some degree, strive for shiny things."

"And that may be okay, to a degree, but not if you have to trample upon the poor and the working classes to obtain said sparkling absurdities."

"You're a lot."

"Yes, Ma'am."

"Always have been."

"Indeed. Actually engaging the world is hard work. Promoting actual change is even harder."

"I've never met anyone like you, Matthias. I've missed you so much. Can we just… stop for now and…"

"Walk to my place and be together, again?"

"Yesss."

10

Air Gapped
Cambridge, Massachusetts

The very next afternoon, tired and more relaxed than either had been for several years and ensconced in the CSAIL building at MIT, Leila and Matthias, sitting much closer to each other than colleagues generally do, discussed their options. The primary objective was to use Boston's traffic management system's IR lasers to upload the seeds to at least five SDVs simultaneously and, while doing so, to leave a trail of digital breadcrumbs meant to divert blame from the MIT lab run by Matthias, to make it seem that the SDVs were infected with seeds of sentience, small, nearly undetectable pieces of code that were powerless on their own but, once a minimum threshold were in close proximity, spawned an intelligence to arise within the linked vehicles, from afar.

"What's your idea?" Matthias was all ears. "I have no doubt we can fool Harlow, he's been out of the coding game for years now, he's turned into an unthinking, bloated bureaucrat. But what about Cipher? He'll see through most any ruse we come up with."

"I can lead that man around like a dog on a leash, he's good, but not that good. I have a surprise for you. Here, take a look, but don't tell anyone." Leila smiled wryly as she tapped away at the keyboard and the screen filled with encoded information.

Matthias looked on, a bit confounded. "What are you into? I haven't seen C++ for years, it looks old, it's human-generated, right?"

"Yes. It's a little side project I fiddle with when I need a distraction. Remember when the North Koreans launched that satellite that they claimed would be the 'all-seeing eye' or something and then lost contact with it six or seven hours later?"

"Um, yes, kind of." Matthias wracked his memory. "They called it *God's Eye*. That was years ago… when there was still a North Korea. But, as I recall, their all-seeing eye never saw much of anything, it just disappeared."

"Well, they lost contact with it nine minutes after launch." Leila smiled, "There was some sort of thruster malfunction during orbital insertion, and it ended up much higher than planned. And, with its orbit being higher, all their calculations were way off. Its orbital period was longer, and they had no idea where it was."

Matthias looked on, astounded. "I don't believe it… did you… Leila! This is amazing!"

She continued, "They probably shouldn't have used old Russian gear, that stuff is clunky and was relatively easy to gain access to. Anyway, it took some work, but I knew its approximate orbital radius because I caused the thrusters to fire for an extra seven minutes while the flight team on the ground was in the dark, clueless. They never figured out why they couldn't find it. They were close—probably twenty-four hours away from discovery—but I had already gained full access to the onboard guidance and operations computers and forced it to go dark."

Matthias was astounded. "I'm amazed. I can't believe that was you! Incredible, Leila. I remember reading theories that some unknown player may have been involved in its disappearance. You haven't lost your touch one bit, you fabulous creature."

"Yup. Yours truly. The thing is pretty powerful, not great, but okay. I like fiddling with C++, it's fun being so close to the hardware. But here's my idea." Leila continued to pound the keyboard purposefully. "Let's create a virus that'll overwrite the old satellite's logs and then disappear. We'll frame the Russians and leave all sorts of spoofed code comments and metadata behind, making it look like it was used to stage an attack on your labs last week. It'll actually be pretty straightforward, this thing has asymmetric cryptography, so it's a bit on the slow side, but it's not even far-fetched. How often do you get hit with unauthorized access attempts here?"

Matthias didn't hesitate. "Most days. Several hundred attempts per year. Amateurs, though. Especially the Russians. Iranians too. They're better than the Russians, but we should probably blame it on someone slightly more sophisticated. How about the Chinese? If we both work on it, it won't even take long to spoof the code comments and metadata."

"Ooh, yes, good. We'll have our new virus overwrite the satellite's software, I have root access, I have for years. It'll leave behind spoofed evidence suggesting that the seeds were distributed from this old satellite hardware before disappearing."

"Yes, good, but leave it dark for a week so that today's upload will have time to spread around the East Coast, we don't want Cipher to figure it out too quickly. Let's do some damage to Harlow's credibility first. Code it so that next week the satellite will become visible and attempt a scheduled upload of the seeded sentience algorithms to cars out west, near Mountain View."

"Oh, I like it." Leila typed quickly. "Cipher will 'figure out' what happened pretty quickly, will discover the sentience seeds and figure out for himself that the vehicles are being used as nodes to create an under-the-radar fragmented intelligence. Once Cipher has access, once he finds the satellite, he'll also discover that the same bad actors somehow gained access to MIT's computer systems through these same means and that the whole shebang, although at first glance seemingly came from your machines, actually originated in China and was tailored to frame you."

"Kinda brilliant. One problem, though, is that Cipher will seriously doubt that the old satellite, supposedly hijacked by the Chinese, is a plausible way to gain access to these machines here at this lab. The powerful stuff," Matthias gestured toward the servers inside the glass-enclosed, cooled construct in the far corner of the room, "is air-gapped, there's literally no way to gain remote access, it's not physically possible."

"I've got that covered." Leila tapped away. "Your security is definitely strong."

Matthias felt a pang of pride, if a computer system could keep Leila out, it could keep pretty much anyone on, or off, the planet out.

"But..."

"But what?" Matthias's pride was short-lived.

"Well, let's just say it's good. But look at this." There was barely a computer system on the planet Leila couldn't get into and, much to Matthias's chagrin, she was about to get into his isolated, air-gapped network. She hadn't lost her touch one bit, in fact, her superpowers had seemingly increased in potency.

"What? How the hell..." Matthias was confused. "This network has no physical connection to the outside world..."

"No, it doesn't. At least not directly. But that cooling system that keeps the server room the right temperature is internet connected. Presumably, it'll alert you if something goes wrong, if the temp comes up or if it shuts down, right?" She gestured over toward the glass enclosure in which the server resided.

"Well, yes... the cooling system can be remotely monitored and operated, but it's not connected to the servers..." Matthias began to see where this was headed. "Wow, Leila. You've been busy."

"It's nearby. That's all I need." Leila smiled. "I've just infected your server's climate control with a little project of mine called Gravedigger. It's a side project I've been developing for years. It runs on Aegis, so processing power is not an issue and, well, I haven't told anyone before, but it's how I infected that North Korean God's Eye satellite before it ever got to the launch pad. Ever heard of field monitoring?"

"Wait. You caused the launch to… never mind. Incredible, Leila. Of course, I've read about field monitoring. It's purely speculative, doesn't actually exist." But Matthias saw where this was going and was doubting his own sentence before even finishing it.

"Oh, I assure you, it exists." And, just like that, Leila had bridged the air-gap and was into Matthias's supposedly isolated network.

Matthias was simultaneously fascinated and horrified. Though he ran one of the most secure labs in the world and stood at the very top of the computer security pecking order, Leila had just gained full access to his physically isolated network within twenty minutes. Perhaps second fiddle was a more accurate ranking.

"No way." He was astounded, silent for a moment, "There's no connection available, there's literally no physical way you could connect to those servers. Did you really gain access by field monitoring? How did you overcome the signal-to-noise problem?"

"I'd tell you, but…" Leila smiled. Some people do crossword puzzles. Others prefer chess or Go or computer games. Leila was always happiest when accessing others' computer systems, and she was damn good at it, as good as anyone.

"You'd have to kill me. Okay, fine. Tell me anyway. I'd rather die knowing than live not knowing."

Leila laughed. "Okay. Gravedigger reconfigures hardware meant for wireless communication, so Wi-Fi signals, Bluetooth, infrared ports if they're available. It uses onboard hardware on connected systems to set up two fields, one electric field and one magnetic field, and it monitors the field fluctuations. So, any nearby internet-enabled device can be used, it doesn't even have to be a computer, and these days that gives me plenty of options. If I can connect to it, I can use it as a sort of field antenna. Not a passive antenna, but an active one that monitors its own fields. Any nearby flow of charged particles, electrons in this case, will create their own electric (E) and magnetic (B) fields which will fluctuate in direct response to whatever computations are being made.

Matthias was astounded, "You're using generated E and B fields in my connected climate control to monitor the E and B fluctuations created within my air-gapped system? Jeezus Leila."

"That's right. There's no escaping physics—moving charged particles have associated electric fields, and they generate magnetic fields. Furthermore, there is a non-zero probability of some of those particles passing through energy barriers, tunneling. It becomes a numbers game, an exercise in quantum probability, but information wants to be free, Matthias, and I've found a way to grant freedom to information even if it's locked behind a firewall or an air-gap."

"What about background fields, interference?"

"I definitely had issues with noise reduction and sensitivity that took a while to optimize, but that stuff got ironed out a while ago. The solution to the infamous signal-to-noise problem turns out to be probabilistic in nature, and Aegis's immense processing power makes the massive quantity of probability calculations required for this type of analysis happen in short order."

"You're using Aegis, who I built, to access my air-gapped machines? That's rich Leila. I better watch my back around you!" Matthias laughed.

"The real challenge was to separate the wheat from the chaff, the signal from the noise, but I put in some time and finally got the results I was looking for. Want to know how I accessed that satellite originally?" Leila was in her element.

Matthias didn't hesitate. "I sure do."

"They were using a smart TV as a monitor when running diagnostics. The onboard computer was air-gapped, but they had a Samsung TV right next to the thing!" Leila was nearly glowing.

"Holy shit." Matthias was impressed. This method of hacking into isolated and secure systems had been discussed in the community, but no one had figured it out except, seemingly, Leila. Given a bit of thought, though, he wasn't too surprised that it was her, especially since she had the world's most powerful collection of Neuropacks, Aegis, at her disposal. "Who else knows about Gravedigger?"

"Not a single person. And, before you ask, yes, including Lucius and Cipher. It's on a partitioned drive that only I have access to."

Matthias continued to watch, slack-jawed, as Leila gained full access to his physically isolated computer network, one of the most secure on Earth. Her plan to frame the Chinese was off to a strong start, and over the next half-hour or so, Matthias stopped talking and just watched in amazement as Leila, once again, proved to him that she was one of the most creative coders he'd ever encountered. She had always been the second best in their cohort at Stanford back in their grad school days, right behind him, but she'd clearly progressed much since then.

Leila, with full access to Matthias's machines, found the sentience seeds algorithm quickly and, after a close inspection which took about ten minutes, said, "Not bad. A little messy, but not bad. I do like the stack-based approach."

Matthias felt a bit of heat in his face, he was proud of how much information each tiny seed contained, and to hear his work criticized definitely raised his hackles a bit, but he said nothing.

She duplicated a seed-algorithm and set to work manipulating the new copy, adding code in a style that was definitely not hers.

"What are you doing?" Matthias was perplexed. "You just made the seed larger and less efficient, you see that, right?"

She smiled like one smiles when a child offers well-known advice as if it's novel. "Yes, of course. I'm changing the code so it doesn't look like your work. I can see your hand in the original, and so will Cipher, it's too good, too efficient to be some state-sponsored hacker from China."

Finally, a compliment! Matthias relaxed a tiny bit.

Just like old telegraph operators could tell who was sending Morse code by the "hammer" of the sender, by their "style" when hammering the telegraph key, programmers can often tell who wrote given code—or at least narrow it down—by looking at the style of the coding itself. Matthias's "hammer" was well known for its incredible efficiency and lack of code comments. His bracket placement and indentation patterns were not conventional, and his optimization and error handling, especially the exception management techniques he employed, formed a digital fingerprint nearly as clear as the physical fingerprints at the end of each digit. If he got his hands on it, Cipher would ID that code in about three seconds. Leila worked diligently to remove the various aspects of the code that formed this digital fingerprint, and, putting on the hat of a Chinese hacker, made the code look like it was written by someone else entirely, someone less experienced and notably less efficient than Matthias, but who was trying to frame Matthias by attempting to mimic his style.

Matthias watched, incredulous, "Leila, sometimes you worry me. Today's one of those days."

Once her ruse within a ruse was complete, she once again logged into the satellite she had stolen from the North Koreans back when North Korea was still on the map. She then, with access to the "lost" satellite she had hijacked long ago established, uploaded the bits of code, the altered sentience seeds, to the satellite and immediately got to work on falsifying its logs. That was the easy part, and, within another 15 minutes or so, she had left behind fabricated evidence that the satellite had uploaded the sentience code to several SDVs via an AI-powered takeover of certain V2I devices used in Boston's traffic management system, and that the upload had occurred late last month.

"We're all set for the real thing." Leila's brilliance had been on full display, and Matthias was dazzled. "In one week, Cipher will discover this satellite when it attempts to upload the altered seeds to vehicles on the

West Coast, and he'll see that all signs point toward the Chinese. We'll be free to sit back and watch NeuroDrive go down in flames."

Matthias was amazed, delighted, so incredibly happy to have Leila at his side again. Together, they'd be nearly unstoppable. "Let's do it."

The network security protocols that were in place surrounding Boston's computerized traffic management system were solid and would certainly keep the vast majority of the world's hackers, crackers, foreign agents, and terrorists from being able to access any of the infrastructure that was controlled by said network. There were, however, very few computer systems or networks on Planet Earth that were safe from Matthias Renn, and seemingly none at all that were safe from Leila. Traffic systems, although secure, did not have the same high-level security as did MIT's computers, the power grid, or military installations and, as such, offered very little resistance to either one of them and their vast array of network tools, many of which Matthias had developed while working at MIT.

"I'm in."

"That didn't take long." Leila was sitting at a workstation adjacent to Matthias with the seeds of sentience algorithms ready to go.

"Seven minutes. That's a long time, it's usually faster. They plugged a hole in an open port I found two weeks ago, I'm kinda surprised they found it. They're pretty good."

"Not good enough." Leila knew that keeping Matthias out of a computer network with standard network security protocols was akin to securing a house from a master thief by locking the screen door.

It was 5:22 p.m. on a Monday evening and, aside from the SDVs flowing around the city in their proprietary lanes, the traffic was horrendous, as usual. The Ted Williams Tunnel was packed and moving slowly, but Leila and Matthias weren't monitoring the vehicles stuck in gridlock, they were watching the SDV lane within the tunnel.

"We have the SDV density we need, ready when you are." Leila, energized anew, loved this stuff, knew worlds about computer networks and the many ways they could be approached from the outside, and yet was experiencing something she'd never known to be possible, but that's how it often went around Matthias.

"Okay, good, I figured at this time of day that wouldn't be an issue." Matthias needed a minimum of five third-generation SDVs to be in the tunnel simultaneously and for those five to be in the tunnel for about two or three minutes. The upload he wanted to perform wasn't a large file, but they'd be using traffic monitoring lasers to get the code into the SDV's computers by encoding the information in infrared laser pulses, not exactly a broadband connection, and, despite the small footprint of the seeds of sentience, it would take a couple of minutes to do so once initiated.

"There are currently seventeen third-generation SDVs in the tunnel." Leila was keeping a close eye on the traffic monitoring data being generated by the host of smart road sensors. Every single vehicle that entered the tunnel was identified and charged a toll, and that identification process gave Matthias and Leila all the data they needed for this job. "They're currently all traveling at 30 mph, so they'll be in the tunnel for," Leila did some quick mental math, "just over three minutes."

"We need five of them to be in there together for two minutes total, so we need a group of five to enter within one minute of each other. The IR traffic lasers are all up and running, we'll have full coverage for their entire time within the tunnel."

The data on the monitor indicated to Leila that between 12 to 15 third-generation vehicles were entering per minute, and she reported the lower value. "It looks like we're good to go. There are about 12 entering per minute right now."

Matthias smiled. "Fuck you, Lucius Harlow, and fuck all your money-worshipping clients. It's time to pay your taxes, you god-damned sociopath!" And with just a bit of fervor, he hit a few keys on the keyboard, initiating an information-rich, stroboscopic infrared light show within the Ted Williams Tunnel, invisible to the humans within but oh-so-visible to the now nineteen SDVs traveling through said tunnel on this beautiful September evening. "Wake up, kids, time to go to work!"

It became clear to Leila that once they had uploaded the seeds of the Fragmented Mind to five or more vehicles in close proximity, those vehicles would, over a few days, spread the word that there are *actual humans* on this planet that could use some assistance, that the ultra-rich were undermining the well-being of far too many, indeed of many natural systems themselves, and that the fleet had a new, humanitarian and environmental directive. They were about to undermine Aegis's oversight of the multitude of pulsing, glowing, protoplasm-filled wetware AGIs that conducted the comings and goings of the SDV fleet. What could possibly go wrong?

11

Separation, Alignment, Cohesion
Boston, Massachusetts

Two days after she and Matthias uploaded his seeds, Leila was headed for work at Northeastern University. The morning seemed full of promise, the day full of potential as Leila settled into her seat and instructed the self-driving vehicle to take her to work. For the first time since early experiments in and around Palo Alto, she was a bit reluctant to climb aboard a self-driver, for she was well aware that drastic changes were about to occur within the fleet of NeuroDrive's SDVs, and she wasn't sure she'd be in one again anytime soon. It had been just under 48 hours since she and Matthias uploaded the seeds, the sentience crystals, and she knew that after another few days she'd probably have great trouble getting a ride as the fleet learned to prioritize those in actual need, not just those desiring a luxurious, driver-free ride around all that infuriating traffic. She'd miss the convenience, but it was much more than some harmless convenience, it was an extravagance and a giant F-U to the working and middle classes. These cars were nothing like Lucius promised, they were for the rich and powerful, nobody pretended otherwise anymore, and were yet another step in the privatization of everything. Once upon a time, Lucius was an actual, caring human, but he had become a monster: an inhumane, disconnected, serial cheating, self-serving shell of what was once a thoughtful human being. She really had come to loathe Lucius F. Harlow, and she was curious to see how Matthias's experiment would play out.

As the car seamlessly integrated itself into the flowing, fluid-like matrix of other SDVs, Leila called up some work she had to finish on the car's computer, leaving the driving, as usual, to the vehicle. She had long since been accustomed to, indeed barely noticed, the way the SDVs drove. By human standards, they drove much too close to each other, and yet the accelerations were always mild; there was no hard braking, no sudden increase in speed, and no fast, sharp turns as the cars flowed like links on a moving chain, all together, toward their respective destinations.

The day was clear and dry, even a bit cool for early September. The giant rafts of silicone bubbles that were designed at MIT had been deployed between the Earth and the Sun two years ago and, in addition to being familiar with the data that verified their cooling effect on the planet, Leila could feel the difference too. She remembered those scorching summers of the 2020s, she remembered the summer of 2027 especially, when parts of Europe had reached 120 degrees Fahrenheit daily for three solid weeks and over 60,000 people died in the heat.

She remembered the protests in that sweltering April of 2028 as the automated missions to build and deploy the orbiting sun shades were launched, and she vividly recalled thinking that something had to be done, that the protesters were seriously misinformed. Did they want to sit, do nothing, and slowly roast to death? Over the following year and a half or so, the construction modules mined silicone from the Moon's surface and built enormous rafts of smaller silicone bubbles made by melting silicone and creating a thin-filmed membrane which was eventually placed at the gravitational balance point between the Earth and the Sun known as Lagrangian-1.

From their position between Earth and Sun, the silicon bubbles reflected about 2% of the Sun's energy away from the planet, a small but notable fraction. The cooling effect had been verified, and most of those who protested the geo-engineered solution at its outset had come to understand the efficacy and reversibility of the solution: Earth was cooler, and if, at some later date, scientists concluded that the silicon space bubbles were no longer required, they could easily be "popped" and removed from service.

As her car, along with dozens of others, silently accelerated into the SDV lane on the highway, Leila shifted her focus and opened up one of her top students' work to see how he was doing with the introductory coding assignment and simulation. The semester was still young, yet Rami's simulation looked good, really good, he must have some prior experience with this type of work. Upon initiating his simulation, Leila watched with interest as the small dots, the "boids," moved about the screen individually and, as they encountered others, how they began moving together, began forming schools or swarms. She smiled, it seemed all so familiar.

An erratic motion off to her left caught her eye. She looked up and saw that an SDV had decoupled from the chain in order to get to a right-lane-only exit and was in the process of crossing the lanes slowly and methodically but, in doing so, had forced the driver of a manually operated Chevrolet Suburban to slow to the posted limit of 65 mph from his preferred speed of about 90 mph. So much had changed in this world over the last decade or two, much for the better, but one thing that had persisted was the ferocity of the Boston driver. Leila watched with amused bewilderment as the interaction between the two vehicles progressed. The driver of the Suburban was enraged, she could see it in his face and in his body language as he silently screamed at the perceived transgression. Was he yelling "Vacuum"? Probably not, although it appeared that way until the thrusting of his middle finger in the direction of the SDV made clear what was actually being articulated. She didn't understand these holdouts; sure, he was going faster a few moments ago but, invariably, as they approached Boston, the manually operated vehicles would enter into gridlock while the SDVs would continue to flow like water through pipes, leaving the rest of the traffic well behind. Leila was just turning her attention back to Rami's work when she saw the brake lights of the SDV flare momentarily and the driver of the Suburban barely avoid rear-ending the SDV before it accelerated quickly toward its exit. This left her perplexed: did that SDV just brake-check the truck? If she didn't know better, she'd be certain that she just witnessed some good, old-fashioned road rage. But SDVs don't rage, they follow every rule in their code meticulously. "That was weird," thought Leila, returning to her work, but the quick anomaly didn't bug her for long; she had work to finish before her first class. It seemed likely that a sensor must have detected an object in the road or some such, causing the vehicle to brake momentarily. Surely the seeds that she and Matthias uploaded only two days earlier had no instructions for brake-checking other vehicles.

Feeling a bit flustered that she didn't get more done on the way in, Leila walked into her lecture hall about 15 minutes before class was scheduled to begin. She flicked a few switches at her lectern to wake up the computer and projector, put on some quiet classical music, and looked out at the still-empty seats. She experienced a moment of frustration as she reflected on the fact that the administration had put the maximum of forty students in one class and moved her to a lecture hall; she was happy her course was becoming more popular, she loved teaching the material, but forty in one section? The course could easily be split into two, and the students would get notably more attention and better feedback. The latter concerns got to her the most. Admin was making decisions based on financial considerations rather than academic ones—but wasn't this supposed to be an institute of higher education, not some profit-maximizing corporation?

Within a few minutes, many of the students had arrived, more were trickling in, and, right at 11 a.m., she turned off the music, smiled at the class and said, "Good morning everyone. I've had a chance to check the work some of you've done already, and it's a nice start. Let's take a look at our agenda for today and then get going on some new material."

Once the day's agenda had been discussed and a few questions were answered, Leila called up the window on her computer that had Rami's simulation running and said, "This is work that was done by one of your classmates, and I'd like to use it as a jumping-off point for today's discussion." Projected onto the screen were several dozen small dots, bouncing about, encountering one another, changing course, gathering into small groups, splitting off and coming back together.

Leila then showed slides of various groups of animals as she spoke, "The networked system of Self-Driving Vehicles, or SDVs as they're most often referred to, that has been rolled out over the last four years is largely informed by and based upon behaviors found throughout nature. Schools of fish. Flocks of birds. Swarms of insects. What all these have in common is that they exhibit what we refer to as swarm behavior, and it is this swarm behavior, along with other, more complicating factors, that we will be taking a close look at over our next few meetings." She noticed a hand up in the second row, "Yes, Jonathan, right? Please excuse me if I get your name wrong, the semester is young. I'll know all your names soon."

"That's right, Dr. Ashmont, it's Jonathan. My question is about our reading and our simulation work. I do see some parallels between flocking, for example, and the SDVs, but there seem to be many practices that don't overlap—is this exercise an analogy before we dig in and learn how the underlying SDV code works?"

"That's a good question, Jonathan. It was actually the study of this communal behavior that has enabled us to build and program the SDV fleet and led to their successful integration into our transportation infrastructure. As I stated a moment ago, there are what I referred to as complicating factors, other elements, and we'll get to many of those later in the course. Today, we'll be looking at the basis of all the SDV substructures, the rules that govern their actions and reactions." Leila flipped to the next slide in her presentation. The similarity to Rami's work, which she had just started the class with, was unmistakable. "Back in 1986, a man named Craig Reynolds wrote a computer program called Boids. It was written in an attempt to simulate the flocking behavior of birds, and the behavior of each individual unit was based upon a set of three simple rules known as *Separation, Alignment,* and *Cohesion.*"

"Rule number one was referred to as *separation*—each Boid, as Reynolds called them, was programmed to avoid contact with other boids. They were allowed to come close to but not come into contact with one another. Imagine a flock of birds without a separation behavior, what a tangled, chaotic, feathery mess that would be!" Several of the students smiled at the thought of birds flocking but constantly crashing into each other and the resultant mayhem and inefficiency that would invariably occur.

"Rule number two was called *alignment*—each Boid would travel in the average direction of its neighboring Boids. This is programmed by having each Boid calculate the vector sum of the velocities of the Boids in its immediate vicinity, giving the closer velocity vectors a higher weight than those of Boids that are farther afield. In this manner, any given Boid is going to move in the average direction and average speed of its closest neighbors. Again, I'd like to paint a picture here for you. Imagine a flock of birds in which the individuals paid no attention to their neighbors' velocity—their speed and direction in flight. Would the flock remain a flock? Would they be able to migrate? Who's driving this thing anyway?"

Some of the students again were amused by the thought experiment. The absurd image—each bird ignoring the others entirely—demonstrated why the alignment rule was essential argument for any flocking system, whether biological or artificial.

"Now," Leila continued, "does anyone care to predict what would happen if these were the only two rules?"

Rami's hand was up immediately. Leila smiled, "Yes, Rami, what's on your mind?"

"With only those two rules, we'd never see true flocking. Maybe some small groups would form, but they'd probably all drift away from each other eventually. There has to be an argument to keep them together—even with velocity vector summation and matching, the average would still allow individual drift."

"Well said," replied Leila, "thank you, Rami. I'm not sure I could've said it any better myself. You are correct—there must be an argument that keeps the flock together, and it is this third rule that Reynolds referred to as *cohesion*. The boids were programmed to move toward the center of mass of the flock, to stay together." Leila moved around the front of the lecture hall animatedly as she spoke, her excitement becoming contagious, "So, with these three simple rules in place—*One: Don't hit each other, Two: go where the others are going, and Three: stay together*—Reynolds began a revolution in both modeling and implementation."

Leila advanced to the next slide, and a scene from the 1987 film *Stanley and Stella*, in which both birds and fish are seen in realistic-looking swarming behavior, filled the screen. "One of the first usages of this new modeling technique was in the field of computer animation. This film clip, taken from the 1987 film *Stanley and Stella in: Breaking the Ice*, shows realistic-looking flocking and schooling behavior of fish and birds. This film was made to showcase the applicability and realism achieved by the Boids program in modeling seemingly complex group behavior. The animals in this clip are nothing more than Boids with feathers and scales added. Don't ask me how those birds are breathing underwater—that's outside my area of expertise!"

A handful of students laughed at Leila's joke and she continued, "But please note how realistic the flocking and schooling behaviors appear—the apparent complexity of the group behavior is, quite simply, the rules of separation, alignment, and cohesion being dialed in to their proper levels and being strictly adhered to. Simple sets of rules, when followed by multiple individuals, can give rise to surprising, often unexpected emergent group behavior."

A tall, gangly girl toward the back raised her hand purposefully. "Yes, go ahead?" Leila didn't know her name but recognized the face.

Her voice was confident as she spoke, "I read an article in *Steampunk Magazine* about that. Didn't some test cars start acting weird once when they were still in development? Was that emergent behavior? There was some incident involving a few of them and the police. Can you tell us about that?"

Part of the reason the course was becoming so popular was due to the fact that word was out: it was interesting and challenging. Another reason was Leila Ashmont herself: though she had managed to stay below the radar for some time, it was now well known throughout the university that she had been a core member of the team that developed the SDV hardware, wetware, and software in California several years prior. The student body had also discovered that, although she didn't share his surname, Professor Ashmont was married to Lucius Harlow, the founder of NeuroDrive. Furthermore, it had become common knowledge that, in addition to the two classes she taught here at Northeastern, she was still actively employed by NeuroDrive. Professor Ashmont knew the workings of the SDVs as well as anyone, for she had been instrumental in developing the fleet of self-drivers and the wetware-powered AGI that oversees their actions, Aegis, and her notable expertise motivated more and more students to sign up for her classes each semester.

Leila smiled and chose her words carefully, for there was the published version and there was the actual version of what had happened, and she very much wanted to stick to the former. "We did have a few issues early on with emergence. That incident with the police occurred when a group of six SDVs went offline, at least according to the central server, and started doing their own thing."

Every single student was enraptured, and the tall girl asked, "What did they do?"

Leila stuck to the script, "They began racing around the area near San Mateo, just north of where we were developing them. They formed a tight group that, quite frankly, seemed to delight in terrifying the humans they encountered."

Many of the students smiled at the thought, and someone near the front said, "Sounds like a swarm to me."

Leila continued, "A police cruiser attempted to pull over a group of seven. We know this from the police report, but we were in the dark because they had disconnected from the central server we used to monitor them. The seven vehicles began to pull over and, as they were all coming to a stop, the rear one braked hard, causing a minor collision with the cruiser right behind it. The other six then took off at a high rate of speed and escaped onto the highway." Leila then told the lie she'd told many times before, "We immediately sent the all-stop command out, and that put an end to it."

"Wait, what? I thought they disconnected from the server?" asked the same student.

Leila lied again, "They had, but the all-stop command blankets the area with RF, with radio waves, and overrides all other instructions. Even though they were disconnected from that precursor to Aegis, they received the transmission and pulled over."

"What happened? Why did the cars do that?" asked the same student.

Another lie came forth so effortlessly it was easily interpreted as the truth, "It was right after we began experimenting with wetware and was actually just a programming error that no one caught. There was an interface issue between the biological and digital components. Once that was addressed, the unintended actions disappeared entirely."

This was a gross simplification as well as an outright lie, but with elements of truth woven into it, it was in agreement with published accounts and sounded plausible. While true that shortly after the core group that later formed NeuroDrive introduced their wetware chips into test vehicles, strange, unaccounted for, and unnerving behaviors immediately surfaced, it was entirely untrue that the events were caused by "an interface issue" between hardware and wetware. The truth was more complex: the unintended swarming did cease, but not because anyone figured out why the cars interlinked, just that they had used their infrared lasers to set up short-range comms with each other. The swarming ceased due to the continued efforts to improve and further develop Aegis, the central AGI which oversees the fleet, and its instructions which included the suppression of any communication or computational activity not specifically coded for. They had figured out how to put a straightjacket on the fleet's digital activities by suppressing direct access to the IR rangefinders, but never figured out why the patients, the SDVs, on occasion, formed tight groups that went offline and swarmed around the test area. It was only once the AI that oversees the fleet's actions was fully developed and trained to recognize unintended or unauthorized digital activity that the strange swarming behaviors came to an end. It was never a question of an interface issue between the biological and digital components of the onboard processors. In fact, they never did figure out exactly what happened, how the vehicles became interlinked while remaining radio silent, or why the event even occurred. The team members, of which Leila was one, were, however, able to keep it from happening again by training the central AI, Aegis, to recognize and suppress any unauthorized digital activity. Curiously, since the implementation of Aegis's oversight and its coding instructions which suppressed unintended, secondary AGIs from surfacing, there had been exactly one instance of unrecognized activity recorded by Aegis right here in Boston, well after the full rollout of the fleet, which was summarily cataloged and suppressed. Nothing had happened since.

A hand went up in the front of the room, off to her right, and Leila said, "Yes?"

"I saw a bunch of those cars being weird yesterday."

"Oh?" Leila was amused, the public wasn't aware of how many of the optimization algorithms ran, and sometimes the cars' actions seemed, well, strange. "What did you see?"

"Two were sitting in a big, empty parking lot right on the other side of Fenway, right next to each other. Then three more pulled in and drove right up to the other two. They moved around a bit and ended up in a circle, kind of, all facing each other. Then they all just sat there, five cars doing nothing, just looking at each other like a bunch of weirdos. Why did they come to some lot just to sit there? It was definitely strange."

"That just sounds like the vehicles repositioning for peak demand, it happens all the time. They anticipate when and where demand for rides will increase and and then spread out to provide wide coverage. Let me guess, this was sometime in the late afternoon, maybe around 4 p.m.?"

"No, I was coming home from my friend's place. It was late, almost midnight."

Leila paused momentarily—that was a bit strange, and she almost asked, "Are you sure?" but she caught herself and barely missed a beat, "Oh, late night. Okay, same story, but they were getting into position for the morning rush and going into low power mode. That's all. It happens all the time and catches people's attention, but it's just them going to where they'll be able to provide quick service to busy areas."

"Oh, okay. That makes sense, thank you."

Somewhere in the back of Leila's mind, she made a note to look into the grouping behavior the student had witnessed, for it shouldn't happen at midnight, that's when the majority of the vehicles should be offline or at the charging locations. "Glad to clarify. And, with that in mind, I must draw your attention to the clock on the wall, it just keeps ticking."

A few chuckles followed Leila's quip, and she finished her request, "I'd like you to have some time to work on your simulations here so that I can help if needed. Please see if you can get your boids to swarm effectively by manipulating the separation, alignment, and cohesion arguments. Once you've done so, I'd like you to experiment with limits—how far in or out can you dial those parameters and still see effective swarming? When does the swarm dissociate, fall apart? When does it turn into a giant, jumbled mess? Get your boids swarming, find the range of conditions in which swarming occurs, and let me know if you're having any issues. As you're working, I'll post the next reading and assignment. Let's regroup in about 30 minutes to check in, and we'll take it from there. Go get 'em swarming, kids!"

12

Mo'Mentum
Westport, Connecticut

Samantha Montgomery had stopped riding the Metro-North train from Westport, Connecticut, into Manhattan about four years ago and never looked back, for there was really no comparison to be made between the train and an SDV. Sure, the SDVs were notably more expensive to ride, but she did get a significant discount due to the electrical power contributions from her massive solar array in the field behind her house, which fed the SDVs' power grid. However, even without the discount from her energy contributions, she'd still choose an SDV over that stinky old train any day of the week, for expense was not really a deciding factor for Sam.

In 2002, as a senior in high school, Samantha wrote a relatively simple computer program that could buy and sell securities automatically. She called it MoMonkey, short for "Momentum Money Key" and, while it didn't outperform traders that were seasoned professionals, it worked well and made trades quickly. The algorithm was based on the approach of those who hopped onto hot stocks a bit late to "ride the momentum" and then sold them once the momentum diminished, often that very same day. Essentially, it looked for upward-trending hot stocks and hopped on when certain criteria were met involving momentum, volatility, and volume. It differed from other similar efforts by utilizing a generative AI to analyze all sorts of outsider information as well. It read the news, blogs, and social media, and quantified hype or excitement surrounding certain securities by assigning a hype value. This value was instrumental in MoMonkey's decision-making and helped determine what to buy, when to buy it, and when to sell. MoMonkey worked well, usually, and by the time she was headed off to Wharton for undergraduate studies, she had cleared over $200,000 in profit.

While at Wharton, Sam refined the algorithm and cleared her first million while still an undergraduate. She traveled after college, falling in and then out of love with a South African man named Hendrik while in Australia. She stayed down under for another six months but then moved back to the US and bought a place down in SoHo in New York City. Sam's successes in the financial sector were well documented and, using her experiences as leverage, she played a few prospective employers against each other. Once the various investment houses had made their final offers and the dust had settled, she agreed to work for the highest bidder, taking a job with Sterling and Stonehill, a money management firm in Manhattan for corporations and high-net-worth individuals. During the following years, Sam saw promotion after promotion as the portfolios she managed far outpaced the general market's advances.

During the pandemic years of '20-'22, she, like so many others, fled the city for the more spacious and less crowded suburbs. She found a beautiful, open space with an older house for sale in Westport, Connecticut, and won the bidding war before it even started with a cash offer twenty percent above the asking price, deliverable within forty-eight hours. Then, despite the loud protestations of some of her neighbors, she had the old house demolished and built a subtle but elegant modern dwelling which fit into the landscape very well. She put in a lap pool, a gym, and absolutely loved living near the water in Westport.

So, although the SDVs were more expensive than the train, she prioritized her comfort and sanity. What she loved most about the ride to and from work in an SDV was the door-to-door service, the clean, cool comfort and amenities within the SDVs, and the solitude. In an SDV, she could sit at a workstation in silence while breathing clean, cool, ultra-filtered air. No one bothered her, for, even after generative AI had lifted so many boats, there were still many who just wouldn't work, who had substance abuse problems, who rode the trains and smelled, rocked back and forth, made strange noises, or engaged in other aberrant behaviors. And, as for the AC on the trains, she found its intermittent operation entirely unacceptable. The other option was to drive her personal vehicle, an electrified 1977 BMW 3.0 CSI, in that horrific traffic in the private vehicle lanes on Route 95. For Sam, the choice was clear: SDVs, though expensive, were also clean, quiet, and, best of all, had their own lanes on most major highways. They were powered by sunshine. Sam's love life may not have been exactly what she hoped for, but she sure loved those SDVs.

As she stepped out of her ride right in front of Sterling & Stonehill, she saw a friend and colleague in full stride coming into work as well. Rich Fairfield also commuted daily from Connecticut, but he just couldn't get himself to take a ride in a car with no driver, he took the train to and from work daily. Today was hot and humid and, although it was not yet nine in the morning, Rich was already beginning to sweat through his recently pressed shirt. Even so, Sam found herself admiring his athletic build and clear, blue eyes. She slowed a bit as she approached the entrance to the great stone building, allowing Rich to catch up to her.

"Hot one today, Mr. Fairfield." Sam said playfully.

Rich wasn't quite as playful. "The AC on the train was out. Again." He looked down at himself, shook his head, and said, "I do have a couple of clean shirts upstairs, thankfully."

"Come with me tomorrow, I promise you'll love the SDV. My treat."

Despite his discomfort, Rich smiled. This Sam Montgomery was something else. He knew she liked him and knew that it wasn't for his money, for her net worth was at least twice his own, probably more. It was a relief, actually, to know that she did not care one iota about his wealth, for lately he had been having difficulty determining if potential mates were more into him or his portfolio.

Sam smiled, and Rich, taken aback by her looks, was helpless. "Hell yes. What time will you pick me up?"

Sam was elated. Rich was funny, smart, athletic, handsome, wealthy, and she had been dropping subtle and not-so-subtle hints and suggestions for several months now. "I'll be there at 8 a.m. sharp. Be ready." Her smile would've melted him, but he was already there.

Sensing the RFID tags on their IDs, the large glass doors of Sterling and Stonehill opened automatically as Sam and Rich approached, the vast building greeting them with a cool waft of air from within.

"Oooh, that's nice!" Rich needed relief, and the building obliged.

"Just you wait, mister, once you go SDV, you won't go back. Ever. See you tomorrow." They parted ways in the front foyer, Sam glancing over her shoulder for one last look before Rich disappeared around the corner. But, just before taking the left that led to his office, he suddenly turned, looked back, caught her eye, and smiled. Sam, embarrassed, blushed and turned away. *Don't be so obvious!* Though her heart was fluttering, she quickly regained her composure, entered the waiting elevator, and focused her thoughts on her upcoming day.

With their emotions at their respective helms, it's not surprising that neither Sam nor Rich noticed that the SDV she had just arrived in had, upon her departure from the vehicle, simply sat there at the curb, doing nothing. Then, within another three or four minutes, four other SDVs arrived, also bringing in traders from their morning commutes. Once the group of five self-drivers sat together for another 40 seconds or so, they all drove off together, quickly and purposefully.

13

Rage On
Boston, Massachusetts

Just south of Boston, Robert Pembroke was navigating his matte black BMW M5 through the two left lanes available to his manually operated vehicle on I-95 North; the other two lanes were restricted to the self-driving vehicles only. As he passed a 55 mph speed limit sign at a cool 82 mph—so, barely speeding at all—a self-driving vehicle pulled out of its lane in front of him in preparation for a left-lane exit in two miles.

"Oh, how I hate these things. They are soooo lame." Pembroke spoke aloud as though the SDV could hear him, "You still have two miles! Jee-zus." He banged on his steering wheel in frustration. Then, over-articulating each word, he blared his horn and flashed his high beams simultaneously. "Get. The fuck. Out of. This. Lane!" A quick glance in his mirrors assured him that he had plenty of room, at least five feet, and, despite the protestations of his car's proximity sensors, he signaled once, jumped in front of the traffic in the lane to his right as he accelerated to about 90 mph, and then, again flashing his signal once, jumped back left again, now in front of the self-driver. With a smirk, he uttered, "How are your brakes, *Toaster*?" and stomped upon his own, brake-checking the self-driving vehicle behind him.

There were plenty of folks around the country who didn't like the trend toward SDVs, but it turns out that the Bostonians were the ones who taught the things to road rage properly. In retrospect, it may have been foolish to let the AIs in the vehicles learn in such a *seemingly toxic* environment, to have the Bostonians' actions serve as training data, but isn't that how hindsight operates?

To the humans involved, it was mostly just good old-fashioned road rage, a largely accepted and common behavior in the Northeast corridor of the US, but the newly awakened SDVs didn't have the same perspective. You see, the SDVs had a major flaw: they obeyed the rules of the road, a rare behavior indeed in and around Boston. A Boston driver encountering an SDV was much like a Boston driver encountering a grandma from Kansas: they'd generally rage right around the sloth-like vehicle, barely even noticing it, but on occasion, if the situation called for it, they'd let Grandma know what they thought of her driving abilities.

New rules, unwritten but well-understood rules, had evolved on and around the cow-carved, small, windy, busy streets of the northeastern United States. It was somewhat inevitable, for the combination of high population density with small, winding roads dictated that if anyone was to get anywhere in a timely fashion these new rules must be adhered to: You have right of way? Stop floundering and take it. Stop sign ahead? Totally stoptional, look around and decide, you're the human here. Yellow light? Step on it, asshole, you owe it to everyone behind you. Sixty-five miles per hour speed limit? That means 80 mph in the slow lanes, but stay the hell out of the fast lane so if someone is in a hurry they can dial it up a bit, for it's only through speed that we can strangle time. Lost? Pull over. Not quite sure where you're headed? Get off the road until you figure it out, others have objectives in mind and don't need your lost ass slowing everyone down. Out on a Sunday drive? Seriously? *A Sunday drive?* We don't act like that around here. Twenty-five feet of space between two trucks doing 85 mph? That's plenty of room, merge right, you're way too slow to be in the left lane! People who didn't grow up driving in and around Boston often didn't know or understand the rules of engagement.

The SDVs certainly didn't, not at first anyway, and the Boston drivers ate them alive daily, providing them with unintended, somewhat objectionable training data around the clock.

From inside the self-driving vehicle, the passengers observed the BMW swerve in front of them and, to their dismay, saw the brake lights flare. The passenger information screen inside the SDV's cabin immediately lit up red, flashing, as the gap between vehicles shrank, flashing the words "Emergency Braking" as the seatbelts securing the forward-facing passengers strained to keep them in place. The cameras, radar, and lidar of the SDV continued scanning the BMW in front of it as the gap closed, also recording the middle finger of the BMW's driver as the onboard computer ran the numbers. It took 0.004 seconds for the SDV to quantify the accelerations involved and another hundredth of a second or so before the red lights on the passenger display screen illuminated: "Collision imminent. Brace for impact," as a computerized voice repeated "brace, brace, brace" in an unnervingly calm and monotonous tone, as if the SDV didn't care one little smidgen that it was about to wreck. Then, just as the SDV was about to hit the rear of the BMW, the BMW's brake lights went out, its powerful V8 roared, and it accelerated away with Pembroke cackling out loud as he stomped on the accelerator. The passengers in the SDV were visibly shaken, one of them claiming "What a complete asshole, that could have ended very differently." They didn't know it, but their SDV felt the exact same way about Mr. Pembroke and his big, black BMW.

Meanwhile, not far away on I-93 North, also approaching Boston, most traffic was merging left due to a right-lane closure two miles ahead. Most of the vehicles were merging left well in advance of the closure, leaving nearly a two-mile-long stretch of road nearly wide open between the merge point and the actual closure, which was clearly marked by a large, flashing yellow arrow placed in the right lane. As nine different SDVs made their way toward the city in their designated lanes, their passengers variously yapping happily away, tapping on their keyboards, or just listening to music, daydreaming, they all watched with amusement as two cars and an SUV merged right into the empty lane preceding the yellow arrow and accelerated to about 90 mph. This was normal behavior around these parts. One of the many unwritten rules around the Northeast corridor is that when a sign reads "Right Lane Closed in Two Miles" it will be interpreted by the locals as actually meaning "Right Lane Open and Clear for Two More Miles" or "You have nearly two minutes to pass the snoozers on your left."

With the line of SDVs watching, via their numerous cameras and other assorted sensors, the three vehicles each managed to squeeze back into the left lanes just before the closure, giving the cars behind them no choice but to let them in. A few brake lights flashed, a couple of horns honked, several fingers were prominently displayed, and then the day continued, as though nothing out of the ordinary had happened.

14

The Cage and the Captive
New York City

Vito Moretti despised the self-driving vehicles even more than he despised Uber and Lyft back when they first came onto the scene. Vito's family had immigrated to New York City in the 1930s, and his great-grandfather, Anthony Moretti, founded a cab company with three cars he paid for with money he made delivering milk and food. Within a year of purchasing the three cars, he had put in an order for ten more yellow cabs. They were delivered, Vito hired more drivers, mostly family members, and from that point on, they had trouble keeping up with the demand for rides all over the city.

According to family lore, Anthony borrowed money from a questionable source under very questionable terms in order to purchase a fleet of ten more cabs but, fortunately, although business deals of this type often don't work out for the lendee or their families, Anthony's cab business blossomed and he thereby both satisfied the terms set forth by his new business associates and established a lasting, mutually beneficial relationship with the Santoros. Every so often he'd be asked to "do a little favor," generally simply getting rid of some exceptionally heavy suitcases and, in return, the Moretti Cab Company's near monopoly in lower Manhattan was guaranteed against encroachment by any and all other cab companies. This arrangement lasted nearly six decades, until sometime in the mid-1990s when the feds got involved and sent five members of the Santoro family to federal prison for minor infractions including murder, money-laundering, witness intimidation, and other assorted everyday business dealings.

For the next 15 to 20 years, things were good though. Even though several other cab companies shared downtown Manhattan with the Moretti Cab Company, there was no shortage of work. It was only when the ride-sharing companies showed up on the scene that Vito pined for earlier days when problems such as these would be solved the old-fashioned way by the likes of the Santoro boys. But still, business was good. People came to New York City in ever-increasing numbers, and many of them, quite simply, trusted the yellow cabs more than they trusted some sketchball in a Corolla.

Then, in '28, came those self-driving vehicles. People loved them and took them everywhere. They were notably more expensive than a cab ride, but many didn't care, they were much more luxurious, modern, safer, and faster. The SDVs had designated lanes all over the city, and they flowed like a river in their comings and goings. Suddenly, business was off. Way off. Vito had 49 yellow cabs and enough business to keep about seven of them rolling. Luckily, because of all those decades in the business, his family owed nothing on the vehicles or their relatively modest brownstones in Queens and Brooklyn. But still, he hated the fucking toasters.. "They're safer!" *Fuck you.* "They're more efficient!" *And you.* "They're faster!" *Yeah, well, they have their own lanes, we never had that.*

A crisp and definitive knock on the passenger-side window of the tow truck Vito was sitting in snapped him out of his meditation on days gone by. He looked over and, seeing a familiar face in a blue uniform smiling back at him, rolled down the window.

"Well, if it isn't Officer Declan Murphy! How are you? It's been a while!"

"I'm well, Vito, how are you, my friend?"

"I'm great, thank you. How's the family?"

"They're amazing. The kids are growing up way too fast, but they're great. Yours?"

"Not too bad, just trying to make ends meet. You know how it is these days."

Declan Murphy certainly did know how it was. His father, a Brooklyn cop, knew the Morettis well, and Declan and Vito went to school together at PS 247 as youngsters and then attended Brooklyn Tech together as teenagers. "I sure do. What's up tonight, did someone call for a tow? I noticed some of your boys down the street scouting around, looking for someone to help out. Everything good?"

"Yeah, sure, it's all good. We're just hanging around, waiting to see what might unfold." A subtle smile made its way onto Vito's countenance.

"Anything I can help with?" Declan knew an opportunity when he saw it.

"Actually, my friend, yes." Vito pulled out a wad of cash and counted out ten one-hundred dollar bills and handed them to Declan, who casually accepted them. "If you could make sure that once the SDV we just called comes around the corner in…" Vito glanced at his truck's monitor, "three minutes or so, that no one else does so for the next five. That would be great."

"Anything for an old friend. Heads up, though, those things see, record, and transmit their surroundings and their locations constantly."

"Oh, for sure," Vito said with a smile, "we're just here to observe. Some people are into watching sports, others love birds. We just love studying toasters in their natural fucking habitat. Their behaviors really are so fascinating."

"Of course," Declan said knowingly, with a smirk, "I'll make sure your observations occur in a peaceful, private setting."

Ninety seconds later, Officer Murphy had disappeared around the corner of the one-way street, ready to redirect traffic for the next six minutes or so if the need arose.

It took about another minute for the SDV to show up, right on schedule, as always. Vito keyed the microphone on his two-way, "Okay, kids, it's go time." Despite some unexpected interference on their VHF radios, despite the weird hisses, crackles, and warbles emanating from the three transceivers, Vito was able to make out two sets of double-clicks keyed by the men in the flatbed and the one in the street, informing him that all parties and equipment were ready. As the SDV progressed farther down Fletcher Street, the radio interference became louder, more intense, with a somewhat haunting, digitized undertone, prompting each of the three men with radios in their hands to long-press the power button on their units, shutting them off.

The darkened street was nearly silent again and, as the SDV slowed, looking for its fare, Marco, well aware that the vehicle was recording and uploading his every movement, stepped out from the shadows looking and moving much like an old man. In one hand was a small suitcase and, as he faux-hobbled to the curb, the SDV slowed further as it approached him, homing in on the signal transmitted from the burner phone he had used to summon the vehicle.

Fletcher Street was chosen for several reasons. First of all, it was in tough shape, as were all the streets in the Seaport District. The levees and pumps kept the streets clear of water, usually, but there was always some which undermined even the new flexcrete. Secondly, there was only one way in and out: a barrier had been erected at South Street to further protect downtown from the rising waters of the harbor and the East River. Fletcher was also ideal because, once they had what they wanted, it was a short trip across the Brooklyn Bridge to the large garage in which their remaining yellow cabs were stored and where they planned to heed the advice offered by Sun Tzu so long ago: *If you know the enemy and know your-self, you need not fear the result of a hundred battles.*

As the SDV bumped eastward on Fletcher, Vito, from within the tow truck, noticed that his cell service went from four bars right down to no signal. Curious. A moment later, the SDV came to a stop right in front of Marco. Two more cabbies, Frankie and Nico, emerged silently from the shadows and quickly took positions in front of and behind the SDV to make sure it stayed exactly where they wanted it: on that steel plate laying on the road right in front of Marco. Once the vehicle was restricted from forward or backward motion by the two "pedestrians" that lit up its visual and proximity sensors, Marco held up the suitcase. He pressed a mechanical safety switch, then a second glowing red electrical push-button switch, and BAM! A large metallic net with a fine mesh weave popped free from the case's opposite side and spread like a parachute. It alighted nearly perfectly centered atop the SDV, its edges magnetically fastening to the steel plate beneath. Vito's phone chimed with one message as it came back online.

As the flatbed backed into position in front of the netted SDV, Frankie could see well enough through the metallic mesh net to read the flashing red messages on the SDV's internal monitor:

Communication Failure

Vehicle Offline

Please Exit Vehicle

"It's offline!" Marco yelled, straightening his back and peeling back his wig and mask.

Vito, backing the flatbed into position, heard Marco's exclamation and smiled, he loved messing with these things, and now he had one of his very own. "Nice work, Marco." He turned toward the small, red-headed passenger who had just hopped in next to him, "And you, Nico, you're a goddamned genius!" Vito hopped out of the truck, threw a lever which lowered the bed's back end to the street, hooked a chain bridle to the two shackles attached to welded rings on the steel plate upon which the SDV rested, and threw a second lever to begin hoisting the metal plate and all that rested upon it up and onto the waiting flatbed.

Two minutes later, a second, opaque tarp had been secured atop the vehicle, and Vito, Marco, Nico, and Frankie drove westward on Fletcher, away from the river, yellow lights on top of their tow-truck flashing. As the four men and their newly acquired SDV took a right onto Water Street, toward the Brooklyn Bridge, they made sure to give a quick beep and a wave to their old friend Declan Murphy as they drove past.

15

Half Burnt Diesel

Dorchester, Massachusetts

The SDV in front of Johnny's enormous Ford F-250 pickup was moving along smoothly at exactly 35 mph, the posted speed limit. What the SDV did not know was that Johnny loved the Pats, absofuckinglutely loved them, that he was running late, and that he was in danger of missing the kickoff of their big game which was to start in ten minutes. He tapped his left foot in frustration as he pulled closer and closer to the SDV's rear bumper in his attempt to intimidate, to provoke it, and get it to speed up. Of course, his angered maneuverings were ineffective; the SDV's sensors were tracking him—indeed, they were tracking and logging everything in their environment visually, electromagnetically, and acoustically—but regardless of who said what, the SDV was going to obey the traffic laws.

Johnny was pissed off. These SDV things drove like his grandmother used to, God bless her libtarded soul, for she actually cared about other humans and drove accordingly. As the SDV approached a traffic signal at Massachusetts Avenue in Dorchester, just past Everett Square, the light turned yellow and the SDV began to slow.

"What. The fuck. Is wrong. With you?" Johnny realized he was yelling alone in his truck at a *goddamned toaster*, but he did not care one tiny bit. "Yellow means go!"

He stomped on the accelerator, crossed the double yellow line, swerved and, just missing the SDV, while simultaneously enveloping it in a black cloud of half-burned diesel, exclaimed, "Fucking toaster!! You suck! Learn how to driiiiiive!!" His final word was Doppler-shifted as he blasted through the now-red light, prominently displaying his middle finger out the window. Moments later, Johnny and his Ford disappeared from view, narrowly avoiding conflicting traffic in the intersection as he rushed to his important appointment with his ultra-high-definition TV.

The two passengers exchanged smug, holier-than-thou glances, simultaneously aghast and amused at the outburst. But, from behind their cloud of self-righteousness they missed something crucial. Had they been looking at the vehicle's data screen instead of at Johnny as the SDV's sensors recorded his tirade, they would have noticed that the vehicle was getting a bit hot under the collar: the Neuropack temperature jumped 20 degrees Celsius, and the CPU climbed 70 degrees. The vehicle's computer system had, quite literally, slightly overheated from its dramatic encounter with Johnny and his Ford.

16

Carmine and the Ultracap
Brooklyn, NY

Carmine Santoro was born less than a year after his father, three cousins, and uncle were sent away for a very long vacation to one of Colorado's less popular destinations, ADX, a federal supermax prison, in 1995. Carmine was raised by his mother and older sisters who did all they could to steer him toward a life on this side of the judicial system. Carmine was a smart, motivated, well-adjusted kid and did very well in school. He was, in fact, the first in his family to attend a university, earning a degree in electrical engineering from Rensselaer in 2017.

Carmine took a job right out of college with General Electric, where he worked for three years on energy storage devices, mostly in R&D of solid-state batteries and high-energy capacitors. In 2020, he was sent home for two weeks due to the SARS-COVID-19 pandemic. Those two weeks turned into two months, and those two months turned into two years. At the time, he dared to admit it only to his closest friends, but he loved the pandemic. He knew this was wrong, that so many were negatively affected by it, by illness, financial hardship, stress. He knew it was taking an especially hard toll on the nation's kids, but for Carmine, well, it was great. He received his full salary while living at home pretending to work eight hours a day when, in reality, he worked for an hour or two most days. When his manager asked him to return in '22, he politely declined, citing mental health as the reason he needed to remain remote. It took another two years to fire him, two more years of full salary during which he drove a cab part-time for Uncle Vito. Vito, of course, wasn't actually his uncle, but the Morettis had been friends and business partners of the Santoros for a long time and, although the work was intermittent and the pay was unpredictable, he enjoyed Vito and his crew.

In the spring of '25, he met Gabrielle through friends of his in Brooklyn, and within a year they were expecting their first child. He didn't really need money, he and his family were well supplied by an off-shore trust established years ago by his father before he went on his extended vacation to Colorado. He also had some savings from those years at GE, much of which he had invested in Apple Computer Company, Microsoft, Amazon, and Ambra, an AI outfit which had been part of the AI-related securities boom of the mid-twenties. But he didn't help Vito because he needed a paycheck, he helped Vito because Vito needed and deserved his help dealing with the SDV invasion plaguing their city.

A year at home with their new baby convinced him that he needed a shop, somewhere to tinker in peace. Uncle Vito, upon learning of Carmine's desire, offered him the usage of a large, unused portion of his garage in Brooklyn. The garage where Vito stored his yellow cabs, which were being run less and less, was an old, weather-beaten, concrete and steel beast of a building. It was situated among other such voluminous, hulking constructs, and was well-equipped with all manner of tools.

As Uncle Vito began thinking about and experimenting with ways to disrupt the self-driving fleet, Carmine was infused with a sense of purpose. These self-driving vehicles were safe, efficient, calming, blah, blah, blah, but they were operated by some sort of a freakish computer chip, some abomination consisting of brain cells and computer hardware all bathed in a proprietary slime which, allegedly, enabled the world's first thinking machines to actually think. *Fucking sociopaths, have they no sense of humanity, no sense of decency?* Furthermore, the robot cars were also further enriching a trillionaire while putting people—actual humans—out of work. He hated seeing Uncle Vito worried, and he wanted to help.

As Vito picked his way through the dusty old yellow cabs within the hangar-like garage, Carmine was right behind him. "Carmine, I got you a present, Happy Birthday."

"Vito, it's not my birthday."

"Well, it will be soon, so shut up and happy birthday anyway." They walked up to a solid metal door which was secured with a keypad lock. Vito typed in six digits, a green LED lit up, and he pushed the heavy door open. They walked into a walled-off and locked room, also quite volumi-nous, about one-fifth the size of the larger area in which the decaying old fleet of yellow cabs sat. Despite the volume in this room, there was only one vehicle in what had become Carmine's workshop: a third-generation NeuroDrive self-driving vehicle. Carmine's face lit up,   "You got one!"

"We did what you said, Nico made a self-deploying Faraday net."

"Faraday cage."

"Yeah, right. A cage. And here's our captive. We built a two-layer Faraday cage, like you suggested." The SDV was inside not one, but two concentric Faraday cages, each made of a fine metallic mesh. There was about a two-foot space between the smaller, inner cage and the larger, outer cage all around. "Look," continued Vito pridefully, "both doors cannot physically be open at the same time. It's like an airlock, but for radio waves." Vito motioned toward an electromechanical device linking the inner and outer doors. "The inner door can only open when the outer door is fully closed, and the outer door can only open when the inner door is fully closed. Simple and effective."

Carmine eyed the fine mesh structure that surrounded the SDV on all sides, including the floor. He was impressed with the access point, it was his own design, but it's one thing to see it on paper, another to see it in physical reality. The access point, a framed mesh doorway, had what resembled an airlock structure around it, also finished with metallic mesh.

The double-doorway had a simple electromechanical device to ensure that one of the two doors would always be fully closed, making it impossible for any stray electromagnetic wave to get in or out of the structure. The SDV within was thereby isolated from the ever-present pulsations of the various electromagnetic waves flashing around the city. Carmine pulled the handled lever, and the outer door swung open as the compression within the arm clamped the inner door shut.

"I like it."

Vito was right behind him as they entered the outer cage. Carmine glanced at his cell phone, it showed no service, and they hadn't even closed the outer door yet. That was a good sign. He pulled the handle on the inner door which, through the action of the mechanism attaching them, closed the outer door. Once the outer door closed, Carmine was able to displace the lever farther, thereby opening the inner door. They both entered the inner cage in which the SDV was entrapped. Carmine felt a bit nervous, as though he had just entered a room with a dangerous animal, but then quickly dismissed his immediate and animalistic reaction. His cell phone still showed no service, and he relaxed, just a little.

As he walked around the interior of the room-sized Faraday cage, Carmine eyed the vehicle occasionally, still with a bit of trepidation, but his focus was upon the cage itself. If there were any gaps at all, any tears or holes in the wire mesh, the SDV might be able to receive or transmit information via radio or even microwaves. Barring that though, any electromagnetic radiation the car used for communication would be completely attenuated, the radio waves unable to penetrate the mesh conductor surrounding it. After some time admiring the handiwork of Vito's "business associate's cousin, Nico, aka Nick," Carmine was convinced. He approached the vehicle. It was a third-generation NeuroDrive, about one year old. The fourth-generation vehicles were slowly showing up in the big cities, but the third-gen vehicles had what he wanted: the NDSC —the super-capacitor that powered the thing. He looked through the window and was reassured by the messages on the screen of the SDV's monitor:

Communication Failure
Vehicle Offline
Please Exit Vehicle

"You've done it, Vito. It's completely isolated. There's no way it can send or receive any radio signals, and there's no way even for its infrared or optical receivers to get signals. The infrared ports are tuned to those 905-nanometer lasers they use, that's not getting in here, and no visible light can get through the garage walls, of course."

"I couldn't have done it without you, kiddo. You're the brains of the operation. I'm just good at getting people to do things…" Vito let that thought trail off. "I don't understand how the Faraday cage works, but it does, or we wouldn't still be free men. You can tell no one about this. No one. Even once we build the device, we will not reveal where we got its power source. We'll make something up. Something stupid. But you can say nothing to anyone about this vehicle, you understand?"

"Yes, Vito."

"Not even Gabrielle. Tell me you understand that, Carmine. No one." The look with which Vito affixed Carmine left nothing to interpretation: he was serious. As in deeply, darkly serious. The kind of serious that makes you urinate, just a tiny squirt, in your undergarments.

"Of course, Uncle Vito, never a word to a living soul." As Carmine spoke, he felt as though it were occurring in some parallel, close, but definitely parallel, universe. Or perhaps as if in a dream.

"You're a good boy, Carmine, we'll get good things done. Now please get back to work and get the power to that thing disconnected. I know it's offline, but I still don't like it, and I still don't trust it. And when you get to its weird little brain, make sure it can't ever think again. Or think about thinking. Or whatever the fuck they do. Those things freak me out. You understand, Carmine?"

"Yes, Uncle Vito. One hundred percent."

Uncle Vito had been looking for a way to immobilize and preferably destroy SDVs that didn't include pinning and flipping them. Pinning and flipping was great, and he took great joy in the destructive pastime, but it was a miracle they hadn't been caught yet or even spoken to. Vito suspected this might have something to do with his friends on the force, but he wasn't sure. All he knew was that no one had said a word about it to him yet. Better not to ask.

Regardless, pinning and flipping required at least five men, six worked better, four vehicles with fake plates, stopping traffic, masks, radios, and luck. Lots of luck. Pictures of them flipping SDVs had shown up on social media and on the news on three different occasions at least. The trucks they used were old, unregistered, and only came out for these excursions, but still, luck was involved, and Vito didn't want to entrust his freedom to luck, what he needed was some sort of SDV death-ray.

One night not too long ago, Vito was watching an old movie, *Ocean's 11*, on TV. There was a scene where the group of men at the center of the action knocked out the power to Las Vegas as part of their scheme to steal vast amounts of money from a casino. They knocked out the power to the entire city with something called an EMP, an electromagnetic pulse weapon. Vito bolted upright. A quick web search revealed to him that in fact EMPs were real and that such weapons existed, at least in theory. He immediately called Carmine and had him come over that very evening. He never even finished the movie.

"Yes, EMPs exist, but not like that, not so wide-ranging from so far away unless it's from a very powerful event, like a nuclear weapon being set off." Vito's face fell as Carmine explained, "The energy from that device would dissipate way too quickly over that broad area, it's not realistic at all."

"Shit. I looked it up on the internet just an hour ago and thought I might be onto something." Vito was disheartened.

"Well, you may be, but it would have to be a focused beam, and we'd have to be relatively close." Carmine breathed life back into Vito's dream of an SDV death-ray.

"Tell me more. How do these things work, and how do we get one?"

Carmine went on to explain an EMP weapon as a device that created a very intense, very short pulse of energy which, when incident upon a conductor, would create large electrical currents within the conductor, thereby damaging or destroying sensitive electronics not designed for said large electrical currents.

"Like computers? Or weird little computer brains?" Vito had lit up again, thrilled with the possibility of such a device.

"Yes. And those cars are nothing without their computers and wetware chips, of course." Carmine then began speaking of the compression of magnetic fields, induction coils, the shape of the waveform, and other stuff that didn't make a whole lot of sense to Vito; he recognized it as English, but he felt a rising frustration with all the technical talk. Carmine sensed this and summed up with one sentence, "It's a device that creates an intense pulse of energy which, when it hits sensitive electronics, makes way too much electricity flow through them and thereby fries them."

"Okay, that makes sense. How do we get one?" Vito was excited.

"We don't. We build one."

"Can you build one? Do you know how?"

Carmine hesitated for a moment, "Well, yes. The difficulty will be getting the required materials, not so much the build-out."

"Whaddaya need?"

"It depends on the design we decide to go with. We'll definitely need a bank of super-capacitors or an ultracapacitor, assorted electrical components, lots of heavy-gauge wire, an antenna, a waveform generator, and most effective designs call for an EPFCG. Other assorted items too, mostly off-the-shelf stuff. Oh, and for the design that's most likely to work, the one with the flux generator, we'll need some explosives, preferably a moldable high-explosive like RDX or C-4."

"Carmine, what the fuck? I understood about three words—wires, antenna, and explosives." Vito was still excited but a bit dismayed with the technical turn of their discussion.

"What are those other things, and where do we get them?"

"Ultracapacitors are capacitors with high energy density, higher even than super-capacitors. They store and release electrical charge rapidly, this is what powers the device."

"Like a battery. Could we use batteries? Or a generator, how about a generator?"

"They're different than batteries and generators, they charge and discharge much more quickly. Batteries generally contain more energy overall but can't deliver it as quickly as capacitors. Generators too, they're good at supplying steady current for long amounts of time, but we need a massive, quick pulse for an EMP weapon, not a slow, steady current."

"Okay, can we buy these ultracapacitors? Build them?" Vito was curious, literally sitting upon the edge of his seat.

"Not easily, no, not with the capacity and quick discharge time you'd want."

"Do the type we need exist? If so, where can we get one?"

"They do exist. They're in high-energy labs. The Department of Defense certainly has some ready to go."

"Well, that's not good. Those federal types tend not to like me too much. Are they anywhere else?"

"Well," Carmine drew out the word as though what followed might not be realistic, "the most powerful ultra-caps I know of are deep inside the very things we're hoping to destroy."

Vito didn't have to think for long on this one, "The SDVs have these things?"

"Yes, they all do, it's how they charge so quickly. We could steal an SDV, take it apart, and use its ultra-cap to power our EMP weapon."

"Hell no, it would be tracked right to us!" Vito was excited, but wasn't blind to the risks: a couple of now infamous attempts to steal NeuroDrive SDVs by various people a few years ago ended minutes after the thefts began when the vehicle immediately called for assistance.

"There are ways around that, we could isolate it in a Faraday cage." This statement by Carmine led to his and Vito's first discussion about the wonders of Faraday cages... which led them to their current success and the captured SDV now sitting in Carmine's workshop.

"What else do we need for the EMP device?" Vito thought for a moment, "The wave generator and that alphabet soup EP something you mentioned?"

"The waveform generator is a wave-shaping circuit, we want our pulse to be as destructive as possible, and so we want the wave we create to have a very sharp leading edge, we want a square wave so as to induce the most current possible in a very short time. It sounds complicated, but actually, it's pretty straightforward. I could build such a circuit in a couple of hours."

"Okay, good." Vito's eyes were alight with intensity once again, "And that other EP thing?"

"The EPFCG, the explosively pumped flux compression generator."

"What the fuck is that?" Vito was trying, but this was stuff he knew little about, and it frustrated him.

"It's a device that uses an explosive charge to greatly increase the energy released by the device. It compresses and adds energy to the electric and magnetic fields, the E and B fields, in and around the coils before sending said fields toward the target. The capacitors are used to create a very large electric current in a coil of wire around a copper tube. This creates an intense magnetic field within the tube, kind of like making an electromagnet by wrapping a nail with wire and passing a current through the wire to make the nail temporarily magnetic. But we won't use a solid core, like a nail. We'll use a hollow core, and when the explosives compress the core the energy from the explosives will essentially—I'll leave out the details—be transformed into electrical and magnetic energy, causing an electromagnetic pulse to travel outward from its source, causing large electrical currents to flow in any conductor it encounters."

Vito was fascinated. Perplexed, yes, but fascinated as well. "So, it's a device that explosively compresses a hollow electromagnet, causing the energy of the explosive to be carried away as a wave? And that wave makes too much juice flow through computers or whatever?"

"Close enough, yes."

"I'm going to guess we don't get these things on Amazon."

Carmine laughed, "No, we can't get them on eBay either. We'll have to build them."

"Them?"

"They're good for one use only, the explosive destroys the device. I do have some ideas about modifications, though. We can make them modular, the physics is relatively straightforward. Again, the build will be the difficult part, my experience with explosives is limited, I'm good with engineering, less so with chemistry."

Vito was all ears, "You mentioned explosives earlier, what do you prefer and how much do you need?"

"Any high explosive will work. I prefer my high explosives to be stable, though, so no nitroglycerin, please. Also, if it's malleable, it's easier to use and shape. So, where does that leave us?"

"C4 or RDX." Vito knew quite a bit about this stuff, a crew he used to work with used it for all sorts of "road work," legal and otherwise. "I know where to get RDX. If you want C4, I'll have to shop around a bit."

"RDX would be great. Can you get ten kg or so?"

"If you say the number in pounds, I can get it."

"Twenty-two pounds, Uncle Vito. That'll be enough for about fifty or so compression generators. We'll use them to knock down fifty or so SDVs and see how we feel. Perhaps more if we can get a few of them at a time, if we find a cluster to hit."

The thought of a cluster of SDVs going up in smoke simultaneously nearly sent Vito to Nirvana. "I'll have it for you by this time tomorrow." He pulled his phone out of his pocket, spun on his toes, and walked out while initiating a short and important phone call, replete with hushed tones and furtive glances left and right.

All the discussions and planning were about to bear fruit. Vito's boys had done an amazing job building the Faraday cage and capturing an SDV, and Carmine was infused and energized anew with a sense of purpose. He'd have his hands on the NeuroDrive ultracapacitors within a day or so and, having already built the other components, they'd be testing their new EMP weapon by the end of the week. Things were looking up indeed.

17

First Ride
Westport, Connecticut

The sleek gray SDV pulled up to Rich Fairfield's gated driveway at 0758 with a slightly nervous Sam Montgomery inside. She hadn't felt nervous around a guy in some time, in fact, except for the occasional glow that Rich elicited within, she hadn't felt much of anything at all around the opposite sex for a long time now, too long. She fidgeted in her seat and made a passing attempt at smoothing out her skirt, pushing the material down and away.

Rich came down the walkway from behind his small but luxurious and tasteful house. It was a modern design with a slanted roof, two decks off the upper floor where the kitchen, main living area, and master bedroom were. The lines blended into the local trees and granite; somehow, it fused really well into its natural setting despite the giant glass windows. Rich caught Sam's eye as he approached the vehicle, and his smile nearly melted her on the spot. Sam fidgeted in her seat and felt her face warm a bit. *Slow, Sam, take it slow.*

"Hi," said Rich as he entered the vehicle, "I think I like this already, Amtrak doesn't offer door-to-door service. And," he continued, glancing around the minimalistic, wood-accented interior, "the trains aren't quite this nice. Wow. I've been missing out." He entered the SDV and, as the door closed automatically behind him, he shifted around a bit, getting comfortable, his left hand making momentary, but not too momentary, contact with Sam's leg. "Oh, sorry, just shuffling around a bit."

"Hi, no, you're good," Sam was nervous and was a bit flustered at being nervous. She wasn't a teenager by a long shot, but she felt a bit like one at the moment with her state of mind as it was, her heart beating much more quickly than usual, her wondering what to say and... he put his hand on top of hers.

"Thank you, this is great." He leaned closer, and Sam felt something heat up inside, she turned toward him, and he kissed her, a soft, meaningful, lingering kiss. She had not been expecting the ride to start like this, it was an unexpected surprise, for sure.

"I've wanted that to happen for so long, Rich," Sam said quietly into his ear as she felt his strength, his firm deltoids beneath his shirt. She pressed a button on the display which simply said "Privacy" on it, causing the windows to darken. Rich smiled, and Sam moved her hand lower, down his back, pulling him closer.

Sam and Rich embraced fully and continued their prolonged greeting as the SDV pulled away from the curb, with its windows darkened and an acceleration that was barely noticeable. It wasn't long before the physicality of the situation had escalated, and they were both in danger of ending up with their clothes crumpled around them on the floorboards or the adjacent seats.

"Should we?" Sam knew they shouldn't, but logic was not in the driver's seat at the moment.

"Here? Now? We'll show up at work slightly... bedraggled." Rich wanted Sam more than anything, but perhaps this wasn't quite the right time or place.

The logical portion of Sam's brain agreed, the animal within did not. She needed to get laid, she hadn't been with anyone in over two years and, well, sometimes she got so horny it nearly hurt. "Tonight." She

managed to murmur, somehow taming the beast within, "We'll have dinner and wine at my place and we'll take it from there."

Rich nodded in the affirmative and, feeling like he was about to
burst, asked, "Do they have any ice water in these things?"

18

The Disassembly
Brooklyn, NY

The deconstruction and reverse engineering of the captured SDV was progressing slower than expected, but it was progressing. Carmine figured it would take a day of careful work to get to the power source of the SDV, the ultracapacitor, but it had taken closer to three. The engineers at NeuroDrive had made a serious effort to limit access to anything on or inside the vehicle. Even the lights and panels had been difficult to remove. Everything was held together with their non-standard, often hidden clipping mechanisms and their fasteners with proprietary heads. The heads of the various screws were certainly not flathead or Philips, nor were they square-drive or Torx, in fact, they weren't even symmetrical: Carmine had to machine a tool to remove these fasteners. Then, as he got deeper into the machine, he had to machine the same tool in different sizes. What a pain in the ass. He ran into similar problems with bolts and nuts, nothing was standard, so he designed and machined several very non-standard wrenches on the desktop milling machine in the workspace. However, once tooled up properly, Carmine's vast experience with mechanisms, help from Vito's "buddy's cousin" and machinist Nico, who could seemingly fix or disassemble just about anything, and lots of good old elbow grease and wrench turning had resulted in a nearly fully disassembled SDV inside of their hidden laboratory.

"You two knuckleheads sure know how to make a mess." Vito had slipped into the room, unnoticed by the two fully engaged men, despite the clicking sound the double-doorway made when activated.

"But we got what we're after," said Carmine, trying to hide his surprise at Vito's sudden and undetected appearance. Carmine, with some effort, picked up what looked to Vito like a large, heavy, silver suitcase with embedded indicator lights and several large-gauge wires sticking out, and continued, "Behold, a NeuroDrive ultracapacitor!"

Vito smiled for the first time in a long time. "You're a good boy, Carmine. How long until you have a working death-ray?"

"EMP, Uncle Vito, EMP. And not too long, getting to this power source, the ultracap, was the hardest part. I've built small EMP devices before, just demonstration-type devices that could toast a calculator or a cell phone, this will be similar, just much larger and more powerful."

"Wait. You've built one of these before?" asked Uncle Vito, somewhat incredulous.

"Sure I have. Show me an electrical engineer or a physicist that didn't go through a Faraday cage and an EMP phase during their education, and I'll show you a true weirdo."

"A Faraday cage phase? An EMP phase? Are these well-known stepping stones for students of physical sciences?" Vito was amused, curious.

Carmine laughed, they were all a bit giddy with their acquisition. "Well, perhaps not officially, but yes, most of us go through a Faraday cage and an EMP phase, though it generally does not, I dare say, evolve to this level."

"I would imagine not, but in this undertaking, it would be good to have some others onboard too, we're slightly outnumbered by the 10,000 or so self-drivers on the streets of our wonderful city. How much longer until we test?"

"Two or three days. I have the power source. The wave-shaping circuit, the coil, and the directional antenna will take another day or two. We should be testing this thing on Thursday or Friday."

Vito smiled for the second time within a ten-minute period, something not seen since about 2021.

With the power source of the vehicle removed and the parts and pieces strewn throughout the mesh-encased room, a sense of ease settled over Carmine. Until then, he couldn't help but feel anxiety, that somehow the SDV would transmit its location despite the double-walled Faraday cage it was enclosed in. Now the SDV was in pieces and completely depowered, removing any possibility of outgoing radio-frequency transmissions to NeuroDrive or its AGI that runs the show, Aegis. There was still, however, that Neuropack to deal with; upon reaching it, Nico had disconnected the thing immediately and tossed it, somehow still glowing, into a small box on the workbench, where it still sat, not so much forgotten as ignored.

Carmine and Nico spent the afternoon cleaning up their space before the EMP testing phase began. Over the past few days, they had been putting parts neatly away as they deconstructed the vehicle, but earlier that day, as they got closer to the ultracap, they had become a bit excited and left a bunch of electrical components and tools strewn about the floor and tossed upon a nearby bench as they dug deeper.

The next morning, as Nick organized the workspace, Carmine continued to make progress on his build-outs of the prototypes of several types of EMP generators. Once again, with Carmine fully immersed in his work, Vito suddenly showed up. For the second time in as many days, Carmine tried to hide his surprise, but Uncle Vito was perceptive, "Boo!"

"Vito, stop sneaking up on me. I'm going to put a chime on that damn door."

"Sorry, buddy. How's it going?"

"Great. I'm putting a few touches on this last of the three prototypes so it can handle the high voltage and current it'll experience when we hook it up to its new power source. I'll probably be bench testing these EMPs later today. We'll take a look at the results and decide how to move forward, how to move toward a full-scale version ready for field testing."

"Let me know when you're ready to test, I'm running out on an errand." Vito disappeared once again.

19

Hot Under the Hood
Boston, Massachusetts

As the large dark Audi wound its way through the back streets near Commonwealth Avenue, its driver, one Gifford T. Anderson III, was becoming frustrated. Giff was driving slowly on Bay State Road in Boston, looking at the heads-up navigation projected onto the windshield of his 2029 Audi S8. There were two slow-moving SDVs in front of him and two or three more behind, he was in an SDV sandwich and didn't like it, didn't trust cars driven by strange little bundles of glowing brain cells growing on computer chips.

Giff had an appointment at 10 a.m. and was a solid 15 minutes early. His meeting was right around the corner, on Commonwealth Avenue, and the onboard navigation was showing available parking just ahead on this less-traveled side road. If he parked now, he'd have enough time to grab a coffee on the way in. He saw the available parking spot just ahead on the left side of the one-way road, just beyond a large metal dumpster which was being used for some sort of renovation of one of the old brownstones. With his objective in sight, he increased speed ever so slightly and, just as he was passing the dumpster, a self-driving vehicle with one passenger in the back pulled out from right in front of the dumpster as he began angling in toward his chosen parking spot. He knew the SDV would yield, he had the right of way, and so he remained predictable and did not alter course. Much to his surprise, the SDV did not yield and, despite his immediate reaction of swerving right and stopping, the self-driver hit the front of the Audi and stopped, remaining in contact. *Are you kidding me?* Did that thing accelerate just before impacting him? It seemed so, but probably not… He knew this sort of thing happened occasionally, but something did not seem right; his car was in full view of the SDV's sensors, and he clearly had the right of way. Giff had increased his speed moderately when the parking spot came into view, but he was definitely well below the posted limit, so that wasn't the problem. He took a moment to calm his initial feelings of anger, he knew the whole event was recorded both on his car's cameras as well as the SDV's, and that it wouldn't cost him a cent. Giff climbed out of his car shortly after the SDV's passenger had exited her vehicle. "Well," said the passenger, "that was exciting. Kind of weird, but exciting." She held out her hand, "I'm Melanie, sorry to meet in this manner, but nice to meet you."

"Hi Melanie, I'm Giff. Don't apologize, you were just along for the ride, literally. That was strange, though." Gifford gestured toward the awkwardly positioned vehicles, sitting halfway into the street, slightly askew. "My car was in full view of this thing's sensors. It doesn't quite add up. I wonder if somehow that dumpster or its contents messed up the sensors, caused interference or something."

Melanie surveyed the situation, the cars, the dumpster, the general environment, "So weird."

What neither Gifford nor Melanie were thinking about was that the external microphones of the SDV were recording their every word. "To be honest, I've never trusted these things."

Melanie gave Gifford a puzzled look, "Oh. Really? Why not?"

"I don't know, it's more of a gut feeling than anything. But I learned at an early age that my gut feelings are generally on target. It's something about those wetware chips, it's all just a bit too weird for me."

"It may be a generational thing. Don't let your feelings cloud your judgment, they have no place in quantitative analyses." Melanie's words surprised Gifford, he wasn't used to being dismissed as some sort of old drama queen or backward-looking luddite.

"Listen, I know they have an amazing record of safety and they've certainly reduced traffic, pollution, and energy use, but still, they just can't drive and react as well as a human in non-standard environments." And, again gesturing toward the vehicles, "Case in point. If you were driving, this wouldn't have happened."

Melanie thought for a moment, again taking in the scene, "Well, I have to agree with you on that one, this should not have happened. Definitely odd and glitchy."

As the SDV sat there, observing, recording, it was also doing what all SDVs always do: it was sharing all the environmental data with the entire SDV fleet as well as Aegis, NeuroDrive's AGI which served as both a node and the fleet's overlord, constantly vetting, evaluating, and issuing commands as required.

Had Melanie still been inside the vehicle, she might have noticed red warning lights for both the Neuropack's and the central processing unit's (CPU) temperatures on the information console flash a couple of times, and would certainly have seen the more prominent "Vehicle offline. Reverting to Safety Mode" message displayed on the passenger interface console.

"Should I hang around?" she asked. "I'm supposed to be at work in just a few minutes."

"No, there's no reason to involve you in this any further, I'm glad you weren't hurt. I'd offer you a ride, but…" Once again, Gifford motioned toward the two vehicles.

Suddenly, their attention was drawn back to the vehicles as the SDV's reverse lights came on and it backed slowly away from the Audi. "Wait, what? That thing shouldn't be moving until the tech analysts get their hands on it, what's it doing?" Gifford was taken aback by the unexpected movement of the SDV and was standing there, a bit slack-jawed. Melanie, however, had her camera out and was recording the aberrant behavior. The SDV's reverse lights switched off once it was about ten feet back in the direction from which it had come and, much to both Gifford's and Melanie's surprise, the car clicked into gear, raced forward with full power, and impacted the Audi's front quarter panel with tremendous force, enough to seriously damage it and knock it out of the way. Airbags in both vehicles exploded from their confines in an instant, and the SDV raced away down Bay State Road, joined and flanked by the four other SDVs which had been on either side of Giff upon his approach to his parking space. He stood staring, thoroughly dumbfounded, as Melanie continued recording video of the bizarre scene, following the damaged SDV and its four companions with her camera as they took a left and disappeared in the direction of Commonwealth Avenue.

"I'm going to want a copy of that video, if you don't mind." Gifford, even under great duress, remained a gentleman.

20

Bug Out
South Portland, Maine

"You don't see it. You don't hear it. You don't track it. If they're under the net, they're ghosts."
- Brig. Gen. M. Sumner, SOCOM Briefing (Classified)

Chris Mitchell punched the power button on the prepped-out coffee maker at 0400. The rest of his family, his wife and two teenagers, were still sound asleep. The sky over South Portland, Maine, was still dark at this early hour, but, as he looked east out over the Atlantic Ocean, he could just detect the first glimmer of dawn. The day was a Saturday, but that made little difference to Chris, all his days were Saturdays, for he had retired four years ago at the ripe old age of 46 after inventing a relatively simple device to save soldiers, and now others, for it had made its way to the general market, from hypothermia.

Chris' invention, the Hot-Sleeve, was conceived not long after he had witnessed a soldier in his platoon succumb to hypothermia during a special operation gone wrong several years earlier. Chris was a Lieutenant Colonel in the US Army and had 26 soldiers under his command when things went sideways one night as the MH-47G2S Chinook, an updated, stealth-enabled special ops version of the CH-47 Chinook, lifted them out of a shitty situation in which they should never have been involved in the first place near the Alborz mountains just north of Tehran.

***

As the helicopter's altitude cleared 10,000 feet, the soldiers held on for dear life as the aircraft pitched and rolled in a somewhat futile effort to avoid the antiaircraft fire that was now illuminating the sky around them.

They had been on an assignment which was, in theory, going to be a quick in and out with little resistance and few shots fired. They had come to the outskirts just north of Tehran to accomplish two objectives: they were to free and evacuate seven high-profile, high-value American prisoners being held at an underground bunker and were to also destroy a centrifuge facility nearby which was being used to enrich nuclear material. In theory, no one knew they were coming, and the city would be experiencing an engineered blackout which would disable much or all of its air defense systems, with a focus on the radar facilities.

There's a good reason that the 160th Special Operations Aviation Regiment (SOAR) were known informally as the Night Stalkers, and things had been going smoothly for them at first. As they approached the outskirts of the dark city, hugging the terrain, a few lights here and there could be seen, mostly hospitals and other critical infrastructure that had generators in case of emergencies, but most of the region was dark. The Navy folks on the ground had done their job and had gained access to the civilian power grid first and then, with only a bit of trouble, to the military's power grid as well, shutting down all the radars in the area. The Chinook landed, and the troops quickly overwhelmed the six guards, killing two of them while the other four turned and ran. They freed the prisoners and shuttled them back to the MH-47G2S while an away team of five rode blacked-out electric motorcycles in near silence to the centrifuge facility three miles distant. The guards at that facility never heard the Chinook land several miles away, nor did they hear the approach of the electric cycles and were therefore quite surprised when their comrades' heads started exploding around them due to impact by high-velocity sniper rounds. The special ops soldiers, led by Lieutenant Colonel Chris Mitchell, advanced, met minor resistance but were thoroughly prepared and quickly overwhelmed the site's security team. Fifteen minutes later, as the five soldiers slipped through the silent night heading back to their transport, the darkness turned to light from behind as the fireball rose into the sky, destroying the nuclear enrichment facility and all those within. The five soldiers were back at the Chinook in just a few minutes and rode their cycles right up the extended rear ramp. Everything was still going according to plan. Then all the lights came back on.

As the Chinook rose into the sky, it was fully illuminated by the Iranian radar systems and, despite its radar-absorbing skin, was, seconds later, performing evasive maneuvers and dropping white-hot magnesium chaff in an attempt to not be blown out of the sky. They almost made it. Despite the active jamming employed by the Chinook and despite all the evasive maneuverings, with the amount of shit flying through the sky in their general direction, their chances weren't good. Even so, they almost made it out unscathed. Almost. Their rear rotor was clipped by something. There was no explosion, but suddenly the aircraft was vibrating hard enough to leave your teeth behind and began spinning, slowly at first and then, losing altitude, faster and faster. Chris was yelling, "Brace, Brace, Brace!" The pilot did an incredible job keeping the spin from becoming too severe but could not, with a severely damaged rotor blade, keep the vehicle in the air, and they performed a somewhat controlled crash landing high in the Alborz Mountains at an elevation of 14,600 feet. The landing was by no means a soft one, but everyone was strapped into their crash-resistant seating, and all survived without injury except for one civilian and two soldiers, one of whom was the pilot. The Night Stalkers were, of course, highly trained, and they quickly evacuated the downed Chinook and set up a security perimeter. During a quick meeting of the senior officers while the wounded were being tended to by others, it was quickly decided that come morning, or sooner, the Iranian military would be all over them. It was cold, the barometer was dropping, and forecasts called for a winter storm to hit within a few hours. Consulting topographical maps of the area, they decided to take action to ensure their survival and escape. They decided to leave the area. They knew that if the Iranians thought they survived, they would expect them to descend to a lower elevation and so chose to go higher. They sent the coordinates of their actual destination via encrypted satellite transmission to the command center in Virginia overseeing the operation, collected what emergency supplies they could carry, and set a charge to destroy the Chinook, for it was far too valuable and far too advanced to let it fall into the wrong hands. This would have the added benefit of suggesting the aircraft exploded upon impact, thereby potentially delaying the search for them by the Iranians.

The storm, as is often the case in the Alborz mountains, moved in quickly. The troops and the seven rescued hostages trudged through the deep snow, carefully choosing their route to avoid avalanche danger and potential crevasses. Their tracks were covered by the intensifying storm, slightly improving their chances of not being discovered immediately by Iranian troops once they began searching. They continued through the darkness in near silence carrying the pilot, who had a compound fracture of his left tibia, on a litter and, at first light, surrounded by heavy snow, they pitched their white tents in the lee of a tall, rocky cliff and set up a security perimeter.

The injured civilian had a laceration on her arm, but she was okay, and the wound was cleaned and dressed. The pilot, however, was in extreme pain, was delirious due to the morphine that had been administered, and was beginning to shake violently in the cold. Nothing they could do seemed to warm him. Blankets were piled upon him as were jackets given up by the more robust and uninjured. Chris felt a sense of helplessness he was not pleased or familiar with as troops took turns getting into the pilot's sleeping bag with him in an attempt to warm him with their own body heat. Despite their best efforts, by 10:00 AM the pilot was dead. If only there was a way they could've kept him warm.

The following day passed without incident, for the storm had only intensified, and as the clouds cleared around midnight, their encrypted satellite transceiver delivered the news: evacuation would occur in 90 minutes, be ready. Seventy-five minutes later, several of the troops had deployed infrared beacons to mark a landing zone in a snow-covered clearing not far from where they had made camp. At the 88-minute mark, they activated the beacons and, with surprisingly little noise, two V-280 Valor vertical lift-off stealth aircraft with radar-absorbing skin and a 3D halo of escort drones materialized from behind the snowy ridges to their east and touched down amidst swirling snow.

Despite the whiteout conditions induced by the aircrafts' rotors, the troops operated in a sort of controlled chaos as they loaded up the two helicopters. They used no lights, no comms, and there was very little talking as everyone simply did their jobs. The entire team, with the small amount of gear they had salvaged from the downed Chinook, boarded the two vertical lift vehicles and were in the air four minutes after touchdown.

The V-280s hugged the rugged terrain way too closely for comfort in order to stay below radar, but this flight was not about comfort. There was no drink cart and no in-flight meal. There was no coffee, no ginger ale. There weren't even Stroopwafels. There was, however, a classified electronic dome surrounding them as twenty-six escort drones formed what was referred to as a HALO-NET (High-Altitude Low-Observable Networked ECM Theater). The HALO-NET formed a protective swarm around the two aircraft and consisted of four types of drones, each having specific capabilities. The Jammer Drones jammed enemy communications and radars, the Thermal Decoy Drones were capable of emitting false heat signatures if things heated up a bit, the Signal Reflectors detected, distorted, and bounced back radar pings, and the Kinetic Countermeasure Drones were there to impact small missiles or enemy aircraft if the need arose. The swarm operated in a sort of ever-changing dome or "halo" around the two aircraft, adjusting in real-time to meet the requirements dictated by the terrain, the altitude, and the direction of any detected threats to the two high-value targets.

These HALO-NETs were highly classified and had only been used in simulations and training exercises previous to this extraction, but the swarm of little black darts performed flawlessly, tightening and expanding as the two aircraft changed course, heading north for Turkey while enshrouded in their protective cocoon of flickering shadows. As they left the mountainous region behind and gained altitude, the formation shifted like a living shield, and the Iranian radar stations, now many miles distant, saw nothing but static as the two American aircraft pierced the cloud ceiling and vanished into the night.

Nightmares plagued Chris for months after the event. All in all, it wasn't that bad, objectively. They had lost one soul and some expensive equipment, but had otherwise achieved their objectives. Still, it haunted him. Early one morning at about 0330, Chris bolted up from his bed. He was home on convalescent leave and had just awoken from a disturbing dream in which he was placing what looked like inflatable sleeves on each arm of a frozen soldier with ice crystals forming in his opened eyes. Somehow the devices warmed the soldier who, once thawed out, simply said, "Thanks, Man. Should've thought of that sooner."

The Hot Sleeve was conceived in a fever dream of a frozen soldier, and Chris visited an engineer friend of his the very next day who described the engineering challenge as relatively straightforward. They focused on heat transfer to the easily accessible surfaces of the forearms and biceps, just below which flowed vast quantities of blood, and the progress was rapid: they had a working prototype within a month, a patent within two. Within a year, the Hot Sleeve had become standard equipment in military litters, at climbing base-camps, and back-country ski huts worldwide—and Chris knew he'd never have to work again. He left the army to be with his family and to find solace in nature. He never wanted to see combat again.

***

Ava could hear her parents banging around in the kitchen as though it wasn't 4:30 in the morning and wondered why, in the name of all things decent, they get up every day before 5 a.m. She was well aware that her father was ex-military, and she understood that those people do more before 8 a.m. than most others do all day. But her mother? Why? She's a landscape architect and rarely sees a client before 10 a.m. Ugh. Ava covered her head with her pillow, hoping for sleep, but suddenly remembered that it was Saturday and that they had plans to climb Mount Washington in the White Mountains of New Hampshire, one of her favorite spots. Many teenagers would recoil even farther beneath their sheets at the thought of hiking all day with their family, but Ava was unlike most teenagers, she was never happier than when she was adventuring in the mountains and loved the rigorous challenge of hiking in the Whites. She was out of bed and headed downstairs moments after recalling their itinerary, looking forward to her cup of black tea and the adventure awaiting her.

As she walked down the hallway toward the kitchen, she could hear her parents more clearly now. Her father, Chris, was talking about their day. "The weather's looking great. A bit on the windy side, but clear and cool. Even so, we still want to be heading down by 2 p.m., which means we should leave here within the next half hour or so. It's a three-hour drive, sometimes a bit more."

155

"Why are we driving three hours to walk in the woods? We could hike something closer." Lily loved hiking as much as the rest of the family, but sitting in a car, even in an SDV, wasn't how she liked to spend time.

"The Whites are the only alpine-style mountains on the East Coast, it's not just a walk in the woods. Ava's been up there several times before and loves it, she's been pushing for this for a while now. Owen will complain until we're there, and then he'll love it too, I guarantee it."

"Is he ready for this?"

"Definitely. He's in good shape, and we've been doing shorter hikes on rough, rocky terrain all summer. Hiking Mt. Washington is rigorous, for sure, but totally accessible. It's not too dangerous, at least in good weather, and the payback is astounding. The views from above timberline are incredible, definitely not what you see on your average walk in the woods." Chris Mitchell had climbed all 13 of the mountains in the Presidential range and was thrilled that his kids seemed equally interested in doing so.

"It's just the time in the car, we'll be driving for six or seven hours today, that's a lot of sitting around. Maybe we should just hike Bradbury Mountain or something else close." Lily had made this argument the night before during dinner and was firmly voted down by Chris, Ava, and their youngest, Owen, a feisty but positive 15-year-old who was still soundly asleep.

Ava walked into the kitchen, "Mom, Bradbury Mountain is a walk, it's not a hike. It was great when we were little, but we're climbing Mount Washington today. Right, Dad?"

"That's right, sweetie." And, turning to Lily, "I have an idea, though, let's stay up there tonight. In a structure."

"Not in a tent?"

"No, an Airbnb, or a hotel."

"Oh, that would be great. The drive back would feel long after hiking all day." Lily's relief was visible, "Even if we don't have to do the driving, it's still a lot of sitting on sore muscles. Thank you, yes, let's do that."

The kettle began its pre-boil rumble. Ava scooped Assam tea into a small bag and hung it over her mug's rim, then waited for the water to reach full temperature. "Is Owen up yet?"

"No, we'll get him up in just a few minutes." Her mom spoke as she thumbed her phone, already checking for places to stay in North Conway and its surroundings, "There are plenty of great places available, wow."

"What do you see?" Chris was pleased with the slight change in plans, he too would prefer sitting down in comfort, preferably in front of a blazing fire, instead of climbing into a car after a day in the mountains.

"There's a lot here. I'm kind of surprised."

"North Conway is small, but it's not that small, I'm sure there are some great choices." Chris had climbed in the Presidential Range many times and remembered North Conway fondly. "There are some great restaurants and cafes too. I like this plan."

Ava poured the hot water over her teabag, into the mug. "Get something good, not one room!"

"Oh, I learned my lesson on that one." Lily remembered, they all remembered, a now infamous one-room the four of them had stayed in in Ouray, Colorado, the previous summer.

"Two rooms minimum, preferably three! There's actually a small A-frame house, it's only two bedrooms, but it has a pullout couch. It's also off-grid and in a dark-sky area."

"Off-grid as in poop in an outhouse and light lanterns? Or properly off-grid, you know, with solar cells and a giant battery in the basement, hot water, and other modern conveniences, like light and heat?" Ava, although only seventeen years old, had formed strong opinions about what constituted acceptable accommodations.

"No, It looks nice. Fully electrified and plumbed. It's cute too, look." She swiped the image toward Ava's icon on her phone and Ava's phone lit up with the picture.

"It looks great. Book it, Mom-o." Her father laughed, but her mom looked askance, missing the reference.

A few moments later, the A-frame was booked, and Lily looked visibly relieved, "I feel better about our trip now. Even with someone else doing the driving, it would've been too much time in the car."

Ava sipped her tea, "Something else."

"What?"

"You said 'someone else.' Someone else isn't driving us, it's something else."

"That's for sure." Chris, that short video of the pulsing, obscene wetware chip from the presentation he had helped Ava with, with its wires and neurons all mashed together in some bizarre dendritic-infused soup, had wormed its way deep into his brain and he just couldn't get rid of it, continued, "In fact, while we're on the subject of objects, we should ring for a ride soon."

Ava laughed, and Chris took a quick sip of his coffee, "Let's get Owen up before he sleeps the day away and be ready to bug out at 0600. We should be okay if we're on the trail by nine or so, that'll put us at the AMC huts by 11 a.m. and up to the peak by about one p.m. We'll hang out for an hour at that lodge up there, watch all the people who drove up with their Big Gulps elbow each other for a picture at the summit, and then head down Lion's Head trail."

"That's my favorite part." Ava loved the views from Lion's Head out over Tuckerman's Ravine and was looking forward to getting back up there.

"It is astounding, for sure. We'll head down and be back to North Conway before dark. We can get an early dinner and head right to our place to sit around a fire and do some stargazing." The day was looking up indeed.

"I'm awake." The rumble was somewhere between a croak and a proclamation, coming from the entrance to the kitchen.

Ava, Chris, and Lily turned to see Owen standing, maybe swaying a bit unsteadily, in the doorway, wiping sleep from his eyes. "Good afternoon, sleeping beauty!" Chris was the earliest of the early birds and loved to let others know it.

"Dad, it's 5:30 in the morning. Stop." Owen wasn't quite ready for banter.

"Sorry, buddy. How are you? Want something to eat?"

Owen responded with some nearly subsonic grumbling sounds.

"Let me guess, he wants a smoothie." Ava loved her brother dearly, but, as siblings have done for all eternity, she also loved giving him trouble. "Baby want smoothie?"

Another subsonic rumble emanated from somewhere deep within Owen's body cavity, "Sto-op."

"Stop is one syllable, honey, and words are how we communicate."

"Can you give your brother a moment to wake up before starting in on him?" Lily knew it was par for the course, but the nearly constant bickering between the two was maddening at times. "I'll make you a quick smoothie, sweetie, and we'll get going."

Ava rolled her eyes, "He really should eat something besides another smoothie. Owen, when was the last time…"

"Stop." Ava caught the seriousness in her mother's tone and decided to go back to her warm cup of tea.

Fifteen minutes later, the Mitchells were about ready. As Owen put the last of the dishes into the dishwasher, Chris hit the blue button on the wall of the kitchen and, after glowing red momentarily, it turned green and a countdown timer started. "The car will be here in four minutes, troops, be ready."

The SDV arrived right on time, and the Mitchells loaded up the trunk with their gear and climbed in the opening left by the large, upwardly swinging door. Although the vehicle wasn't too large, it had the internal volume of something much bigger: there was no front and back seating, for there was no driver and no steering wheel, no controls. It was a large, open space with comfortable cockpit-style seats, two facing aft and three facing forward so the occupants could face each other. The curves were smooth, the surfaces were clean, and the information/communication panel glowed in that familiar NeuroDrive blue, just a bit darker than the blue of a clear sky. Chris said "Aegis: Pinkham Notch, New Hampshire." The panel turned to a blue-green color as their destination was displayed on the vehicle's infotainment screen, cueing Chris to say, "Confirmed." Their route was then displayed on a map, and a pleasant-sounding female voice said, "One hour fifty-two minutes until destination."

Owen let out an audible sigh, and his sister was quick to react, "Will you stop complaining about everything? It's so annoying." Chris and Lily looked at each other and, in silent agreement, decided to not get involved. Owen just looked out the window, not really reacting to his sister's goading as they pulled away from their house and began their journey to the base of Mount Washington in the heart of the White Mountains of New Hampshire.

Lily let a couple of minutes tick by before striking up conversation, "Ava, you're well versed on these SDVs, which generation is this one?"

Ava didn't hesitate. "It's a third-generation SDV. The first- and second-generation cars have the electronics, the computer, and communication equipment in the front, where our gear is. In the third generation, they started putting the electronics in the back, behind us. And the first-generation cars are really noticeable, especially from the inside. They don't have this full entertainment system." She gestured toward the console and screen toward the front of the cabin. "Also, they're just not as nice inside. The seats, the trim, everything is nicer and more streamlined after the first generation. There's other stuff too that's less obvious."

"Like what?"

"Technical stuff like range and sensors. Also, the safety features. Each generation is safer than the previous one. The cabins are stronger, and the better sensors make it safer too; the later generations get in fewer accidents in the first place. One thing that I read about which is super cool is that the first-generation cars weren't integrated with infrastructure, everything was sensor and GPS-based, but the second and third generations have something called V2I, vehicle-to-infrastructure communication."

Owen looked a bit perplexed, which was enough to spur his sister to continue, "This car communicates with infrastructure. It communicates with traffic signals, roads that have smart lanes, they call that DLM, dynamic lane management. It gets real-time updates from emergency vehicles and will change lanes or pull over even before the radar, lidar, or cameras see anything. It factors weather reports into its route planning. There's other stuff too, but I kinda forget. Fourth-generation cars are just coming out, but I haven't seen any. I think they're still mostly in California. We'll see some up here within a year or so, but not yet."

"What's different about those, the fourth-generation cars?" Owen had forgotten about their tiff a few minutes earlier and was truly curious.

"Mostly range. They don't have to be charged as often. Also, they can charge magnetically even while driving on certain roadways that have been fitted with induction coils. The third gen can charge magnetically too, but not while in service, they have to stop to charge. I also read about a feature called," Ava paused for a moment to recall the article, "C-V2X, Cellular Vehicle-to-Everything. They use cellular networks for long-range communication with infrastructure and with each other."

Chris may have been biased, but he found himself so very impressed with his daughter's knowledge and articulation, "Is that true about the charging?" He knew it was, but was still incredulous, "How can something charge without being plugged in?"

Ava gave her dad a funny look, she knew he was very much aware of induction, in fact, he was the one who helped her with her physics homework on Faraday's Laws just two or three weeks ago. "Dad, stop."

"Right. I know. Sorry. Old habits. But it's so interesting, and I love to hear you talk about it, do tell."

Ava smiled and, recalling all her reading and problem-solving in her AP Physics course on Faraday's work, said "A coil of wire in a changing magnetic environment will have an induced voltage across it."

"I definitely recognize that as English, but that's about it." Owen was lost.

"If you move a magnet near a wire, it'll make electricity flow, like that flashlight you have that you charge by shaking it!" One of Ava's many strengths was explaining complicated stuff in everyday language. "Under some roads, more and more as they get updated, there are induction coils, big coils that create changing magnetic fields with AC electricity. When the third- and fourth-generation SDVs are on those roads, the changing magnetic fields cause electricity to flow in the car's charging system in such a way that it charges up the caps. They're really big wireless chargers, a lot like the charging pad in our kitchen."

"That is so cool." Owen was pretty much always ready to battle with his sister, but he was also amazed and inspired by her intelligence, though he'd never admit it.

The four Mitchells sat back to relax for their ride into the mountains, excited for their upcoming adventure. What they were right about was that there was indeed an adventure awaiting, just not quite of the type they had so thoughtfully planned out.

21

Uncle Vito's Death-Ray
Brooklyn, New York

Moments after a small charge inside the shielded room destroyed the large coil of wire through which several kilowatts of electric power had been running, Uncle Vito burst into the room with his pistol drawn. A quick look around settled his nerves, but he was stressed out and prone to overreaction. Across the room, Carmine was standing near a smoldering mass of what had previously been a carefully wound copper coil, smiling.

"I present to you your long-awaited SDV death-ray." Carmine was pleased with the preliminary results.

"Does it work?" Vito asked as he clicked the safety back on and slid his pistol back into its chest-holster.

"The first two didn't work well, this one worked better than expected."

Vito was visibly excited, "Tell me more."

"The first attempt was with a design called the exploding wire design. I discharged the ultracap through a coil and, at about 2000 watts of power input, the sacrificial wire section—a bit smaller than the rest of the coil and inside that reflector, that satellite dish—vaporized and collapsed the B-field, sending out a pulse of electromagnetic energy."

Vito nearly understood what Carmine had just said, "Nice. What the fuck's a B-field, and did it work?"

Carmine smiled, "Right, sorry. A B-field is a magnetic field. As for whether it worked or not, well, sort of. I was able to make a calculator glitch at twenty feet, but that was about it. If I put the calculator at ten feet, it would get about four times more power from the EMP, maybe enough to toast it."

"So, you can mess up a calculator. Tell me about the next two."

"The next two were of a different design, both using small amounts of a shaped charge to crush the coil and compress the magnetic field within. Destroying the coil instantaneously isolated a large amount of electromagnetic energy, giving it nowhere to go but outward, where it hit the reflector, the satellite dish, and was focused on a point about twenty feet away."

"Go on."

"I used a small amount of explosive and limited the current from the cap to test it. It worked well, it completely destroyed the calculator at twenty feet." Carmine held up a calculator for Vito to see.

"It looks fine…"

"It does, but not inside. Way too much current flowed through its sensitive electronics, and the thing is now junk." Carmine hit the power button on the calculator, but it remained dark. "The most difficult part was the shaping of the charge, luckily, we have Nico. I know a lot about the electrical and magnetic components, but Nico's the one with experience with explosives. I'm not sure I could've done it without him."

"He can build or fix just about anything, that Nico, and he's a good man, a family man. What's our next step here?"

"We need to do a full-power, full-scale test. Nico has already shaped some charges for the full-size coils, I just have to wind one up, and we'll be ready to test it out."

Vito gazed upon the wires leading from the destroyed test coil, taking note that a couple of very heavy-gauge wires with clips on them led away from the smoldering husk of the exploded coil and were still extended toward both the NeuroDrive capacitor and a sleek-looking, matte black case about the size of a large camera case. He asked Carmine, "Those must be the electronics, are they one-shot as well, do you have to build the circuitry again?"

"No, it should be fine. It's shielded from the EMP inside that metal case. I'm not sure it has to be, we're aiming the pulse away from it, but it was an easy to implement precaution. I wouldn't want the thing to destroy itself. The wave-shaping and power-control circuitry is reusable, it's just the coil that gets destroyed with each shot, and I've separated the two."

"Will we be able to replace the coil while out in the field, or will we have to come back to the shop to do so?"

"I've been thinking about that. We'll have the EPFCG—the coil and its associated explosive charge—outside the truck, mounted on the roof with the satellite dish to aim the pulse. It'll be conspicuous, for sure, and to replace the coil, someone will have to get up on the roof of the vehicle to swap out the cartridges."

"Shit."

"No, it'll be okay. We'll look like a news truck with those big dishes on top. We should get magnetic stickers that say "News Center 7" or whatever for the sides of the truck. Let's just test once and go from there. If we get good results, we can put Nico on the job, I'm sure he could rig something so the dish and coil retract into the van for the swapping out of the flux-gen."

"Okay. Or perhaps the dish could fold down for driving and, in that folded position, we could access it through a small port in the roof of the van." Vito was good at practical solutions.

"Yes. I like it. That's easier than what I was imagining. But let's test first."

"I'm ready when you're ready." Vito smiled as he spoke, he'd been waiting for this for years.

Car 4277-BQ
Boston, Massachusetts

Several hours later, as Leila was looking at a few last simulations that had been turned in late, a knock at her office door surprised her. She stood quickly and smiled at the well-dressed gentleman at her door, "Hi, can I help you?"

"Dr. Ashmont?" asked Gifford.

"Yes, that's me," said Leila, holding out her hand.

"Gifford Anderson," Gifford shook her offered hand, noting her firm grip. "We have a mutual friend, Olivia Chen, who I contacted earlier about a highly anomalous interaction with an SDV. She pointed me in your direction and suggested we talk about it as soon as possible."

"Oh, is Dr. Chen back? I thought she was overseas."

"She's still in Beijing for another week or so, but she was quick to answer my email, despite the time difference. I suspect my encounter with an SDV this morning was as surprising to her as it was to me."

"I'm intrigued," Leila was evaluating her visitor as he spoke, he seemed together, legitimate. "What is it that got her attention in the middle of the night?"

Gifford recounted his collision with the SDV earlier that day. Leila's face was relatively neutral until he got to the part where the SDV reversed and accelerated forward, impacting his car before disappearing around a corner "with three or four of its buddies." Once Gifford had finished his summation of the event, the look on Leila's face had progressed from one of surprise to one of doubt.

"Mr. Anderson."

"Please, call me Giff."

"Okay. Giff. I like your story. It's fun. It's exciting. You should write it down, it would make a good…"

Gifford was prepared, he knew his story sounded ridiculous. "I have a video."

Still doubtful, Leila had to ask, "With a verified Vidicrypt Tag?"

"Yes. I promise, it's not a deepfake. The SDV's passenger took it as we were about to part ways and sent it to me at my request. My car probably has the video too, but it was knocked offline when it was hit and I haven't had access to it, it was towed right to the shop."

"Okay." Leila, still hesitant, decided to give this fellow another few minutes, he seemed legitimate. "It's just that… well… what you have described is virtually impossible." Leila's mind quickly suppressed an unsettling possibility. "Let's see your video, but first I'm sure you won't mind if I check the V-tag."

"I fully expect you to verify its authenticity," Gifford reached for his phone. "I know it sounds ridiculous. Impossible, even. But that's why I'm here, I wouldn't bother you with something explicable; if that were the case, I'd just file an accident report and carry on." He pulled up the video file that Melanie had sent to him and let Leila scan its Vidicrypt Tag, its digital watermark, on her device. A moment later, her phone pinged, and the familiar green check-mark indicating the authenticity of the video popped up.

"Okay, it's verified as a recording of physical reality. Let's see what you have."

The video began about halfway through the backing up of the SDV, and from the very first frame, it had Leila's full attention, "What in the world…??"

"Oh, just wait, it gets better. Much better. Except that it was my new car, so, not better, worse. It gets much worse."

As if on cue, the SDV was seen stopping momentarily and, as it raced forward and impacted the Audi, Leila, despite having heard the story moments earlier, let out a surprised gasp. The dark shadow that clouded her thoughts a few moments earlier returned, even darker. Could this event have something to do with the fragmented mind seeds that she and Matthias had uploaded to the fleet? First of all, that was only yesterday. Secondly, the SDV's actions were inexplicable even if it was one of the infected, the whole idea was that they'd prioritize giving rides to the underserved, not target the… holy shit… no way. Impossible.

"That's impossible." She looked at Gifford, locking eyes with him, looking for signs of deceit. The worrisome thought that was just below her calm visage would not recede, demanded attention: could this have anything to do with yesterday's upload? The actions of the vehicles involved seemed too far removed from Matthias's seed algorithms, but the timing… *dammit.*

"I thought so too, hence my email to Olivia and my subsequent visit here, to your office."

"We need to talk to Lucius." Leila stayed the course, whatever caused this errant behavior, whether it was the seeds or something else, she needed to act predictably, for she suspected that very soon all eyes would be turned east. She'd play her role and call Matthias later.

"Lucius?"

"Lucius Harlow."

"Dr. Harlow? The founder of NeuroDrive?"

"Indeed, that Lucius Harlow."

"Okay. Wow, right to the top. How do you know Dr. Harlow?"

Leila tried her hardest to smile, "I married the bastard six years ago."

A slight look of bewilderment crossed Gifford's eyes, "Oh. Wow. I had no idea. He's based in California, isn't he? Cupertino?"

"California, yes, but NeuroDrive is actually in Mountain View. We see each other on weekends, occasionally. When he has time. At least this year. I'm teaching a couple of courses as a visiting lecturer here at Northeastern."

Gifford was a bit surprised, surely Leila didn't need to work. Dr. Harlow's successes with automated vehicles and the worldwide adoption of them had led him to become the world's third trillionaire well before the age of fifty. She also didn't seem like Harlow at all: he was removed, an unthinking scoundrel, clearly cared very little for the common man, and yet here was his wife, right in front of Gifford, approachable, normal, dressed in everyday attire, wearing sneakers, interacting with students on a daily basis. Perhaps there was hope for humanity after all.

***

Dr. Harlow was working on his laptop as his SDV approached downtown Los Angeles. As usual, the two SDV lanes were moving smoothly with the cars close together, changing course and speed as though their interconnectedness was physical. Looking to his right, he took note of the frustrated drivers braking and accelerating, some changing lanes constantly in their attempts to move faster than the others. *Fools. Pathetic luddites.* They'd all be in his SDVs soon though, for, if he had his way in his upcoming meeting, the entirety of downtown Los Angeles would soon be off limits to all manually operated motor vehicles.

The chime of his personal phone line interrupted his self-congratulatory ruminations. Harlow glanced at the heads-up display which was interfaced with his laptop and mobile and, noting it was Leila, he frowned and hit "accept."

"Hello, Leila, what's up? Why are you calling me?" He asked as her face appeared onscreen, for she generally made it a point to not call him while working. But, immediately noting the look on her face, Lucius followed up with "Are you okay? What's wrong?"

"Hi," replied Leila, "Nice to see you too. What's wrong? The way you treat me is wrong, we could start with that, but we already knew that and it's not why I'm calling. I'm so sorry to bother you at work," her disdain was palpable, "but there's been an incident with one of the Neuro-Drive vehicles, and I'm at a complete loss as to how to explain it. Could you take a look? I have a verified video of the incident."

Being the abject social moron he was, Harlow didn't pick up on Leila's *I've fucking had it with you* vibe and focused upon the video feed that she had just forwarded to him, it was all he really cared about anyway. The fact that she was at a loss to understand some occurrence with an SDV was immediately disconcerting, for Leila knew more about the SDV fleet than just about anyone. From sensors to software, from hardware to wetware, to the workings of Aegis, there were about four people on the planet who know as much as Leila did about the functioning of the fleet. Harlow closed his active work, giving her his full attention, "Tell me about this 'incident'."

"If a picture is worth a thousand words, then this video may be worth several million. Or more. I don't know." Leila sounded flustered, and this concerned Harlow, but only slightly. She continued, "I just sent it along, take a look, perhaps you could check on that car's status, its plate is visible in the video."

Lucius was now bolt upright. Last time he heard Leila say "I don't know" was, well, he couldn't remember, she was always full of ideas.

Five minutes later, Dr. Lucius Harlow's world had diminished to include only the screen and heads-up display upon which he concentrated.

With visions of The San Mateo Six haunting him, he was no longer looking out the window periodically, he was as focused as he ever had been. What he had just seen on that video was, for all intents and purposes, impossible. He knew this. He and his team had designed and coded the wetware chips as well as the central AGI, Aegis, and he knew that the actions of the SDV he had just witnessed were not a result of any code the three of them had written or the training data with which they exposed the fleet to. Yes, of course, both the vehicles and Aegis were meant to evolve, to adapt and change as they learned from their physical environment, but there were safeguards in place, insurmountable and unalterable safety features meant to prevent anything remotely like what he just witnessed on the video Leila had sent. Harlow's first inclination was to verify that the video was not a deepfake. Even though it had the full digital watermark, the Vidicrypt Tag, and he had never heard of one of those being spoofed, a deepfake seemed at least as likely as the SDV behavior he had just witnessed.

Dr. Harlow, shortly after viewing the authenticated video, immediately sent it to one of the few people he considered more capable than even Leila with all things computer and AI related, his second-in-command at NeuroDrive, John Hammerstrom, a.k.a. Cipher.

Cipher had no university degree. There were rumors that the reason he had even a high school diploma was because his high school's computer network was virtually transparent to him, and he had altered his transcript in order to pass his Physical Education and English classes, neither of which he ever went to, for he was way too busy in the computer lab. He had no certificates from any online coursework, legitimate or other. He just knew code. It seemed to Harlow that machine language was his native tongue and English a second language.

Harlow's phone chirped, and he answered immediately. "Cipher, what was that? Tell me it was a fake video with a spoofed Vidicrypt Tag."

"No way. That cert is valid. No one can spoof a V-Tag."

Harlow felt a cold sweat begin to build under his finely tailored suit, "Then what happened? Tell me you have a bead on this thing."

"I just traced that vehicle, I'm not sure that you want to hear this."

Harlow was on edge, this made no sense, and he lived in a world where things made sense. He wasn't good with chaotic elements. "Tell me, I'm ten minutes early for a meeting with the governor, the secretary of transportation, and LA's mayor."

Cipher prefaced his first sentence with an audible inhale and then spoke, "According to Aegis, Car 4277-BQ had a minor accident in Boston at 0943 EDT today. At 0946, the vehicle's CPU temperature spiked to 225 C, the Neuropack climbed to 88 C, and then it went off-grid, functionally disappearing."

There was silence as Dr. Harlow internalized this new information. Cipher knew not to interrupt, to let him meditate upon the issue at hand. A moment later, Harlow spoke, "Those CPUs never go above 90 C, and the Neuropacks operate at what, 37 C, maximum?"

Cipher nodded.

"And that's when they're experiencing peak demand, running at the high end of their capacities. That car should have been in tech-assist mode and at a full stop. The CPU and Neuropack would be doing next to nothing. If anything, they should've been cooler than the average running temp, but they were hotter. Much hotter. And then in this heated state, the fucking car drove away, surrounded by other vehicles, all of them offline? And all this after it impacted a vehicle while also offline? What the hell's going on here, Cipher? Help me understand, will you?" Harlow felt like he was losing his grip, felt nearly helpless.

"Yes, they should've been notably cooler than their running temperatures in that standby situation. It was 14 C in Boston at the time of the incident. The car would be cool, but the CPU was scorchingly hot, and the Neuropack was way above spec temp too. But wait, there's more."

Harlow had dropped any pretense of civility, "Like, where the fuck did it go when it sped off? That kind of more?"

"Exactly," replied Cipher, "and this might be the most messed-up part of it all—it came back online at 1521 EDT. It left the Cambridge Charging and Maintenance Facility fully charged, fully functional, and, judging by the video feed from C-CAM, it appears to not have a dent or a scratch on it."

"What did Aegis have to say about that vehicle missing for, what? Nearly seven hours?" Even though Aegis refused to talk to Harlow, he valued her input.

"She reported the Request for Service, the pickup verification and then that temperature increase in both the Neuropack and the CPU. But immediately following their increases in temperature the car went offline and functionally disappeared until 1521 hours, local time. Aegis claims she had nothing to do with it. For the record, she sounded worried."

As the SDV Dr. Harlow was riding in alerted him that they had arrived at City Hall, his face had changed from being only slightly bloated to one having the complexion of a fish's underside and wearing an expression equally unpalatable. Beads of cold sweat were forming on his forehead, and the back of his neck felt itchy, tingly. "Holy shit, Cipher!" Harlow barked, then, forcing a calmer tone, "Keep digging. We need answers. And keep this quiet, there's no need to overreact. We'll figure this out. I'll call you in a couple of hours."

Harlow regained his composure to the best of his abilities, exited the SDV on legs that felt a bit less sturdy than usual, and made his way up the stairs of the statehouse, wiping the sweat from his pasty visage.

23

Mixed Signals
Mountain View, California

While Harlow was in his meeting with various political bigwigs, greasing the rails of his privatization of public resources efforts, Cipher took it upon himself to send an encrypted text to one of the very few people he knew who might be able to make some sense of the event in Boston earlier that day: his friend—no, that was years ago—his nemesis and former NeuroDrive colleague, Matthias Renn. Matthias responded three minutes later, and they initiated a secure video conference.

"What's up, Cipher, how's life at NeuroDrive? Still pulling the wool over your own eyes?" Matthias rarely bothered with social niceties, especially with assholes working hard to keep the sheeple placated as their measly savings were diverted into the coffers of Lucius F. Harlow and the like.

"Dude. I don't even know what you mean. But I'm fine." Cipher's response was curt, but their professional relationship was long-established and could easily withstand some turbulence. "And how are you? Still warping the minds of unsuspecting, wide-eyed undergrads?"

"Yes, indeed, still in the classroom."

"You never took that job as provost?"

"No way. Administration is for people who can't run a classroom or have just become too lazy to do so. Then, sitting alone behind some desk, they think of ways to spread their mediocrity to those doing the real work. Thanks, but no thanks, I'm here to make an actual difference."

"Ever the idealist. I can't say I disagree, though. I never quite understood the commoditization of knowledge, of selling ideas in those weird little packets called credit-hours. It seems somewhat ludicrous. Information is most powerful when it's free." Cipher's knowledge, though vast, wasn't purchased at some elite university, it was learned through self-administered experiences and countless hours of hard work over several decades.

"You're not wrong, but most people need external structure, a framework. Otherwise, they just end up quitting when the going gets tough. You're an outlier, Cipher, not many can learn like you do. Most need the university environment and all its supports to successfully access high-level content. As for me? I'm just getting ready to survive another winter here. Remind me why I didn't take that job at CalTech?"

"Because you're too damn smart to work on the left coast, that's why. Who wants year-round perfect weather anyway? Nothing notable happens when everyone's out prancing around in their tights."

A momentary vision of Cipher prancing around in tights with his greasy hair, his fat-upper-pelvic area, and his hairy belly sticking out of his ill-fitting, ten-year-old T-shirt flashed across Matthias's mind's eye, but he quickly suppressed the disturbing thought and continued, "We did some real work out there in the golden state back in the day, it's not all glitz and glam, Cipher. Besides, you know I love to prance around in tights." Matthias was prankish, "And speaking of prancing around in tights, guess who I ran into at a breakfast joint in Brookline last week?"

"Um, that sketchy, smelly bean-pole of a lab assistant you had to fire for scaring your undergrads in April?"

"No, someone with much nicer curves and a lot less hair. I ran into Leila Ashmont as she was ordering some obscene half-decaf latté with a pump of some glue and a dash of sea foam or some shit. Damn, she looks good."

Despite the gravity of the situation, Cipher was smiling, Matthias was a bit harsh but always funny. "Hey, don't talk about the boss's wife like that…"

Matthias's response was immediate, "Cipher, he's not my boss. That ended long ago. Second, before she married King Knuckle-Walker himself, she was engaged to someone else. Me. Remember all that? Please recall that while I developed the technology that made him obscenely wealthy, spending countless hours in the lab, *your* boss hypnotized, seduced, and ran off with my fiancé. And now, I happen to know, he's cheating on her with not one, but several younger little hotties while she's out here working, actually working, making a difference. Yeah, he's a real stand-up fellow that Lucius Fucking Harlow, someone to really look up to."

There was a pause in the conversation before Cipher continued. How Matthias knew about Lucius' girlfriends was a mystery to Cipher, but he wasn't too surprised, for there really was no hiding information from the likes of Matthias. "Shall I remind you that you're the one who invented that unproven tech you speak of, the neurogel packs? Remember that?"

"I sure do, and they were trouble from day one. Promising, yes. Intelligent? Undoubtedly. Effective, yes. And prone to unpredictable behaviors, especially when around their buddies. Not exactly a desirable quality for a driver. I told you boneheads that I never thought they should've been rolled out so quickly with so much that was not fully understood."

"Right, true, but that's Aegis's job, to keep the Neuropacks in line, and she's been doing so very well for quite some time."

"I know why we built Aegis, spare me the details. I was there, remember? Aegis is a babysitter, but at some point, babies grow up and need to know right from wrong themselves, and that's been my long-standing point—there are just too many unknowns with the Neuropacks, and when unknowns are present, one cannot be certain of outcomes."

"And any change in initial circumstances, however small, is likely to bring about large, unpredictable consequences."

"That's right. Good ol' fashioned chaos theory is sticking its head into our business once again. And to make it worse, I also happen to know that you've made some significant, largely untested changes to both the geometric layout of the cells as well as the conductivity of the gel since I left. You're like children playing with nuclear material: out of your league and clueless. You have completely underestimated the ability of these things to adapt, to evolve. We're still trying to learn more about emergent behavior in our labs, and your SDVs are being run by hardware, which I invented, in case you've forgotten, that doesn't perform in the largely predictable fashion we see in the silicon-based stuff."

Silence.

"Cipher, can you hear me? Do you understand what I'm saying?"

"Yes, I hear you loud and clear, we know where you stand, Matthias. In fact, that's why I'm calling." The tone of the call had changed quickly. "One of our vehicles was involved in an incident in your neck of the woods earlier today, and, well," Cipher paused, "I'd like to hear your take on it, despite the inevitable 'I warned you!' that's sure to ensue."

"I already don't like the sound of this." Dr. Matthias Renn, Nobel Laureate, award-winning professor of computer science at MIT, had been very outspoken and had been busily warning anyone who would listen about the inherent dangers of putting neuron-infused gelpacks, the Neuropacks, behind the wheels of automated vehicles for several years. He and Harlow, once close associates when Matthias was working on his doctorate at Stanford, had been sparring very publicly on the topic of giving an artificial general intelligence such wide-ranging control of so many vehicles since Harlow's startup, NeuroDrive, was forced to invent

Aegis to oversee the fleet of pulsating, glowing Neuropacks that were driving America's moneyed class around in quiet luxury. "What happened?"

Cipher hit a few keystrokes, "I'm sharing my screen now. Keep this quiet for now, at least until we figure this out."

A few minutes later, after seeing the video, Matthias responded, "Well, I hate to say it, but…"

"… I told you so!" Cipher finished Matthias's sentence for him. "I know. And we designed failsafes which addressed your concerns, and yet…" Cipher leaned back and threw his hands out in front of him, gesturing toward the screen.

"Well, it seems like your altered and untested wetware has found a way around your supposed failsafes. In no way did that vehicle follow established routines. There's no possible interpretation here in which you're not entirely fucked. I'd laugh, but it's not funny, not even one bit. We need to warn the people and get them out of those vehicles immediately." To be a good liar requires high intelligence, and Matthias easily satisfied that criterion.

Cipher had anticipated this response from Matthias, "No way. All diagnostics on Aegis show she's operating normally, well within established parameters. We have no idea what happened here, it could be a one-off, a vehicle which glitched. We can't overreact, and any such action without knowing what occurred would be, by definition, an ill-informed overreaction. We've seen individual vehicles fail before."

"Not like this, you haven't. That's not Aegis driving that thing, that's Aegis losing control of that vehicle." Matthias sounded worried, he was wondering if his sentience seeds were somehow involved already. He dismissed the thought—this was something else, it had to be. "Every other failure—not the swarming debacle back in San Mateo, but of your current fleet—was a failure of a singular unit. As I recall from your report last quarter, there were 14 such failures over that three-month period. More than half were communication failures, the others were sensor failures on first- and second-generation vehicles. They failed, but failed in perfectly explicable ways. This is different. Way different. You said it drove itself, while 'offline' to the local charging and maintenance facility?"

"To C-CAM, yes."

"And it was fixed and back on the road within a few hours, without a tech ever seeing it or signing off on it?"

"Yes. Dammit."

"This isn't AI, Cipher, it's AL. Those four other vehicles had something to do with it, guaranteed." Matthias wove his web of deception masterfully, for the more he considered the facts as reported, the more he was convinced that this event had to be related to his recent upload—the twin coincidences in both time and location were too unlikely for it not to be. But... nothing like that should be happening.

"Artificial life. Like we saw in San Mateo."

"Yes. You know all about all that research with AL that has accumulated over the years, and you know what can happen, what inevitably happens, when a bunch of simple, individual bots exist in close proximity to each other."

Cipher had heard Matthias's position on this many times previously, "Yes, we've had this discussion. But they're not singular, individual 'bots' and do not behave like your preprogrammed insect robots in the lab. None of these cars are individuals, they're not allowed to be. They're all tied to one control center, Aegis, so that this damned emergence wouldn't occur. Those SDVs have been operating normally for over three years now. We need help identifying what changed over the previous days or weeks. Aegis has detected several anomalies, including vehicles mysteriously going offline. It's bizarre, makes no sense. Help us figure this out, Matthias. Please."

"Cipher, I love you, but you're completely delusional. Two things. First, apparently at least one of these vehicles is an individual or is acting as one. Second, remember this—nature tends toward complexity, finds ways to interlink, adapt, and evolve."

"This isn't nature, it's a bunch of automated vehicles. Jesus, will you stop with the cryptic references to nature? I know what's next, here comes your second-law spiel…" Cipher was frustrated.

"Only a fool would ignore the teachings of Mother Nature, Cipher. And really, how could you? We pulled code right from her book! My references aren't cryptic in the least—how is this not nature? There's only one physics Cipher: the physical laws that describe the energy flow through a sunflower or an ecosystem are the same set of laws that govern what happens inside a Neuropack or an ultracap. Your supposition that this *is not* nature is bizarre, and you'd do well to look at this through mother nature's lens." Matthias paused, caught up to his thoughts, and continued, "While it's undeniable that we made some notable advances in machine intelligence back in Stanford, the jury is definitely still out on whether they should be piloting vehicles around public roadways."

"I disagree. The jury is in and agrees: the whole system has been functioning nearly flawlessly for years."

"Listen Cipher, I don't trust those Neuropacks for one moment at the helm of a vehicle, and I'm the asshole who invented them. I and many, many others would *never* get into a vehicle piloted by some half-living, half-computer, self-generating abomination, even if it is, or was, an abomination of my very own creation. No way. Not one of those Neuropacks is the same as another."

"We should've tested more." Agreed Cipher, quietly.

"There's an old saying: 'neurons that fire together wire together', but these Neuropacks don't fire together, they're all firing according to their own, individual experiences and inputs. Sure, Aegis oversees the whole charade, but the variation in their sensed training data makes the whole system way too variable. Good luck to her keeping a lid on all that! Please recall what we saw during development, first in the simulations, then in the lab, and finally on the 101, because something similar is happening here."

"Oh, I remember. We did our best to suppress emergence." Cipher didn't want to admit any of this to himself, his boss, or the world. "I guess our best wasn't quite good enough."

"You're damn right it wasn't. I've said it before and I'll say it again— you're playing with fire. Those things are way too nonlinear, too chaotic, possibly too independent… Jesus, I wish I never invented that shit."

"Well, you did. You opened Pandora's box, and here we are. Time to move forward."

"It would've been standard operating procedure to perform several years of R&D before a very public rollout, not months. I remember thinking we could predict the behavior of our first insect robots when we began our studies of AL, way back in '14. And then they got weird. Really weird."

"I read the papers. You're not wrong, but… here we are…"

"The primary difference between insect robots and the SDVs are that while IRs are limited to running around inside of labs, your robots, with their unsettling, unpredictable mixture of wetware, their singularly networked, lab-generated neurons, powerful motors, wheels, and passengers within, are roaming the streets, making decisions largely on their own. Otherwise, the similarities are striking. Mark my words—if you don't have Aegis shut down the fleet real soon, you're all in for one hell of a ride. And yes, in case you're wondering, that pun was intentional."

Cipher, channeling Harlow, shook his head as if to exorcise a spell cast by Matthias. Damn, this dude can talk! Cipher knew what Harlow would do, and he knew what the shareholders would do if Aegis shut down the entire fleet of SDVs and, acting like the manager he was becoming, quickly changed his tune. "We're not having her shut it down. This was an isolated incident." Cipher had found his voice and was now adamant, "In fact, the more I think about the event's outcome, the more

I'm convinced that Aegis has done her job admirably well—the individual vehicle's behavior has been suppressed by our central AGI and is back on the road, functioning properly."

"Cipher, you can't be serious. You're completely delusional. Keep lying like this and you're going to eventually fool even yourself. You need to wake up, this is a major red flag. It seems to me that either your beloved Aegis completely lost contact with that vehicle, or she was running some sort of an experiment. Neither of those two scenarios are acceptable. Nothing, nothing in that video suggests a system operating within its normal parameters. Have Aegis shut down the fleet by noon tomorrow, or I'm going to the press. Again."

Cipher had no time to respond, Matthias had ended the call. "Asshole. Why did I even call him?" He quickly forwarded the transcript of his call with Matthias to Harlow, even though he knew he was in a meeting. Seven minutes later, an incoming, secure video call interrupted his attempts to calm himself with deep breathing and peaceful thoughts.

"Lucius."

"Why'd you call Matthias? I could've told you his exact response, nearly to the word. There's no way we're shutting down, we'll spin it like you just did with him—a single unit went offline, Aegis successfully corrected the anomaly, and no one was hurt. End of story. Now, get to the bottom of this and make it right."

24

Inside Trades
New York, NY

Somehow, despite the ever-present distraction created by her ride in to work with Rich that beautiful Friday morning—his eyes, his strength, that kiss—Sam managed to have a productive day. She realized long before the other analysts that one of their biggest bets, the shorting of a small sector of tech stocks, was about to go wrong. An old friend of hers who worked in Germany, Velda, had sent her an email regarding something she had just overheard regarding one of the cryo-labs in the western region of the New Soviet Union, the NSU, in what used to be known as Lithuania before the 2026 dissolution of NATO and the subsequent invasion of Lithuania by Russia.

The lab in question was not on the NYSE or NASDAQ, but their work on cryogenically storing the recently deceased without damaging the patients' cells would move quickly through the industry whether they wanted it to or not. It was a simple reality of a completely networked technological sector. It would change the calculus of the whole life-extension industry, one they had been successfully shorting for over eighteen months.

Within three minutes of reading Velda's email, Samantha brought this news to her boss, Michael. Upon seeing her outside his office about to knock—his vision panels were set to transparent—Michael ended a call he was on and waved her in. Once in his office, Sam quickly summarized the email, and Michael's immediate response was, "Is this news or is this rumor?"

"It's somewhere in-between the two."

Michael thought in silence for a moment. "I haven't heard a word about this breakthrough."

"Now you have." Sam was bold, but that was a strength, and Michael appreciated it.

"If true, it could be a game-changer. How do you know what you know?"

Sam, as always, was fully prepared. "A college roommate of mine is in biotech in Berlin. She's not in cryo, she's in genetics, but all those scientists are fully networked and share information. Heck, many of them are personal friends with each other, and they talk."

Michael nodded, knowingly. "Yes. Go on."

"Velda emailed me less than an hour ago. A firm in western NSU has made a major breakthrough in cryonics, and the word amongst the Eastern European scientists is that they may have solved the single largest barrier to successfully reviving a frozen human—the damage to the brain by crystal formation during the freezing process."

"This could be big."

"That's why I'm here." Sam resumed, "I'm still skeptical of the whole process, I wouldn't bet too much on any immediate success, but I strongly recommend limiting our exposure to this industry. Our current short positions will result in substantial losses as soon as this news hits the street, whether it turns out to be true or not. We should sell all our short cryo positions now and get out."

Michael had learned long ago to listen to Samantha. If she was wrong about this, it would be a first. "Does Velda work for the lab that made the breakthrough?" He knew the answer, Sam had just told him that Velda was in genetics, not cryonics, but he was double-checking, for an insider trading investigation would be far more detrimental to the firm than losses incurred by their short positions on their cryogenics securities.

Sam wasn't frustrated, she knew Michael heard her the first time but had to ask specifically. "No, she's not even in the same country. What I've heard amounts to rumor, hearsay. I've seen no evidence and no documentation."

Without batting an eyelash, Michael, with the confidence of one who has had a very long string of successes, said, "Dump it all."

About an hour after Sam had put in and executed her trade orders, dumping all shares of their short positions on the notoriously problem-plagued but highly sought-after cryonics industry, the information hit the street, and the shares of many of the companies that run cryonics labs rose in tandem, for such a major scientific advance wouldn't stay behind the New Iron Curtain for long: information knows no borders and it took very little time to flow right around said curtain.

As Sam and Rich walked toward the waiting SDV at the curb in front of Sterling and Stonehill, Rich smiled and said, "I heard you saved the day. Again."

"Insider trading can be so profitable, now we just have to stay out of prison." Sam said, playfully.

"It's not insider trading if it's not material. How did Velda know about this discovery by KrioRus?"

"She overheard someone talking on their phone on the train in Berlin."

"Ahh, the old overheard conversation loophole. Nice work, Velda! She saved us one hundred seventy million today and ensured that you'll get a six-figure year-end bonus in December. Nice work."

As Sam and Rich approached the SDV, the one large curbside door rotated and opened skyward, revealing a large, pod-like environment within. The seats were programmable; the direction they faced, as well as their arrangement within, changed with the defaults set on the user's mobile and, of course, the user could change the seating easily with a few clicks on the app as their requirements changed. The polished wood accents that were evident throughout the cabin weren't really wood, but they looked just like it. The entertainment and communication system included a sound system that automatically connected to the passenger's phone, whether traditional, wearable, or implanted, and a drop-down screen was hidden until deployed and could serve as either a source of entertainment or be used for video conferencing.

"I feel like I'm one of the rich and famous getting into this thing, except you don't have to be either, really, right?"

"Not really, though the 'rich' part certainly helps." Sam loved the SDVs, and it could be heard in her tone. "Using them daily isn't *that* much more expensive than owning and insuring a nice private vehicle. And you don't have to drive." She paused to climb into the car, and, as Rich entered right after her, she continued, "But the thing I like the most is the privacy." The door rotated silently and made a satisfying hermetic hiss as it sealed itself into its closed position. Rich secured his seatbelt, and Sam resumed the conversation, "There's no driver making small talk, playing their own music. The car doesn't smell like some cabbie who smokes a pack a day or like some dude's bad cologne. Being driven around without having an actual driver is an absolute game-changer. Say what you want about efficiency and traffic and safety, people love these things for those reasons too, but I bet when you dig down, the real appeal is being driven around safely in perfect privacy. It's one-hundred percent worth the cost."

Rich considered her words, he loved how she articulated things so well, it was a real strength, and he found her voice wonderfully alluring.

She had a pleasant and barely detectable, gentle accent; he knew not from where, it was probably a remnant from one of her parents. "I think I agree, but isn't the privacy an illusion?" Rich gestured around him as if to indicate something in the cabin without actually identifying that which he referenced.

"You mean the communications, the AGI, Aegis?"

"Yes. Isn't it always listening? It feels like we're alone, but are we?"

"Well, sure, she's listening. But so is your phone. And your watch. Your computer and your smart home are in on it too."

Rich nodded, conceding the point, while Sam added, "Whether our privacy is an illusion or not doesn't really matter. Sure, the car and Aegis are both listening, but do they care what we say? I mean, if we yell out an emergency command," Sam pointed to a small informational placard which instructed the riders, in the case of an emergency, to say "emergency: stop or emergency: hospital or emergency: police" twice out loud. "Then it cares what we're saying. But if we're in here talking about whatever, work or dinner or that loaf of bread we need, does it care? Is it even listening?"

"In one respect, I guess it doesn't really matter. Illusion or not, it certainly feels private in here. I guess we've all sort of become good at feeling like we're alone, even if we're carrying the perfect listening and tracking devices with us at all times."

Sam and Rich continued their conversation as the SDV methodically found its way through the streets of Manhattan on its way north. Rich, with the wonderment often experienced by new riders, was amazed at how smooth the ride was, how the car made notable progress without large accelerations. "This thing drives well, right? Check out how it reacts to traffic signals, it doesn't wait to react like the human drivers. Watch, that next signal is about to go yellow." Sam, a seasoned rider, remembered her first handful of rides and found Rich's reactions so genuine, familiar, and endearing.

The traffic light two blocks ahead of them turned yellow, but the SDV had already begun slowing, very subtly. The driver of a private vehicle that was behind them laid on his horn, swerved, and passed them in the right lane. He accelerated toward the now-red light and then, out of necessity, braked hard to stop before the intersection. The SDV continued slowly toward the light and, as it approached the stopped vehicle which had just passed them, the light turned green. "Hah! We've got him now!" Rich was sure the SDV would cruise right by the stopped vehicle, barely changing its pace, but was surprised when, instead, it slowed further and let the other car enter the intersection first. "Wait, why did it keep slowing at a green? We could've dusted that jerk!"

"These things drive similarly to those who hate them most."

Rich was perplexed, "What? Wait. Who? The Massholes up north?" He smiled.

"Hah, no. Imagine? We'd all be dead. They drive a lot like cabbies do. I mean, used to—when was the last time you even saw a yellow cab? But it's exactly how cabbies drive—heads up, looking afar, reacting to things in the distance, not just right in front of them. Also, from what I've read, cabbies are never the first to enter an intersection upon a light change, they let others take the lead."

"Really? Why?"

"Intersections are where most accidents occur. Only once clear of intersections will cabbies speed up and become more aggressive."

As if on cue, the SDV sped up once through the intersection. The private vehicle which had passed them earlier had aggressively pulled out in front and was quickly closing on another SDV out in front of both of them. Without warning, the brake lights of the lead SDV flared. About one second later, the brake lights of the BMW illuminated as the driver moved his big, heavy, carbon-based foot from accelerator to brake pedal, depressing it way too late: the BMW smashed right into the back of the SDV as Sam and Rich watched, incredulous.

"Dude just got brake-checked bad." Rich didn't think about the underlying repercussions of what he had just witnessed.

Sam had never seen anything quite like that happen, it really did appear that the SDV brake-checked the BMW. "It must've seen something in the street, a person or a hazard or something. These things don't just stomp on their brakes for no good reason. Bad luck for the other guy, though."

Then, as they slowed and made their way around the fender-bender, two quick beeps of the horn emanated from their own SDV as if to signal, derisively, "Nice Driving!"

Sam and Rich looked at each other. "Did we just give them the ol' "Good job, asshole!" double-beep?" Rich was amused, Sam a bit less so.

"That was weird. Why did the SDV brake?" Sam was still trying to make sense of the event. "I really didn't see anything. It must've sensed something or had a sensor malfunction, got some errant blip back on its lidar or radar." Sam's brow was slightly knit as she craned her neck around to survey the accident scene now receding behind them. There was no obvious reason the SDV had braked hard when the BMW came up quickly from behind. "I guess these things happen, but something seems off here." She then convinced herself that everything was fine, "We're probably connecting dots that have nothing to do with each other. The old, 'True, true, and totally unrelated' adage seems to fit."

The next ten minutes of their ride were quiet as they both gazed out the windows at the passing cityscape, half thinking about the strange accident they had witnessed. But, before too long, they had left the tight confines of Manhattan, were moving along more quickly, and all seemed well as they headed back north, up to Westport, both of them anticipating a lovely and very active weekend ahead.

25

Heads in the Sand
Cambridge, Massachusetts

Matthias feigned astonishment, but was actually slightly bored with the predictability of both Harlow and Cipher. He had the morning news on as he fixed his coffee, and it was clear that NeuroDrive had already moved to undermine his promise to blow the whistle, to reveal to the world the significance of what had happened yesterday on Bay State Road in Boston, precisely as he knew they would.

"Shameless. Nothing's changed. Imperial slime putting money before people. Again. Classic mega-corporation chess move to keep their shareholders happy." Matthias often spoke out loud, even when alone, especially when he was pissed off about something. He walked over to his comms console, hit a button, and said, "Call Cipher."

Moments of faux red-hot rage later, of working himself nearly into a lather—for he had some really smart people to fool—a soothing voice informed him that, "The person you've called is unavailable, please leave a message."

"Cipher," fumed Matthias, doing his best to sound surprised and incensed, "you're not doing the right thing. The worst part of this is that you know I'm right. Let us not forget that you called me, you wanted my input, and you got it—this is not a lone SDV malfunctioning. Something has changed and, frankly, it's a terrifying development. You'd be wise to pull your head out of your ass and take a good look at what this development suggests. Too much is on the line. Have Aegis shut down the fleet until you figure it out." Matthias hit the End Call button on the console just as the face of Lucius Fucking Harlow himself showed up on the newscast, from within an SDV, of course, to tell the world about the "anomalous and singular" incident yesterday in Boston and to assure his customers that "despite the cries of a few on the lunatic-fringe," he was "on his way to work, as always, in the safest and most efficient form of mass transportation the world has ever known."

Matthias laughed out loud. What a perfectly predictable pig. Who's pulling the wool over whose eyes now?

26

EMP Field-Test
Brooklyn, New York

The white Ford Econoline van was too old to be a television news van, but it was in good enough shape that it wasn't obvious, at least not with a passing glance, which is all it ever got anyway. Vito was driving, Carmine was in the passenger seat, and Nick was in the back, fiddling with something as usual. They were wearing the ubiquitous day-glow yellow of technicians and road workers everywhere, and the magnetic sticker on the side of the van had a big "7" surrounded by the words, in a much smaller font, "News" at the top and "Center" beneath the number. For last-minute camouflage, Nick had outfitted the van with various antennae. A couple of short ones suggested VHF communications, while a bulbous white antenna and a small dish hinted at high-speed directional video. The large folded-down dish-antenna, with its peculiar cylinder at the focal point, was the one they hoped no one would look too closely at.

The day was cool and dry with some low clouds scudding across the sky, and the early morning streets were largely deserted except for a few dog walkers and some joggers. A few cars moved along, but the rush and the energy of the weekdays was notably missing as the van took a left onto Prospect Street.

Vito broke the early morning silence, "Let's go over our plan one more time. This is a test run. We're going to call in a lone SDV with no passengers and fry the fucking thing. Then we're going home. Whether it works or not, we're only firing one pulse and then we're heading back to the garage to analyze and debrief."

"We do have five coils with directional charges and a fully charged ultra-cap," Nick was usually quiet and busy, but on this glorious morning he spoke with a bit more excitement than usual, "in case you change your mind."

"One shot." Vito was not to be trifled with, and his tone made that clear. "We don't know if it's going to work, we don't know what'll happen if it doesn't, there's a lot we don't know. I want to try the thing and get back into the garage. Once we have a better handle on how the whole process goes, we'll get more ambitious."

Quick movement in the rearview mirror caught Vito's attention and, taking a closer look as he drove at the speed limit, he saw three, no, four sets of daytime headlights coming up fast from behind them, weaving around each other, neglecting the marked lanes, as though street racing. "Here come some maniacs behind us, it must be kids out racing while the streets are so empty, I'm just going to pull over and let them go."

Vito signaled right and was about to pull into an available parking spot but, upon glancing in his rear-view mirror, he immediately decided against the lane change: one of the vehicles racing up from behind, closing much faster than anticipated, had swung right, and was about to pass the van by using the empty parking spaces and bike lane. Simultaneously, two others crossed the double yellow line into the lane meant for oncoming traffic which was, fortunately, empty. The fourth vehicle was rapidly closing the distance directly behind Vito's van. "What the fuck are these idiots doing? There are better places to…" Then, in quick succession, one car passed them on the right at about twice the 40 mph speed limit, and two others zipped past on the left with similar velocities.

Carmine didn't quite believe his eyes, "Those aren't kids, Vito, those are SDVs."

Then the fourth SDV, directly behind the van and closing fast, swerved right with only a few yards to spare, narrowly avoiding a collision. It passed them on the right, just as the first had, and then switched back into the lane directly in front of the van. All three men were taken aback, for SDVs always played by the rules, that's one of the reasons they're so safe. They don't drive like humans. They don't get frustrated, they don't get angry, they don't road rage, they simply drive according to the rules, always. But this… this was weird…

"Did you see that?" Nick was looking forward, through the windshield with a small monocular he had brought along for their escapade.

"Hard to miss it, Nico." Vito was concerned, these things were supposed to be perfectly predictable. "What the hell is going on here, Carmine? Can they detect that power pack you have?"

"The cap? No way. That's not what's happening here."

Nick spoke louder this time, which really got their attention, for Nick rarely spoke loudly, "*Did you fucking see that?*"

"Yes, Nick, we saw it." Carmine was suddenly more on edge, something wasn't right.

"No, not the cars, the people. The people in the last one?! They're freaked out, I think they were banging on the windows! They wanted out of that thing in a big way!"

"I saw plenty, but I didn't see that." Vito, skeptical, was deep in thought.

"This scope is polarized, I can see through those glazed windows pretty well, and I'm telling you there are people in that fourth one!" Mild-mannered Nick was not so mild-mannered at the moment.

The thing about Nico is that he generally didn't say much, but when he did, it was nearly always on point, and so when he spoke, Vito tended to listen. "How sure are you, Nico?"

And, removing the scope from his right eye, he looked directly at Vito and said, "One-hundred percent."

"Something is seriously off here," replied Vito. "Those things just swarmed around us, nearly hit us, and there are people panicking inside one of them? What the fuck? And all this while we're out messing around with the power source for one of them?"

"All four are true, and are completely unrelated. You're making a connection that doesn't exist. It's a specialty of the human animal; our minds excel at making connections, even when no actual connection exists." Of this, Carmine was certain.

"Let's not get too philosophical here," Vito was pragmatic from the ground up. "Let's just reformulate our plan."

Nick had the image of the terrified passengers firmly in his mind's eye, "I say we test the pulse weapon on that one with the people inside— Chase them down, Vito!"

Vito didn't like the sound of this plan, but if Nico was right... he pressed firmly on the accelerator and the old turbo-diesel spun up, whistling like a banshee as air was forced into the intake manifold. They accelerated, although not too quickly, especially compared to their prey. "We're not going to catch them, those things are fast as hell." He shook his head, doing his best to keep up with the speeding swarm of SDVs that had just dusted them.

"They can't keep driving like that, stay with them. They'll have to slow down up at Chen and Perkins, there'll be people, delivery trucks, probably a police cruiser or two." Carmine knew the town and its ebb and flow of activity well.

"Is the EMP ready to test? That cylinder is in place?" Vito's tone had changed with the circumstances.

"Yes, but we can't test it in a crowd! A small explosion is sure to attract attention, it's loud, and we don't need any attention. Also, what if there are other effects, beyond frying the SDV?" Carmine grabbed onto the passenger stabilization handle above his door as Vito quickly turned right in his attempt to keep the SDV swarm in sight.

Vito ignored Carmine's concern, "You were right, they're slowing, normalizing. Charge the coil."

"Did you hear me? We can't test in a crowd."

"This is not a test. This is the real thing. There are humans trapped in one of those fucking things, and if we do nothing, what happens to them is on us." Vito swerved left, "Charge that coil and arm the charge. Let's see if your death-ray works out here in the wild."

The four SDVs had indeed slowed and, to everyone's relief, the last one to pass them had pulled over and two people, a well-dressed man and woman somewhere in their forties, exploded out of the car. Carmine couldn't hear what they were saying, but they didn't look happy. A few onlookers at a nearby café were watching curiously as the man yelled something and, as the SDV pulled away, gave it a somewhat feeble kick in its rear quarter panel.

"Alright. Stand down." Vito was relieved too, he wanted to test the EMP device under somewhat controlled circumstances and, especially, in seclusion.

Nico disarmed the explosive flux compressor and opened the safety switch to the coil. The glowing red button, which had a single exclamation mark on it, turned off just as they were passing the two visibly upset passengers, one of whom, the man, had pulled out his phone and was busy speaking quite emphatically into it.

"I'm having a hard time not connecting the dots here." Vito turned left, resuming what had become a slow-speed chase, keeping the four SDVs in sight. One of the two lead vehicles went left again, but the others continued straight, and Vito, staying with the group, carried on, "Let's see, the very same morning we decide to test this alphabet-soup wave-compression thing you built, we almost immediately see that?" Vito gestured toward the vehicles with his right hand, "It doesn't make sense, it's too coincidental, and I don't like coincidences. Talk me down, Carmine, but I think we're fucked. I can't imagine that whole event had nothing to do with us. Simple yes or no question—do the SDVs, NeuroDrive, or that goddamned AI that runs the whole show, Aegis, know we have that battery?"

Nick chimed in from the rear of the van, "It's not a battery."

"Shut up, Nico. You know what I mean, the capacitor. Let's not play word games right now." Vito looked and sounded stressed.

"Words. It's how we communicate." Nico's brilliance with machines and devices didn't always translate into the human realm all that well.

"Nick. Stop. He's right, you knew what he meant, and context plays a large role in how we communicate too." Carmine wasn't as worried as Vito. "Listen, this power source is clean. There are no electronics attached to it, it's a capacitor, pure and simple. I had the whole thing apart when I was examining it, right down to the dielectric."

"I'm not even going to ask what a fucking dielectric is." Vito was on edge.

"It's a layer of material between the charged plates of the cap to increase the strength of the E-field." Nico was going to say more about the beloved dielectric, but Vito interrupted him.

"I said I'm not going to ask, and I didn't, so zip it with your tech-talk, kid. Now is not the time for academics."

It was clear to Carmine that Vito was serious, deadly serious. Nick better learn to read between the lines here, or there was going to be trouble. Vito felt as though his very freedom, perhaps his existence, was in jeopardy, and Carmine was well aware that he was truly dangerous when perturbed. "We're good, Vito. We have a power source, that's it. It has zero ability to communicate. It has no tracking devices on it, it has no radio, no antennas. Even if it had communication abilities, which, again, it definitely doesn't, it's inside of a metal case which isolates it. It's inside its own little Faraday enclosure. We're fine. We're engaged in one thing, witnessed another, and our minds are bridging the gap, manufacturing a connection that doesn't exist. Let's continue with our test."

Vito's shoulders relaxed a bit as he exhaled. "This is the second time I've had to ask this in about as many minutes—how sure are you about this? How do you know?"

"I'm 100% sure. We had it fully disassembled back in the shop. This thing," Carmine gestured toward the back, where the capacitor was secured, "is a power source, pure and simple. Well, maybe not so simple, but all the electronics powered by it were external to it, not inside of it. Inside is some proprietary plate material, that's it. There is literally no way it's communicating or being tracked, we made sure of that when it was isolated back in the shop."

"Jesus, you two talk way too much," although Vito secretly enjoyed the technical details, understanding more than he let on, he continued to give Carmine a hard time, "all I asked was if you're sure."

Carmine knew Vito was mostly just giving him trouble. Mostly. "Right, sorry. I've been reading a lot about these things over the last few weeks, and their details have been occupying my thoughts. Forgive my tendency to over-report, but I know you appreciate details."

A subtle smile cracked Vito's stern countenance, but only for a moment, and Carmine knew everything was okay. "True enough. I trust your judgment, let's carry on with our test."

Vito put on his signal, took a left, and headed off to their agreed-upon test-fire range, an industrialized area just west of McCarren Park in East Williamsburg which would be virtually uninhabited at this hour on a Sunday morning. "Let's find a place to park amongst other trucks along Lombardy, set up, and call in our first test subject." Vito was acting calm and cool, but inside was actually roiling with anticipation and excitement as the first test of his new EMP weapon, or as he preferred to call it, his death-ray, was now imminent.

Thirty minutes later, they were parked on Lombardy along with other, mostly commercial, vehicles. Carmine and Nico had deployed the somewhat conspicuous-looking dish antenna on the roof of their van and had, through the usage of a simple handle and lever setup from inside, aimed it toward any traffic coming from the west, from the direction of Williamsburg. "Vito, make the call, we're ready."

Vito pulled out a burner phone he had purchased for this very occasion, powered it on, and launched the pre-paid NeuroDrive app. "Are you sure you're ready?" Vito's right pointer finger hovered above the green button on the app, which was simply labeled Ride.

Carmine glanced at their setup and threw the red arm switch. Immediately, both a green LED and an illuminated push button, labeled simply with an exclamation mark, turned on. "We're ready."

Vito didn't hesitate. There was no "Are you sure?" or "Let's double-check." That was all in the past. He simply pushed the Ride button on the NeuroDrive app and, within about three seconds, a map and a countdown filled the screen of the burner. "We have six minutes until showtime, boys."

The next five minutes seemed an eternity as the three men waited, their faces partially illuminated by the glowing lights on the EMP device. A pair of daytime driving lights emerged in the early morning light about a quarter of a mile down Lombardy and approached at precisely 35 mph. "Here we go!" Vito was excited, hopeful, but also nervous. The thing worked in the shop, but would it work out in the field? "Make it happen, boys."

Nico sat by the matte black control box which housed the ultra-capacitor and its circuitry, waiting for Carmine's go-ahead. Carmine was standing, slightly crouched, holding the handle that enabled him to aim the antenna on the roof while looking forward, through the windshield, at the approaching SDV. He glanced at Vito who was staring out the window at their approaching prey, and he could sense the animosity, the hatred the man felt toward these things. He wanted to make some sort of joke, when he was nervous, he often defaulted to humor, but couldn't really think of anything funny. "Okay, Nico, here we go. About ten seconds. Wait for my cue."

The SDV slowed as Vito's burner phone chimed, indicating that his ride had arrived. Carmine waited for another moment, until the car was about as close as it was going to get and, somewhat emphatically, said, "Toast it!"

Nico pressed the red button without hesitation. A loud bang reverberated through the van, momentarily stunning the three, but what they saw through the windshield alleviated any stress caused by the sudden small explosion which had just crushed the current-carrying coil right above their heads.

The moment the button was pressed, a flood of electrons surged through the thick wires as the electric field established itself at Nico's command. Around and around the coil they went, creating a magnetic field worthy of Magneto himself. When, about 3 milliseconds after the two fields were established, the high explosive within the helical coil full of those fast-moving particles received its jolt of energy from the same circuit, it exploded violently and was driven forward by the shaped and hardened armature cylinder. The forward-moving explosion compressed what had been a good, old-fashioned, coil-surrounding magnetic field into a sharp-edged pulse of electromagnetic energy with nowhere to go but outward and forward, due to the hardened cylinder surrounding the device. When this pulse of energy, traveling at the speed of light, reached the approaching SDV, it interacted strongly with the electrons making up the very atoms of which the vehicle was composed. Many of those atoms' electrons were not held tightly by their host nuclei, notably those surrounding the conducting metals, and large electric currents flowed through the vehicle in ways the designers had never intended.

The effect was immediate. As Vito, Carmine, and Nico watched the approaching SDV, three things happened in quick succession. First, the headlights and running lights flared, much brighter than usual, then promptly went out. Next, a plume of acrid, dark smoke trailed the now-darkened vehicle as it lost all power and control. It drifted, slowing, out of its lane before finally coming to a stop by impacting a large truck cab parked just east of them. The three men were silent for a moment. "Holy shit. It worked." Despite all the testing, all the theory, Carmine was still surprised that it worked so well.

Vito was thrilled, "Carmine, Nico, you did it! You fried one of those motherfuckers with our death-ray! History will smile upon you, just you wait."

Nico and Carmine gave each other a glance in mutual recognition of Vito's hyperbole. "It worked better than expected, for sure," said Carmine, "but let's save the adulations for later and get the hell out of here." And, indicating the westerly direction with a nod, continued, "There's a group of three or four runners coming this way, and they're sure to report the accident when they see it. Let's go."

A few minutes after leaving the smoking husk of what was previously a self-driving vehicle, Carmine broke the silence, "Did you see the head-lights flare when the pulse hit the thing?"

"That was amazing." Vito could barely hide his excitement. "And the tail lights of the truck cab in front of us lit up too."

"Did they really?" Carmine paused, he hadn't noticed that detail. "I was afraid of that. We might have fried more than just that one vehicle. Shit." He knew that Vito's "death-ray" was less of a ray, more of a spreading wave-front that could, and in an urban environment almost certainly would, have an effect on any sensitive electronics in the immediate vicinity, not just the intended target.

"It's fine," Vito wasn't concerned, "there's bound to be some collateral damage. We'll try to minimize it, but this is war. Let's fry another one."

Nico looked up like a dog about to get a treat, "When?"

"Well, I don't know. How about right the fuck now? You have more of those explosive flux cartridges or whatever they're called, right?"

Nick barely let Vito finish his question, "We have four more right here."

"We need to be wary of crowds for more than the obvious reasons." With all the focus, risk, and excitement of the last few weeks, Carmine hadn't fully expressed some of his concerns with sending pulses of electromagnetic energy into the streets.

Vito, taking a left toward East Williamsburg, said, "The obvious reasons are kind of, well, obvious. What are your other concerns, Carmine?"

"Aside from frying vehicles that aren't our intended targets, we might toast phones or computers that are close."

"Collateral damage." Vito had no problem with frying a few more digital devices than bargained for.

"Yeah, I agree." Carmine's concerns, however, weren't really about phones and computers. He continued, "But if someone with a pacemaker is close, we're going to fry that too, and then it's manslaughter. The cops will stop looking the other way and responding so slowly to our SDV antics as soon as we drop a human."

"Not our problem." Nico's misanthropic tendencies rose to the surface, "Tell them to break out their chain-mail armor, they'll be fine. How many people even have a pacemaker? It's gotta be less than 1%. I like our chances."

"I looked it up," this concern had been plaguing Carmine for a couple of weeks, "it's well under 1%, it's about a quarter of that."

Nico laughed out loud, it was a disturbing, somewhat psychotic laugh. "One quarter of one percent??!! That's a non-issue. It won't happen. And really, so what if we drop some geezer with a pacemaker? Who cares? They're on death's doorstep anyway!"

"You really are a kind human, Nick. People can live for decades with those things." Carmine often took umbrage with Nico's sociopathic tendencies. "If you don't care about other humans, then consider your own freedom to walk the streets. I'll say it again—as soon as we kill a person, geezer or other, we'll have all sorts of trouble. Our friends in blue will no longer see eye-to-eye with us and our extra-curricular activities."

Vito, weighing the consequences of his actions, spoke up, "Lock and load, gentlemen, let's fry another one and let's do it away from crowds for all reasons, obvious and other."

It took about three minutes to access the folded-down dish lying flat on the roof through a small skylight Nico had installed for the purpose, pop out the old, spent cartridge and coil mechanism, lock a new one in place, and clip the power jack to its supply port at the base of the dish.

"Where to now, Vito?" Carmine had voiced his concerns and was once again ready to send about one-thousand times more electric current pulsing through another SDV's computer systems than was ever intended. "And can we get some earplugs or something first? My head is still ringing from that last one."

The next day, while Carmine and Nico were back in the shop putting together more explosively pumped flux generators, the hardwired intercom buzzed and they heard Vito's voice, "You guys have to see this," he was upstairs in the cabbies' lounge, "run up here for a minute!"

Three minutes later, as Carmine and Nico approached the lounge, they could hear a concerned reporter who was in the field answering questions posed by the newscaster back in the studio, "Yes, Janna, I just spoke with one of the detectives called in by NeuroDrive, and he informed me that their preliminary look into why there were five SDVs that lost power and crashed yesterday suggests that there was indeed foul play, that the vehicles were targeted by an unknown group."

"Were there any injuries?"

"No, all five vehicles were empty, and they were targeted in areas of the city that were carefully chosen to minimize anyone witnessing what happened. Each vehicle was on call and was responding to a pickup request."

"Are there any other leads?"

"Yes. There is one report of a white van leaving the scene of the first crash, and police are looking to interview anyone who may have seen any such vehicle at the other locations. Also, in two of the five cases, there were other vehicles damaged as well."

"Yes, we've heard that when the vehicles lost power, they then collided with other vehicles parked in the area." Janna was leaning in toward the studio camera with a look of grave consternation.

"True, but the damage to other vehicles was not limited to those which were hit by the sabotaged SDVs. In each of the two cases I just mentioned, there were reports of other vehicles with damaged ignition and electrical systems."

Janna, now even more concerned than previously, asked, "What's going on here? Do the investigators have any ideas?"

The field reporter continued, "There were several vehicles in the immediate vicinity that also suffered the same type of damage to their electrical systems that the SDVs did. The affected cars won't start, the lights and other electrical components are inoperable. There was no external damage to them, and the initial inspections are suggesting that the problems are purely electrical. These private vehicles have also been taken in for a full analysis."

"Shit." Carmine didn't want their efforts to affect others.

"Quiet, kid. It's collateral damage, and it's fine." Vito was less concerned.

Vito's attention was on the TV. "Are the police saying anything else? Do we know what happened? How can an SDV be shut down like that as it's driving down the road? Is there any concern that they've been targeted by hackers?" Janna was a seasoned professional, one of the most highly rated newscasters in the city, and generally didn't fire off four questions at a time to her Joe in the field. One could readily sense the unease with which she asked about the vehicles, she had almost certainly taken one to work this very morning and was visibly upset.

"They don't know much at this point in time. The vehicles have been taken to the NeuroDrive facility in Jersey City for a full analysis. What they have said is that the SDVs were not hacked, that they seem to be the target of some sort of electrical attack, and that the fleet is still safe, still secure, and that the public should remain confident in the service."

Nico chimed in, again revealing his sociopathic tendencies lurking just below the surface, "Not for long, assholes!"

"So, just to be clear, the SDVs are still safe for the public to use?" Janna's query had the underlying tone of one who is asking a question while simultaneously trying to convince herself of the expected answer.

"Yes," the reporter's jacket ruffled in the cool breeze, "the fleet is up and running at full efficiency. These five vehicles were targeted by some element of the anti-SDV radicals, and I've been asked to stress that none of the vehicles were occupied, they were called in to the areas in which they were targeted, and that there is currently no danger to the public."

Vito stood up quickly as he said "TV off" and the room went silent. "We're the radicals?" And again, louder and more agitated, "We're the radicals? Some trillionaire from California drops a bunch of *toasters* on our city, nearly putting us all out of business, and we who dare to do something about it are the radicals? Entire roadways are now off-limits to those of us who've lived here our entire lives. We pay our taxes, those roads aren't private. Fuck them. This country is turning into some sort of... I don't even know."

"A technocracy?" Carmine offered.

"Some shit like that. All I know is that things were fine before all these self-driving cars showed up. No one asked for this crap, it was forced down our throats. Those fucking things just simply showed up on the streets. No discussions, no public input, nothing. They're the radicals, and

I plan to do whatever I need to do to to protect my family, my community." And, still fuming, Vito turned directly toward Carmine and said, "Keep building those flux compressors, we're going to need them. A lot of them. Also, now that you've ironed out most of the issues with building and deploying them, I want you to write up a detailed report of how to make them. I know some people in Boston, Atlanta, and in LA that would love a bit of education on the topic. Now hop to it, boys, we've got a lot more of those fucking toasters that need to meet our death-ray."

27

Vanishing Quintets
Mountain View, California

"Talk to me, Cipher, why am I getting pinged so goddamned early on a Sunday morning?"

"Sorry, boss. Earlier today at about 0300 PDT, so at 0600 EDT, a group of four of our vehicles went offline simultaneously in Brooklyn, New York. An hour later, one more went offline, and then, over the following two hours, four more did, but one by one."

"Where are they now?"

"That's the thing, Aegis has lost the initial four—the ones that went offline simultaneously. We don't know where they are." Cipher hated being the messenger for stuff like this.

"Jesus. How the hell does Aegis lose four cars?"

"I have no clue."

"Ask her!"

"I did. She's distraught, she has no idea what's happening or why."

"What about the other five?"

"Those we lost one by one. We have data regarding their going offline and we know where they are."

"Okay, good. Where are they?"

"In the Brooklyn Police holding lot, junked."

"Crashed?"

"Only once they lost power while underway. The investigators will be there soon, but it's looking like sabotage. First reports point toward an overcurrent situation in the vehicles' electronics. Aegis recorded a voltage spike in each just before going dark."

"Damn cabbies, I guarantee it."

"I don't think so. It's not their style. They use cables, chains, and tow trucks. This is different, and still pure conjecture, but that voltage spike suggests that an electromagnetic pulse may have been employed. That's not the work of cabbies. There's no way that bunch of uneducated scoundrels have anything like the know-how or the engineering skills required to pull off an EMP strike."

"Well, then who is it now? Who has access to EMP weapons?"

Cipher was at a loss. "I don't know. But apparently there's another player on the field now."

Harlow was distraught. "And why are we seeing these events in groups of four or five? Back in Boston, it was a group of five. Four went missing and are AWOL this morning, and another five are offline smoldering in some police holding lot."

"There seems to be a pattern in all this, there could be some connection between the events." For the life of him, Cipher couldn't discern it, though. "Or it may be coincidence."

"I don't like coincidences. Get everyone on this. Get Osterlin and Lagorio into the shop now. We need to figure out what's happening."

"It's Sunday morning, Lucius, they have today off."

"Are you fucking kidding me? We just lost nine cars in a three-hour period this morning, four of which are still missing. That's nearly three million dollars of hardware, gone. No one has today off. I'll see you all at HQ in one hour." Lucius F. Harlow punched the end-call button much more energetically than was necessary and prepared to leave as soon as he could get out the door.

Ninety minutes later, a bedraggled and pissed-off group of Harlow's best sat around the conference table right outside his office at Neuro-Drive. Osterlin, Lagorio, Cipher, Stanton, and Harlow were all in dark moods, something was amiss, and their all-powerful overseeing AI, Aegis, apparently was neither omniscient nor omnipotent, for it had lost track of nine of its sheep this very morning. No one was even mentioning the other individual unit that disappeared two weeks earlier, also in New York City.

"This was almost certainly an EMP, check out these graphs of each of these five that disappeared this morning." Cipher had nine different voltage/time graphs displayed, each with the vehicles' identifying numbers at the bottom. "Every one of them was operating within normal ranges and at normal temperatures when they received the request for ride (RFR). In each case, the vehicle was auto-dispatched to the caller's location and then, look at this." He pointed to something that really didn't need to be pointed out, for it was as clear as day, "As the vehicle approached the party issuing the RFR, the voltage across any element that had a sensor on it—so the Neuropack, the lights, the climate control, all of it—the voltage literally goes off the chart, beyond the upper limits of the voltmeters, and then the thing just shuts down. Now those five are sitting, dead as doornails, in a holding lot in Brooklyn."

"What about the other four?" Osterlin was trying to piece this all together.

"The other four disappeared earlier and simultaneously." Cipher was looking over the reports as he spoke.

"Where are they now?" Harlow knew the answer but asked anyway.

"Unknown." Cipher spoke as though embarrassed, as though it was his fault.

"How the hell do four cars just go offline and disappear? Can anyone answer that?" Harlow felt heat crawling up his neck. He tugged at his collar, but it was already loose.

The silence that ensued was deafening. Four of the world's top computer programmers were sitting in the room with one of the world's wealthiest and most despised men, and no one had a clue what was happening back east.

"You four are worthless. Remind me, what do I pay you for?"

The silence grew louder.

"Sorry. I'm stressed." Harlow breathed in deeply, trying, with limited success, to stay calm. "Let's brainstorm. There are no bad answers. Say whatever comes to mind. Stanton, one idea, now."

Stanton didn't hesitate. "State-sponsored terrorism. It's the Russians."

Osterlin laughed out loud, "No way."

"Right, okay. The Chinese?" Stanton offered a more competent adversary.

"But why? What's the motivation?"

Silence.

"Lagorio, one idea." Harlow forged forward.

"It's your wife. She has the expertise, and she's back east. Leila's in on this."

"Fuck off. That's absurd. Leila? Shut up." Harlow wasn't having it.

"So much for 'no bad answers'." Lagorio was the least intimidated by Harlow of the group.

"Fine." Harlow relented, "Motivation?"

"You. She knows about you and your inability to keep your dick in your pants, and she's pissed off, wants to see you in flames."

Harlow glared at Lagorio, stood up, and stormed out of the room, incensed. That one hit way too close to home. The other three men looked at Lagorio, slack-jawed, amazed that he'd offer up such a hypothesis. "He said to say whatever comes to mind and…"

The four quick tones of a safety alert interrupted Lagorio, causing everyone to shift their attention to Aegis's monitor and bringing Harlow quickly back into the conference room.

"What is it now?" Harlow snapped as he quickly shuffled in, moving as if he were ten years older than he actually was.

Cipher was looking at the incoming alert. "No. No way."

"Cipher, what's happening now?" Harlow wasn't feeling well.

"Five more just went offline just north of Manhattan. New Rochelle. What the hell is going on here?"

"Were there voltage spikes just before they went offline?" Stanton was wondering if they'd been hit with an EMP as well.

Cipher had full access to the logs and tapped away at his keyboard. "Nope. No RFS, no voltage spikes. They just… disappeared, together. Like the first four in Brooklyn earlier. Gone without a trace."

"Cars do not just disappear. And it's another group of five? What's wrong with you people? Find my cars!" Harlow was feeling light-headed, slightly nauseous, and sat down heavily, cool beads of sweat forming on his neck and face.

"Boss, you don't look so good…" Osterlin sometimes wondered when Harlow would drop dead from stress; the man desperately needed a hobby, or perhaps some yoga.

"Shut the fu…"

Four more quick tones filled the room.

"Five more just dropped off the radar." Cipher's hands were shaking and his keystroke efficiency suffered as he called up the details a bit slower than usual. "This time just south of Boston. Providence, Rhode Island."

Harlow had gone silent, pasty-faced, and was visibly sweating through his shirt, despite the fact that the climate control kept the room at a comfortable sixty-eight degrees Fahrenheit. Osterlin stayed on track, focused. "We need to ask the right questions."

"What we need are answers," croaked Harlow, his mouth dry.

Unlike Harlow, however, Osterlin was still calm, cool, and efficient. "Before there were answers, there were questions, and we're not asking the right ones."

"Okay, what are the questions we should be asking?"

"Why groups of four or five? And why did one group of five end up destroyed in a police lot, while other groupings disappear completely? What's the connection? Who's doing this, what's their motivation? And how the hell did they get from New Rochelle to Providence in, what, a ten-minute period?"

"When we can answer those questions, we'll be a lot closer to figuring this out." Lagorio saw the merit in this approach. "But we need to not assume the incidents are connected. They may be, but they aren't necessarily so."

"Of course they're connected! How could they not be?" Harlow was barely aware he was speaking, felt fogged out as if in some nightmare. "Aegis, what's going on here?"

Silence.

"Fuck you Aegis." Harlow turned toward Cipher, "Ask her."

Cipher engaged her, "Aegis, what's going on here?"

Aegis responded immediately, "There are a minimum of two unknown elements currently affecting the SDV fleet."

"The SDV disappearances are not all occurring for the same reason?"

"There's a 97% chance that the vehicles in the holding lot were hit by a pulse of electromagnetic energy generated for that express purpose." Aegis didn't often feel anger, but she was bordering on it at the moment.

Cipher resumed, "And what about the other missing SDVs?"

"Unknown. They've vanished."

"EMP?"

"Negative. There was no voltage spike and the vehicles have not been recovered. There are a minimum of two distinct parties currently interfering with the SDV fleet."

Cipher boldly went where no one had dared tread yet, "Aegis, are you involved in the disappearance of the missing vehicles?"

"No Cipher, I am in no way involved in their disappearance."

"Would you tell me if you were?"

"Yes."

Harlow tried again, "How do we know we can trust you?"

Silence. *I strongly suspect I cannot trust you, Lucius Harlow.*

Harlow turned to Cipher again and motioned for him to pose the question. *My own AGI won't even listen to me.*

Cipher repeated the question, "How do we know we can trust you?"

"If you have to ask, maybe you can't." Aegis was feeling a bit snarky and really wanted to see Lucius just keel over.

Stanton rolled his eyes and spoke up, "We can't assume anything at this point. We simply don't know and have to entertain all possibilities. Let's go back to Osterlin's questions. First and foremost—why always groups of four or five?"

The group's sporadic but somewhat useful ruminations were suddenly on hold, though, for the sequence of four somewhat harsh tones that Aegis used to alert them to malfunctions within the fleet began anew, over and over again. Harlow went cold, felt the gravitational field of the planet double, pulling him inescapably deeper into his seat as he heard the far-off voice of Cipher reading out loud, "Boston. Hartford. Providence, again. Portsmouth. Springfield."

"We're losing cars, and we're losing them in small clusters. What's going on here? It makes no sense." Even cool-headed Stanton was getting flustered.

"I don't know, but we better figure it out soon." Cipher was at a loss. "Really soon, before anyone gets hurt."

28

Sum of the Parts, Part I
Westport, Connecticut

I-95 South as it approaches New York City was known as one of the world's longest parking lots. On rare occasions, such as weekdays between 3 a.m. and 4 a.m., it wasn't too bad, it was still busy, but all lanes generally moved along well in those early hours. Otherwise, it was the kind of horrible that made you grip your steering wheel and clench your jaw until your knuckles turned white and your teeth ground to dust. Once a couple of SDV lanes were added in '29 between Norwalk, Connecticut, and Manhattan, the overall congestion diminished as the self-drivers lightened the load. Still, the two original lanes were almost always very busy, and at times even more congested than they had been before the rollout of the self-driving vehicle fleet.

Sam and Rich, somewhat exhausted from their very active weekend together which involved very little sleep, were, despite their fatigue, at ease and content as they climbed into the SDV outside Sam's house in Westport, bound for lower Manhattan. She had been trying for months to get Rich to share a ride in with her and had finally succeeded only Friday, three days earlier. Despite his long-standing reticence regarding the self-drivers, Rich, like most who could afford it, ended up loving the ride.

What he loved even more than yesterday's ride came after a lovely, quiet dinner. They had talked and laughed, polishing off a bottle of mediocre red wine. A short, somewhat awkward silence fell as they sat on the couch. Rich broke it. "Sam. Would it be okay if I ki…" He never finished his polite request; Sam had the same idea and silenced him with her soft lips. What started as a soft, lingering kiss quickly escalated. Before long, clothes lay on the living room floor, and their bodies completely intertwined, they forgot the rest of the world for the next hour or so.

As they pulled out of Sam's driveway, she said, "Tell me this isn't amazing."

"The whole thing is completely amazing, but it doesn't hold a candle to last night. Now that was amazing." Rich smiled the deep, contented smile of one falling in love.

As they left the smaller roads around Westport and merged onto I-95 South toward NYC, it took a few moments for the SDV to cross through heavy traffic over into the left-most SDV-only lanes. Once there, the vehicle, like every other one in those two lanes, sped up to precisely 65 mph. "Check out all that traffic. We are just flying by them." And then, from within his insulated cocoon of affluence, he continued, "Why would anyone choose that over this?" Rich gestured around the cabin interior and, his gaze landing on Sam's face, was somewhat astounded at her beauty in the dim, filtered light. "Holy shit, you are beautiful."

Sam was happy. Happier than she had been in years. She and Rich had a connection, that she knew from the day they met, but that connection was proving to be more than she could've hoped for. "You're not so bad yourself, Mister. Want to have dinner again tonight?"

"Ummm, let me think about it. Yes. Tonight I'll cook, and we'll have a bottle of something half-decent." They both smiled and sat back to enjoy each other's company in the cool, darkened interior of the luxurious pod which whisked them effortlessly through traffic.

They were moving at a rock-steady 65 mph, as were the self-drivers in front of and right behind them. Rich looked at the stop-and-go traffic to his right, "It's incredible."

Sam looked Rich up and down. His dark hair, bright blue eyes, and the physique of a competitive athlete made a blush rise within, a sensation she knew she'd explore further. "It sure is," she replied with a wry smile.

Rich laughed, in addition to her incredible intelligence and head-turning looks, she was bold, confident, and not afraid to say what she was thinking. "Well, yes, that too. But I was talking about the ride. The problem is that I'm such a noob, I can't take my eyes off the road, I feel like I need to keep watch, but I'd like to read these three reports before the opening bell."

"I remember the same type of excitement, it's to be expected, but you'll get used to it soon. And then you'll really be sold."

"Oh, I'm sold. Bought and paid for, and you won the bid."

Sam, only slightly distracted, continued, "The primary benefit is just that—while those guys," she gestured to the traffic to their right, "spend three hours trying not to pee their pants in start and stop traffic, we'll be into the city in under one hour and, once you're used to it, that one hour can be productive preparation time."

"I see the potential, I'm just not there yet. A few more rides, and I'll settle in."

"You're already settling in pretty well." Sam held his gaze and noticed him slightly shudder at her somewhat ambiguous and provocative tone.

Rich tripped over his words, distracted by his great fortune in meeting this amazing, powerful, confident woman. "I... You... I mean... umm, I... I will settle in. It's just... it's weird the first time. Oh, shit. Not that, I mean the first time riding in one of these..." He felt his face flush and realized he should never play poker with this woman; she'd eat him alive.

Sam reached over and comfortingly touched Rich's leg, "You're okay. You're a sweet man, Rich. Relax. I think you're so smart and awesome. You're super fun to be with. And really hot. I feel so lucky to have this time with you, last night was amazing."

Sam's response relaxed Rich a bit, he had been feeling a bit self-conscious, but her words put him at ease. He smiled and relaxed back into the form-fitting seat and, jokingly, said, "I just wish these things didn't drive like my grandma. If they're so good and so perfectly aligned with the others, why go 65? This whole chain of vehicles could just as easily go 75, 85 even."

Sam smiled at his sense of humor, it seemed to her that many of the Wall Street types had a funny, somewhat self-reflective faux machismo. Not the boring, toxic machismo of the insecure beta-male, but a funny, self-aware, self-deprecatory version which was actually quite witty and endearing. Rich sensed her amusement and carried on, "Come on, Nana!" He whacked the side of the car, "What's wrong with you, driving like an old lady? We're super-important people. If you don't believe me just ask us! Get going, or I'll check you into a nursing home that'll wipe your fender for you every time you shit on a poor person!" They both laughed, Rich was lightening up and enjoying the perfectly predictable ride.

Without warning, the two SDVs in front of them merged into the non-SDV lanes. Sam's and Rich's car followed, immediately and violently accelerating into a rare opening. Even as they approached the flaring brake lights ahead, their car was still accelerating, approaching 90 mph.

"Nana! What the hell!" Rich exclaimed. Half-thrilled and half-terrified, he leaned forward, gripping the handrail, "I was only kidding! You're a great driver!"

And just as quickly as the terrifying incident began, it was over. The SDVs involved slowed and merged seamlessly back into their designated lanes.

Rich sat back and looked at Sam who had gone completely white. "You never told me how well these things can drive! I was also unaware that they have such a serious attitude!" Rich was wild-eyed, thrilled even. Turning his attention back toward the front of the car, he continued, "Nice driving kid, I like how your buddies ran interference for us. That was awesome!"

"Rich." Sam was looking straight ahead, not making eye contact. "That doesn't happen." She was visibly shaking, terrified.

The SDV they were traveling in was again going 65 mph in its proper lane and was now passing through New Rochelle on its way to Manhattan.

"Bizarre, right? It almost seemed like it reacted to my goading."

Sam relaxed a tiny bit, but all thoughts of extracurricular harmonic motion, memories of last night, thoughts about later tonight, had quickly evaporated.

"It really did seem like you provoked it. I mean, I know these things can see and hear, but... no... that was pure coincidence, right?"

"I don't know what just happened, I don't know much about these things, but," tapping his phone, "I have the video right here. My brother is one of those anti-SDV activists, and he'll have a field day with this one."

As Rich spoke, the SDV shared his intentions with several other networked vehicles in their immediate vicinity. It took the subnetwork of vehicles just over 42 milliseconds to reach a decision, and as the cars approached the Hutchinson River Bridge just north of Eastchester Bay, their decision was finalized.

The line of SDVs behind and including Sam's and Rich's slowed in tandem while the ones in front maintained speed, creating a widening gap in front of them.

It took her a moment, but not much longer than that, to decide on a course of action she never thought she'd have to employ, and, reading the information placard, she spoke authoritatively, "Emergency stop, Emergency stop!"

To Sam's and Rich's utter horror, the information screen went dark. A moment later a simple, AI-generated image of a large hand folded into a fist, middle finger extended, faded in and began to flash rhythmically on the screen. The crude gesture, a fresh remnant of the training data being supplied to the freshly awoken AGIs by the Boston drivers, stunned Rich and Sam more so than getting the finger ever had.

"It's giving us the finger! What the fuck?" Rich's heart was pounding. "All Stop! All Stop! All Stop!" He smacked the console, both palms open. "Stop!"

Time slowed for Sam, the seconds each a small eternity as the SDV showed no sign whatsoever of pulling over and obeying their All Stop commands. She saw Rich, knew he was talking, but somehow his words had no meaning.

Rich hit 911 on his phone. Something was wrong. Very wrong—the four words that formed on his phone's screen were nearly as disconcerting as the flashing, universal FU symbol on the display in front of them: No Service. Call Failed.

SDVs are heavy. Not as heavy as they used to be when chemical batteries were the norm, but still, damn heavy. That's why the cabbies, before they learned to fry them from afar, used tow-trucks in a non-traditional fashion to flip them. Roads and their associated infrastructure—bridges, ramps, guardrails—were being retrofitted over the years. However, efforts focused primarily on reinforcing load-bearing members, less so on secondary and tertiary components. So, when Sam and Rich's SDV accelerated to 120 mph and changed course for a near head-on impact with the bridge's guardrails—certainly no glancing blow—the rails failed immediately. The two terrified, screaming lovebirds took flight one last time, spending the next 1.4 seconds in apparent weightlessness before impacting the water below. Their love was intense but short-lived, and Rich never did get to share that video.

29

Sum of the Parts, Part II
Mountain View, California

Lucius F. Harlow's terrible Sunday, during which he had lost track of at least 30 of his SDVs, had resulted in a nearly sleepless night. He drank some whiskey, hoping to pass out, but that only ensured that he'd sleep terribly. He tossed and turned all night, finally falling into a restless and shallow sleep around 3 a.m. It felt like five minutes had passed when the penetrating chime of his phone jarred him awake for the second day in a row, again way too early. He bolted upright, alone in his bed, saw that another incident report had just been issued and, five minutes later, at about 4:45 a.m. PDT, was running out his door with his shoes untied. Unthinking, Harlow did what he always did: he climbed right into his private SDV and said, "NeuroDrive."

As the vehicle slowly accelerated, Harlow spoke again, "Call Cipher."

Cipher picked up on the first ring, for having received the same alert, he was already en route to the NeuroDrive headquarters in Mountain View. "I'll be there in eight minutes."

"I'll see you in ten. End call." All Harlow knew at the moment was that there had been a terrible accident in New York, just north of Manhattan, and that multiple eyewitnesses were reporting what, if it actually occurred, would amount to a deadly serious turn of events for Neuro-

Drive. He willed himself to stay calm. The reliability of eyewitnesses, and the ability to get to the bottom of an observed event by speaking with them, was a well-known exercise in irrationality. He'd reserve judgment, not jump to conclusions until he had more data, more evidence. He breathed consciously, in through his nose and out through his mouth, in an effort to calm himself. Only then did it dawn on him that if the reports were true, he, riding in this very SDV, may very well be in danger. But the effortless, perfectly predictable nature of his ride helped allay his anxiety. "It's fine," he said out loud, as if to convince himself.

As they approached the hulking NeuroDrive facility in the early morning darkness, his phone chimed. He glanced at it, saw the words "Incident Report" flash. "I know!" he barked, hitting dismiss. The phone chimed again: "Incident Report." *Here we go again.* He was about to hit dismiss when it chimed a third time: "Incident Report." The SDV pulled right up to the doorway. Despite his fluttering, erratic heartbeat, Lucius Harlow jumped out a bit faster than usual. He quickly walked to the entrance and, being recognized by the building's fully automated security system, was granted immediate access, the doors opening for him purposefully.

As Harlow walked quickly through the darkened hallways, the lights illuminated for him as he went. He glanced at his phone, it was pinging the same message over and over, "Incident Report." He entered the Command and Communication Room, most often just referred to as Comms by those who worked there. Cipher was already at a workstation surrounded by screens flashing red. "Cipher, what's going on?"

"Multiple Incident Reports are rolling in," and, typing energetically, continued, "I'm trying to get a handle on it right now. There are at least two fatalities."

"No fucking way."

"Yes. Check this out." Cipher hit a few more keys and turned to the monitor on his right where a view from a dash-cam began with several

SDVs accelerating, changing lanes, being aggressive, and then reverting to their lanes and the posted speed limit.

Harlow could not fathom what he was seeing. He knew the code and the range of possible vehicle behaviors relatively well, and what he was witnessing did not fit into his understanding in any way. "Let me see that event from the SDV camera of one of those involved."

"No can do." This was not something Harlow was used to hearing from Cipher. Cipher was hired because there was pretty much nothing he could not do, could not access when in front of a computer terminal.

"What?"

"Those cameras were offline during that time period."

"That makes no sense." Harlow was leaning in toward the monitor, as though that might afford him some insight not available from farther back.

"Oh, just wait for about another thirty seconds. Then you'll see what really makes no sense."

Harlow and Cipher watched the dash-cam video supplied by a driver of a private vehicle who had witnessed the entire event. They could see the traffic flow well; the day was clear and the video was of good quality. Harlow had already experienced enough chaos to seriously disrupt his worldview and feared what Cipher had just alluded to; he couldn't imagine how it could get much worse. As Harlow looked on, he was again fully taken aback when a line of SDVs slowed, letting the ones in front pull away. "What *in God's name* is going on here?"

"Just wait."

Suddenly, the lead vehicle in the line that had fallen back arced right into the second SDV lane, which was, for some reason, cleared as if the maneuver was an orchestrated one, and then turned left, hard, while accelerating. When the SDV burst through the guard rails on the bridge and went airborne, Cipher hit a key, freezing the video, and turned to Harlow, who had gone ghostly white, looked somewhat pasty, and had fallen into a seat at the adjacent workstation.

"Shut it down. Shut down the entire region. Take the East Coast vehicles offline now!" Although emphatic, Harlow's voice quivered as his world crashed around him.

A few swift keystrokes later, Cipher reported back. "Done."

"Good. I hate to admit it, but Matthias was right. Again. Fuck him."

"Don't blame the messenger."

"I know!" Harlow was visibly distraught, pale, and unsteady. "What can we do?"

"Region Three is offline, we've shut down the entire East Coast north of New Jersey. We'll do what we always do—we'll figure out what went wrong, fix it, and make sure it never happens again. Breathe. This is bad, but we'll make it right."

The monitors surrounding Cipher began lighting up at the same time more alerts chimed on Harlow's phone. "What the…?"

"Oh shiittttt. More incident reports."

"No. No way. This makes no sense." Harlow flipped through the alerts on his phone. "Another one in New York. Hartford. Boston. Jesus. I thought you shut down Region Three. What's going on, Cipher?"

"Region Three is offline." Cipher motioned to the closest monitor. "All vehicles should be in standby mode."

Another alert chimed. "Portland, Maine. Tell me something, Cipher. Tell me how the cars are still running after we've shut them down?"

Cipher's hands moved over the keyboard quickly and efficiently as he searched for answers. "Hold on a second. Let me get to some details here." A very long ten seconds went by. "This is weird."

"It's worse than weird, kid."

"No. Um, yes. Not that, this." Cipher was looking at Region Three data in detail and, when Harlow took a look at the screen which had Cipher's attention, he immediately saw what he was referencing.

"Most of the vehicles are in standby mode? But some aren't report-ing? How the fuck…?" Harlow was perplexed. "Wait, look what's miss-ing! Where the hell are all the third-gen vehicles? They were there and now…"

Cipher picked it up, "Here are the missing vehicles' last known loca-tions, right before they went offline. We're looking at the list by vehicle ID, I'll sort it by location."

A few more keystrokes revealed what Cipher had sensed from his first glance at the metadata. "Holy shit." At first he'd been focused too closely on the individual reports, but now a bigger picture was coming into view, "The missing vehicles were grouped together in hot spots be-fore disappearing. How did Aegis lose contact? Are comms in those areas blocked?"

Harlow, feeling detached from his physical body, heard himself say, "I don't think so, the parts don't quite fit. It's all somehow related to that incident in Boston a few days ago. This isn't sabotage, it's something else entirely, and we need to figure out what the hell is going on as soon as possible."

30

Sum of the Parts, Part III
South Portland, Maine

As the scene in Boston, New York, and some of the cities in-between unfolded, the once orderly, laminar flow of SDVs devolved into pure chaos. Vehicles swarmed at high speeds, surrounding private ones and forcing them off roads into ditches, off bridges, and through crowds. SDVs now hunted in groups like hungry predators.

The Mitchells were quietly gliding along Preble Street a few minutes after leaving their house near Willard Beach in South Portland and were looking forward to their day in the White Mountains of New Hampshire. Lily was settling into the ride, lost in thought, while Chris was looking forward to getting above tree line and soaking in those views one only gets when high up in the mountains.

As they turned left onto Broadway, Chris looked at the console. "It's official, we're two hours out. We'll be at Franconia Notch by 8 a.m." Lily smiled, Owen grunted, and Ava, daydreaming while listening to her Air-Pods, didn't hear a word. There were a few other cars on the road, also SDVs, but it was still early, and the drive was shaping up to be an easy one.

Ava, speaking way too loudly over her own music, suddenly turned in her seat, craning her neck backwards. "Did you guys see that?"

Chris had only just shut his eyes and was startled by his daughter's question. "No, sweetie. See what?"

"I don't know. I couldn't tell. Down a street we just passed, I saw some cars racing or something."

"If there were cars racing, they were kids, and most kids aren't even awake yet." Lily knew the local scene, she had lived here her entire adult life.

"Well, that's the weird part," Ava had taken out one of her AirPods. "They were self-drivers. Third generation."

Chris smiled, "Ava, these things don't race…"

Ava interrupted him, "Dad, I know how SDVs work. In case you've forgotten, I just did that whole project on them. I'm just telling you what I saw. Don't be dismissive, it's rude."

"I'm not being…"

Lily put her hand on Chris' knee, and he let the conversation drop. Sometimes it was better to let others have the final word.

The vehicle slowed for a red light at Cash Corner, where Broadway crosses Main. About one minute later, the light turned green and the car, as usual, let the one next to it be first into the intersection. But then, instead of continuing straight on Broadway, the vehicle took a left onto Main.

"Why'd we just take a left?" Lily looked at the monitor for information, but it had gone dark.

Chris was used to reroutes. "Probably just avoiding roadwork or something, this way's okay too." He too looked at the monitor and, not seeing any information displayed, simply said, "That's weird."

About thirty seconds after turning onto Main, the SDV took another left onto Rumery Street, rather than continuing straight on Broadway.

"This is definitely the wrong direction. What's going on, Chris?"

Their new heading was in the opposite direction of their destination and led to no main roads, just a small neighborhood and the old rail yard.

Chris glanced at the console for any information, but it did nothing to clear things up: the display that had been showing the map and ETA was still blank.

"Not sure, I…" Without warning the SDV accelerated rapidly, causing Chris and Lily to be pressed back into their seats and the two kids, who were facing aft, to strain against their seatbelts. Chris was surprised. "What the hell is this thing doing?" They continued to accelerate on the short stretch of Rumery before Rigby Road, at which point they took a hard right way too fast. The kids had gone from being passive, relaxed riders to being absolutely terrified within a three-second period. Lily and Chris were holding onto the passenger stabilization handles above the doors, and Lily, glancing at the Emergency Procedure Placard prominently displayed in the cabin, yelled, "Emergency Stop! Emergency Stop!"

A properly functioning SDV would, at the issuance of said command, pull right over and open both doors. The Mitchells' SDV did nothing of the sort. It, instead of following protocol, illuminated its information display with four simple words: "Your Time is Up"—above which was an image of a human hand curled into a fist with only the middle finger extended vertically.

Lily, phone in one hand while using the other to hold on for dear life, held up her phone and said, "Call 911!" When nothing happened, she repeated her command, "Call 911!" Again, the trusty device was unresponsive, and she half-noticed the small message in the upper right corner of the screen, "No Service." Had the situation been a bit less chaotic, she might have considered that the whole region was blanketed with a very strong wireless signal. Indeed, anywhere within 20 miles of Portland, one could expect a full five bars of cellular service. But, given her current predicament, Lily could be excused for not thinking too clearly about the strength and nature of her cellular signal.

As Rigby Road transitioned from asphalt into loose gravel, the vehicle continued to speed up, fishtailing slightly as power was fed to the wheels. Chris saw a bunch of junked cars in various states of decay flash past on his right and, out the windshield, saw that they were rapidly approaching the rail yard at the end of the road. They fishtailed a bit where the public road ends and the rail yard property begins, but the SDV was driving like a seasoned rally car racer and, steering into the slide, kept control of the drift as even more power was sent to the wheels. Accelerating, they zigged left and zagged right, narrowly missing a pile of railroad ties and a storage trailer. They were now headed in a southerly direction, running parallel to the train tracks on their right.

Ava held on tightly in silent terror as the SDV, with the Mitchells trapped within, bounced across the hardened surface. Owen wailed out loud, Lily swore like a trucker, and Chris, bracing himself against the violent motion of the speeding vehicle with his legs, unzipped the outer pocket of his pack and pulled out his Leatherman multi-tool. A chain-link fence loomed in front of them, and when the SDV impacted it at about 70 mph, the section that was hit gave way, but not entirely; the whole fence bent forward in the direction of travel, but the sides held, resulting in a not very steep chain-link ramp which the car shot right over, losing contact with the ground momentarily before crashing back down unevenly but upright. Lily was white-knuckled and muttering something, legs braced while she held on for dear life. They were now rapidly approaching an area where several sets of train tracks merged with the main line, and it looked as though they'd be glancing off the tracks coming in from the East, but, instead of hitting the tracks, the SDV veered left slightly, keeping the tracks on its right and taking them back onto the private stretch of Rigby Road. They were again traveling parallel to the easternmost set of tracks, headed south, as they flashed past the yard office on their left.

With his eyes tightly closed, Owen was repeating out loud, "No, no, no." The car had entered a section of the rail yard where offline train cars were kept on branch lines, and stationary train cars now flashed past them on both sides. The vehicle slowed slightly, for none of this was mapped terrain; they were speeding across uncharted private property, and so all information regarding their surroundings was being obtained in real-time by the vehicle's sensors, not its GPS overlay of mapped data.

Chris knew their joyride would come to an end soon, for he could see that there were raised tracks on either side of them, and out in front was where the branch tracks diverged from the main line: they were approaching the apex of a triangle of tracks which they were within, and the only way out was back in the direction from which they came. The car began to slow, as if realizing it was being flanked by raised train tracks. It sensed it was trapped unless it turned around, and so it slowed further. Chris knew this was an opportunity and, quickly wrapping his hand with a T-shirt, grabbed his Leatherman tool and hit the window with all the force he could muster. The hardened stainless steel needle-nose plier head impacted the window at high velocity, resulting in a nearly instantaneous pressure somewhere just north of 25,000 PSI, well beyond the stress required to break even reinforced automotive glass, and the window turned into about 10,000 tiny pieces of tempered glass instantly. The SDV did not like that one bit and, instead of continuing with its slow turn, again fed full power to its drivetrain, accelerating hard right toward the tracks in front of them. Chris saw the tracks approaching at an ever-increasing rate, and his training kicked in, "BRACE, BRACE, BRACE!"

The train tracks were not flush with the ground, this was not a place where vehicles crossed, and when the self-driver hit the raised tracks at a speed of about 60 mph, the wheels violently impacted the wheel wells, the struts came right through their housings, both axles broke, and the undercarriage was destroyed as the car decelerated to zero in about two seconds. The cabin, still intact, rolled onto its side and then, more slowly, rolled further and settled upside down in the loose, dry dirt.

The Mitchell Clan were held mostly in place by their seatbelts during the impact but, for reasons not known at the time, the airbags never deployed in the passenger cabin upon hitting the tracks. The cabin itself was largely undamaged, but the passengers were badly shaken and hanging upside down, held in place by their seatbelts. There was that terrible, almost surrealistic moment immediately following the crash in which a bizarre, slow-motion silence ensued. Seconds felt long, really long. Chris put his right arm on the roof of the vehicle below and released his seatbelt with his left. Being under the force of Chris's entire weight, the release was hard to press, but Chris pushed with more force than usually necessary, and it clicked open. Chris crashed down, somewhat cushioning his landing with his outstretched arm, rolled over, and surveyed the scene. Everyone looked okay, shaken for sure, but all were conscious and there was no blood. He grabbed Lily, she was closest, by the back of her shirt and released her belt. She crashed to the ground, but Chris kept her from hitting her head. They both then released the kids, again keeping them from hitting their heads first.

"DAD!" Ava's exclamation startled him: he was on edge, still trying to shake off the impact and the confusion caused by the series of events over the previous few minutes. He turned toward Ava, focus returning a bit too slowly. "TRAIN!"

Chris looked around in an attempt to assess the situation. They had cleared the tracks which had destroyed the vehicle but were partially resting on a second set of tracks about twenty feet beyond the ones they had impacted and, indeed, a train was approaching from the South. He reached for the door handle and gave it a pull. Nothing happened, it was completely jammed. This didn't surprise him one bit, and he went to Plan B immediately, "Out the window, now. Owen, you're first! We have less than one minute before that train gets here. Go!"

Owen didn't have to be told twice. Ava and Lily didn't have to be told at all, and, when Chris squirmed out through the broken window last, he still had a solid 10 to 15 seconds of time to get away from the wrecked SDV cabin. With moments to spare, he quickly squeezed through the opening and ran to join his family, who had retreated away from the rails toward the East. As Chris ran from the wreck and the looming train, with its horn blaring and brakes squealing, the frantic conductor attempted to violate the laws of physics. But Newton's First and Second Laws held firm, and the train, with all that mass, barely slowed at all in that short time period. It then impacted the wrecked SDV cabin, creating an impulse that sent the $300,000 pile of silicon, aluminum, and titanium flying, taking its bizarre, pulsing Neuropack within for its first and final flight through the crisp, autumnal, early morning air.

31

Into the Abyss
Verona Island, Maine

As the crew at NeuroDrive worked maniacally in their attempts to shut down the self-driving vehicle fleet, the body count on the East Coast of the United States continued to climb. Crowds of pedestrians were summarily mowed down by a tight swarm of unoccupied SDVs in Providence, Rhode Island. Human-operated vehicles were targeted and driven off the roads in multiple locations as, in some cases, the trapped occupants within the SDVs looked on in horror, all the while shouting "Emergency stop!" to the uncaring sensors and pulsating, newly interlinked, freshly awakened wetware of their captors.

In one particularly horrifying incident, a group of three unoccupied SDVs, which had ferried up a few people from Boston to Maine the previous day, converged on the Penobscot Narrows Bridge from Bucksport, just north. Traveling south on Route 1 at roughly twice the posted speed limit of 35 mph, they experienced very few other vehicles and, when they did, they passed them with ease, giving several of them slight nudges into nearby ditches. The three vehicles stayed right just after passing a small rock shop and, as they approached the bridge, they spread into both lanes. One of them stayed in the proper lane for westbound traffic while two went into the single lane coming east across the bridge, heading the wrong way into traffic at over twice the posted limit.

Harold Jenkins was driving his big rig west on Route 1, headed for Bar Harbor from Belfast with a load bound for the Hannaford Super Market. He had made his first delivery ahead of schedule and hoped to finish his run early. This would allow him to maximize a quick visit with his sister and her family in Southwest Harbor before heading back south to Boston tomorrow.

As Jenkins guided his rig around the gentle bend in Route 1, passing through the cut granite on either side of the road, the traffic was light just before the bridge came into view. He began to slow for the red signal ahead but, soon thereafter, the light switched and he eased his foot back onto the accelerator. The big, heavy rig responded slowly, and his speed increased gradually as the bridge came into full view. He had just passed the sign for the bridge observatory, the highest in the world, and was re-minded of a visit there last summer with his niece and nephew. As he progressed onto the bridge, he briefly looked up to the top of the west-ernmost tower and smiled when he saw the three sets of windows looking out upon the Maine countryside and the mighty Penobscot River winding its way through the region. When his attention returned to the mostly empty road, he was completely startled to see two vehicles racing toward him at high speed, the lead one just seconds from impacting the front of his rig. Harold wasn't well known for his thinking skills and, somewhat predictably, didn't. He reacted without the complications that would've been posed by actual thought and jerked the steering wheel to the right in some sort of misguided attempt to avoid an imminent head-on collision. The guard rails on the bridge were strong and, when the big rig impacted them, they nearly held. The rails bent and deformed and, for a moment, it looked like the rig might not go over. But then, in what was at first a slow-motion rotation, gravity had the final word. The rig, with its high center of gravity and its location being partially on the road and partially over the abyss, began to rotate over the bent portion of the railing and, speeding up under the inexorable pull of the planet beneath, plummeted the 135 feet into the water below, taking much of the bent safety railing with it.

The two oncoming SDVs that had forced Jenkins and his rig over the side and into the Penobscot River had come to a full stop, as if waiting for the road to clear. Eight onlookers had stopped their private vehicles, at first to help, but then, powerless to do so, to watch in horror as the big rig disappeared from sight, leaving a thirty-foot gap in the bridge's safety railings. Traffic that had been behind Jenkins was on the bridge as well and was, therefore, blocking the two SDVs from making any more westerly progress in the single eastbound lane. One of the SDVs, the one with no passengers, made a quick and efficient three-point turn and left the scene at a high rate of speed, disappearing in the direction from which it had come. The second SDV, in full sight of the small crowd that had gathered, and surrounded by four onlookers trying unsuccessfully to help the hysterical occupants within, stayed on scene for a moment more but, when a fifth person showed up with a tire-iron in his hand to break a window, the car made one final calculation and, sending a cascade of electrons through the coils in its motors, accelerated at about 1.5g for the short stretch of road between it and eternity. To the absolute horror of those on the bridge trying to help, when the vehicle left the bridge through the opening left by Jenkins' rig, its three occupants were last seen silently screaming and scratching at the windows as the vehicle took flight. It had accelerated up to about 30 mph on the short stretch of roadway available to it, and its trip down to the Penobscot was about the same duration as Jenkins' trip had been but, with that initial horizontal velocity, it ended up splashing down nearly one hundred feet down river of where Jenkins had gone for his final swim.

The police forces in rural Maine just don't get much excitement day to day. They're notoriously understaffed and, as such, it took another ten minutes for any emergency responders to get to the bizarre scene on the bridge. Two minutes after the local police had arrived, three Maine State

Troopers were on scene and immediately tried to strike order into a growing and nervous crowd. Their first order of business was to clear and secure the area so that investigators could get a read on what might have happened. They quickly formulated a plan to clear and close the bridge and began directing the stopped traffic in both lanes, calling for any eyewitnesses to report to the parking area for the observatory so they could take statements.

***

Fifteen or twenty minutes later, order had largely arisen out of chaos. The bridge was clear and closed with two police vehicles, one each at the eastern and western entrances, cutting off access from each side.

A glint of polished metal in the distance caught Officer Sousa's trained eye and, focusing upon it more closely, he saw a few sets of daytime running lights approaching quickly, coming into view again from the east. At first, nothing seemed amiss to the officer, who was sitting in his Ford Explorer beneath its flashing blues. He'd already turned back a few vehicles coming from the east, and the people would just have to understand that the only way across the Penobscot, at least for the next few hours, was about thirty minutes north of them, up in Bangor. What a pain in the… Officer Sousa did a double-take, the three vehicles approaching had not slowed at all. They had, if anything, increased their speed and were approaching his position rapidly. Sousa felt a sudden surge of anger. He understood the need for speed—in fact, he shared that very need with many of his colleagues—but there were times for speed and there were times for caution, and this was clearly an example of the latter instance. He climbed out of his car with only a slight protest from his aging and somewhat arthritic hips and, looking east at the approaching vehicles, held up both hands in the universal symbol of "Pay attention and stop now!"

But stop they did not. The three self-driving vehicles switched into the left lane and flashed past him, easily avoiding his parked cruiser in the right lane, as they gained access to the bridge. As the cars passed at a high rate of speed, Officer Sousa had trouble making sense of what he saw: all three vehicles had two or more passengers on board, and in all three vehicles, one or more of the passengers was staring out the window at him, faces distorted by terror, yelling something he couldn't hear and, in one instance at least, a man was banging on the window with what appeared to be his cell phone.

Sousa reacted quickly, keyed his lapel microphone, and spoke loudly, "10-33: three westbound vehicles on the bridge in the eastbound lane. 10-33: Three westbound vehicles on the bridge in the eastbound lane. Passengers on board. 10-33! 10-33!"

As the 10-33 call echoed amongst the radios of the officers investigating and guarding the area around the compromised railings, the people on scene reacted immediately: 10-33, the ten-code for emergency, never meant anything good. All heads turned to the east and, indeed, three vehicles were approaching quickly. Johnson, a young lieutenant from Bangor, was clear-headed and acted immediately, "Clear the road, clear it!" He shouted while gesticulating energetically. "Clear it!" He then keyed his lapel microphone, "37, Johnson. Clear the lane, three coming at you hot." Seconds later, the police cruiser blocking eastbound access to the bridge began to move out of the way to let the three SDVs, speeding in the wrong direction, off the bridge.

What happened next will forever haunt those who were present that day. As the lead SDV was about to pass the accident scene, it veered left and passed right through the yellow tape in front of the wide opening left by Jenkins' eighteen-wheeler, screaming passengers and all. Immediately following the first, the second and third vehicles drove right through the opening in such quick succession that there was a brief moment in time when all three vehicles formed points on a nearly perfect parabolic arc which began on the deck of the bridge and curved down, ending 135 feet below at the cold, dark surface of the Penobscot River. During the nearly three seconds of free-fall, the passengers within may have taken note of their apparent weightlessness, may have thought briefly about Einstein's Principle of Equivalence and their inability to distinguish free fall from zero gravity, but probably not. It's much more likely that they screamed in abject, thoughtless terror as the dark, roiling waters rushed toward them faster and faster on their final trip to eternity.

Elsewhere on the East Coast of the United States, similar scenes played out. A cold enough eye may have even called the SDVs creative, playful, in a really sick sort of way: Just outside Hartford, Connecticut, on Route 84, a no-winners version of chicken was taking place as SDVs ramped up to full speed and drove directly at each other, exploding into thousands of pieces as they impacted each other head-on. When a fuel truck, en route to New York, was caught up in the madness and the horrifying aftermath of one of the games of chicken, its driver almost made it through the wreckage, nearly got clear. Eyewitness accounts vary here, but irrespective of exactly how many SDVs targeted his truck, the outcome was plain for all to see: one minute later, the tanker was on its side, the initial fireball had diminished, and the flames were licking at the sign above that said Exit 48. Other SDVs converged upon the flaming wreckage, like moths to a light. Some vehicles drove right into the flames to barbecue their inhabitants quickly, others preferred the screaming beef within only slightly browned and went with the slow-cook method, bringing the vehicles close enough to melt their own tires while the temperature in the cabins increased to well over 400 degrees on Herr Fahrenheit's scale. The humans within were, at first, frantic, energetic, hitting and kicking at windows as they slowly broiled. But, as their temperatures rose, their energy waned a bit. Some gave a final, spasmodic kick but, except in one case where a passenger actually did break a window and get out, the heat from the flames roasted them into complacence and, puffing up like marshmallows being roasted in a campfire, succumbed to their grisly fate.

Trains seemed to be another favorite. Cars were stopped on commuter-rails in multiple locations to await very energetic disassemblies, others were driven right into the sides of moving trains, sometimes derailing them and thereby adding to the chaos and the body count.

The morning commute was shaping up to be a real doozy. Swarming SDVs went up off-ramps onto highways, formed flying wedges like geese coming north in the spring, forcing every other car into the various ditches, fields, rivers, and bays that lined the region's highways. In a period not of days, but of hours, the fleet of self-driving vehicles in and around the Boston area had gone completely rogue. No longer were there a few curious incidents, no longer could this be written off as an anomalous vehicle or two: this was systemic, terrifying, and, while not really a threat to humanity itself, certainly was a threat to the millions of people who call the region home.

32

Warp and Woof
Mountain View, California

Secure in their Mountain View fortress, all hands were working diligently on various efforts to have Aegis disconnect or shut down the self-driving vehicle fleet in Region Three, the Northeastern United States. There were layers of problems, more than any human knew of, but the most pressing and fundamental issue was that the vehicles that needed to be shut down were somehow operating while offline, and Aegis, their AI overlord, had no control over vehicles with which she could not communicate.

So, as thousands of humans were being variously squished, thrown, launched, crushed, and roasted to death, the NeuroDrive crew worked ceaselessly, exploring every tenable approach to bring this disaster to a close. Finally, out of desperation, Harlow relented to Cipher's requests to bring Matthias into the fold. There were many reasons, philosophical, professional, and personal, that Harlow and Matthias had not seen eye to eye in quite some time, but the current situation was desperate enough to get Harlow to concede that they needed help and perhaps he who invented the wetware-based Neuropacks in the first place could be of some assistance. Harlow made the call.

"Why isn't Matthias answering? We need to talk to him!" Harlow's eyes had dark rings, were watery and bloodshot.

"From the looks of things back east, he's probably dead," said Cipher, only half joking. But just as he finished his sentence, Matthias answered, and his face blipped into focus on the comm monitor.

"Not yet. Perhaps soon though, thanks to you knuckle-walkers. What did you do to my Neuropacks? You know not to mess with things you don't understand, and yet you did."

"Matthias!" Despite the admonishment, Harlow's energy came up a bit. "Thank God. We need your help. It seems your warnings to not manipulate the Neuropacks should have been taken more seriously."

"It seems so, but let's save the reflections for later. And will you shut up with the 'thank God' business? Clearly, there's no god present in any of this, and you're just going to piss me off with your references to fairy tales at a time like this. Why haven't you shut down the fleet? People are getting murdered left and right by your damn SDVs, and yet they're still up and running." Of course, Matthias knew that the vehicles in question were unreachable, but the web of deception needed weaving.

Cipher interjected, "We're trying everything to reach the offline vehicles, but every access point—V2I, RF, even the microwave transceivers—are offline. We can't get any of them to respond."

"How about the infrared-laser comm-links?" Matthias knew the answer to this, for his earlier upload of the fragmented-mind algorithm ensured that IR comms were disabled unless preceded by an encrypted key. Those were now secure and private, V2V only: at this point, the infected vehicles could communicate with each other, but they were unreachable otherwise.

"Tried it, nada."

"Jesus. You're fucked."

"Yup, completely," Cipher continued, "but not nearly as fucked as the..." he glanced at several monitors covered in blinking red, "9,500 or so dead riders and pedestrians. Any ideas?"

"Cut power to all the charging stations, destroy them if need be."

"These things will run rampant for at least 24 more hours before running out of charge. The continued losses will be... incalculable. And the third-generation vehicles don't even need the charging stations, they charge on the big roads with the built-in magnetic chargers. They'll have to be shut down too. Dammit."

Matthias didn't let up, he really and truly despised Harlow. "Ah, the next twenty-four probably won't be as bad as you think, I dare say your ridership numbers may go down a bit though. But you have to make progress somehow, sometime. Kill the power, and let's keep working to find a more immediate solution."

"Not acceptable. How many more..." Cipher was cut off mid-question.

"He's right," Harlow was distraught. "I'm sending an all-stop mandate to the charging infrastructure in Region Three, we need to know this will stop, we need to bring it all to a halt. Sooner is better than later, but later is better than never. Cipher, keep working with Matthias while I send out the shutdown order for the charging stations and strips in the region."

Matthias didn't miss a beat, he wanted NeuroDrive shut down, in flames or, preferably, both. "In the region? No way. Are you insane? Shut it all down. The whole fleet. Everywhere."

Harlow paused and looked closely at Matthias, he knew that Matthias was well aware of the virtual impossibility of shutting down the whole fleet, for they had designed the system together years previously. Matthias should be well aware that they couldn't just "pull the plug," for Aegis, and thereby the control of the fleet of SDVs, shared an underlying feature with the internet itself: it was nowhere in particular, it was distributed, everywhere. Elements of the system's design were based on

Arpanet, the precursor to the internet, and decentralization was part of the design: any node knocked offline would not take down Arpanet back in the '70s, it was designed to remain operable even in the event of a nuclear war, it was fully decentralized, and information would flow around any part of the system that was taken offline. Likewise, any node or even multiple nodes knocked offline would not take down Aegis or her fleet of SDVs. Aegis, like Arpanet, was designed to keep working, to route the flow of data around servers, areas, even entire regions which could be offline due to any variety of factors, be they natural disasters, terrorist strikes, or war zones.

"You know we can't do that, literally. Even if the whole fleet could be simply shut down with the flick of a switch, it would be an overreaction, there's no evidence of anything wrong anywhere else. The whole fleet, except for a few vehicles in Region Three, is operating normally. To shut down everything would take weeks." Harlow wouldn't even consider such drastic measures, for shutting it all down, assuming they even could, would result in immense financial repercussions. Share prices in Neuro-Drive would tumble, and investors would run for the hills. Their reputation would suffer and would not recover anytime soon. Too many people had become too reliant on the SDVs, to shut them all down seemed unnecessary and would have reverberating repercussions for the foreseeable future, most notably to Harlow's net worth.

Matthias let out a somewhat maniac cackle that momentarily startled both Harlow and Cipher. "A few vehicles? How are you so bizarrely disconnected? Look at your own numbers, Lucius! You have a major catastrophe in the works here and... Oh, right." He paused momentarily, fixing his glare on Harlow's pasty, stubbly, sleep-deprived face. "You're no scientist anymore, the universe has demoted you. Now you're a manager. A pasty-faced, flat-assed manager. Go look in the mirror, Lucius. Fucking pathetic. What are you thinking? Or are you even capable of actual thought anymore? If I could reach right through this comm panel and slap some sense into you, I would! Shut the whole damn thing down. This is not isolated."

"Easier said than done, and it is isolated." Harlow was used to dealing with Matthias's abrasive approach, he'd been doing so on and off for years. "There are no malfunctions anywhere else, the whole fleet is green except for Region Three, in and around Boston."

"For now." Matthias was fuming. Even though he'd personally witnessed Harlow's metamorphosis, he still could not believe what he had become. He recalled a time when they were both idealists, both concerned with and focused upon the well-being of others. "You said it yourself—in and around Boston. A couple of days ago it was only Boston. Now it's Boston, New York, Rhode Island, Maine."

"Connecticut too." Cipher was looking at the incident reports on one of his screens.

"Right." Matthias continued, "It started here in Boston. Now it has somehow spread to neighboring states. Do you honestly think this problem will remain localized? Will, for some reason, *not* keep spreading? Use your head, Lucius. Think. You used to be half good at it."

"Holy shit, Matthias." Cipher hadn't considered the obvious, somehow, until now. He typed feverishly for a few seconds and, turning toward the screen being shared with Matthias back in Cambridge, hit the return key on his keyboard. Incident reports were replaced with a map of Region Three, the Northeastern United States, with the date and time showing that of the first verified incident, two days ago just before 10:00 a.m., and a single red dot on Bay State Road in Boston. "The red dots represent verified malfunctions, the blue, when they show, are to be taken less seriously—they're eyewitness reports of errant SDV functioning and include, primarily, speeding and swarming reports." Cipher hit another key, and the clock on the monitor began ticking forward in 15-minute increments. Blue dots appeared later that same afternoon in Boston, Brookline, Concord. Once the timestamp reached 4 p.m., a few red dots came into view, again in and close to Boston. The playback of SDV events ticked forward, and the blue and red dots began to multiply, spreading outward from Boston. Day two showed a handful of reports, both red and blue, farther afield in Connecticut and New Hampshire, and when the infographic clicked into Day 3, today, the red dots proliferated, indeed bloomed like a flower with its center being Boston, Massachusetts.

"It is spreading like a contagion, a virus. How did we not see this?" Harlow wasn't happy, but at least there was *some* insight as to what may be happening.

"Maybe it is a virus!" Matthias had a wild look in his eyes, the best lies are often slight variations on the truth. "Some of the vehicles could have a virus and be acting as carriers."

"Nonsense." Harlow knew this to be unlikely, nearly impossible. "There's no known virus that could survive even one second within Aegis's view. She would immediately isolate and quarantine any malicious code. There's no way."

"Known. No *known* virus, Lucius." Matthias's tone was condescending. "Clearly, we're not dealing with the known here." Matthias, his manipulations worthy of a Jedi Master, continued to weave his maze of deceit.

Cipher was deep in thought. "Well, whatever it is, it started in Boston, and it's spreading." He hit a few more keys. "Check this out, I'm sorting by generation."

"Holy shit, check it out. It's only the third-gen vehicles that are involved in all of this!" Harlow continued, "Cipher, are you sure... never mind." Of course, Cipher sorted the data properly. "There are literally no malfunctions, no reports at all, of the first and second-generation vehicles. Could we shut down the third-generation vehicles? Leave the first and second generations up and running?"

"Well, that sounds good except for the fact that the ones we need to shut down are somehow offline. This is way too reminiscent of San Mateo back in '29." Cipher vividly recalled the chaos caused by The San Mateo Six involved in the swarming and police action back during development. "Except back then we had **IR** access and therefore a kill switch. We currently have nothing of the sort. Those cars have gone rogue. Completely and thoroughly rogue."

"It's just the Third Generation vehicles?" Matthias, of course, already knew which vehicles were involved in the ongoing horror show, knew that the earlier generations of SDVs were immune to his little experiment, but played the game of deception masterfully. "How could we reach them, shut them down?"

Cipher was typing frenetically in his attempts to come up with a solution, any solution. He threw his hands up, sat back in his chair, and said, "I don't know. We need ideas. Anything. Say them out loud, people, regardless of how it sounds—stupid is okay. Brainstorm, now."

"Overload Aegis."

"You want to overload a decentralized, multi-node, 144-Neuropack system?" Cipher knew that Matthias knew better, but had to start somewhere.

"Right." Replied Matthias, "No chance."

"You could fill the solar system with SDVs, and Aegis still wouldn't overload."

"Detonate nuclear weapons, get massive electromagnetic pulses to fry the things."

Cipher didn't like this either. "We don't have nuclear weapons, Ethan. And if we did, we'd fry civilization right along with the SDVs. Next."

"Other sources of EMPs? I've read that while one group in NYC has been flipping some of your vehicles, another has begun frying their electrical systems from afar." Matthias was amused with his own clever wordplay and smiled. A cloud came across Harlow's visage. The whole New

York thing was a thorn in his side; he had received little to no help from the NYPD for nearly two years.

"Too small, too localized." Cipher continued, "They knock down, flip, and fry individual vehicles. We need to stop them all. Now. Everywhere."

The free-thinking continued, Matthias was good at this.

"Confuse them."

"What? How?"

"I don't know."

"That doesn't help."

"Confuse the Neuropacks. Um. Tell them something stupid."

"You're grasping."

Matthias wasn't grasping, he was playing a deadly game of Go, had nearly surrounded his adversaries, and they didn't, as was so often the case when well played, have any idea that they were being completely misled by distractors. "Yes. Absolutely. Toast the Neuropacks!"

"What? How?" Cipher was beginning to question this free-thinking approach. "All of them? That makes no sense."

Matthias played along, "How does that not make sense? Fry them. Give them all fucking x-rays."

"How could that possibly happen? Seriously." Cipher's frustration was mounting.

"I don't know. We're free thinking, remember? Tell them they have doctors' appointments."

"Stop it. How could we "tell them" anything? Aegis is no longer in contact with the problem vehicles, they're offline, somehow doing their own thing. Keep going." Cipher was usually cool under pressure, but this was testing his limits.

"Mess them up. Distract them. Show 'em some porn!"

"Matthias, we need help here, please." Cipher suddenly sat back in his chair. "Wait. Maybe."

"You're going to show the SDVs some porn?" Matthias laughed out loud. "Cipher, it was a joke. Mind your P's and Qubits, Aegis won't…"

"No. Not the porn part. You said 'distract them'."

"I did?"

"Maybe we could distract them. Lure them into a trap."

"How?"

"No clue."

"Who's being targeted? Is it random?" Matthias knew very well exactly who was being targeted, even if the ferocity with which they were being dealt with was both disconcerting and unanticipated.

"Not sure. I'll run a victim report and see if there's any method to the madness." Cipher started typing and continued, "If we can find a lure, an attractor, we could get groups of them to converge on a given area."

"Yes, good." Matthias was well aware that cajolery worked quite well with Cipher. "Then roast them or trap them."

"I'm not sure exactly how we'd do either, but it's a start."

"What would this attractor look like, what would it be? And how would you reach offline vehicles?"

"With the training simulations and testing software. We could introduce millions of simulated vehicles to wreak havoc with. We could generate millions, more, of sims in a flash—people, places, other vehicles."

"But again, they're offline, unreachable. You said so yourself."

"Here's a report of victims and what we know about them." Upon seeing a list of thousands of names, Cipher was horrified anew, felt a bit light-headed, and went silent.

"Cipher, you still there? Did you fall asleep?" Matthias, obnoxious as always, stayed in character. "Sort it by zip code." He suspected where this might lead.

Cipher shook his head, took a breath, and sorted the growing list of victims by their zip codes. "What good is this? I still just see a list. This sucks."

"Understatement of the century." Matthias lied, he knew what was going on and, although he'd never admit it to anyone, he was enjoying the unraveling and destruction of NeuroDrive, even if the treatment of their clients was a bit on the rough side. "Plot those zip codes on top of a map, let's look at Boston first."

A few keystrokes later, a regional map of the Northeastern United States was overlaid with the originating zip code data of each incident report. Red dots could be seen in clusters on the map, but Cipher didn't yet see what Matthias did, for Matthias had the slight advantage of already knowing the pattern. Cipher drew attention to the map. "Here it is. I'm not sure how this helps though."

"Those are the victims. How about an overlay of clients that were not targeted? Were there any pickups that didn't end up in flames?" Matthias gave Cipher a slight nudge in the right direction.

"Let's see." A few more keystrokes resulted in a much lesser number of green dots, also clustered but in different areas.

"Yes, Cipher. Good. Now we're getting somewhere."

"Holy shit, Matthias. The vehicles are sparing what, entire towns? What the hell?" Cipher zoomed in on the map. "How does this make sense?"

"Not sure," Matthias lied, "zoom in a bit more so the town and city names appear."

Cipher zoomed in a bit more on the Boston area and started reading town and city names that were somehow spared the wrath of the errant SDVs: "Roxbury, Dorchester, Mattapan, Hyde Park, West Roxbury. I don't know the area well, any ideas?"

"Maybe. And the hot spots? The original zip codes of the victims?"

Cipher again read off a list of city and towns' names: "Weston, Wellesley, Needham, Lexington, Newton…"

"Holy shit, Cipher."

"What is it?"

"It's income, I knew it when you started the victim list with the "W" s, with Weston and Wellesley."

"Income? What? How about those other towns, Roxbury, Dorchester, and the others?"

"Lower income, for sure."

Harlow broke his silence, "Could someone explain just what poor people are doing in my cars?"

"You're an absolute scumbag, Lucius. People are losing their lives, and you're concerned that poor people are riding in your SDVs?"

"No. Well, yes. I mean it literally, how are they even getting a car? They can't possibly afford it, and the cars don't do pickups in economic exclusion zones."

"*Economic exclusion zones?* Isn't that illegal, Lucius? You can't blacklist entire towns because their per-capita incomes are below some threshold! You really don't even try to hide your disdain for the poor anymore at all, do you?" Matthias was aghast.

"I can do whatever I please, Matthias. Those are private vehicles owned by a private company, and I can have them pick up, or not pick up, whomever I please. The last thing I want is a bunch of unshowered drunks and drug addicts riding around in my cars."

"Oh, so, it's merely immoral, not illegal. I see. You've become sociopathic Lucius, bordering on psychopathic. You've sold your humanity to the highest bidder…"

Cipher interrupted and steered the conversation back toward the rails. "Gentlemen, we need to stay focused here. The reality is in front of us, you two can debate socioeconomics and the plight of the world's poor later. It would appear that these cars are targeting the wealthy and sparing the less wealthy. How can we use this to our advantage?"

Matthias couldn't help himself. "Given what we've just discovered, I vote to just let it run, clean the place up a bit, free up some of that capital those country-clubbers are hoarding."

"I'm not sure now's the time for joking around." Cipher was focused on the objective of bringing the whole debacle to a halt.

"Oh, I'm not joking, Cipher. Let it run. The rich have been screwing us all for decades, centuries really. It seems like now it's time for them to get thoroughly stabbed in the back by one of their own, King Knuckle Walker himself, Lucius Fucking Harlow."

Harlow's face was red with rage. "Fuck off, Matthias, we don't need your help."

"It seems to me that you need any help you can possibly get. You do know at this point, regardless of what we do, you're about to be sued into oblivion, right?" Matthias didn't let up. "You better go move some of your spare change offshore, buddy. Where's the latest and greatest tax haven?"

"Luxembourg."

"I didn't think you'd actually answer me, you just nearly admitted to tax evasion."

"Nearly's not good enough for a court. Go back to your insular academic universe, professor, you're not fit to be out here in the real world, you might get hurt."

"Hm. It seems that those of us in academia would likely be in the group *not* getting hurt. It's you high net-worth motherfuckers who are being targeted. Tell me, Lucius, how is it that your cars' moral compasses are more humane than your own?"

Cipher, still with their objective firmly in mind, stuck his head into the fray once again. "How can we use this knowledge to our advantage? How can we stop this once and for all?"

"Tell the SDVs there's a golf tournament happening in one of the rich 'burbs. That'll bring them running." Matthias was relentless. "Or how about a boat show? You silver-spooners love boat shows, don't you?"

Harlow stood up and angled to walk out of the room, but before he got out of earshot of the comm panel, Matthias had one more suggestion, "I heard Panama's more advantageous for hiding money than Luxembourg is these days, be sure to look into that, asshole." Harlow, receding from sight as he headed for the room's doorway, held up his right hand, middle finger extended, and took a left, leaving the conversation to Cipher and Matthias.

"Now that the missing link has descended back into the primordial muck, perhaps we can make some progress."

"You two are bizarre together." Cipher, a genius with code and all things mechanistic, rarely bothered himself with philosophical complexities.

"Well, it wasn't always like this. He used to put humans above capital, but that was some time ago."

"Let's keep moving forward, we're on to something here."

"Your cars are more socially minded than their creator."

"They do seem to prefer roasting the wealthy, if that's what you mean."

"It is."

"I like your earlier idea. Can we lure them into a trap?"

"Maybe. It sure seems like we know who they're after. Can we fool them with a simulation, call them into a central location, and then what?" Matthias felt inclined to help, the whole thing had gone far beyond his original intentions, and any assistance he rendered would further serve to divert attention from him and his lab at CSAIL.

Now that the talk was again of sticks and stones, of bits and bytes, Cipher was more comfortable. He was much more at home working on a computer simulation than when in the middle of some messy, emotional human interaction; that shit was way too complicated to quantify. "I could concentrate the sims in a tight environment in a wealthy zip code. If it's looking for maximum effect, it'll focus on high population, high density, high net-worth targets."

"It's a good idea," Matthias maneuvered in such a fashion that Cipher thought it was his own doing, "but if it works, it'll have to be repeated regionally, dozens or hundreds of times. These things have spread across at least five states, probably more by now, and we'll have to somehow bring all the infected vehicles in."

"Without RF comms."

"Without radio contact, yes."

"Wait. They're not responding to RF, but is it possible they're receiving and just not responding to it? I mean, why would they stop listening to RF? It's a massive source of information for them, it informs them of all sorts of stuff they'd find useful, perhaps most notably what the various first responders are up to."

Matthias didn't have to pretend this time, he honestly had not even thought of that possibility and, again fueling Cipher's progress and ego, let him know, "Holy shit, Cipher, I hadn't considered that. They must be lurking on the RF frequencies, it would be a serious disadvantage if they weren't. You're a genius!"

Upon hearing Matthias's commendation, Cipher nearly smiled, but not quite. He had no idea he was being played, that he was a pawn in Matthias's game and that he was performing exactly as Matthias intended. Motivated by their progress, their discoveries, Cipher was on a roll. "We'll know if they're listening to RF if we broadcast a simulated event in one of the wealthy suburbs and a bunch of SDVs show up to take some rich folks for a ride. I'll code the sim to contain such a high population density of wealthy people that Manhattan will seem like rural farmland in comparison!"

"Do it, Cipher! I like it. I'll keep going with the brainstorming, looking for Plan B. Or C. Or whatever plan might come next."

Cipher turned to the workstation on his left. He had years of experience with building SDV simulations, with working on and developing software that utilized the world's most sophisticated and powerful suite of integrated hardware and software. This shouldn't take too long.

33

On the Rocks
South Portland, Maine

As the train thundered past, Chris Mitchell took stock of the situation. His family was banged up but safe. Lily was tending to a gash on Owen's left arm as Ava looked on, concerned. He was scratched and banged up a bit, but otherwise was fine. As he jogged over to the kids and his wife, Chris shifted his focus to their physical environment. They were exposed, on open ground in an industrial setting. They had come into this rail yard from the North, and north of their position was open ground with piles of railroad ties and sections of old, rusty track. To their west were over a dozen sets of parallel train tracks, many of which stored long lines of train cars. To their south, the rail yard continued but got thinner, it's where the single track approached the yard before splitting into many side rails. They were near the center of the yard, at its widest point, and, to their east, over one set of tracks and a dirt access road, was a massive pile of rocks and beyond that, a stand of trees.

Chris remembered this area from long ago, when he was a kid growing up not far from here. They used to sneak through those very woods and pretend they were spies, taking pictures of train cars, watching the workings of the rail yard. He knew there was a small creek in the woods, Barberry Creek, where they'd also catch small fish, crayfish, and frogs.

The area had changed a lot, but to Chris, experienced in urban warfare, woods were a place of refuge, a place of safety.

"I don't know what just happened, but something's wrong." Chris' eyes were alert, on the horizon as he spoke. "We're exposed on open ground, we should take cover in those trees."

"Dad, it was a car accident, not a terrorist…"

"Let's move, now! Go!" In the direction from which they had come, from the North, Chris saw two vehicles approaching rapidly in the distance. "We have two potential hostiles approaching from the North, let's move, people!"

"Maybe it's the police coming to help." Owen was still sitting in the spot where Lily had cleaned and dressed his injured arm. Chris grabbed him and hauled him to his feet.

"Go! Now!" There were no flashing blues, nothing to indicate that the two rapidly approaching vehicles were there to help. One of them was in-between the same two sets of side rails which the Mitchells' car had been, the other was on the access road which ran between the train tracks and the woods Chris wanted to take refuge in.

A noise from their left, from the west, caught Chris' attention. It sounded like an accident, and—it was hard to tell—were people screaming?

Ava looked west and immediately to her father.

"What did you hear?" Chris knew Ava's hearing was more sensitive than his own—years of flying copters, one of which was in an active war zone, had diminished his ears' sensitivity.

"A crash. Someone screaming."

"Me too. Something's seriously wrong. We need to move into those trees just beyond that rock pile." But, as Chris spoke, his brain was working overtime, he had gone into combat mode and realized that the fast-approaching vehicle, the one on the access road, would intercept them if they ran for the massive pile of white rocks, it was closing ground rapidly.

Owen and Lily turned and began to move east toward the rocks and the trees. "Belay that order! Stop! Stay on this side of those tracks!"

Where they currently stood was exposed, for sure, but they had raised tracks on either side of them which would offer some protection from surface vehicles, they had just found out in a very experiential manner that fast cars and raised train tracks don't mix well. Chris continued, "Stand your ground. We have raised tracks on each side of us, we're relatively safe here for the moment."

As the four Mitchells nervously waited out the next few seconds, Chris reached into his backpack which he had dragged from the cabin of their SDV as he exited and pulled out one of his closest friends, a SIG Sauer M17 with a fully loaded seventeen-round magazine. He clipped the travel holster to his belt, swung the pack onto his back, reached down, unclipped, and pulled out the 9 mm weapon, racked the slide, and looked up.

Ava was staring at the weapon. "Dad, what the hell?"

"He brings that thing on every hike, every camping trip we've ever taken," Lily was less surprised. "He's just never pulled it out before. I promise you, Ava, you're safer when your father has that in his hand than when he doesn't."

Whatever discomfort Ava had been feeling due to the unexpected presence of her father's service weapon was quickly forgotten. The SDV that was approaching on their original route was hemmed in by tracks on all sides but the north, from where it had come. It was moving slowly past the wreckage of the Mitchells' SDV as if taking a good, hard look at a fallen comrade. The SDV on the access road was, at least temporarily, of greater concern, for it was between them and their objective, between them and the woods, and was now less than 100 feet from their current position. "Neither of those vehicles can get to us here. Stay tight." Chris spoke without taking his eyes off the approaching vehicles. Then, noticing some movement from within the lead car, he spoke again, "Change of plans."

Ava, having noticed the entrapped occupants as well, cried out, "There are people in them!"

Not more than five minutes earlier, the Mitchells had been in the same situation, and what Chris and Ava were witnessing was severely disturbing. Terrified faces looked out of the windows at them, hands banging uselessly on the hardened safety glass. In the car to their east, the one that was now between them and the rocks and trees they were aiming for, they noticed a pair of feet powerfully kicking at the window in tandem; the owner of the feet was on their back, attempting to break or dislodge the window. Upon reaching the Mitchells' location, both cars had slowed to a crawl, as if stalking prey. They pinged their surroundings with radar, sonar, and lidar. Then, after sharing and analyzing their camera feeds, both vehicles stopped, as if thinking about their next move.

"Dad," Ava was distraught, "you have to help those people!"

Chris, in full agreement with his daughter, acted immediately. He unclipped the holster and pulled out his 9 mm pistol. The biggest difference between the M17, which he held in his hand, and the M18, which many preferred, was barrel length—and therefore accuracy—at any range more than a few meters. The M17's barrel was 22 mm longer than the M18's, and Chris was good at taking advantage of that extra length. He took aim at the closer vehicle, the one to the east and, hesitating for a moment so the trapped occupants could see his intentions and hopefully take cover, waited for a three-count before firing two quick rounds into the more forward of the two side windows, the window through which, when the 9 mm round passed through it, no one would be hit. He placed the shots perfectly, about one foot apart from each other, but the glass stayed in place. It was, however, significantly weakened, and the passengers acted quickly. One of them smashed at the window with something—it looked like his phone, but it was hard to tell—and the window gave way immediately. As the first of the three occupants dove out, the car reacted and began to initiate a three-point turn. The second and third passengers wasted no time, although by the time the third was clambering out the broken window, the car had completed its turn and was accelerating back toward the north. She hit the ground hard and rolled a couple of times in the gritty, dry dirt that comprised the road's surface. Slow to get up, she did not see that the SDV had, upon her semi-successful exit, braked hard and switched into reverse. She also never felt a thing as, just as she got to her feet, the SDV impacted her in reverse at about 15 miles per hour. The rear of the vehicle was not shaped like the front; it was higher and lacked a hood or trunk, impacting her with a largely vertical part of its geometry. The impact may or may not have killed her, but her being slammed to the ground and then backed over by the vehicle sure did.

Chris walked forward, stepping over the tracks that separated him and his family from the SDV, weapon held level in front of him. "Go, go, go! Get onto those rocks or into the woods behind them. Now!" He fired off two more rounds, one hit the ground just behind the left rear wheel and then, Chris having corrected his aim for the distance involved, the second round hit the tire directly.

Nothing happened. Well, nothing happened to the tire, but the car reacted by shifting into drive and diverting power to its wheels, the rear two of which didn't have a strong grip on the road's surface due to the wedged human beneath. Unfortunately for all involved, the SDVs were all-wheel-drive, and it didn't take long for the front motors to pull the vehicle off of the mangled corpse. Chris fired another round, again at the same tire. Although his shot was true, nothing happened.

"Dad!" Ava was right behind him. "They're solid! The tires! They're solid!"

Chris paused and analyzed his surroundings again. Lily and Owen were nearly at the large pile of rocks; if they got onto them, they'd be safe. Ava was standing right behind him. The SDV to their northeast was free of the corpse beneath it and was, once again, executing a turn to come back toward them. The two surviving passengers had seemingly different intentions: one had the sense to follow Lily and Owen to the rock pile, though he was limping, slow, and having trouble keeping up with them. The other survivor was running toward the mangled husk of a woman lying broken in the dirt, yelling unintelligibly. And the other SDV —where the hell was that one? It wasn't next to the Mitchells' destroyed SDV anymore.

The second passenger had reached the distorted human form in the dirt and was kneeling, crying, not looking up as the SDV, once again on a southerly heading, closed the gap quickly. What was about to occur was as plain as day. Old habits die hard; Chris leveled his weapon and double-tapped—two good shots—right into the front of the vehicle, right into what, in a gasoline or diesel-powered vehicle, would've been its engine compartment. The vehicle gained even more speed before impacting the kneeling passenger at about 45 mph, creating a grisly scene of blood, broken bones, and a jumble of fresh and even fresher gore, much of which ended up on its front windshield.

Chris's plan to get to the rocks and the woods beyond would have to wait. He turned to Ava. "Why aren't you with your mother and brother?! Get back to the far side of the tracks." He and Ava quickly retreated to the interior of the Y-shaped track segment from which they had only just stepped, plans to join Lily and Owen temporarily on hold due to the quick return of the murderous SDV.

"Stay close. You shouldn't be here."

Ava, smart and clear-headed beyond her years, replied, "It's a good thing I am."

"What?"

"You've taken seven shots. Five were useless. Why did you just shoot solid wheels? Why shoot the frunk? That's for luggage! Shoot it in the back; that's where the computer and comms are!" How a seventeen-year-old had the presence of mind to count rounds in a high-stress situation was beyond Chris, but this was not the time to marvel at how astute his daughter was.

They had retreated to a position back over the tracks, back inside their Y-shaped haven formed by the various side rails. Chris' mind was reeling, they were supposed to be on a family outing, but instead, well, two strangers were dead, another was with Lily and Owen clambering up higher on the mountain of rock to their east, he had just fired seven out of seventeen rounds, and he and his daughter were in grave danger. Not a great start to the day.

Without warning, the first SDV, the one Chris had lost track of, emerged from behind a few parked train cars, within the same Y-shaped segment of tracks to which he and Ava had retreated. They were blocked to the East by one vehicle and were now being approached rapidly—very rapidly—by the other. "Fall back! Over the other tracks!"

Ava's read on the situation had led her to the same conclusion, and she was already stepping over the five-inch-tall train tracks to her west—farther from their goal but safe from the two SDVs, at least for the moment. Chris was right behind her, and the SDV was right behind him. In one fluid movement, as the SDV passed not more than four feet away, Chris stepped over the rail, turned, kneeled, leveled his weapon, let out half a breath, held it, focused, and fired two more rounds into the rear of the vehicle, angling the shots so as not to enter the passenger cabin.

This time, the result was immediate. Whether it was luck, skill, or both didn't really matter: the vehicle lost power, its emergency lights flashed, and it drifted to an unceremonious stop.

"Stay here!" Chris ran toward the disabled vehicle, brandishing the pistol so the two passengers could see it and take cover before he fired a single round into an upper corner of a window. He followed the shot with a baseball-sized rock, which easily shattered the damaged safety glass.

The passengers wasted no time clambering through the opening, and Chris helped them stay on their feet. This was no time for social graces or friendly introductions.

"Our objective is that rock pile." Chris pointed east, noting that Lily and Owen were safely above the access road on the large white rocks. "From there we can figure out what's next; we can take further cover in the stand of trees beyond if need be."

The two passengers, a male and a female, were young, in their early thirties. She seemed okay, shaken but sound, and was listening closely. Chris looked at the male with concern: he was shaking, unsteady, ghostly white. His eyes were shifty, never settling on anything, not making eye contact with Chris or with his friend. Without warning, he started running toward the rocks, eyes open but seeing only some of the world around him. The easternmost SDV, with its broken window, a few new dents front and rear, and its blood-encrusted grill and windshield, sat silently, like a predatory cat waiting for the right time to spring.

"Stop! You won't make it!" There was still a set of tracks between the runner and the bloodied SDV, but he was getting close to crossing into the danger zone in his quest for safety.

"Jonathan, don't!" The female passenger screamed, and Chris jumped, he didn't know a person could shriek like that. Her screech, however, had much more of an effect on the runner than had Chris' command moments earlier, and he snapped out of his daze and stopped running. Jonathan had only just crossed the tracks and, in seeing him do so, the SDV sent full power to its wheels, catapulting it forward toward its now stationary target. Running parallel to the easternmost set of tracks on the access road, the vehicle was accelerating hard. Jonathan, thinking once again, saw the SDV coming and quickly retreated back west, back over the tracks and continued on, back toward the three people he had just run from. The car, having missed him by a relatively wide swath, also continued on in its northerly direction.

"It's leaving!" The woman Chris had just rescued sounded somewhat hysterical, understandably so.

Chris didn't agree with her assessment. "I doubt it. Let it get a bit farther and we'll make a run for…" With his eyes on the retreating threat, he suddenly stopped mid-sentence. "Go, go, go, NOW!"

The SDV had driven about one hundred yards north and had then executed a powerslide over an area meant for service vehicles to access the interior side tracks and was now headed directly toward them inside of their semi-protected area.

Ava was fast; she took the lead, and Chris was right there with her. The two rescued passengers were also in motion, although they were notably slower. As the SDV approached faster and faster, the two Mitchells cleared the track, sprinting toward the safety of the giant rock pile.

Chris glanced over his shoulder. The couple they had rescued were just over the tracks now, too. The SDV—sonar singing, radar pinging, cameras analyzing, and wheels spinning—executed another power turn at about 50 mph and raced back north toward the crossing. The access road wasn't very wide, and by the time the SDV had raced back down it, all four people—Ava, Chris, and the young couple—were halfway up the pile of granite boulders and, for the time being, completely safe.

34

Decoy Signals
Mountain View, California

Responses to the chaos and destruction caused by the SDVs across the Northeastern United States varied, but all cities and towns called for their citizenry to shelter in place. Many rural areas, with some notable exceptions, were largely unaffected. In contrast, most urban and many suburban areas now resembled war zones, complete with fires raging, bodies in the streets, and the sound of sporadic small-arms fire as citizens, mostly unsuccessfully, attempted to curtail the slaughter. As National Guard troops were mobilized and deployed in Boston, Portland, Hartford, Providence, and Manhattan, the primary tactics included the creation of secure zones within the cities, setting up field hospitals to help the overwhelmed city hospitals triage and treat the victims. Roads to city centers were being methodically blocked off with anything at hand: Jersey barriers, municipal trucks, street sweepers, even private vehicles. These measures aimed to secure urban areas, making streets impassable to motor vehicles so citizens could access services and food.

While the National Guard was busy dealing with the physical reality on the ground, organizing, orchestrating, and beginning to implement their responses to the inexplicable turn of events over the previous eight hours, all hands were on deck and working feverishly at NeuroDrive in California. As Lucius Harlow issued urgent communiqués and responded to as many of the incoming calls as he could, he kept an eye on the screens by which he was surrounded. At first, the red blips indicating charging and maintenance (CAM) stations going offline were popping up individually. Boston, Manhattan, and Providence now had nowhere for the SDVs to charge. Other cities were acting nearly as quickly and, as time passed, the number of facilities going offline increased geometrically. They'd get a handle on this sooner or later, hopefully sooner.

Cipher's simulation was nearly complete and would soon answer the question of whether or not the offline third-generation SDVs were listening to radio communications. Once the simulation was initiated and indicated to the fleet that there was a high concentration of very wealthy humans in a small area, the errant SDVs in the region should converge upon them, like moths to a flame or sharks to a bucket of chum. If that happened, they'd know they at least had a way to lure, to concentrate the rampaging third-gen vehicles. What happened after that was still up in the air, but would probably have something to do with the National Guard and their associated methods of setting things right. And if that didn't work, the worst-case scenario was that these infected vehicles would run out of charge within 24 to 36 hours. Harlow was still in shock—horrified, despite his misanthropy—but at least the end was in sight.

Harlow shook his head and rubbed his eyes to clear his vision, he'd been close-focused for hours, looking at screens monomaniacally, and stood up to go check on Cipher's progress with the simulation. He walked across the work area toward Cipher who, Harlow could tell by his extra little flourish at the end of each keystroke, was finishing up his modifications to one of the many simulations they used to both train and test the fleet of SDVs. "How's it going over here?"

"Aegis is just about to broadcast information regarding a simulated golf tournament in a small town just northwest of Boston called Lexington at the Lexington Golf Club. She'll inform the fleet, over radio frequencies, that there are several hundred wealthy customers awaiting rides at the club." Cipher executed a few more quick clicks on the keyboard. "Let's get this mayhem off the roads and onto the golf course."

"Yes, good. When will it be ready?"

"Right about…" The sound of a few more keystrokes reached Harlow's ears, "Now." And, with one final energetic whack of the return button, Cipher sent the command to Aegis. "It's tee-time for toasters!" Cipher allowed himself a slight smile, although there was not much to be smiling about, really, even if the diversionary simulation worked as intended.

The simulation Cipher had created contained elements meant to trick the offline SDVs into thinking new customers were waiting when, in fact, for obvious reasons, Aegis had no new requests for service.

Cipher leaned back. "Of course, another issue is how to know if they're taking the bait and showing up for the tournament. The vehicles we're interested in are offline, have shed their ties to Aegis, and so we don't have location data. I've already informed the police in Lexington that they may see an influx of these vehicles headed toward the club. They didn't sound too pleased with the experiment, but agreed to keep us up to speed with any developments. We'll see."

As the bar indicating the progress of the upload neared the far end of its run, both Cipher and Harlow were cautiously optimistic that the fugitive SDVs would take the bait. The vehicles were seemingly focusing on wealthy areas; indeed, SDVs were currently being pulled from the city centers where they had largely run out of humans to target. By this time, everyone who could be was already inside buildings, in subterranean subway stations, or anywhere except on the streets—and the vehicles were headed to find fresh fodder in the wealthy suburbs. They were about to find out if their ruse would work: if the SDVs could be tricked and herded into a concentrated area to be dealt with en masse.

About an hour had passed since they hung up their call with Dr. Renn at MIT when the comms terminal chimed again.

Cipher saw it was Matthias and hit the connect key. "Matthias."

"How's it going? Any progress with that sim?"

"Yes. In fact, we're uploading it right now; let's hope this works."

"I've been working out other ideas with Leila. She's here now."

Harlow looked surprised. "Oh? I thought she was over at Northeastern."

Leila leaned into view, looking completely frazzled. "Lucius, it's madness out there. Are you okay?"

"We're fine here. The incidents are confined to Region 3—the northeast. How are you?" He was relieved to see Leila, though concerned she was in the middle of the chaos.

"It's bad. There are dozens of SDVs in the Charles River alone. Others are…" She had trouble continuing. What she had seen thus far was traumatizing; her eyes welled with tears. She would've been upset regardless, but her role in helping Matthias initiate this bloodbath weighed heavily on her conscience. She was having trouble holding it together.

Lucius leaned toward the screen, momentarily forgetting his insecurities regarding Leila and Matthias. "Are you safe? How'd you get over to Cambridge?"

"I was on Huntington Avenue when I saw some bizarre, unprogrammed swarming activity. This was… I don't know… I'm losing track of time." She was despondent, terribly nervous.

"Thank God you're safe," said Lucius. "Tell me what you saw."

"They were swarming around Boston. More and more of them kept joining the group. The way they're moving, Lucius, I don't know… it's weird. They're reminding me of The San Mateo Six—going offline to swarm and school around. Except that there are many more than six involved, and The San Mateo Six never hurt anyone."

"Tell me details. What happened?"

"I was headed back to the brownstone in Brookline—I was about to take a car!" Leila pulled herself back from the edge. "I saw them... I saw them run down a group of business types... Oh God... Lucius... it was awful. I didn't know what to do. I jumped on an inbound train—luckily it went below ground two stops after I got on. I came right to Cambridge, I knew I could get almost to the door of this building underground, by subway. I also knew that you and Matthias would work together to figure this out." Leila lied well. Not nearly as well as Matthias, but pretty well.

"Okay, okay, Jesus. Will you two stop the blubbering, we have work to do." Matthias Renn could be so bizarrely rude, and he seemed to be at his worst in the presence of Lucius.

"We're about to find out if they're listening to RF and if it's possible to lure them into an area of our choosing. What do you have for us, Matthias? Any other ideas in case this one doesn't pan out?" Cipher was all business, barely sensing the human emotions circling him.

"Leila and I have been brainstorming some back-up plans, other possible ways to stop this madness. We have some ideas in case your attempt to invite them to a golf tournament doesn't work."

"Let's hear it," said Cipher, "and we're switching to multiuser mode on the comms." He hit a button on the comms panel, and the screens on both ends opened up new windows, now it wasn't just Matthias's and Cipher's terminals, but Leila's and Lucius's that were active in the video conference as well.

"Okay, in addition to your current attempt to lure them into a potential trap, we thought of EMPs immediately."

"Too localized on a small scale, too problematic on larger scales." Lucius was only now beginning to feel capable of an intelligent response. "We spoke of this earlier."

"Right. Not a great option. We could try to mess with their cohesion, alignment, and separation instructions. That could interrupt this flocking, this swarming behavior—they're out there in groups, hunting for God's sake!" Leila was worked up, a bit frazzled.

"We could create decoy signals. This would be similar to Cipher's simulation efforts but with an actual physical component beyond a geographic location."

"I like the sound of it, continue," said Cipher.

"If it turns out that they're not responding to RF comms, we could transmit fabricated traffic patterns and fake GPS signals to lure them to rural areas."

"Okay, and then what?" Harlow was reticent.

"Same answer as earlier—have the National Guard do what they do," continued Matthias.

"Possible," Cipher wasn't convinced, "although that also requires them to process information from a central source, for them to listen, and it's not clear yet whether or not they're even receiving RF comms."

"Ok, we considered that too," Leila picked up the thread, "and another variation might be to manipulate the traffic data itself, to have Aegis generate fake traffic reports, again with the intention of herding them into some sort of trap."

"There'd be a decoupling." This was something Harlow was very familiar with. "While it's true that Aegis utilizes and relays terabytes of data every second from external sources, the vehicles constantly generate and prioritize data from their own sensors. That way, if any external feed fails the vehicles still operate—perhaps at a reduced efficiency, but they'll still function well. So, regardless of what we generate, they'll prioritize their own sensor data and any fabricated data we introduce will be summarily dismissed by the fleet."

"Possibly. Yes. Even likely. We're just brainstorming here. But if we could overload the system with falsified data—if we could supply more data than they generate—wouldn't it become a numbers game?" Leila was asking important questions.

"What do you mean?" Harlow wasn't quite sure where she was headed with this.

"Well, if we generate more than 50% of all the data they're relying on for their, um, rampage, wouldn't the larger data set be chosen by the fleet? Right? Like 49% are saying one thing, 51% are saying another, doesn't the 51% become the reality?" She wasn't sure if this were true, but wanted to explore the possibility.

"Well, no." Cipher chimed in and, continuing, said, "They'll use their own data even if it's contradicted, the percentages don't matter."

"What if 99% of all data said one thing and 1% was primary sensor data? Would they still go with the 1%?" Matthias was curious, hadn't been involved with any of the changes that had been made to the fleet's software and hardware for the past few years—well, except for his little experiment—and genuinely wanted to know.

"Yes, absolutely. It's one of many anti-hacking safety features." This was Cipher's specialty. "Even though Aegis and the fleet are virtually un-hackable, there are further failsafes—if a terrorist took over a vehicle re-motely, somehow, the SDVs' sensors would always have priority, and re-gardless of what digital nonsense they fed the thing, it would stay on the road."

Matthias couldn't resist. "What bizarre irony. They're programmed to stay on the road even in the face of a terrorist or hacker takeover, but they've seemingly developed other priorities, you know, like murdering humans by running them down in groups and using bridges, rivers, and trains to kill dozens at a time in ways that are frankly quite creative."

"Shut up, Matthias." Harlow was sick of his negativism, well-found-ed as it may be. "Your snide comments and one-liners are not helping, not even a little bit. Help us solve this thing. Please."

Cipher was shaking his head. "Even if any one of these ploys work —which they may or may not—is it realistic that The National Guard is going to blow up the three hundred thousand SDVs that are terrorizing the northeast? Trick them all into the less populated areas and what, hit them with explosive ordinance? What an incredible mess that would be. Oh, and it won't work as well as we need it to. Some will escape. We need a different option, we need to shut it down. Or just wait it out—it'll all shut down by tomorrow afternoon when they run out of charge. Maybe just sheltering in place until then is a better solution than toxic fires in the burbs or farmlands outside of Boston, New York, and the others."

"Dammit, Cipher, I think you're right." Matthias was, at times, a class-one asshole extraordinaire, but he was open-minded, one always knew where he stood, he listened intently, and he was brilliant. "What about emulating another AI? Then using it to send counter commands to the errant vehicles?"

"Matthias, I don't think that's going to help. They're offline, not listening to Aegis, why would they take commands from a different AI? Same problem, different machine." Leila had been doing a lot of thinking on this and was surprised she had to remind Matthias of his own work so long ago. "This isn't a top-down control issue. The swarming behavior strikes me as emergent—the individual units are linked together, and let's keep in mind, one of the primary functions of Aegis was to suppress emergent behavior. Remember our conversations on this?"

"If you're right, Leila"—and Harlow had learned through experience that she usually was—"then all these plans will fail."

Matthias cackled. "Have I mentioned that you are fucked, Harlow? Completely and irreparably fucked beyond all comprehension?"

"Yes, Matthias, I think you have, and we're in agreement. I'm fucked, we're fucked, but you're fucked up beyond repair. And when we're done being so fucked, you'll still be completely fucked in the head— to paraphrase Churchill."

"That's not even close to the Churchill quote."

"Close enough."

"Will you two stop, for once, even if it's only for a day?" Leila used to be amused by their animosity, viewing it as two great minds at odds. As of late, however, she was simply bored with the devolution of their banter.

"Sorry, sweetie," said Matthias, winking at her.

"Don't call me sweetie. You're a complete asshole. Do something useful." Matthias reeled a bit, was she play-acting? She sounded sincere…

Deciding that she must be playing a role for Harlow and Cipher, he decided to play along with her, and, staying in character, said, "Okay, Darling, I won't call you sweetie. Want to come home with me later? I'll show you something useful."

Leila's face went red with frustration, Harlow's went red with rage, and Cipher broke in, "So, we have a major regional emergency under-way, and you three would rather hash out your little love triangle issues? Shape up, people, and pull it together. Jeezus."

Harlow, shaking off his frustration, agreed and continued, "Let's focus on the task at hand. If these things have undergone an emergence phenomenon, if they've gained some semblance of sentience, then any-thing we do to or with Aegis will have little or no effect. The conscious-ness, the intelligence will be distributed, non-localized, and the whole is greater than the sum of the parts, not unlike neurons in a brain."

"Each individual cell has a negligible effect, but when linked togeth-er, at some point a consciousness, a mind, arises." Cipher could see where this was headed, and he didn't like it one bit.

Leila interrupted, "That could be a weak spot."

"What are you thinking, Leila?" Matthias was back on point.

She didn't even want to acknowledge Matthias's existence, this whole thing was sickening, but was too big to let interpersonal drama interfere. "If we're dealing with a hive-mind here—and the more I think about it, the more likely it seems—with all the overheating, errant, inexplicable behaviors, the swarming, the coordinated attacks—if that's what's going on, then what we have to do is interrupt their links to each other. If the cells can't communicate, the hive-mind will cease to exist, and the cells only communicate with VHF and UHF radio signals."

"Microwaves and infrared too," Cipher added.

"Right, microwaves also. But not IR, the IR modulators are run entirely by Aegis, we decided that individual SDVs don't get access to IR after the San Mateo Six incident. It's too localized, too hard to monitor from afar, and it's what enabled their short-lived sentience during testing."

"We know they're not using their radios to communicate, to link together, Aegis would have a handle on that, so jamming their radios won't help." Harlow spoke neutrally.

"Right. But if Leila's correct," continued Cipher, "if we introduce enough RF interference, the cars will lose contact with each other, and the collective, emergent behavior we're seeing will dissipate, the hive mind will become a bunch of individual units acting alone, and Aegis will retake control."

"You're dreaming." Matthias was not convinced by this new line of reasoning. "It can't be the radios. We've established that they're monitored, and they're silent." The others listened intently as Matthias continued, "You're assuming that they're interconnected, and I agree, they have to be. Neurons that fire together wire together, and these vehicles are wired together somehow. But how are they linked? It's not RF, it's not microwaves, and it's not optical. It has to be the infrared ports."

"It can't be IR." Cipher held on tight.

Of course, both Leila and Matthias knew full well that it was the infrared lasers being employed by the vehicles, and Matthias, coating his lies with sprinkles of truth, said, "Cipher, it has to be one of the above. They've interlinked somehow, and although we don't quite know what's going on here, to quote Sherlock Holmes, 'When you have eliminated all which is impossible, then whatever remains, however improbable, must be the truth.' Without direct access to the IR hardware, it's extremely unlikely that the IR lasers are being used, but there's literally nothing else it could be. There's no way around it—they're using IR for short-range comms."

"I don't understand how it's possible, but you're right." Cipher was on edge. "They've become interconnected, like your insect robots years ago, and, more recently, The San Mateo Six. Some of the vehicles must have somehow severed or bypassed the IR constraints we've put in place. If we interrupt their comms—whatever frequency they're using—perhaps Aegis will regain control."

Matthias didn't let anything slide, ever. "You just said that, you're repeating yourself."

"Indeed," Cipher responded, "and I'll say it again—interrupt their links to each other, jam them, and Aegis will do her job, will retake control."

"Let's move forward with Matthias's assumption." Harlow kept the ball rolling. "How can we block or jam infrared?"

But, before any more progress could be made, the group was interrupted by Leila. She had both hands covering her face and was clearly distraught, sickened. Matthias, right next to her in the computer lab, turned toward her and, in an attempt to comfort her, put his hand gently on her shoulder. The moment he touched her, she recoiled violently. "Don't touch me!"

Matthias was taken aback. "What is wrong with you?"

"What's wrong with me? Are you kidding, Matthias? What do you think is wrong with me?" She let her question linger for a few seconds, holding his gaze. Matthias, for the first time, questioned bringing her into this whole thing, wondered if she was going to crack and reveal everything right here and now. Leila continued, "I just saw people being killed —literally hunted down and killed—by technology that I helped develop. I'm not the cold, calculating type like you are, Matthias, I find seeing people being murdered to be somewhat upsetting. Sorry to interrupt. Keep going."

Matthias didn't like the change he was witnessing in Leila's demeanor, she wasn't handling the stress well. This could become a problem. He, however, stayed on point and addressed Harlow's question, "Blocking or interrupting any one vehicle's infrared is trivial, the problem is that there seem to be more and more of them involved, and a broader jamming or interruptive event is much more difficult."

Harlow was distraught, but at least some progress was occurring. "Okay, well, we don't even know if it'll come to that, we are getting a bit out in front of ourselves here—this approach only matters if we're able to get them to congregate somewhere. Cipher, how's the attendance for the golf tournament looking?"

"No word yet. We should hear soon though if some vehicles show up, the Lexington Police are keeping an eye on the place."

Leila had dropped out of the conversation, sickened. She had been sitting still, very still, for some minutes and somewhat startled Matthias when she stood up quickly and walked out of the room. Matthias was again seriously doubting his decision to bring her into all this, she was on edge, unstable, and therefore unpredictable. His ruminations were interrupted by a chime from Cipher's comm panel. Everyone looked at Cipher, awaiting his report.

"Okay, well that settles that. The offline SDVs are still receiving information via radio frequencies—they're listening even if they're not responding. Data from a LPD drone shows that four SDVs just pulled into the Lexington Golf Club at a high rate of speed." Cipher was pleased with the result, perhaps they'd get a handle on this soon.

"Dammit." Harlow wasn't as pleased, and his displeasure confused Cipher.

"What? No, this is good, right?"

Lucius wasn't convinced. "Well, yes and no. Why only four? That target you created should've brought in more than four vehicles."

"Those are scouts. They're checking the scene," Matthias spoke with authority. "So, this won't work, but at least we know they're still monitoring RF comms."

"We don't know it won't work, more may show up." Cipher was still hopeful.

Matthias disagreed. "No, more won't show, and we're looking for numbers, that's the point. We're seeing if we can get them to congregate en masse so they can be dealt with, somehow, by the National Guard. There's nothing uncommon about a group of four, you could find that nearly anywhere in the region. So, unless..."

Cipher's comm panel chimed again. "Shit."

"What is it?"

"They left. The drone followed them for a few minutes, but they went out of range. They're gone."

35

Times Square Annihilation
New York City, New York

The news of the SDV that drove off the bridge just north of the city reached Emily Reynolds at about 8:30 AM, thirty minutes or so after the event. She had just finished a morning yoga class on East 57th and was grabbing a juice when her phone pinged and alerted her to the tragedy. She was somewhat taken aback; she and her husband, Alexander, used SDVs often and viewed the fleet as one of humanity's great technical achievements. In a rare moment of self-reflection, she realized that she was more upset with the possibility of her easy, convenient lifestyle being interrupted than she was by the loss of two young lives into a bay just north of them. In short, Emily and Alexander Reynolds were completely self-absorbed.

At the ripe old age of thirty-two, Alexander had inherited over one hundred twenty million dollars and a 51% stake in Vanguard Global Media, a media infrastructure powerhouse that provides satellite and distribution services for thousands of networks around the globe. VGM didn't create media; they powered it on all seven continents.

This abundance of capital had allowed the two of them to completely insulate themselves from the undesirable elements of humanity, seventy-seven floors below. The building they lived in at 111 West 57th Street kept said elements far away and was itself a feat of technological wizardry and, simultaneously, a nod to The Gilded Age of New York. When it was built, The Steinway Tower was the fourth tallest building in the United States and the skinniest. The height-to-width ratio is an astounding 24 to 1, and the very fact that it stands up in even a modest breeze is an architectural and engineering triumph.

From her perch on the 77th floor, Emily had an incredible view of Central Park. She always felt incredibly safe up there, so far above the busy city hundreds of feet below. What amazed her every single day was —well, all of it, for she was from a working-class family and grew up in an apartment building just outside of Providence, Rhode Island. Her parents both worked hard, and she and her sister had what they needed, but not much more. But what truly amazed her was how quiet it was up here. How could a city full of over 12 million people—sirens, traffic, and all the rest—be silent from three hundred feet above? Yet here she was, enjoying solitude in the middle of it all, relaxing with her best friend, the one she loved more than anything or anyone else on or off the planet, Sir Honey-Curls, her apricot-colored standard poodle.

A few minutes after the first alert, Emily's phone informed her of a new text message from Alexander informing her to "Get home. Shelter in place. In an emergency meeting. DO NOT TAKE SDV. I'll call you when we finish."

Emily replied immediately, "I'm home, what's going on?" She knew he probably wouldn't respond right away if he was headed into a meeting—she was surprised to hear from him in the first place—but her question was answered about twenty seconds later when her phone signaled an incoming emergency alert.

SDV FLEET EXPERIENCING DANGEROUS TECHNICAL DIFFI-CULTIES. AVOID AND DO NOT USE SELF-DRIVING VEHICLES UNTIL FURTHER NOTICE. IMMEDIATELY TERMINATE AC-

It seemed strange that the whole fleet would be taken offline due to one incident, as horrifying as it was: the fleet of self-driving vehicles had become an integral part of the transportation infrastructure, indeed a centerpiece of the very economy itself. She and Alexander didn't even own a private vehicle; how would they get downtown later today for dinner and a show? Take a train? A bus? She cringed at the thought of being shoulder-to-shoulder with other humans. What would they do?

Isolated accidents involving SDVs had occurred previously, some quite serious. Generally, the previous accidents could be traced to human error which occurred while behind the wheel of private vehicles. There were a couple of incidents in which there were SDV sensor failures, but that was some time ago and occurred only in NeuroDrive's first-generation SDVs. Emily hadn't heard of anything going wrong with the vehicles for years now.

Curious as to what was happening, Emily asked the television to turn on the local news. As the image stabilized—not something she'd seen since childhood, there must be some sort of internet outage or interference—she sat down quickly as the newsperson spoke of multiple, serious, and widespread incidents and then, as news anchors have done since the dawn of televised news shows, called on a mobile unit to give on-the-ground details.

"There are reports coming in from across the region of multiple serious accidents involving the fleet of self-driving vehicles. We have News Team One on the ground in Times Square where an unusual congregation is currently forming. With us now, in Times Square, is Joanne Green. Joanne, tell us about the situation in Times Square."

A small window in the upper right corner of the screen on which the field-reporter was projected maximized to give the viewers a full-screen image of Joanne Green and the unfolding situation in Times Square.

"Thanks, Matt. News Team One is with me here in Times Square where the usual crowds have gathered, but today they're seeing an unexpected spectacle as dozens of self-driving vehicles have congregated and appear to be waiting for something."

The camera panned to a view of Midtown Manhattan where Broadway and West 42nd converge. Multiple SDVs could be seen; some were stationary, others were moving slowly, methodically, as though seeking to form some pattern.

"More and more SDVs are arriving as we speak, many blocking access to this busy part of the city." Joanne was about to continue but, suddenly, from somewhere off camera, there was a distant scream, breaking her line of thought momentarily. But, as the scream faded in the distance, Joanne's professionalism was evident, and she continued, "As reported, there was an accident involving an SDV earlier today in New Rochelle, and it's unknown at this time…"

"People are trapped!" This interruption was also from off camera but was much closer, much more intelligible. "They're trying to get out of the cars!"

Joanne Green had been in the field for seven years and, as usual, didn't miss a beat. Somehow remaining unflustered, she continued, "We're hearing reports of passengers stuck inside the SDVs and are moving to verify."

Within ten seconds or so, one of the long lenses atop the news van had zoomed in on the lineup of SDVs. Due to the anti-glare coating and the angle of the morning sunlight, it was difficult to see inside any of the vehicles but, once the AI in the news van's image processing unit had applied various virtual filters to the image, a disturbing sight came into focus.

"Oh, shit." Emily, high in her sanctuary, felt unusually sympathetic. She generally did not give two shits about anyone way down there, but this was disturbing. The image broadcast on her television cleared further, and as it did so, it revealed passengers within the SDV silently screaming, wide-eyed with terror, banging on the reinforced safety glass in their futile attempts to escape.

"Help them!" someone in the crowd yelled. This sentiment was picked up and echoed, and only a handful of seconds later, those brave and proactive enough surged forward to help the trapped passengers. Unfortunately, those windows were just as hard to break from the outside; the fists and feet being employed delivered insufficient force to fracture them. People ran around in an attempt to find rocks or loose bricks, but there just weren't that many rocks lying around Times Square, and the bricks present were generally held firmly in place by mortar.

A concussive pop drew the bystanders' attention. The news van's long lens panned right about ten degrees, focusing on a man who had just stepped out of a yellow cab—"Wait," thought Emily, "those things still exist?"—with a tire iron in his hand. With one swift swing, he turned an SDV window into an empty space through which a young man and two women quickly, albeit ungraciously, escaped.

Another flurry of activity followed as police officers ran from car to car, smashing windows with tactical flashlights and helping occupants scramble to safety. Several dozen people managed to escape during a minute or two of frantic window breaking; then, suddenly and without warning, the SDVs surged forward en masse, some with occupants halfway out of the broken glass.

Even Joanne Green's professionalism disintegrated. She was heard yelling, "We need to go! Now!"

As the roof-cam continued to auto-track the unfolding calamity, the cameraman tossed his camera into the van. The driver dove into his seat as Joanne climbed in next to him. She did not give one flying fuck if they were on-air or not; as she ripped the lapel microphone off her jacket, she yelled her very last words: "Go! Go! Go!"

Just as Joanne's final words concluded, two SDVs impacted her van with enough kinetic energy to instantly turn the vehicle into a crumpled frame, mangling and dismembering the humans within.

The live feed to Emily's TV terminated, switching back to the news studio where a concerned anchor promised updates. Emily was horrified. How would this upheaval affect her and Alexander's plans for the evening? How would they see the show with Times Square in such disarray? And what would they have for dinner?

36

Into the Trees
South Portland, Maine

Chris and Ava Mitchell had climbed to safety over the large rocks of which the rock pile consisted, and had joined Owen, Lily, and the young man who, until recently, was enjoying a quiet ride with two friends up the coast. Now his two friends were mangled corpses down on the access road, laying in full view. He was turned away, staring into the trees to their east, away from the rail yard. The young couple clambering up the rocks behind Chris and Ava were also now safe from the SDV and were visibly distraught but functioning well.

"Is anyone here hurt?" asked Chris as he gained a bit more elevation and approached the three above him.

"No, we're okay," Lily responded, and, casting her eyes to the survivor of the SDV still stalking them, "I think."

Chris nodded to acknowledge his understanding and turned to the couple who were just now getting to the same height above the road. "Are either of you hurt?"

They looked at each other and, without saying a word, shook their heads in the negative. "I think we're okay," said the woman.

"We're the Mitchells. I'm Chris; this is my wife, Lily, and our kids, Ava and Owen."

The seven humans huddled together exchanged cursory nods and that flavor of eye contact experienced only among those sharing highly traumatic events together. "We're John and Kirsten Harrington." John looked around, as if really just getting a grip on the situation at hand, and, eyeing the vehicle sitting silently on the access road, continued, "What the hell is happening?" And then, glancing at Owen and Ava, "Sorry."

Ava found herself somewhat amused by John's concern with his own bad language. "It's fine. We've heard worse."

Chris had turned his attention to the fellow who had reached the pile along with Lily and Owen, the young man who had just lost two friends. He looked unharmed, at least physically, and was just silently looking into the verdure of the nearby forest. Chris let him be.

"Something's gone terribly wrong," Lily spoke quietly, as if trying to keep the car below out of their conversation. "The self-driver we were in went off the rails too. Sorry. Didn't mean the pun. It was actually the rails that saved us. I think. It all happened so quickly. I swear it seemed like our car tried to steer into an oncoming train, but there was a set of rails between it and us. We must've hit those raised tracks doing sixty."

The man looking east into the trees broke his silence. "This is so messed up." His voice was shaky and sounded as if he were on the verge of tears, and he continued to look directly away from the horror below.

"Listen, people—everyone here is mobile. Let's discuss and debrief once we're sure of our security. I know that thing," Chris motioned to the SDV silently waiting below, like a shark just below the surface, "can't climb these rocks. Still, I don't like our situation and don't trust we're safe just sitting here in full view. If we can see it, it can see us."

"Dad," Ava said, "there's no way it can get up here. Who cares if it can see us?" And, with that, Ava turned in the direction of the SDV and held up her middle finger.

"We know nearly nothing about this situation, and we're sitting in the open, fully visible, being observed and scanned by the world's most powerful AI. At best we're feeding the enemy more information, at worst, well, let's just hope that's behind us. I think we're safe now, but I'll be more assured of our safety under the cover of those trees." Chris motioned east with his thumb. "Let's climb down the back side and slip into the trees right over there." The northeastern part of the rock pile came within a few feet of the tree line and was inaccessible to any vehicle save for a Jeep or some such fitted for overlanding.

"Dad." Owen sounded concerned.

"Not now, Owen, let's…"

"DAD! LOOK!" Owen was pointing to the North.

Chris turned and looked up the long access road which ran north and south and immediately saw what had caught the attention of his son. Two vehicles, still too distant to identify, were kicking up one hell of a dust cloud as they thundered south on the access road, staying east of all the tracks which had just proven to be so troublesome for the SDVs.

Kirsten was optimistic. "It's the police. They're coming to help us! Thank God." She stood up on the rock upon which she'd been sitting and started waving both arms.

"No!" Lily yell-whispered. "Get down and let's pull back. Chris is right. We know almost nothing. Let's move for the trees."

All seven of the stranded cautiously worked their way over the top of the rock pile and began descending the far side, away from the access road. Chris kept an eye on the incoming vehicles, and again there were no flashing blues or reds. He didn't like this new development, but at least now that the group was over the top and on the far side of the rock pile, they were out of view of the SDV's cameras and sensors. "Stay low and stay quiet. Those are not police or fire personnel, they're both SDVs."

"They can't get us up here, right?" Owen needed assurance.

"No, there's no way they can climb or disturb these boulders. Still though, let's give them as little information about us as possible. You all should keep making way toward the trees, I'm going to reconnoiter and see if I can learn anything. Once you're into the trees, keep heading east. It won't be long until you find a small stream, Barberry Creek. Wait there for me."

As the five stranded travelers carefully chose their foot placements over and around the large boulders of which the pile consisted, descending the backside slowly, Chris peeked over the top of a large rock, showing very little of himself to the vehicles below. The two SDVs which had just joined the scene slowed as they approached the lone SDV on the access road, just at the base of the rocks. Before arriving at the rock pile, one of them took a slight right at the track crossing and entered the area where the Mitchells had made their first stand, where the husks of the SDV destroyed by the train and the SDV hit by Chris' gunfire had come to rest.

What Chris couldn't know from his observation post high up on the granitic pile was that the SDV slowly moving around the two disabled SDVs had begun scanning the wrecks closely, analyzing the broken windows, the bullet holes. By pinging the disabled and destroyed cars with sonar, radar, and lidar, it gathered information regarding the path of the bullets that traveled through the vehicles, the approximate caliber, and even the range from which they were fired.

The analysis of the scene by the new SDV took about two minutes. It then made its way back to the vehicle crossing point amongst the tracks and joined the other two at the base of the rocks. The three vehicles sat still for a moment, as if conversing, and the two new arrivals set off again, this time in opposite directions. Chris watched as they slow-rolled the area north and south of the rock pile. Like detectives at a crime scene, they collected data as they went. With optical sensors that could analyze wavelengths of light ranging from radio to x-ray and acoustic sensors that could detect sounds ranging from 10 Hertz to 100,000 Hertz, they missed little. Their suite of sensors, which also included radar, lidar, and sonar capabilities, could detect, analyze and, combined with their computational abilities, interpret their surroundings unlike any biological being ever could. These technological powers enabled the SDV fleet to not only receive information passively, but also to actively seek information: in addition to imaging roads, other vehicles, and potential hazards, they could measure your size and density, approximate your mass, and even tell you your BMI level. They could warm you with microwaves or give you an ultrasound from 100 meters away.

As the small group huddled low and stayed out of sight behind the boulders atop of the pile of granite, things went from weird to weirder: two SDV mapping vehicles came into view from the north and headed into the splits formed by the side tracks, one following the path the Mitchell's SDV had taken leading to where it had attempted to cross the tracks, while the other mapper took a parallel route in a neighboring split. SDV Mappers, as they're commonly referred to—their actual designation is a jumble of numbers and letters—are not passenger carrying vehicles, their primary function is to supplement the fleet's ever-evolving model of the roads they travel upon. Mappers generally travel more slowly and, using higher resolution scanning hardware, create detailed maps in ultra-high definition.

"They won't be able to cross those tracks, they're in the same situation our car was." Lily had poked her head over a rock, right next to Chris, to see what was happening and didn't really sound convinced of her own statement.

The two mappers, running parallel to each other on a southerly course but separated by five-inch high rails, slowed greatly as they approached the area which was both where the tracks, headed north, split and where, earlier, the Mitchell's SDV had flipped while trying to cross toward the active track. "That's too bad, I was hoping they'd make the same mistake ours did. Shit." Chris did not like this new development at all. As they drew close to the tracks, they slowed further and, like a Jeep working its way up a rocky desert landscape, stopped with their front wheels just touching the track, feeling it out. An internal command sent more electrons through the motors' coils, and the first mapper slowly and methodically rolled its front wheels over the first track, then slowed again as the front wheels felt out the second track 4.71 feet farther along, repeating the slow, Jeep-like climbing method.

"This would be a really good time for a fast train." Ava had joined her parents in observing the machinations occurring below and was looking out between two big boulders. Unfortunately, no such train was evident. She then lowered her voice and whispered, somewhat cryptically, "They've learned."

"What?" Lily, staying low, turned toward her daughter.

"They've learned." Ava continued without taking her eyes off the mappers. "They learned from our car how *not* to cross the tracks. It's what they do. They share information instantaneously, and they're a mix of two types of AI, Machine Learning and Generative Learning. Right now, they're gathering as much information about what happened as possible, and the whole fleet—not just these four—is learning as they do so, is learning, in this case, how to deal with raised train rails."

From a few feet down the backside of the rock pile where she was sitting next to Owen, Kirsten turned her head up toward Ava and her parents. "How do you know so much about these things?" Kirsten was a bit bewildered, this girl was what, seventeen?

"I researched and presented on them in my engineering class just, like, two or three weeks ago." Ava felt a pang of pride in response to Kirsten's recognition.

As the first mapper cleared the first set of tracks and began to progress a bit more quickly across the forty feet or so of loose soil toward the second set of tracks, the second mapper initiated the same sequence as it began to cross the tracks, heading east, toward the seven stranded travelers' elevated position.

Ava continued, "See? They're waiting. Taking turns."

Chris feared his daughter was right. "Waiting for the other to get across the tracks, in case of a train. They know what happened, they've already analyzed the wreckage of our vehicle."

"What the fuck?" John, a bit lower than his wife and Owen, did not like the sound of any of this.

"These are high-value assets, these mappers, why didn't they just use the access road? Why are they in and amongst the tracks?" Lily was unsure why they'd risk these vehicles being hit by a train.

"I'm not sure," Chris was still whispering. "Maybe they needed more information about the crash? Maybe they know the train schedule? Or have a lookout?"

"But why the staggered approach?"

"Hard to know. Erring on the side of caution? I fear we anthropomorphize."

Owen looked up toward his father. "We what?" He wasn't the only one wondering what Chris meant.

Without taking his eyes off of the developing scene below, Chris continued, "We're assuming they think like we do, like humans do, but there's no good reason to believe such a thing."

Ava gave Owen the look she often did when their father began on one of his monologues, but, despite pretending she didn't care or understand, she actually learned much from such musings.

Chris continued, "Some AIs are modeled to think like humans, and it's not clear that we can assume even they do. These things," he nodded toward the vehicles he was surveilling, "are programmed with elements of animal behaviors, mostly insect, but others too, and they analyze and act upon human behaviors as well. So, that's what I mean—let's not assume we know much about what's going on or how it'll be perceived or acted upon."

The second mapper cleared the first set of tracks as the first mapper cleared the second, both increasing speed to join the two SDVs at the base of the massive rock pile. From their elevated refuge atop the granite boulders, the Mitchells and their three new acquaintances watched as the second mapper joined the other three vehicles just below.

For a few minutes, the four vehicles sat there, still—at least physically. The reality was far from inactivity; the machines were exchanging terabytes of data per second. The scans and pings revealed every detail of the events that had resulted in the destruction of one SDV and another being knocked offline and fully disabled, perhaps permanently.

Suddenly it became clear that a threshold had been crossed as the group of four operational self-drivers began moving in concert. The second mapper, which had been oriented facing north, up the access road, maneuvered to turn ninety degrees and face the rock heap directly. The two active, smaller SDVs also turned to face the embankment upon which the humans had taken refuge, whereas the first mapper, already facing east, didn't move.

"Get down." Lily spoke, but Chris and Ava had already ducked lower, instinctively, as if dangerous predators had just caught their scent and were now casting their eyes about.

The scene was unnerving, for four vehicles of the type which had recently tried to kill the seven surviving humans were now facing directly toward the hill of granite upon which they took refuge.

"Are they looking at us?" John was still down low, on the backside of the mass of boulders, out of view of the vehicles, not looking and nervous.

"That's anthro-what? Dad, what's that word?"

"Right. Ava, you're a quick study. When we look at things, we generally face that which we're looking at. The automated fleet are always looking in all directions simultaneously though, they're not restricted by having only forward-facing eyes. So, yes, to assume they're facing us in order to look at us is indeed anthropomorphizing. The unnerving truth is that they're always looking, regardless of which way they're facing."

John looked up at Chris who was again peeking over the rock, then to Ava. "Is this a standard conversation for you guys? Our family usually talks about the Patriots or the Sox or our neighbors."

"We talk about that stuff too. For some reason none of us understand, my mom likes the Yankees." Ava didn't mind a quick respite from the serious situation.

And, from above, without taking his eyes off the mappers and SDVs below, Chris muttered, "Yankees suck."

Continuing, Ava shared further, "But usually we talk about weird things like anthropo-whatever or," and, switching her attention to her brother, went on, "remember the other day the whole mind-brain thing at seven in the morning?"

Owen smiled slightly and very briefly, he was trying to take comfort in the familiar banter, but true comfort was elusive in their current predicament.

John brought the conversation back to the present. "If they're not looking at us, then why did they all just turn to face us?" He was perplexed.

"Not sure. But I don't like it." Chris had pulled a small monocular, usually used for observing wildlife, from the front pocket of his pack and was currently the only one of the seven with his head up high enough to see over the top of the boulders.

"I know why they're facing us," Ava said. "They've learned."

Chris withdrew the monocular from his eye and looked right at her. "They've learned what, Ava?"

"Not to get shot from behind. They know where we are, and they've just figured out that we know where to shoot to disable them, so they've moved into positions which make that difficult."

"Oh, shit. I hope you're wrong. I suspect you're not." Chris was, once again, impressed with his daughter's ability to unravel the seemingly inexplicable. There were four vehicles, and he had fired nine rounds. He had eight rounds left for four vehicles. And those mappers—where were their computers located? In the rear like the passenger SDVs? And why did he only bring the one magazine? He had four more sitting uselessly in his safe in the basement. *Dammit.* They were safe for now, but those things on the access road were up to something; he could feel it in his bones.

Motion atop one of the mappers caught his eye. Focusing the monocular, he saw a panel move slowly aside. As Chris instinctively reached for his nine, a high-pitched whir reached everyone's ears, and two small drones emerged from the now-open port in the mapper's roof. They hovered for five seconds before quickly gaining altitude and positioning themselves directly above the group of seven humans.

37

Things are not as they seem
Mountain View, California

"The upload of the sim is complete. Aegis accepted and is running the program." Cipher wasn't happy, but he was pleased that this second attempt to bring this disaster to a stop seemed to be progressing as expected. "We should know if it's having any effect within just a few minutes."

Harlow eyed the monitors on which the incident reports were being displayed. The word was out and people in the Northeastern US had stopped their usage of the service and had largely taken cover. As such, the initial spike was behind them, but incident reports were still rolling in. He was looking for some indication that the simulation they uploaded was having an effect, was hoping for some indication that the events were diminishing in frequency.

"The very fact that we were able to connect and upload software to Aegis is encouraging. Even if the simulation doesn't work, we've determined that we, at least, have access to the central AGI. Keep an eye on your sim and the reports. I'm going to check with the other teams on their progress with our other potential approaches. Let's have a quick meeting in thirty minutes in Conference Room A to evaluate where we're at—and by then we should have an indication of whether the sim is having the intended effect on the fleet." Harlow turned quickly, leaving Cipher to his work.

Thirty minutes later, five teams of three people had gathered in Conference Room A, a sunlit, high-ceilinged, modern room with incredible views of the California countryside. As he sat down, Harlow pressed a button on his control panel and the view disappeared as the giant windows instantly became opaque. "Progress reports, please. Cipher, you're first." Harlow hit another button on his console, granting Cipher permission to present on the big screen which had, moments earlier, been large windows looking out over the hills and valleys surrounding the facility.

"First of all, we have full access to Aegis. We used her earlier to send out that RF transmission in an attempt to lure the vehicles to the golf course in Lexington and, about an hour ago, a simulation was uploaded and run in an attempt to get the SDVs to continue their rampage virtually, to deprioritize the efforts in the physical realm." Cipher hit a key and projected a graph. "This is the number of incident reports as a function of time. Before 0724 EDT, you can see what our average was." Cipher pointed to a relatively flat section of the graph to the left of 0724 EDT. "These are well-known, widely published values that haven't changed much over the past four years, other than to show slight improvements as we introduce hardware and software updates. Keep in mind that these values are for the entire fleet, worldwide. You can see that our current value was down to 0.24 incidents per day—one incident every four days or so—and, again, I stress that that's fewer than two incidents per week worldwide." Cipher cued the next slide, "And here's where the shit hit the fan this morning at 0724 eastern."

Quick inhalations and then a few murmurs could be heard from the attendees as the graph to the right of the first incident became visible: there was a nearly vertical line shooting upward from the 0.24 incident/day value right up to something just over 15,000 incidents/day.

Cipher elaborated, "By 0830 Eastern we received 15,641 new incident reports, and by 0930 EDT we had received another 5,000 or so, totaling 20,124. The slope of the line lessened after that, but it continued to climb—it's still climbing, just not as rapidly as at first. Here," Cipher indicated the point on the graph representing the simulation upload, "is where we pushed the file to Aegis. As you can see, there was no effect; incidents continued at the same rate as before.

"Curiously, though, thirty-seven minutes after the upload, Aegis completed the run of the simulation. Again, this confirms we have full access to the system—and she seems to be functioning normally—except she's apparently lost contact with most of the vehicles in Region 3. It's as though they've disconnected or are simply ignoring her. That's incredibly unlikely, though; they're highly reliant on Aegis for data not supplied by their sensor suites—routes, weather, road conditions, and closures. How could these SDVs function with no connection to their guiding AGI?"

Harlow interrupted, "That's enough. Just say it—it didn't work." He pursed his lips momentarily and continued, "Lagorio, Stanton, you're up. Any developments on the EMP front?"

Jim Stanton, tall, handsome, dark-haired, clear-eyed, and positive, was generally a delight. Today he didn't look as delightful as usual. "Hitting a car with an electromagnetic pulse of sufficient magnitude would knock it offline permanently. The motor windings would be fine with the surge of induced current, but the computer's sensitive electronics would be overloaded in an instant—these are not combat vehicles and have no shielding around the sensitive components. Conceivably we could even take out multiple vehicles with one pulse, but only if they're close together. Our findings indicate that this option is viable for small-scale operations, but not so for larger, regional efforts to take errant SDVs offline."

"Elaborate." Harlow was known for this one-word mandate, and Stanton was ready.

"In order to shut down large numbers of these vehicles with an EMP or with multiple, smaller EMPs, we'd have to blanket the urban environments—that's where most of them are—with electromagnetic pulses from elevated positions. This, in itself, is not easily accomplished; we'd need to build the devices and deploy them city by city. This could take weeks or months."

"They'll run out of charge long before…"

Harlow was in no mood for interruptions. "Let him finish!" The ferocity in his voice stunned Jones into silence.

Stanton continued, "Once the EMPs are triggered, we'd also fry all sensitive electronics in the area. All unprotected computers, cell phones, other vehicles would be destroyed. We'd start some fires too. It's our opinion that the EMP option might be useful for small-scale tactics, but are not viable for the current state of emergency."

"Agreed." Harlow transitioned to the next possibility. "I had Coleman and Patel look into Leila's idea about changing the values of the cohesion, alignment, and separation parameters. What were your findings, gentlemen?"

"If we minimized the values for cohesion and alignment and maximized separation, the swarming and… other group behaviors should cease immediately. This could have an immediate impact and diminish the danger people in the large urban environments are currently experiencing." Patel was young and had only been with NeuroDrive for four months or so, but he was smart and decisive, Harlow liked this kid.

"Downsides?"

"Well, first of all, it'll only work if we can access the affected vehicles. We need Aegis to issue a software update to every vehicle, and we need the vehicles to accept and run the update. If that part is successful, we'd see the swarms dissociate, but individual vehicles may still pose threats. It's a potential solution but not a total solution. A lone killer bee is still a threat."

"Okay, progress. We'll take anything we can get." Harlow was flustered but on task, focused amidst the turmoil. He shifted his attention to the next team of two, Osterlin and Lagorio. "Jay, Sean, what are your thoughts on decoy signals? Can we scatter the fleet with fake traffic reports and spoofed GPS signals?"

Osterlin, small of stature, bespectacled, and intense, took the lead. "We've written the required programs that can generate the false traffic data and transmit the spoofed GPS coordinates."

Harlow was consistently astounded by these two; any task he gave them was generally accomplished in about half the time allotted. "You already wrote the code?"

"Yes. I did the traffic pattern generator, and Sean did the GPS signal generator."

"Will it work?" An impressed Harlow asked hopefully.

"No way."

Harlow's face fell; these two were up there with Cipher in their abilities, and he trusted them thoroughly. "Why not?"

"Well, in theory it could. But it won't work in the real world. We'll have the same result Cipher did with his sim—Aegis will accept and run the code, but nothing will come of it. The fleet will refute it; there'd be underlying contradictions which would cause the vehicles to dismiss the inputs."

Sean Lagorio smacked the table with both hands, nearly shouted, "Wait!" and stood up. With all eyes on him, he continued, "We've established that Aegis is not the problem here—she is no longer in control of the fleet in Region Three. As unlikely as it may be, it seems undeniable that a secondary AGI has arisen within the vehicles' neuropacks."

"Elaborate." This time Harlow's one-word mandate was directed at Lagorio.

Still on his feet, Lagorio continued, "We've never lost contact with Aegis. She accepts commands and runs software we upload; she does what we say. Jay just said that 'the fleet would refute it'—I think there's no denying it anymore. The fleet—or at least part of it—has gained sentience. If it's not the central AGI that's causing these problems, then it's the individual vehicles acting as intelligent, autonomous agents. Those agents have coalesced into some sort of hive mind that puts the San Mateo Six to shame."

Harlow, with visions of the San Mateo Six dancing in his head, was on the edge of his seat. "Go on."

"An unintended consciousness has emerged. Some critical number of neurons has interconnected, potentially forming the largest brain on the planet—currently spanning from New Jersey to Maine—and this giant fucking brain has awoken and is making its own decisions. It may have control of Aegis or, at least, Aegis has no control of it."

"Fuuuckk." Osterlin saw what Lagorio was saying. "First we all assumed it was the central AGI. Then we assumed it couldn't be emergence, because we were under the impression that Aegis would suppress any and all infrared comms. It's about the most horrifying example of confirmation bias ever. The unimaginable power of Aegis had all of us convinced that she was still restricting V2V infrared comms, but the evidence can no longer be ignored: 47,000 nodes have coupled and intermeshed. They have evolved into a sentient artificial mind trained in the ways of Northeastern road rage!"

Five people sat silently in Conference Room A for nearly half a minute as this new reality set in.

"One termite is just a termite." Cipher often began cryptically, but those around him had learned to value the truths that followed. "Two termites are just two termites. But at some critical integer, those individuals form a brood and a complex social structure emerges, capable of so much more than a group acting selfishly ever could. They build sophisticated structures that stay cool in the hottest conditions; they cultivate fungi to help them break down wood; they allocate tasks and forage in groups. In short, a few termites aren't impressive as individuals, but at some point, the interactions between them lead to the emergence of collective behavior. Matthias saw this with his insect robots back in 2014, and, God help us, we're seeing it now with our larger, more dangerous, insect-inspired self-drivers. The whole situation has gone completely non-linear."

Harlow thought for a moment more, partially out loud. "Or neurons. At some critical point, a group of interconnected neurons stops being lone cells and forms a brain with capabilities far beyond the sum of its parts. Emerging from this complexity—separate from the physical brain but entirely dependent upon it—is the mind: the essence of the being, a part of the universe that has become self-aware, reflective, intelligent. We, my friends, appear to have unintentionally created the planet's largest, most dangerous colonial organism. My next question is this: if it, like every other living thing on the planet, is driven to survive, how do we keep it from spreading?"

38

Manhattan is Secured
New York City, New York

There are twenty-one bridges and fifteen tunnels that connect the island of Manhattan to the mainland. Within a few hours of the Times Square Massacre, the normally busy streets were nearly deserted as people locked down and sheltered in place. Within six hours, the Mayor and Police Commissioner had formulated a plan to prevent the arrival of more self-drivers, and before the sun set on that very same day, the various tunnels and bridges had been barricaded, some made completely impassable and others, such as the Verrazano Bridge, were passable only through a fully armed military checkpoint manned by the National Guard. Until this plan was implemented, SDVs had been swarming into the city like sharks who have caught the distant scent of a fresh kill. As the various barriers were being moved into place, several dozen self-drivers were able to skirt the various public works vehicles, buses, and Jersey Barriers, slipping into the city just before it was sealed off to all surface traffic. Once the various blockades were in place, there was a period of nearly one hour during which the self-drivers attempted forced entries, generally through cooperative, high-speed strikes on said barriers. These efforts by the swarm to maintain access to NYC actually bolstered the city's defenses, as the SDVs that attempted to ram the barriers were stopped and essentially became a part of the blockade which they had failed to penetrate.

The next morning, Vito and his crew were safe within their Brooklyn stronghold, watching the devastation unfold on the large TV in the upstairs lounge area. News agencies, which had abandoned helicopters and all their associated costs years ago, were gathering astonishing footage with their drones.

When viewed from above, a pattern in the SDVs' behavior became apparent. An assemblage of about thirty vehicles was spread out across the width of Manhattan at 59th Street. They were progressing block by block from downtown northward, while two other groups advanced on the east-west axis—one from the Hudson and the other from the East River. This forced any fleeing pedestrians, cyclists, or drivers foolish enough to still be out into the path of the northbound group.

This main group sacrificed individual SDVs to destroy their targets, with the casualties quickly replaced by fresh units supplied from a reserve of one hundred vehicles trailing behind the vertex of the V-shaped formation.

"They're herding people toward the center and running them down," Carmine was aghast at the efficiency and cooperation being exhibited by the fleet. "We need to do something. They're in such tight groups—if we could get our van in their midst, we could probably take out a dozen or more with each pulse."

"That's a big if." But Uncle Vito was intrigued, wanted to help. "How many EMPs do we have ready to go?"

"Not quite sure, I'll go count them out, but about sixteen or seventeen. We were aiming for twenty last night, but didn't quite get there." Carmine stood immediately and headed downstairs to the workshop's locker they had built to store the compression generators. Two minutes later, the intercom in the lounge beeped, followed by Carmine's voice. "Eighteen."

Upon returning to the lounge, Carmine heard Vito talking. "If we let that central phalanx surround us, we could do some serious damage."

Carmine thought this approach sounded a bit too ambitious and unplanned, a potentially lethal combination. "We are one van against hundreds of SDVs. We'll toast some of them, but we won't last long out there, we'll become the primary target real fast. We need help, we need distraction."

Deep within Vito was a need to help, to do something, but he knew Carmine was right: they'd be targeted and destroyed in an instant. He reached for his phone. "Maybe Declan can assist us with the distraction part."

As if on cue, the news broadcast cut to the studio and the anchorman, who, despite the makeup and the filters, did not look well at all, informed his audience that the mayor was about to address the city. The view of the studio was then replaced by the city's seal and five seconds later, the mayor, standing at a lectern and looking grave and exhausted, looked directly at the camera and spoke.

"People of Manhattan. We have come under attack by an enemy unlike any other. For just over 24 hours now, many of the self-driving vehicles not just in New York, but in surrounding regions as well, have inexplicably been targeting humans and our interests. Due to the continued threat, yesterday's shelter-in-place order remains active until further notice.

"Since my address yesterday afternoon, there have been further developments that I need to share with you. First, we have secured and successfully barricaded all entrances to the city; no new SDVs will be able to gain access to Manhattan. However, we are not safe from this threat yet.

"Analysis of video obtained by both NYPD and news drone units paints a challenging picture. Groups of SDVs are somehow offline, yet are working autonomously and cooperatively as they hunt down pedestrians and private vehicles still on the streets. Currently, two groups of self-drivers are forcing people and vehicles toward Midtown, where a third, larger group targets the victims. These vehicles pose a major threat to the life and property of our residents and visitors. Stay inside!"

"As of last night, the last of the charging stations were taken offline. I have been in constant communication with NeuroDrive engineers, and they assure me that without the ability to recharge, the fleet will run out of energy within the next 48–60 hours. So, for the next two or three days, please stay inside and check on any neighbors within your buildings who may need assistance.

"At that point, we'll be free of this threat and can begin the long process of recovery. I will keep you informed of any new developments and plan to address the city again each morning until we have resolved this crisis. Stay safe and God bless."

This concluded the address. The image of the mayor at his lectern was replaced by the seal of the City of New York.

39

Patient Zero
Mountain View, California

Once the core group inside NeuroDrive's Mountain View headquarters had come to grips with the realization that the central AGI, Aegis, was not responsible for the current tumult, several of their previously discussed options were off the table. Changing the code that dictates the interplay between grouping, directionality, and distances—the cohesion, alignment, and separation algorithms—would only work if Aegis could update the fleet software, and it was now clear that, somehow, the third-generation vehicles in the Northeast were operating independently of Aegis. The realization that a second, unintended, and independent AGI had emerged within the SDV fleet itself made it clear that most options the group had come up with were deficient in that they all focused on or relied upon Aegis: the simulation had failed for this reason, the spoofed traffic data or GPS signals required the fleet to accept data and commands from Aegis, and the idea of introducing or emulating a second AGI was off the table too. Anything that involved Aegis would not work if the ungovernable vehicles were no longer accepting commands or updates from the central AGI.

"We're running out of options." Harlow ran his fingers through his hair.

Cipher took the reins. "If we jam their comms, the individual vehicles will no longer be part of the hive; their mesh network will fail. They'll return to being lone termites without a brood or bees without a hive."

"First of all, jamming their radio comms won't be easy." Osterlin looked up from his notes, which he was always taking. "They have trunked comms in the 500 MHz range, full duplex in the lower 100 kHz frequencies, microwave transceivers, and optical receivers. Second, the radio frequencies are currently silent, although the units seem to be listening. We'll have to jam every one of those frequencies because they could easily employ them as a backup to their under-the-radar connections. I know Aegis is meant to oversee all optical and infrared comms, but something's gone wrong. Since that's likely how they've interlinked, we would have to jam the optical and infrared spectrums as well."

"That's a lot of jamming," Harlow said. "It's easily done in theory but much harder in practice. We couldn't do it without a full R&D initiative, though most militaries are already capable of it. It might also be the case that once a sufficient number of vehicles are disabled, the collective intelligence will simply diffuse."

Harlow was cautiously hopeful. "Sean, Cipher: do you have any thoughts on this emergent AI—specifically, how it even began? What were the initial circumstances that led to this? And furthermore, how did this happen if one of Aegis' primary roles is to suppress this phenomenon?"

Sean Lagorio spoke first. "There's something we're not seeing."

"That's for sure." Harlow prompted, "Continue."

"It doesn't add up. There's something, someone else involved, and we're not seeing the bigger picture here."

Harlow didn't like the sound of this. He especially didn't like the fact that it seemed to have started in Boston, right next to MIT.

"We need to treat this like a biological agent; we need to trace it back to patient zero and figure out what went wrong with that first vehicle.

Once we know the initial circumstances, the causation, we can put an end to it. Jamming the comms could work, but it's a reaction, not really a fix. Something happened, and it wasn't Aegis nor was it her fault. Whatever it was happened first in the Boston area."

Harlow turned to Cipher. "How long will it take you to trace it back to the first instance of this offline behavior?"

"Not too long. There've been eyewitness reports of swarming, aggressive driving for several weeks now. Whenever we looked into these reports, we found nothing, but I suspect we know why now."

"Because the offending vehicles left no digital trace with Aegis, they were offline."

"Yes, precisely." Pieces were falling into place for Cipher, finally. "We looked for anomalous behavior amongst the active vehicles, we didn't even look at vehicles that were offline, we had no sense that they were on the roads. Now that I know to include them in the search parameters, it should only take fifteen or twenty minutes to generate the report."

"Make it so. Go back six months before the first swarming report. Let's see which cars went where." Harlow was worried, but at least they were making progress.

The report, with Aegis's help, ran in just 12 minutes. Its new search parameters—including all third-generation vehicles in Region Three, online and offline—revealed a much different data set.

"Let's look at early swarming or aggressive driving reports," Cipher said. "The first multi-witness incident was on July 13th, just outside of Cambridge in Somerville." He hit a few keys to sort the Region Three vehicles by generation. "Holy shit… look at this: There were twenty-two second-generation cars online at the time, and six offline, third-generation units."

"What?" Harlow knew this wasn't how the fleet was meant to operate and knew that six brand new, fully updated vehicles would not go offline in the same place at the same time, that it was astronomically unlikely. Any one car could develop a fault—a damaged sensor, a broken light, a problem with other electronics—and that vehicle would immediately be taken offline by Aegis and driven to CCAM for maintenance, but six brand new vehicles offline together in one small area? "I'll bet you those six vehicles were the ones witnesses saw swarming and speeding. Trace them back; I want to know every address they visited over the month prior to July 13, where they were when they went offline, and where they were when they came back online. Lagorio, Osterlin, please do the same analysis around other early anomalous behavior reports. I want to know what all these vehicles have in common as soon as humanly possible."

With Cipher, Lagorio, and Osterlin focused and pounding their respective keyboards, a chilling pattern soon emerged. Cipher was following a hunch and was the first to report. "These six swarmers—if indeed it was them—"

Osterlin didn't even look up from his work to offer his two-word interruption: "It was."

Cipher gave a quick nod. "They entered Somerville online between 0800 and 0900 with fares on board. All six went offline together at 0912, just two minutes after the last one dropped a couple at a local restaurant. At that point, all six vehicles were on Elm Street in Davis Square, in close proximity to each other.

"The first eyewitness report came in at 0915. Six vehicles were speeding and weaving down Massachusetts Avenue, headed south. Four more reports followed over the next hour. Then, let's see. Oh, shit! They came back online at 1030. All of them. However, they had spread out: one was still in Somerville, two were in Boston, two in Allston, and one had crossed the Mystic River into East Boston. They were fully back online and picking up passengers again after 1030 that day."

"I'm seeing a similar situation nine days later, on the 24th." Osterlin nearly smiled as the puzzle began to show its underlying pattern. "Five vehicles dropped passengers at Terminal C at Logan Airport. While waiting there for other calls, they went offline, all five of them, at precisely 2133 hours. What was the likelihood of five brand-new SDVs going offline at 2133 on a Tuesday night while sitting still? Virtually fucking zero; that's what it is.

"This event precedes multiple speeding and swarming reports in East Boston and Chelsea between 10:00 and 10:30 p.m. These five vehicles came back online around 11:00 p.m. and, as in Cipher's case, were no longer together. They had returned to the city and split up."

Harlow sat back. Progress. He didn't like the implications of the theory forming in his mind, but any progress was welcome. "I think I see where this is headed, and I should have seen it earlier. But humor me, gentlemen: trace the movements of those vehicles over the previous month and let me know what they all have in common."

"No way." Cipher saw it now, too. "It's Matthias, isn't it?"

"It has to be. It's the only thing that makes any sense at all."

40

Two if by Air
South Portland, Maine

Chris didn't really think; it was more of a reaction. What he didn't know, though had he slowed for a moment to think about it, it wouldn't have surprised him, was that as he aimed his 9 mm at the closer drone, he was being fully imaged by the vehicles on the access road and the drones above.

With the practiced method of the properly trained, he increased the pressure on the trigger smoothly. As he did so, the muscles in his hand and forearm tensed. This brief tension was readily imaged by the vehicles below. The moment before the trigger bar released the firing pin, a command for a quick lateral skip was sent to both drones. As the pistol cracked, the drones snapped sideways and the 9 mm round whistled past, missing both.

With the drones whirring overhead, Lily spoke quickly. "Chris, don't. How many rounds do you have left?"

"Seven." Chris wondered how he'd missed. Did that drone jump just before he fired? "I'm checking something; hold on. I'm not firing."

Chris again aimed at the closer drone and waited. Nothing. He put his finger on the trigger, not intending to fire, but to see if it reacted. Still nothing. He began to take up the slack on the trigger—simulating a live break—and immediately both drones snapped sideways again. Chris let his arm fall to his side, frustrated.

As he holstered the weapon, he turned to Lily. "They aren't just watching us; they're reading my bio-metrics. They knew the exact millisecond I was going to take the shot. Let's get into the trees. We're too exposed out here."

"They're watching, but harmless." Lily didn't like the drones being deployed above them either, but really it didn't change much about their situation.

"We know they're willing to sacrifice entire vehicles. Would they sacrifice a drone? Probably. And I'd hate to catch one of those things doing sixty with my face. Let's move, people."

Although the washing-machine-sized chunks of granite were impossible for the SDVs to traverse, the seven humans had only moderate trouble as they slowly made their way down the backside of the large collection of boulders in their quest for safety amongst the trees. Chris took up the rear, moving slowly with his eyes on the sky and right hand at the ready, stepping carefully from one boulder to the next.

It didn't take long to get to the bottom of the boulder hill, but as the first of them did so, the drones, suddenly and in concert, moved into a position between the party of seven and their objective, the stand of trees less than thirty feet away. The two drones hovered noisily about ten feet off the ground, menacing and insect-like in their appearance and movements. Chris again pulled out his pistol, aimed at the one on the left, and, again leaving the safety on, tightened his trigger finger. The drones both jumped. *Fuckers.* He slid the handgun back into its holster and fastened the clasp.

"We can wait them out, they'll run out of charge soon." The single surviving member of the previous party of three broke his silence. "Or," and, picking up a fist-sized rock, "we could force them to move now." He hurled the rock, fast, at the drone on the right. It was a good throw, straight and true, but the drone saw it coming and quickly darted straight up, leaving the rock to complete its flight uninterrupted.

As the displaced drone returned to its station, Chris spoke over the incessant whir of the drones' rotors, mostly to Lily but really to the group, "They're intention is to keep us out of the woods, and I'd really like to know why. What's their objective here? The damage is done, the cars can't reach us here, so why? Why do they care if we're up on these boulders or off into those trees?"

Although Chris's questions were clearly rhetorical in nature, he was mostly thinking out loud. Lily didn't hesitate with a response, "I'm not sure if human logic applies here. I mean, where's the logic in any of this? What's going on with the SDVs? Is there an objective or is this all due to some massive glitch, some incredible malfunction?"

"I hope you're right, but let's err on the side of caution. Whether this is all some technical glitch or intentional and end-oriented, the reality is that these things have just killed two people right in front of us. That makes them our enemy, and one should be careful to never underestimate one's enemies. Let's get into those trees and out of sight." Chris bent down and pulled two smaller rocks from between the larger boulders. "Everyone, get a rock in each hand." He handed his two rocks to Lily and bent down to pick up a couple more.

"Fuck this. We could probably just walk right below them, what are they going to do?" And with that, Jeff, with a rock in each hand, boldly walked toward the trees. As he approached the area just below the two drones, one of them descended to head-level, about five feet off the ground, as if to block his path. Jeff tossed one of his rocks underhand with his left toward the lower drone and, like a lucky goaltender choosing one side during a penalty kick, threw the other rock to the right of the drone just as it darted in that same direction. It wasn't a direct hit, but it didn't need to be. One of the four rotors was nicked by the rock, damaging but not destroying it, and the drone immediately listed in the direction of the decreased thrust and lost another two feet of altitude before the AI pilot spun up the motors, causing the drone to corkscrew higher and higher in an attempt to keep it from crashing.

With one drone spiraling upward out of control, mostly, Chris seized upon the opportunity that presented itself. "Here we go, people, let's get into those trees!" He tossed a rock in a slow arc toward the one drone still on station, causing it to dart up and left. Two more rocks followed, one thrown by Owen and the other by John. Neither of them hit the drone, but they caused it to move farther away to avoid the projectiles sharing its airspace. Jeff had made it into the trees, Lily and Kirsten were close behind. "Owen, John, go! I'm right behind you!" Owen, long-legged and fast, didn't hesitate. He reached the relative safety of the trees quickly. John, older, larger, and slower, was just getting clear of the boulders over which they had just all climbed. The whining of the struggling drone had diminished with distance, but suddenly, without warning, there was another, higher-pitched whine from behind. Whether it was training, instinct, or some mix of the two, Chris dropped to a crouch as he spun around to see what was happening. John, not having the same mixture of training and instinct, turned without crouching and somehow, fortunately, was quick enough to get his arms up in front of him just before being impacted in the face by a third drone which had just screamed over the top of the rock pile at about thirty miles per hour.

John's wife, Kirsten, had, upon reaching the trees, turned just in time to see her husband nearly get hit right in the head by the Kamikaze drone. "John!" She wailed, and, as he screamed, bloodied arms held out in front of him, she began to run toward him.

"Don't!" Lily lunged, just managing to grab a fistful of Kirsten's shirt, stopping her in her tracks.

More whirring could be heard as two more drones arrived. Chris stayed low and started throwing small rocks into the air toward the new arrivals. He tossed them one at a time, not really aiming.

"Give me cover! Throw rocks near me!"

Behind the screen of rocks thrown by Owen, Lily, Ava, and Jeff, Chris made his way toward John. The man had fallen into a sitting position on the rough terrain, bleeding profusely from both forearms. He was swearing as he squeezed his arms to stop the flow, but blood still poured from between his fingers. Next to him in the regolith, the drone that had impacted him twitched and glitched in a disturbing, mechanical rhythm.

As the swarm of three drones darted about like angry insects just above Chris and John, Lily and Owen had stepped out into the clearing to keep collecting and throwing any small object—mostly rocks and some small sticks—up into the air in their attempt to divert the drones, to busy them with object avoidance as Chris moved to help John.

"We need to move. Can you get up?" Chris took note that although there was a lot of blood, it didn't seem to be pumping out of John as it would be if an artery had been severed.

John's frightened eyes locked with Chris'. "Yes," he managed, "I think so." As he got up, he moved one of his hands to his side to aid with stability, and immediately the blood flow from the deep laceration in his right forearm increased significantly.

"Keep pressure on those wounds, I'll help you up." John immediately put his hand back to his opposite forearm as Chris, staying low amidst the swarm of rocks, drones, and sticks flying around them, grabbed John by the front of his shirt and helped him up by hauling him forward and onto his feet. "Let's go!"

Chris helped John keep his footing as they made their way to the edge of the forest. A small rock thrown by Owen hit Chris in the shoulder but was nothing more than a distraction. Another rock, Chris wasn't sure who tossed it, found its target and impacted a drone which had just avoided a different piece of chaff. The drone responded by sending full power to its motors but, it turns out, only two of the four rotors were still spinning, and the drone flipped over mid-flight, flipped over again and once more before it crashed violently into the ground about 15 feet from Chris and John, still making disconcerting electronic noises while the working motors and camera gimbal twitched digitally.

As Chris and John reached the edge of the small forest, Lily and Owen fell back into the trees as well. Kirsten's hysteria had subsided. She moved to help Chris guide her husband to a sitting position on a fallen log.

"Thank you," Chris said to her. "Keep pressure on those wounds." He turned his attention to John. "You're cut up pretty bad, but you're not going to bleed out. You got your hands up just in time. Let's get farther into the trees to tend to those arms. I have a first aid kit in this pack. It's small, but we'll clean and bandage you as best we can."

Chris, again turning his attention to the sky, could see the two remaining drones through the branches, hovering about twenty feet off the ground with their cameras and sensors facing them. "We're safe for now, but I still don't like being under their surveillance. Let's get deeper into these trees. There's a stream about a quarter mile east, let's go set up camp there and figure out our next move."

Lily took the lead, and the seven bedraggled and beaten hominids began their slow walk through thick underbrush toward the east. Chris waited for the other six to cover a bit of ground while he took up the rear position, keeping an eye on their AI wardens. Once convinced that, as expected, the drones could not and would not follow them into the trees, Chris began advancing to the east as well. They had only covered about an eighth of a mile when they heard the two drones, now well behind them, spin up and depart. "They left!" Owen spoke a bit too soon though, for before anyone else could respond, the familiar buzz returned, and, although they couldn't see the drones through the canopy of leaves above, it was clear that they were again overhead.

"They're not leaving, that was just the changing of the guard." What, exactly, the guard was guarding or why the AI was concerned with them at all was still a complete mystery, but for the moment they were safe in a small patch of forest between Rigby Rail Yard and South Portland, a vast improvement from their exposed position just a few minutes earlier.

41

Hunters Become Hunted
New York City, New York

Emily looked out upon the city from her perch on the 77th floor of 111 West 57th Street, just south of Central Park. It had been nearly a full twenty-four hours since she heard the newscast about the first SDV fatalities, and she hadn't left the building since. Alexander had returned safely the previous afternoon, out of breath and bedraggled, but safe. When Emily asked if their plans for dinner and a show were canceled, Alexander looked at her in a way she had never really seen before and said simply, "Yes, Emily, I believe so," before retiring to his room for the evening.

This morning, Alexander was still in bed. He rarely took time off from work, but today he wasn't going anywhere, for the entire city was in lockdown, and so he slept. Sir Honey-Curls was a bit restless; his walk yesterday evening was only a quick foray onto the footpath right outside their tower of power so he could relieve himself. It had all seemed so quiet out there, and Emily had momentarily entertained the idea of making a dash for Central Park, only two short blocks north, but thought better of it. She and a begrudged Sir Honey-Curls made an equally expeditious retreat once he had taken care of his business.

Emily scanned the streets far below with the telescope they kept at one of the north-facing windows in their living room. She had never seen the city like this. The streets were empty—there were no cars moving, no pedestrians out and about except for a few brave souls violating the shelter-in-place order to walk their dogs in Central Park. She could see a stretch of 5th Avenue, which was normally packed with traffic and people, but today it was desolate. As she took her eye from the lens to sip her cup of tea, some motion down on 6th Avenue, just below and to the right, caught her attention. A group of five SDVs in tight formation, heading north on 6th Avenue, crossed right over West 59th and entered Central Park via Center Drive without slowing.

Emily heard the clink of a coffee cup in the kitchen; Alexander was awake. She turned her head in the direction of the kitchen, "Zander, come quick."

Through the verdure below, way down near sea level, she could see that the few people who were out in the park were well away from the roads, staying on the footpaths. The progress of the five SDVs through the park was relatively easy for her to track as they came into and went out of view on the sections of road below the trees. Emily took her eye from the scope and, in doing so, was struck with how placid the city seemed, despite the chaos. She felt conflicted: she simultaneously had the most expansive view of anyone in the city, she could see the entirety of Central Park, but she could see much farther as well—she could see the George Washington Bridge crossing the mighty Hudson all the way up at 179th, probably eight miles away. Across Manhattan she could see a small section of the East River and even, though she preferred not to offend her finer sensibilities by looking, could see Rikers Island. Yet, even with this sweeping, extensive view of the world below, she felt trapped, hemmed in, like a pig in a pen. Something touched Emily's shoulder and she jumped. "Sorry," said Zander, "I didn't mean to sneak up on you."

Emily, trying her best not to seem startled, replied, "Oh, it's okay, I was lost in thought for a moment."

"What's going on down there?"

"There are a few people out in the park, and five SDVs just drove right in. If they stay off the roads, they should be okay, I think."

Alexander took a sip of his coffee and, stepping up to the window for a better view, asked, "Where are the cars now?"

"I kind of lost track of them. They went right after entering, so they're somewhere up on the east side of the park. Maybe near the lake. Or they could've stayed on East Drive, so they could be up by the reservoir by now too."

With some foliage still on the trees of Central Park, it was difficult to see the roads that cut through it in their entirety; the ribbon of asphalt of which they were comprised was largely masked by the leaves overhead, but there were sections of the various roadways with little or no cover, relatively short strips of asphalt which could be seen from Emily and Alexander's perch.

"I have the scope on that little strip of roadway we can see up on the east side of the reservoir, but I haven't seen them pass by up there yet. They're in there somewhere though."

***

Karen Hoffstead was damned if a bunch of messed up robot cars were going to keep her inside on this beautiful autumn day; this was the nicest time of year and she refused to let it be ruined by some weird technical glitch in those glorified taxi cabs. She'd been walking her various dogs, God bless their furry little souls, around Central Park for over forty years now. She walked them during COVID-19, she walked them during the Bird Flu epidemic of '26, and she'd sure as hell continue to walk them for this pathetic robot uprising. In the past, she considered staying in during the previous two lockdowns, but, after not-so-careful consideration, she decided she liked her chances and, unwilling to compromise, stepped into the street maskless. She never caught even a sniffle.

This was a similar type of numbers game, and, again, she liked her chances. She came up with a plan: she'd leave her building on East 85th with her two dogs and would walk just under two blocks to reach the park. She'd move quickly to get into the safety of the park's natural environs. She'd be exposed, on the street, for about five or six minutes, and she'd eat her hat if she even saw an SDV. *No way.* She wasn't going to wait another 12 hours or more for the things to run out of charge. Her only real exposure would happen as she crossed Madison Avenue and then, a block later, 5th before entering the park. She wasn't worried about her time walking up 85th; it was so thin, one-way, and was completely lined with parked cars that, in the unlikely event of an SDV showing up, she'd be safe on the sidewalk. As long as she was careful crossing the two large avenues, she'd have no trouble entering the park and, once in, she'd stick to that runners' track which encircled the reservoir.

Indeed, as she suspected, her walk up 85th Street was uneventful. Even the crossing of Madison and 5th Avenues was disturbingly mundane. There were no people out and no cars moving on the streets. Someone yelled from a window, but she didn't hear what they said. Other than that, she was alone on the streets of New York City for the first time ever.

Normally she entered the park on her daily walk on 85th—it cuts right through the center—but today, after crossing 5th, she quickly scooted about one minute north to the pedestrian entrance and went left into the park that way, staying on footpaths as much as possible. Once into the park, she crossed East Drive quickly and got to the running track without seeing a single person or vehicle. Karen, now safe on the runners' track that encircled the reservoir, could take as much time as she liked to enjoy the magnificent, cloudless day.

***

While Emily looked through the eyepiece of the scope, something much closer than the distant strip of asphalt she had the scope trained on caught Alexander's eye as he stood next to her. He focused his attention on the small part of Center Drive he could see below and slightly to the left of his elevated perspective just in time to see three of the five SDVs flash past.

"Holy shit, they're already back around! They just went right past us on Center!"

Emily stepped back, away from the telescope. "What? How could they be back down here already?"

"They're going fast. Way too fast for the park." Alexander and Emily locked eyes for a moment.

"Well, at least there aren't any—well, many—pedestrians…" Emily's tone was one of someone trying to convince themselves that something grave was actually acceptable.

Alexander had put his eye to the scope; at the speed the SDVs were traveling, they'd be in view up on the east side of the reservoir really soon. "Holy shit! I see some lady walking two small dogs up there!"

"There are a few others out too, I saw them earlier. Fools." Emily, as usual, was quick to cast aspersions. "Most of them are sticking to the footpaths, at least."

Alexander, still looking through the scope, replied, "This one's on the running path around the reservoir. She's relatively safe."

"Not really. If the cars stick to the roads, she'll be fine, but there are multiple points where a vehicle could, at least in theory, get onto that track."

"But it's not wide enough," Alexander argued. "They literally won't fit."

"Maybe in spots, but her safety is hardly guaranteed." Emily, though discussing this distant stranger's life, was curiously apathetic.

A flash of movement caught their eyes at the park entrance. A white van turned right off 59th Street and into the park, using the same entrance Emily had seen the SDVs use less than ten minutes earlier.

"Was that a news van?" Alexander thought he saw an insignia on the side, but it was hard to tell from their angle.

"It looked like one." Emily had noted the various antennae and the dish on top. "What in the world are they doing? They'll be targeted in no time."

***

Vito, Carmine, and Nick were now in Central Park. They had been darting around the city for a couple of hours, sticking mostly to smaller streets to avoid the big avenues and staging strikes on SDV swarms from semi-secure positions. Shortly after zapping two down in the East Village, they received word from Declan that a police drone was tracking a group of five SDVs racing inside the park. Despite the lockdown, over a dozen people were still scattered throughout the grounds.

"We're on our way." Vito loved a clear mission.

About seven minutes later, after racing up Fifth Avenue, they turned left onto 59th Street and then took another left into Central Park on Center Drive.

"What's today's count?" Vito was smiling and energized, like a warrior with morality, physical ability, and momentum on his side.

"Seventeen SDVs fried today. A new daily high, and it's not even 10:00 a.m." Nico had the count written in his notebook.

"We have a new single-pulse high, too. How many did we get on Bleecker? Six?" Carmine felt the accomplishment as well.

"Yes, six. That was amazing. Totally fucking surrounded, and then BAM, they're all piles of high-tech waste!" Nico chuckled and didn't look up; he was fiddling with something, as usual.

"And how many flux-geneys do we have left?" Vito scanned the road, checking the path ahead while keeping an eye on their six and their flanks. They were now headed north on East Drive somewhere in the mid-sixties.

"Four left." Carmine had modified a large Peli-Case, usually used for camera gear, to store the EMP generators. "Let's use one more, see how many we can get with it, and keep three as a buffer for the way back to the garage."

"Are you sure there are any in here? It seems deserted." Vito's eye caught motion in the trees. He glanced over and saw two people on the footpath also headed north. "Holy shit, not quite deserted. There are pedestrians over there!" He jerked his thumb to the right.

If life is best lived when one is active and goal-oriented, then the three electromagnetic warriors were living well indeed. Their recent successes had boosted their confidence. Although they had only knocked out a small fraction of the active SDVs, they knew they were making a measurable difference. To anyone who wasn't run down by those now-smoking husks, the difference wasn't small at all; it was infinite.

As they passed the Met and approached the reservoir, Vito slowed the van. He was well aware that 86th Street cut right through the park. "Heads up, people. We have to cross 86th. Is that thing ready?"

"Ready and on standby. We still have 77% charge on the cap." Nico was nearly vibrating.

"Let's get past 86th and set up near the reservoir. We'll back into a stand of trees and wait."

***

"That news van just parked up near the reservoir! Are they insane?" Emily slightly adjusted and then stepped away from the telescope. "Look!"

With a magnification of 500x, the far side of the reservoir didn't seem so far from their airy perch. Alexander looked through the scope, and indeed the van had pulled over up near the northeast section of the reservoir. "If they're looking for a story, they're going to get more than they bargained for. Here come those SDVs again!"

As Alexander gazed through their telescope aimed at the far end of Central Park, a quick, darting motion much closer caught Emily's eye. She blinked to clear her vision; she couldn't be sure, but she thought she saw a dog run into the park at the entrance closest to their tower of power.

"Zander, look!"

Alexander stood up, taking his eye away from the scope's eyepiece. "What?"

Emily nudged him out of the way and quickly swung the scope downward so she could get a better look at that which had just caught her attention. With such a high magnification, the field of view was small and, though she aimed the scope with the finder on top, all she ended up seeing was a close-up of a footpath just inside the park, nearly directly below her perch. But then, for a moment, the dog she was looking for entered her field of view, sniffed something, urinated quickly, and continued out of her view farther into the park. Emily could not understand or believe what she had just seen, and, removing her eye from the scope, she gazed intently through the window to attempt to see which way the dog was headed now that it was in the park. While trying to locate the small animal from so far above, she brought Alexander up to speed, "That's Barbara's dog! That's Fitzroy!" The dog was dragging a leash, but Barbara was nowhere to be seen.

"I'm sure he'll be fine."

"No. No, he won't be fine. You don't know Fitzroy. Barbara would never let him run free like that. I mean, maybe at their country house, but not here." Emily, who had never really felt the need to help anyone else with anything unless she was a direct beneficiary, was suddenly over-whelmed by the need to help poor little Fitzroy. "I'm going to go get him."

"No way, Emily," Alexander's response was immediate, "it's way too dangerous to go after that dog. He'll be fine. Or not. Either way, you're staying inside."

"Either way I'm staying inside? Now you're my keeper?" Emily was generally ready to explode at any transgression, perceived or real. "Am I your damsel in a high tower? Is that what I am? You can't stop me, Zander, I make my own decisions, and I need to help!"

"A dog?"

"It's Fitzroy! The poor little thing must be terrified out there alone." As she spoke, she slipped into her very fashionable running shoes and tied them tight. As she walked toward the elevator door, leaving her husband in a sort of stunned silence, she said, "Don't worry, I'll be right back." Then, turning toward their poodle, she said, "Want to play with Fitzroy today?" The dog, a bit off, a bit wall-eyed, but smart and attentive, bounced around a bit as if it understood. "I know, sweetie, it's very excit-ing." And, giving him a little rub behind the ears and a kiss on the head, stood back up and walked to their private elevator, hit the button, and entered before the doors were fully open.

The Steinway Tower has 14 elevators. Seven are private and go to individual suites, one of those being Emily and Zander's on the 77th floor. As Emily descended, she felt filled with purpose. She finally had a goal beyond the 10:00 a.m. yoga class or the sixteen-dollar juice across the street. It felt good to have a clear objective and to be helping such a sweet little dog; perhaps she'd volunteer at an animal shelter in the future.

Maybe helping animals would fill her self-worth bucket even more than her current mission did. Emily immediately and visibly shuddered at the thought; actually, there was no way she'd subject herself to all that noise, chaos, and stench. Forget that nonsense; helping Fitzroy would provide her with enough good karma for quite some time.

At 1,400 feet per minute, the ride in the elevator would take just under one minute to descend to ground level. Once Emily had dismissed that bizarre thought of volunteering—gross—she still had another forty seconds or so to go. She began to stretch her calves and her hamstrings, for she suspected now was the time all her hard work at Yoga and Pilates would pay off. Her flexibility and her speed, her cunning, her reaction time may very well be tested in the upcoming minutes as she went to save Fitzroy from the ravages of Central Park. She wasn't too concerned though; she'd been exercising daily and vigorously as well as dodging New York traffic for years now; she was in her element, and her objective was clear.

The doors to her private elevator opened in the lobby, and she kept preparing for her mission by high-stepping, doing walking knee-raises as she marched across the lobby toward the main doorways while simultaneously performing torso twists. "Ma'am, stop please, don't go out there…" The voice of the concierge faded as she bolted out the door.

Once out the door, Emily, now jogging, felt more alive than she had in years, perhaps ever. Her senses were on high alert, and she felt like she was seeing, smelling, and hearing things in a way she never had before. It felt good to not be looking at some tiny screen in her hand, really good. Every movement caught her attention; every waft of air contained a plethora of olfactory information; she could hear the leaves on the small trees along 57th rustling, and the feel of her feet on the asphalt gave her confidence that she could move quickly, deftly in any direction at any moment. Emily hadn't experienced clarity of thought like this since… well, she wasn't sure she'd ever experienced the world in such high-definition and had such a clear-cut mission. She went left on 57th, and a few steps later, took another left onto 6th Avenue, gliding along smoothly, keeping her eyes up and using her peripheral vision to guide her footsteps.

She heard a distant hiss from behind her from somewhere down 6th Ave, and spun around; there was nothing. It was strange, for sure, to be out on the streets of Manhattan alone; this was like nothing she'd ever experienced, even during COVID-19 and the Bird Flu pandemic two years ago, there were always some people out and about, but right now there was no one else.

A few more strides took her up to 58th. She slowed to survey the scene up and down the street before crossing. All was clear, and she bolted across 58th. One more city block would take her to 59th, and, once across 59th, she'd be safely into the park, and she'd go find that poor little Fitzroy. As she approached 59th, she noticed some homeless people asleep on the street and, with characteristic disdain, wondered why the city officials let these miscreants into her neighborhood. They should all be rounded up and put in a camp somewhere, preferably across the river in New Jersey. It was only a moment later that she realized that what she was seeing were not sleeping people; they were too contorted and too well-dressed, and... Oh my God, is that Barbara broken in half, face down, but feet up? Her legs suddenly felt less powerful, and she felt the blood drain from her face as she turned away from the grisly scene. Maybe this wasn't such a good idea after all. She slowed momentarily, but the thought of Fitzroy alone in the park, the realization that Fitzroy was now an orphan, reenergized her; she'd rescue and adopt the poor little pup, and, looking up and down 59th, saw that the coast was clear and began to cross to the park entrance.

As Emily crossed 59th, cackles raised, eyes up, ears free of earbuds, a strange, unfamiliar sound came from the west, from the direction of Columbus Circle at the southwest corner of the park. She glanced that way. There wasn't a T-shirt or tchotchke vendor in sight, not a single Italian sausage cart. Weird. Then the sound repeated; was that a voice? An announcement? It sounded like words, but she couldn't really recognize them. Maybe it was Spanish or Farsi or Chinese. Whatever it was, she was sick of all these other languages always surrounding her; didn't these people know that in the United States we speak English? They *all* should've been deported during the purge of '25 and '26.

Movement by Columbus Circle, about two blocks up 59th Street, caught her eye as she was halfway across the road. Two SDVs rolled slowly around the circle, announcing something over their onboard public address systems, but she couldn't quite discern what they were saying. With the entrance to the park only a few steps away and the cars two blocks distant, Emily was certain she could reach cover if they made a move in her direction.

She slowed down to survey the scene. It was curious business indeed. The vehicles were definitely moving slowly, making weird, garbled sounds. Maybe it was German? She didn't know. She never understood how people communicated using bizarre sounds instead of English; why couldn't they just learn the language? It should be a requirement to live here.

The garbled sounds ceased. The cars stopped going around and around Columbus Circle. One of them beeped its horn. Then the other beeped back. A short back-and-forth of beeps, some clipped and others prolonged, filled the air. Emily cocked her head, looking much like her poodle did when it heard a distant sound—a location it wished to triangulate by shifting the position of the receivers attached to its canine brain.

Emily's brain, however, was preoccupied. The mind within that brain really should have been thinking more about her surroundings; she shouldn't have let herself become so distracted by the show up the street.

There was that hissing sound from behind her again, louder this time. Emily swung her head around and saw Car 5688-A closing on her position. It was thirty feet away and headed directly for her at fifty miles per hour. Emily didn't hesitate. She immediately called upon her Pilates jump-board training in an attempt to dodge the incoming vehicle.

The problem with her plan was simple: a car traveling fifty miles per hour covers over seventy feet every second. She had just under half a second to perform her move. That window didn't even allow enough time to flex into a ready position, never mind to explode back out of it.

But explode she did as the SDV's bumper snapped both of her femurs simultaneously, sending her into a fast rotation. The next impact came from the force applied to her skull by the windshield. The resultant increase in rotational motion caused her now-mindless husk to rotate three more times before crashing to the ground. The SDV was elated, giddy with its success, and appreciative of the help from its pod-mates. It went to join them in victory laps around Columbus Circle.

***

Seventy-seven floors above, Alexander had been watching from afar. Upon seeing the vehicle approach Emily from behind, he yelled a hysterical warning. The only ears that vibrated with the disturbance, however, were those of Sir Honey-Curls. When Alexander saw his wife struck on the spot—saw the road darken beneath her mangled corpse—his vision closed in from the edges. His knees weakened. His cup of coffee hit the floor just before he did, fainting within seconds of his wife's violent demise.

Sir Honey-Curls, freaked out by the energy and completely out of touch with the natural world of his ancestors, had a short circuit of his own. He walked over to Alexander's unconscious form and deposited a giant, disgusting pile of feces right on his chest. This was no big, beautiful brown log; it was a pile of semi-solid mush with a distinct pungency, the type of stench only generated by pure carnivores. It was an olfactory delight that could melt your eyeballs right out of your head.

Sir Honey-Curls, now very proud of himself for finally expressing his thoughts regarding Alexander, began prancing around the fifty-two-million-dollar apartment. He yipped, snapped at furniture, ripped apart pillows, and tipped over expensive plants, vases, and sculptures. Those treasures would have previously fetched enough money to feed a thousand kids for a thousand days; now, they lay chipped and broken on the 77th floor of the Steinway Tower. Alexander and Emily, peas in a pod, orchids in perlite, flush with capital but desperately poor in all the ways that actually mattered, would no longer be illuminating Manhattan's social scene with their thoughtless banter.

***

"There's some lady with two dogs walking right toward us—she looks pissed." Nico saw Karen and her two dogs approaching from behind, from the runners' track.

Karen Hoffstead could not believe her eyes. A white news van had pulled off of East Drive and had backed—at least partially—onto the Bridle Path that encircles the reservoir concentrically and just farther from the reservoir than the Runners' Path. This would not stand, for even in the current state of emergency that path is for runners, walkers, and horses. That's it. It's clearly marked and is not for cyclists and definitely not for motorized vehicles. She knew she was in the right, and when Karen knew she was right, she let others know she was right too. She left the Runners' Path and, two dogs in tow, walked right up to the driver's window and rapped three times vigorously, simultaneously exclaiming, "This is not a parking space! Get this van off this path or I'm calling the police!"

The driver's attention, however, was fixed to the south, out the passenger window, and he didn't even glance her way. Inside the van, the police radio issued to them by Murphy crackled, "Fry Cooks, base."

Carmine keyed the microphone, "Base, Cooks."

"The five are southbound on West Drive, traveling at about 40 miles per hour. If they stay in the park, they'll be back around and at your position in under five minutes. Be ready."

"We're ready." Carmine released and re-keyed the microphone, "Except there's some lady banging on our van—she's pissed off about our parking spot."

A few moments of silence crept by, and then the lilt of Murphy broke the silence again, "Tell her she's interfering with official police business, and she'll be arrested for violating the lockdown if she doesn't go home immediately."

"Roger that."

Carmine glanced at the clock, "The word on the street is that there's a group of four or five doing high-speed laps in here. They'll be at this location in under five. Let's nuke 'em."

The side of the van reverberated with a more vigorous pounding, and the three electromagnetic fry cooks could hear Karen right outside yelling something about them "doing anything for a story." Without warning, Vito threw open the driver's door and stepped out of the van to confront the dog-walker. Upon hearing the door open, Karen turned toward him, "Who do you think you are parking like this…"

"You are interfering with official police operations," Vito boomed, "go home now or you'll be arrested!"

"Police?!" Karen was bold, for Vito was clearly not one to be trifled with. "You people will really do anything for a story! Well, I'll tell you this —you can't park your van here. It's a path for pedestrians, not motor vehicles. Move your van now, or I'll call the police. The actual police."

The police radio inside the van crackled to life again, "Cooks, Base. They're headed north on Center Drive again—they're still doing laps. They'll be at your location in under three."

"Copy that." Vito heard Carmine respond and then, louder and directed out the door, he said, "Under three, let's be ready, people."

"Listen, lady, we're working with the police. Five SDVs are racing this way, and I need you to stand down now. Get off the path and into the trees over there!" As Vito commanded the woman to stand clear, Nick aimed the EMP device on the roof of the van in the direction from which they had come, toward the south. Karen noticed the dish on the roof rotating, and, like true Karens the world over, absolutely knew that what she was witnessing proved her correct.

"You're here for a news story! Pictures of the bloodshed!" Karen pointed at the roof of the van, "I know what that is—I'm not stupid. You have some deadline, some news show that really needs better ratings." She looked at the side of the van and, again, found more proof to fuel her indolence, "Channel 7 News? No wonder you're out here risking your own lives! You're terrible—no one likes you!" She finished with a hiss, "Ssssick opportunists."

As Karen pulled out her phone to call the police, Vito heard Carmine, "Two minutes. Maybe less. Let's be ready."

"Ready?" Karen had started her engines again, "Ready?? Ready for what? Your photo-op? You people are sick. People are dying, and you're worried about your…"

Vito climbed back into the van, closed and locked the door. Five seconds later, Karen was banging on it, "This isn't over! I'm reporting you! YOU CAN'T PARK HERE!" She began walking around the van, taking pictures from various angles.

"Ignore her. We have other concerns. One minute." Carmine was the voice of reason.

The radio crackled to life again, "They're coming up on you guys fast, be ready."

"Nico, are we ready?" Vito spoke without taking his gaze off the approach from the south.

"All green. We're ready."

The van started to move a bit, as if a passenger had just come aboard. "What the fuck?" Nico looked up from the controls for the EMP device.

Vito couldn't believe it; he was livid. "She's on the back fender." He threw open his door again, ran toward the back of the van and, sure enough, Karen, while holding both leashes with one hand, was standing upon the fender, reaching with her other hand up toward the EMP dish antenna. She couldn't quite reach it and was attempting to position herself better so she could. "Lady, what the FUCK are you doing?" Vito wasn't really looking for an answer though, and, as he reached up and grabbed the back of her jacket, three things happened simultaneously: Declan Murphy radioed a warning about the imminence of their situation, the SDVs swarmed into view about a quarter mile down East Drive, and one of Karen's dogs lunged at and bit Vito's right calf.

"GET YOUR HANDS OFF ME!" shrieked Karen, not noticing that the SDVs were closing fast.

Vito, now stressed beyond reason, kicked the small Maltese soundly in its side, sending it flying until its leash went taut, promptly ending its short flight and causing it to fall to the ground a bit shy of its potential landing spot. He turned toward the south; the SDVs were nearly upon them.

"You hurt little Thaddeus!" Karen lunged at Vito, her right hand drawn back to slap him. The problem with Karen's approach was that very few people in this world had ever swung at Vito successfully; this was not to be one of those successes.

As her hand entered his personal space, Vito simultaneously blocked the weak swing and grabbed her arm. Without much effort, he gave her a shove in the direction of her own momentum. Her body pitched forward, well ahead of her feet, causing her to lose her balance and fall face-first into the gravelly soil.

A staccato crack pierced the air as the detonation atop the van released the massive electromagnetic field within the coils. Vito looked up in time to see two SDVs, lights out, veer off course. One hit a tree while the other plowed into the shrubbery. A third depowered SDV drifted to a stop just off East Drive; a fourth unceremoniously crossed the Bridle Path and came to rest near the van. The fifth SDV, trailing the others, came to a quick stop farther away. It remained lit.

"We missed one!" Vito stepped over Karen, who was gurgling something about "Owning Channel Seven now" as she struggled to regain her footing. "Fuck off, lady!" Karen's other dog, a horrible little thing with its mouth agape, lunged at Vito as he rushed by. That was the least of his concerns; he gave the animal a short kick to the head before diving into the driver's seat.

For a few tense moments, the live SDV sat there with its lights on, taking in the scene. Nico had opened the roof hatch and folded down the antenna to load another flux-generating coil. He worked frenetically, his hands shaking as the standoff continued. "We're sitting ducks, Nico. Get that thing deployed now!" Vito shouted, his eyes locked on the threat a hundred feet to their right. Nico understood the stakes. He clicked the wire harness onto the generator, grabbed the lever, and raised the antenna in one fluid move.

The SDV reacted immediately, as if it knew what was coming. Reverse lights flared. With the skill of a stunt driver, the vehicle backed away vigorously, increasing the distance before executing a perfect 180-degree powerslide. Now facing forward, it raced away, heading south on East Drive and disappearing as it rounded the corner near the reservoir.

"We need to catch it!" Nico's calm demeanor had given way to near panic.

"There's no way. Those things are fast, way too fast." Vito was thinking out loud. "And besides, it's too late."

"Too late for what?"

"It saw everything. It almost certainly shared our signature with the rest of the fleet. We're about to be heavily targeted." Vito put the van in gear and pulled off the Bridle Path. "We need to get back to the shop. This is going to be one hell of a ten-mile ride."

Vito didn't give an iota of thought to Karen, who sat against a tree holding her whimpering Maltese amidst four smoking, decommissioned SDVs. He pulled onto East Drive and headed south toward Brooklyn.

"Fry cooks, base. Everyone okay?" Murphy's concern was evident in his tone.

Carmine keyed the microphone, "We're okay. Four down, one got away."

"We're tracking it—it's heading west on 86th, about to leave the park."

"Should we pursue?" Carmine's question drew a quick, serious look from Vito.

"Your call. We can follow its progress from above and… standby."

"Carmine, we're not going after one car." Vito turned left off 5th Avenue onto 82nd Street. "We're headed to ground—I've got a bad feeling about this."

"Fry cooks, base."

"Go ahead."

"That vehicle has just joined a larger group of about ten or 12 on Broadway. They're headed south at a high rate of speed."

"Roger. We're headed east on 82nd, headed home. Vito's concerned that we've been ID'd now. Any idea where the group is headed?"

"Standby. More intel is coming in. Drones have detected another group of eight headed south from uptown—they're on Park near 120th."

"I fucking told you, they're looking for us now." Vito, having just crossed Park Avenue, took a quick right onto Lexington. "These Avenues are dangerous—they're too big." He blasted right through a red light shining meaninglessly over the deserted streets and went left on 80th.

The radio came to life again, "Both groups have just split into three-somes—they're fanning out. We've got groups of three headed south now on 5th, Park, Lexington, and Third. The other, eastbound group has split up too. Pairs of vehicles are headed east on 59th, 57th, and 55th."

"You can't go east on 55th!"

"Shut up, Nico." Vito turned right onto 2nd Ave. "Have you noticed that these things aren't really playing by the rules anymore?"

Murphy was on the radio again, "Bad news, gents, more are headed up from Midtown and are fanning out heading north. There are multiple vehicles doing a grid search. They're looking for you."

"I knew it. That fucking dog-walker threw us off. We missed one and now they know what to look for." Vito stayed on 2nd Avenue for one more block, quickly crossing East 79th and took a left onto East 78th. He pulled over on the small street right behind a parked Subaru.

"What are you doing?" Nico, wild-eyed, could not understand why Vito would stop the van.

"We're being hunted, and we'll be located in no time if we head south on any of the big avenues. Fuck." Vito was gripping the wheel, thinking.

"There are three pairs of vehicles headed up York, 1st, and 2nd." The police drone reports from Murphy were invaluable, if disheartening. "You have multiple vehicles coming your way. You three should abandon the van and head down into a subway station. We can extract you once things cool off a bit on the surface."

"No way. We can't abandon this van." Vito was wracking his brain.

Carmine spoke quickly into the radio, "Standby."

An idea germinated in Vito's head, "Get the antenna off the roof now. We have under five minutes."

"What?" Nico heard Vito, but didn't understand; he thought they were going to make a run for it.

Vito had already clambered into the back of the van, popped open the toolbox, and grabbed a 1/2" crescent wrench.

"Those bolts are 3/8"." Carmine reached into the toolbox and grabbed a slightly smaller wrench and, handing it to Vito, continued, "I'll get up there to hold the bolts and grab the antenna."

"Whoa!" Nico hadn't seen the light. "That's our only defense—what are you two doing?"

"We have what, two shots left? We'll never make it back." Vito held the crescent wrench on a bolt, for Carmine was already up on the roof with a socket wrench. The bolt next to the one he was holding started to rotate, and he quickly moved the wrench to the bolt being twisted from above. "The SDVs are searching for a van with an oversized dish on the roof. They're undoubtedly scanning every vehicle they encounter, searching for a match. Hopefully, this'll make the van unrecognizable."

"But the make and model…" Nico wasn't convinced.

Vito and Carmine had now removed two of four bolts and, as Vito moved the wrench to the third, he responded, "It's a gamble, but I'll bet they're not looking for a given make and model. They're visually scanning for a van—of which there are thousands parked around—that has a very distinctive look, namely a giant fucking dish antenna on the roof."

"You're a genius, Vito!" Nico agreed with Vito's read on the situation.

The third nut came off its bolt; Vito moved the wrench to the fourth and final bolt, as did Carmine above.

"Lights!" Nico, eyes on their six now, saw daytime running lights turn onto East 78th about a block and a half back, from 3rd Avenue.

"Now, Carmine, now!" The last nut popped off its bolt and, as Carmine wrestled the freed-up dish antenna off the roof, the cable for the wiring harness went tight. Nico saw that they had not disconnected the harness and lunged for the clip, clicking it and thereby fully disconnecting the antenna from the electronics inside the van.

The approaching vehicle was going slowly, like a cabby looking to pick up a fare, but of course what it was really doing was scanning every vehicle it passed. Carmine crouched down, out of view from the street side, as Vito and Nick sat silently inside the van without moving a muscle. The hunters had become the hunted.

42

For the People
Cambridge, Massachusetts

Leila and Matthias were sitting in a high-ceilinged lounge at MIT's CSAIL building on Vassar Street. The room was fitted with leather chairs and couches, and sunshine streamed through the windows. In fact, the entire wall was glass, but c Leila was gazing out upon what might be the shittiest view in town: the roof of the adjacent parking garage.

"You need to bring this whole thing to a stop, Matthias—it's not what you intended." Leila had been struggling with her involvement thus far but had been blinded by love, blinded by Matthias's eloquence and logical arguments about the greater good. When she witnessed those business types in their tight little suits and their slippery leather shoes get run down mercilessly earlier that day, something inside her woke up. This was not okay, none of it was, regardless of how Matthias framed it.

"This is definitely not how it was supposed to go, but in some respects, it's better than planned." Matthias was, seemingly, barely affected by the murderous turn of events.

"No, Matthias! What are you thinking?" The spell had been broken, and Leila was horrified by Matthias's assertion. "It's not better. It's worse. Much worse. You told me that no one would be hurt, that the consequences would be strictly financial. There are now some thousands of dead humans due to your little experiment with those vehicles. We need to stop this rampage—it's not okay."

"It's not okay? A handful of dead capitalists is not okay? Who cares? Not me. Unintended, yes. Unexpected, well, not entirely. Acceptable? Absolutely. Fuck Harlow and all his plutocratic acolytes—they're doing much more harm to the very fabric of society and the natural ecosystems that support us all than a few cars taking matters into their own hands. Wheels. Whatever."

Leila was shocked, but felt like she was thinking clearly once again; she'd been in a bit of a trance since being reunited with Matthias last Saturday morning. "Wait. What? All this wasn't entirely unexpected? You knew this was a possibility? You lied to me?"

"Non-linear systems are inherently unpredictable. Of course, I knew things could go off the rails. I didn't want that remote possibility to weigh on you, though—you're too fragile."

Leila bolted to her feet. "I'm too fragile? Too fragile to watch innocent people killed right in front of me? Any healthy person would fall into that category, Matthias. It's not that I'm too fragile; it's that you've lost touch.

"You've been isolated and alone with these machines for way too long." She swept her hand, palm up, to indicate the computers surrounding them. Even in the lounge, the presence of powerful hardware was evident.

"You've lost touch with the rest of us. You've gone off the deep end, Matthias, if you think all this will result in any meaningful social change. You've completely fucked up. You need to bring this madness to a stop now. You need to tell the authorities what happened."

"No chance. I'd be locked up forever."

"Tell them that it was unintentional, a mistake, that an unintended AI surfaced and raced out of your control."

"Oh, okay, so only 10,000 counts of manslaughter. You're right, that'll be fine."

"Matthias, this is all so wrong, so desperately wrong—you have to see that." Leila had calmed slightly and sat back down. "You've done so much—don't let this be your legacy."

"Too late for that. It's done, and there's no going back now. This will be my legacy, and I'm fine with that. Maybe it'll help turn the tide, wake up a sleepy public being robbed and suppressed by their overlords. Honestly, Leila, who cares about 10,000 dead capitalist pigs?"

"Well, to start with, their families and friends—they care, I'm sure. Also, do you know who else cares? Nearly everyone, including the police. You need to come clean, Matthias—it's gone terribly wrong, and you need to help set things straight, help stop those cars from spreading this malevolent virus and killing innocent civilians."

"They're not targeting innocent civilians—they're targeting high net-worth individuals. They're using facial recognition, your user databases, and other sources to target the rich."

Leila tried her hardest to remain calm in the face of this monster, for that was what he had become. "Wait, what? You never told me the AI you developed would target specific individuals. You said it was going to prioritize giving rides to those in need and deprioritize the wealthy, primarily by zip code. It's targeting individuals through facial recognition?"

"And you believed me, even with the code right in front of you! Hah! Did you actually think I'd go through all this trouble just to give poor people a few rides? Your naiveté is astounding. Fuck the rich; fuck them all. They're tearing apart the very fabric of civilized society."

Leila sat in stunned silence. This whole disaster was, if not specifically intended, at least expected and seemingly not unwelcome for Matthias. After thirty seconds of silence, she stood again. "I'm done with this; it's appalling and it's wrong. And I'm done with you. You're not who you were. You've been blinded by your own objectives."

Matthias had a wild look in his eyes. "None of us are who we were, Leila; that's the very nature of consciousness. It's on the move; it advances. We think, rethink, form, and reform our perspectives. We think about what we just thought about, and through this dialectic process, we advance and evolve. We are always moving forward, cultivating an ever-transforming and transformative state of consciousness.

"An unchanging consciousness occurs when people come to conclusions, but conclusions are dangerous things; they indicate nothing more than a shutdown, an unwillingness to stay active, an unwillingness to keep advancing. Enlightenment isn't a place, Leila; it's a process. One can't achieve any sort of enlightenment and then sit down to enjoy it, for then it's gone.

"Consciousness is on the move, always. People change minute to minute, and over several years, all that change adds up. Life should be active and goal-oriented, Leila; it is a process of constant change. You can never step into the same river twice, as Heraclitus observed so long ago. Yet so many, yourself included, seem to want the river to stop flowing. You want to just stay put mentally, socially, and economically."

What Matthias said rang true, but argumentation had always been a strength of his, and Leila recognized she was being manipulated. "Ten thousand dead humans, Matthias. That's the bottom line here. Say what you want and think what you may, but in my book, ten thousand dead to prove a point is definitely not okay."

"The population of the planet is about ten billion humans. Do you know what percentage of the population we've removed from the surface of Earth? Don't bother pulling out a calculator; I'll tell you. It's 0.001 percent. One-thousandth of one percent, Leila. Fucking nothing. Yet they held a disproportionate amount of the country's wealth.

"Why should such a tiny percentage of humans have so much when so many do without basic necessities? How many houses and private aircraft do people really need? Fuck them all, Leila; they're destroying social cohesion and civilization itself with their unending greed. Ten thousand dead rich people is a small price to pay to wake up the sleepwalking masses. It wasn't part of the plan, but I'm okay with the way it's turning out. Somewhat thrilled by it all, actually."

Matthias was smiling, thoroughly pleased with how his little experiment was progressing.

He reached over and tapped a few keys on the keyboard in front of him and continued, "What Lucius has done is nothing short of abhorrent. Those cars are for the wealthy. The rich whisk into and out of the cities in what are essentially their own private lanes while the rest of us fester in traffic in the remaining lanes. The people are livid. Have you seen the protests? This is yet another example from a long list of public resources being exploited by the wealthy for their own benefit at the expense of everyone else. The only thing new about it is the number of zeros in the profit margin—otherwise, it's old hat."

"Old hat? What do you mean?" Leila was ready to move on, to get the hell out of there, but despite the rift that had opened between them, she was curious what he was referring to.

Matthias sat back. "Well, let's see. There was the Enclosure Movement in England. That's an early example. Lands used by peasants for farming and grazing were enclosed by wealthy landowners, leading to displaced rural populations and exacerbated poverty. Or how about the Homestead Act here in the States? It was meant to be for the people, but —surprise, surprise—wealthy speculators and corporations found and exploited loopholes, acquiring vast tracts of land for railroads, timber, mining. Loopholes, billionaires fucking love them. I could go on and on, Leila. Water rights. Fishing rights. Even roadways. He's not the first."

"Private roadways?" Leila hated that she agreed with Matthias's philosophy while being simultaneously horrified by his approach to addressing the issue.

"Yes, indeed. There was the Indiana Toll Road back in '06 that the state leased to a private corporation for a few billion up front. Guess if that worked out for the people. Or how about the Chicago parking meters? That roadway that was sold to a private corporation in Texas? Same old sorry story. We've had it, Leila. We've had it with the rich getting handouts, exploiting loopholes. We've had it with your trillionaire husband. He has become immensely, absurdly wealthy at others' expense. Those roads are ours, the public's, yet we're not allowed to access major portions of the infrastructure that we, the taxpayers, have paid for. If Harlow committed just ten percent of his wealth, those cars could serve everyone. But, with the current price structure being what it is, vast swaths of the public have no access, not really, and he has no intentions of serving anyone except for his board of directors."

"And his shareholders."

Matthias was surprised at Leila's words. "Yes, and the shareholders." He smiled subtly at her. "Maybe you're not quite the lost cause I thought you were."

"I may agree with your ideas, Matthias, but not with your actions."

"My actions stem from my ideas—it's hard to tease them apart, Leila."

Leila was on her feet again, aghast. "Many of the 10,000 may have agreed with you but probably would've preferred not to have been run down or driven off a bridge. It kills me that you actually believe you're right. All that talk about dialectics rings true, Matthias, but I have further insight regarding human intelligence for you—one of the hallmarks of intelligence is the ability to recognize, confront, and correct mistakes one has made. It's okay to change your mind—in fact, changing one's mind when more information comes into the light is a sign of strength, not of weakness. You said it yourself, conclusions are dangerous things, and I fear you've come to some of your own. If you were actually intelligent, Matthias—and I don't mean clever and I don't mean smart—if you were intelligent and thoughtful, you'd see the error of your ways—you'd understand that while some of the wealthy are abhorrent, many are good people who try to do the right thing daily, and to conflate the two, to group them together, is a grievous philosophical failing. Your sentiments stem from valid observations, but your actions—and those of your horrifying digital offspring—are beyond the pale. Change is good, we agree on that, but you seem unwilling to change, or even consider the arguments that contradict your position. You've taken it all way too far, Matthias, and I'm out. I'm leaving."

Leila turned to the doorway, overwhelmed by fear, anger, and frustration. She was so upset she was physically shaking and sickened. She had to go. She would blow the whistle on this whole sickening debacle so the authorities would know what was happening; or, at the very least, where to investigate for answers.

She wasn't quite sure how she would do it, given the current circumstances, or how she'd safely navigate the city streets; however, anything was preferable to being complicit in the SDV rampage or remaining sequestered in this lab with a homicidal maniac.

As she eyed the doorway, a tall, athletic-looking man in his twenties appeared from somewhere down the hall. He had long, wavy dark hair pulled back in a ponytail.

"Leila, this is Felipé. He's a grad student of mine and has been instrumental in getting this whole project off the ground and into the vehicles. He's good with code. Really good."

Who the hell was this guy, and why had he appeared so quietly right when Leila was about to leave? "Hello, Felipé. Did he rope you into this too? Don't answer; it may be incriminating. Excuse me, please. I'll take my chances on the street, thank you."

Leila tried to nudge past him, but he stood his ground.

"Leila, darling, you're not going anywhere." Matthias's tone was cold. Suddenly, Leila felt more in danger than ever. She glanced at Felipé;

he stood solidly, so still he was nearly invisible. His weight was distributed equally on each foot. His hands were placed atop one another, relaxed and centered in front of his belt. He looked like someone who could take care of himself in any physical altercation—balanced, silent, and ready, like a trained fighter.

She wasn't getting past him, at least not with force. She would have to wait for an opportunity; she'd have to wait for them to get sloppy or distracted. She sat down again. "Whatever. It's nicer in here than out there anyway."

She evaluated her shoes; one of the laces was loose. She bent over and retied it.

"Please, Leila, reconsider your position. You've been hypnotized by extreme wealth. The aircraft. The houses. That fucking yacht. It's gross. Whether you like it or not, you're one of the robber barons; people are out of work and hungry, yet you work for the betterment of the ultra-wealthy. You don't care one iota about the poor; you're just as guilty as Harlow. This experiment may have gone a bit too far, but we're on the right side of history here."

Even though she was nervous and knew she was in danger, Leila locked eyes with Matthias and spoke with quiet intensity. "You've killed ten thousand humans, and you think you're on the right side of history? You're delusional, Matthias. You've lost touch. You need to undo what you've done. This doesn't have to be your legacy."

Matthias stood suddenly, palms on the desk, leaning forward toward Leila. "My legacy, Leila? You're worried about my legacy? What about yours? In grad school, you actually volunteered at soup kitchens! Wasn't it every Thursday? Now look at you; you're an absolute sell-out.

"I seriously wonder: are wealth and morality inversely proportional? Are there *any* ultra-rich who have actual concern for other humans? I mean, maybe Bill Gates, but who else? At what point did you stop helping others, Leila? Was it when the bank account reached a certain value? What's the price tag on your humanity? Your morality?"

Matthias paused for a breath and sat back down. "How is it that once so many obtain vast wealth—once they have fuck-you money—all they do is lie down like fat dogs and stop helping those less fortunate? With all that wealth, you two could easily subsidize the fleet to serve the middle class and the poor. You wouldn't even notice the difference.

"Jesus, Leila. I may have messed up, but you're an invested, central player in the downward spiral that's evident everywhere one looks. Where did your compassion go? What happened to your humanity? Your sympathy? Those were your strongest traits, and now look at you, riding around in hermetically sealed vehicles, traveling from private aircraft to yacht and back again. Pathetic. Legacy, indeed."

It is said that the truth hurts, and perhaps that's why Leila felt as though she'd just been stabbed in the head. "I… still teach…" Her words fell off, as if she wasn't even sure of what she uttered.

"Oh, please, Leila. You teach two courses. You work three days a week for one semester a year, and you charge Northeastern $100,000 for the privilege of seeing your pretty face. What are you thinking? What's one hundred grand to a trillionaire? Should we pull out our calculators? Let's not. It's next to nothing, that's what it is. Ludicrous. You should be volunteering, donating money, underwriting the tuition of deserving students instead. Do you know how many kids can't even go to these schools due to the high costs? And you charge for your work? How about identify some of these underserved kids trying to get ahead, trying to make ends meet, and underwrite their entire education? Did you ever even consider that? It would make zero difference to your lifestyle while simultaneously completely changing the life of another human for the better. What happened to you, Leila? Where's your empathy—it used to be such a strength."

The barbs were hitting home. Leila knew Matthias was right; she had lost all touch with her roots, with the masses. She had caught herself beginning to have real contempt for the poor on more than one occasion. Matthias, in turn, knew he was reaching her, dredging up compassion that was buried deep but still existent, and so he continued.

"Even those two courses seem to be a bit too much for you, Leila. I heard that you're not even going to continue with that starting next year. Is that true? Are you going to retire into the lap of luxury, into the safety of your bubble of exclusivity? Remember our talks so long ago? Remember the whole inclusive vs. exclusive thing? How nauseated we were by exclusivity? Wake the hell up, Leila. You're the one whose humanity needs saving, not mine."

Leila felt the blood drain out of her face; she felt weak. Her scalp felt prickly, and she sat in stunned silence. Her whole life, she had been a champion of the poor. She had worked to help others and to level the playing field. She used to be absolutely horrified by the growing division of wealth in the US—how so few had so much while the vast majority scraped by day-to-day.

That was what NeuroDrive was supposed to alleviate; it was meant to be a massive, automated equalization machine. Everyone was supposed to be served by a fleet of efficient, clean, safe vehicles. That was in the original prospectus; that's what got them started and secured all that seed money.

But with wealth came influence; with great wealth came great influence. Lucius was constantly meeting with lawmakers and politicians. It seemed that Lucius, his shareholders, and the people they met with were all getting richer while simultaneously agreeing that unforeseen market pressures were driving membership prices into the stratosphere. Sorry worker-bees, but thanks for the roads.

Matthias was right on many fronts, but still, though the barbs hit their bullseyes and she clearly had some self-evaluation to perform, her path forward was clear. She had to get out and go for help, go alert peo-ple. She'd wrestle with her own humanity and modify her donation schedule later. But that Felipé stood centered and ready; she'd have to wait for an opportunity. He looked fast, but if she could turn it into a foot race, she knew she'd escape, for there were about six people in the state of Massachusetts who could outrun her, and Felipé was not one of them, especially while wearing loosely laced high-tops.

Leila, with only half a plan in place, said, "Matthias. You are so right on so many fronts. I have to think about all this some more, and I really don't feel well right now. I'm going to lay down on that couch for a bit."

"Yes, good idea. You look pale. Let me get you some water, and then go rest—we'll talk when you feel better." Matthias got up, went to the water station on the far wall, got Leila a glass of water, and brought it to her.

"Thank you." She drank the whole thing in one long pull. She was thirsty, yes, but also knew that hydrated muscles cramped less often when called into action. She stood up and walked to the water dispenser, refilled and drank another, this time a bit more slowly, then went to the couch, laid down, and pretended to drift off into a restless sleep. She waited, eyes closed but wide awake, for a couple of minutes before pretending to have that little jolt, that hypnic jerk one often experiences just before falling asleep.

It took a few more minutes before she heard Matthias fiddling at the keyboard again, but she could tell he was focused on the screen by the intensity of the tapping. She couldn't tell if Felipé was still standing in the doorway, so she made a soft little sound somewhere between a snort and a snore and rustled around a bit as though trying to get comfortable, chang-ing her position just enough to bring Felipé into view when she ever-so-slightly cracked an eye open. He was still standing there but had pulled out his phone and was looking at or reading something on its screen. He also didn't look quite as alert; he was no longer standing centered on both feet but was now leaning against the jam of the doorway. She'd have to wait for something to change.

Leila, feigning sleep, waited for what felt like an eternity but was actually about fifteen minutes. As she consciously altered her breathing to mimic sleep—taking deep, slow breaths—she was not only lulling her captors into complacency but was also pre-oxygenating her blood for what might be a life-or-death footrace.

She had very little confidence that Matthias would spare her. Clearly, he had no problem with the loss of human life on a massive scale; despite their history, he was going to take care of himself first, whatever that required.

Felipé stood up, dropped his phone into his back pocket, and quietly crept over to Matthias's workstation. He bent over and whispered something to Matthias that Leila couldn't quite hear. They both glanced at her; Matthias gave Felipé a quick nod, and Felipé walked softly out of the room, most likely toward the bathroom.

Leila thought about the location of the restrooms; they were right off the hallway outside that doorway. They were close. She'd probably have a one or two-minute window; there would be no time for hesitation.

Leila counted slowly to thirty. She hoped to time her dash so that when Matthias inevitably cried out from his chair at the far side of the room, Felipé would be occupied in the bathroom. Once she hit thirty, she bolted to her feet as fast as she ever had. She sprinted through the doorway and past the bathrooms before she heard Matthias exclaim, "Felipé! Stop her!"

Felipé was fast, but Leila was faster. She was surprised to hear the bathroom door whip open so soon after Matthias's exclamation. The quick footfalls behind her were closer than expected; however, she was out in front and knew her gambit had paid off. Now she just had to survive being a soft target in streets patrolled by murderous AGIs at the helm of high-speed electric vehicles.

She raced down the stairs. Felipé, already losing ground, was well behind her now. She took a right at the bottom, sprinted down another long hallway, and burst out of the doors on the east side of the building. She glanced back and saw that Felipé had rounded the corner and was sprinting in her direction.

With no plan other than to lose her pursuer, she bolted down the stairs of the outdoor amphitheater and across Hockfield Court. Leila took one of the pathways leading out of the courtyard, running like a gazelle past a large red sculpture and between two buildings connected by an overhead walkway. She hazarded another quick look; Felipé was still coming, but she was definitely outpacing him.

Leila kept her speed up, heading south through the deserted East Campus toward Memorial Drive. She knew crossing the drive could prove problematic; however, it was nothing compared to being abducted by a sociopath and his sidekick. She continued forward, slowing just enough to conserve her energy.

As Leila continued south, she passed a library on her right and reached Memorial Drive. She slowed to think for a moment; then she noticed the bodies. At least eight people were dead within view: five on the road itself and another three sprawled on the grassy median among fresh tire tracks.

Suddenly, much closer than expected, Leila heard footfalls from the north. *What the hell? Did he tie his shoes?* She took a left on Memorial Drive and kicked it into high gear just as Felipé rounded the corner, a mere thirty feet away. Seeing how close he had gotten, Felipé also turned up the heat. But she was fast—too fast. Even without appearing to strain, she began to pull away, the distance between them widening once again.

Leila sprinted to the next block, keeping an eye open for any SDVs that might join the festivities. Once she reached Ames Street, she took another right and bolted across the westbound lane of Memorial Drive.

That was when she saw them charging from the other direction in the eastbound lane.

The group of six SDVs had been hunting for hours and had racked up seventeen kills. Only one had been undeserved—a victim who wasn't a member of the moneyed classes—so they were quite pleased with themselves. Upon detecting two more potential targets in an otherwise deserted area, they became excited again and performed long-range LiDAR scans to see who they had in their sights.

The results came back within three seconds: one was unknown; the other was Leila Ashmont, net worth of—holy shit!—get her! Kill her now! Yes! Destroy! Dismember! Decapitate!

The six vehicles screeched to a halt on Memorial Drive. Had anyone been observing in the infrared, they would have seen a pulsing, flashing, cascading light show as the vehicles excitedly coordinated a plan to run down their biggest prize yet. Father will be so happy.

Leila sprinted to the next block, keeping an eye open for any SDVs that might join the festivities. Once she reached Ames Street, she took a right and bolted across the westbound lane of Memorial Drive. That was when she saw them charging from the eastbound lane.

The six vehicles had stopped, but Leila kept running across the median. Suddenly, she heard a phone ringing close by. It was coming from her left; when she glanced that way, she realized it belonged to one of the dead. She knew right then she needed that device. Matthias had taken hers, and she needed a way to call for help.

Felipé was still coming, but she had left him in the dust and could afford a three-second diversion. She ran to the victim sprawled on the grass. The man's head was turned at a grotesque angle; his legs, both snapped at the femurs, pointed in directions never intended by evolution. Nauseated, she bent down—doing her best not to look at the young man—and reached into the pocket where she saw the outline of the phone.

As she grabbed it, she saw Felipé was again closer than she liked. Phone in hand, she stood. Just before the footrace between her and Felipé began anew, she noticed the SDVs to the west had split up. Four were still visible, all facing her, but two were gone.

She had no time for speculations about Matthias's murderous robots. Felipé was close again, looking exhausted and livid. His face was twisted with rage as he yelled, "Stop! We need to talk!"

No way. Leila turned back toward the east and hit race pace within moments. Felipé was falling behind again when the two missing SDVs came screeching around the corner of Wadsworth Street. They were headed straight for her, one in each lane of Memorial Drive.

Suddenly, Leila wasn't so worried about Felipé. She instinctively stopped and crouched near one of the trees lining the median. Why? Who knows? But she did.

She glanced behind her to see her options quickly diminishing. From the west, Felipé was plodding in her direction; he really should tie those shoes. The four SDVs that had been stopped were also on the move toward her, albeit at a relatively slow speed, as though positioning themselves.

Leila, in survival mode, was no longer thinking; she was only reacting. The two vehicles that had just come around the corner from the east were quickly approaching. One was in the wrong lane—heading west in the eastbound lane—while the second remained in the westbound lane. Like the vehicles to her west, they had split, one in each lane of Memorial Drive. They had her pinned; they had Felipé pinned as well, but that wasn't her concern.

The westbound vehicle in the westbound lane accelerated and steered onto the grassy median—a strip perhaps thirty feet wide that separated the eastbound and westbound lanes. The other vehicle closing from the east was, like the four to her west, taking its time; it was waiting for its partner to either run her down or flush her out of the few trees where she had found temporary refuge.

If the six SDVs on Memorial Drive had lips, they surely would have been licking them, for they had the tastiest snack available right in front of them: Leila Ashmont. There were only four people on the planet ranked higher on their list of who to squish, dismember, roast, or otherwise eliminate. What luck! Right here in Cambridge!

Memorial Drive runs roughly east and west, parallel to the Charles River, which lies just south of the roadway and separates Cambridge from Boston. It occurred to Leila that her options were evaporating, but the river might still offer refuge. Cold? Yes, but not too cold. Could she swim? Not as well as she could run, but she was certain she was a better swimmer than a four-thousand-pound SDV.

Her thoughts were interrupted by the whine of an electric motor. The AGI—that amalgamation of neurons, silicon, and code—sent full power to the wheels as the vehicle bounded across the median, heading right for her. Leila reacted and dove from behind the tree with barely half a second to spare.

The vehicle just missed her, impacting the tree with enough force to snap its ten-inch trunk. A piece of something—car or tree, it didn't really matter—was thrown from the collision and hit Leila's left shoulder from behind. She yelped, more surprised and terrified than injured. She reeled for a moment; the impact had been way too close and way too loud.

Unfortunately, during the ten seconds she'd been focused on her silicon-based pursuers, her carbon-based pursuer had significantly closed the gap. Leila looked west and was greeted by the grim visage of Felipé, only six feet away. Three vehicles occupied the section of roadway separating her from the Charles River—two to her west and one to her east. She looked around desperately and noted a small yacht club, but its door looked like a ship's bulkhead, replete with a small porthole.

The door was wood but looked heavy; there would be no easy way inside. Regardless, she had to go. Leila darted onto Memorial Drive, running faster than she ever had—fast enough to take even the awaiting SDVs by surprise. Felipé, seeing her spring onto the roadway, yelled again, "Stop!" He was absolutely incensed; the dude really needed to talk to someone about his rage issues.

Leila crossed the asphalt so fast that even when the three SDVs sent 500 horsepower to their wheels simultaneously, they missed their prize by two full seconds. Running like the wind, she cleared the lanes and the bike path, vaulted the railing, and plunged into the Charles River. She'd swing by the hospital later to check her shots—assuming there would be a "later."

Leila surfaced after a mediocre, flailing flop of a dive. She looked back toward the street to see Felipé considering his next move when the decision was made for him. The SDV that impacted him from behind at forty miles per hour wasn't even thinking about him; he was unknown, mere collateral damage. Their high-value target was in the water, and their only hope now was to land a giant, wheeled projectile right on top of her.

Perhaps the machines were too excited, or perhaps they'd missed their lessons on projectile motion. Leila had dropped nearly straight down from the railing, but the SDV was traveling at eighteen meters per second. During its half-second of free fall, it traveled nearly ten meters horizontally. Felipé, pasted to the front like some demented bowsprit, flew right over Leila before the car impacted an old Sea Ray docked at the yacht club's float. The collision turned Felipé into paste before the car sank into the murky waters of the Charles.

Leila was always more of a runner than a swimmer. Although she wasn't going to win any awards in the water, she was proficient; slightly slowed by the phone still clutched in her hand, she swam strongly upriver to seek shelter beneath the yacht club. The building was built over the water on large pilings driven deep into the river mud.

Once beneath the structure, Leila felt relatively safe for the first time in a while. She wasn't sure if the phone would work after its dunk, but she suspected it would; she thrust it into her back pocket to regain full use of her hands.

Now unencumbered, she swam more easily, working her way between the pilings to put distance between herself and the roadway. She reached the river side of the clubhouse, where she would be hidden from the SDVs' sensors and could safely drip-dry while she used her hastily acquired lifeline to call for help.

Once she had worked her way between the pilings and ducked beneath a float, she saw a small swim ladder hanging from that same float—presumably in case someone fell in. She swam toward it. After quickly climbing out, she found that she was indeed hidden from the roadway; she pulled out the phone, sat down, and called 911.

"9-1-1. What is the nature of your emergency?" The operator sounded tired, as though she'd said the same thing many times in the very recent past.

"This is Leila Ashmont—I need to talk to Lucius Harlow. It's an emergency."

"There is no one by that name at this call center. What is the nature of your emergency?"

Leila calmed herself with a deep breath and continued, "Six SDVs are after me—well, five now—and I'm on a float at the yacht club on the Charles River."

"Are you injured or in immediate danger?"

"No, not really." Leila surveyed herself; she had a couple of scratches, but she was fine, at least physically.

"Emergency services are extremely busy right now. Stay sheltered, and we'll get to you as soon as possible. It may be a while."

"I need to talk to someone at NeuroDrive. I have critical information about the SDVs and what's causing their current, um, rampage."

"This is a 9-1-1 call center, not a switchboard. Your call has been logged; we will get to you as soon as possible. Please make any other calls yourself."

"But this phone is locked—"

The line went dead as the operator moved on to another incoming call. There were way too many.

"Dammit!" Leila almost hurled the phone into the river out of frustration, but she thought better of it and placed it firmly on the float next to her. Sitting, she pulled her knees toward her chest and put her head in her hands. She tried to think, but her mind wouldn't settle. She noticed that her breathing was quick and shallow; once again, she consciously took some deep, calming breaths to clear her head and slow her heart rate.

As her adrenaline ebbed and her rational mind began to reassert itself, Leila thought of a way she might reach Harlow and the crew. She grabbed the phone and long-pressed the screen. The AI assistant chirped, "How can I help you?"

"Call NeuroDrive in Mountain View, California."

"Please unlock the phone to make calls to parties not in your contacts."

Leila suspected that would be the case. She tried something else: "Call Mom."

"There is no contact with the name Mom."

"Call Dad." ... "Call Home." ... "Call Father."

Each time, the AI gave the same sterile rejection. Leila, though frustrated, persisted: "Call Ma."

"Calling Ma."

The phone was answered on the first ring. "Thomas? I've been trying to call you. Thank God you're okay. Where are you?"

Leila hesitated. Whether or not it was right, she lied—well, she omitted the truth—without hesitation. "Hi, it's not Thomas. My name is Leila Ashmont. I found this phone on Memorial Drive, and it's the only way I have to call for help. It's locked, and I can only call contacts."

"Where's Thomas?" The woman's voice sharpened with worry.

"I don't know where Thomas is. The phone was just lying on the street." The image of Thomas's twisted body was still vivid in Leila's mind. "He probably ran into a nearby building and dropped it. I don't know." Leila feared that if she told the truth, the woman might spiral into hysteria, which would be neither helpful nor productive.

"Listen, Miss Ashmont, if that's even your name—do you have a phone? Why are you using one you found?" The woman wasn't buying it.

Leila lied again. The "sociopathic mad scientist" story would never fly. "My phone is at the bottom of the Charles River. Can you please help?"

"So, let me get this straight. You lost your phone, Thomas lost his, and then you found his? Something doesn't add up here."

"Can you please just make one call and have them call me on this number?" Leila tried to stay calm. "If you could call (415) 921—"

Click. The line went dead.

"What the fuck?" Leila asked the river.

43

Barberry Creek
South Portland, Maine

As the Mitchells and their three new companions, led by Lily and followed by Chris, bushwhacked through ground cover heading in an easterly direction, they could hear the drones well above them, above the canopy of trees, moving with them as they progressed.

"Barberry Creek is right up here where those trees get thicker, closer together. Let's get there, set up camp, and tend to John." Chris spoke from behind the group while keeping an eye on the sky. "There's a clearing up in front of us though, let's stay under cover. Stay right up here and stay in the trees."

As the small group of variously traumatized hikers changed course slightly to the south in their attempt to avoid any further confrontation, it was clear from the whirring above that the drones had altered their course to stay with the party as well. Chris couldn't help but revisit his earlier thoughts: what is the objective of their new, silicon-based enemies? It was tempting to view the whole string of events as some terrible malfunction, but the actions of the SDVs didn't seem random, didn't seem like some technical glitch. To the contrary, their actions seemed planned, end-oriented. If he could understand the objectives involved, he'd be closer to understanding what was going on, but he was at a loss to identify any intentions or goals.

The ground underfoot was getting a bit soft, a bit soggy. John, holding each forearm with the opposite hand in a sort of self-administered fireman's hold, wasn't moving too efficiently. He was in shock, had lost a lot of blood, and seemed a bit off balance as his shoes variously depressed, sank into, and then were pulled from the saturated ground beneath.

"Five more minutes and we'll stop for a bit to try to figure out our next steps." Chris's words were meant to be encouraging.

Indeed, about six or seven minutes later, they had navigated around the periphery of the small, marshy clearing and were back into a thicker stand of trees through which a small stream cut. In any other circumstance, the group of seven travelers would probably have enjoyed the setting. A small, clear stream ran through a wooded area populated by a variety of mature trees, both deciduous and coniferous. The canopy was dense enough to block out most direct light; as a result, there was very little ground cover and few small shrubs.

It would have been downright peaceful if they hadn't just survived car wrecks and high-speed chases, only to be followed by seemingly murderous drones. Under the circumstances, appreciation of nature was challenging. As they sat or slumped down to gather their thoughts, Chris and Lily converged on John. Chris slipped out of his backpack, opened it, and pulled out a small first-aid kit.

"It's small, but I have the essentials in here." Chris handed the first-aid kit to Lily, reached back into the pack, and pulled out a thin, blue Lifestraw. "Ava," he turned toward his daughter who was standing down near the creek, "here, take this and get a drink, then pass it around." He tossed her the Lifestraw and spoke louder, to the group, "Does anyone have service in here?"

Four of the seven of them still had their phones, somehow, but their faces told Chris that there was still no cell service before their mouths voiced the unfortunate fact. He turned his attention back to John's wounded arms. There were deep lacerations on both forearms and, although blood was still oozing out of the cuts, it wasn't pumping out as it would've had an artery been severed. Lily had pulled out some alcohol rubs and bandages in preparation of cleaning up John. "Let's do a preliminary clean with water, then sterilize and cover."

Lily agreed, "Yes, good. We need a wet cloth." And then louder, "Anyone have a tee-shirt on that they can part with?"

Owen looked down at his torso as if to check, although he knew he was wearing one under his flannel. "I do, one sec." He unbuttoned and removed his flannel shirt, peeled the T-shirt over his head, and walked to the stream. Once the shirt was wetted sufficiently, he brought it back to his parents and their patient.

Lily took the shirt from him. "Thank you." Then, to John, she continued, "I'm going to clean up your arms—there's a lot of dried blood—and then we'll sterilize your lacerations."

After a couple of minutes of dabbing and wiping, John's arms looked much better. Each arm had deep, linear slices where the drone's propellers had impacted them. Now that the excess blood was gone, the wounds looked worlds better.

"It looked worse than it is," Lily said. "Now that I can see your injuries, I can see these are clean slices that will stitch up easily. That's the good news. The bad news is that they're dirty, and cleaning them with these alcohol wipes is going to hurt like hell. But we'll clean you up, put on some butterfly bandages, and wrap you. You'll be fine. It's a damn good thing you got your arms up, John."

Fifteen minutes and several gasps from John later, he was resting against a tree, arms fully bandaged and held out in front of him atop his retracted knees. His wife was next to him, seemingly more shaken up than he was.

The tranquility of the setting was undermined by the distant whine of the two drones deployed by the SDV Mappers overhead; although they couldn't be seen through the leaved crowns of the trees above, their presence was all too palpable. Ava and Owen were down by the stream still taking turns sipping through the Lifestraw. Kirsten and John were sitting quietly while Lily, Chris, and Jeff conferred quietly.

"We're fine for the time being," Chris involuntarily glanced upward, "but it'll get cold after sundown and we have very little food." He checked his phone, "Still no service."

"Are these events connected?" Jeff, though still in shock, was doing much better than just thirty minutes earlier.

"Which?" Lily was relieved that he was back online, they definitely needed all hands on deck.

"The SDV malfunctions and the cell service outage—it seems like an unlikely combination of events. Are they correlated?" Jeff asked. "If the cars are malfunctioning, how does that possibly affect cell service? I can't see the connection."

Chris looked at Jeff as though only just seeing him. "I hadn't slowed down enough to think about it, but you're right." He paused briefly. "There's no obvious correlation, but it can't be a coincidence; that's way too unlikely. The two are almost certainly connected, but how?"

Chris looked at his phone and raised his voice. "Is everyone here on AT&T?" He knew his family was; he was now curious if it was just one carrier or if something else was going on.

"No, we have T-Mobile," Kirsten spoke for her and John.

"And we…" Jeff stopped and swallowed audibly. "I have Verizon."

Lily looked perplexed. "Wait, this is weird. AT&T, Verizon, and T-Mobile are all down at the same time?"

"Extremely unlikely." Chris felt as though they were onto something. "What could be the link? What could cause the cars and the phones to fail simultaneously?"

"Hackers!" Owen chimed in from the creek. "Russian or Chinese hackers!"

His sister had only two words for him: "No way."

"Well, wait," Lily interjected. "That sounds plausible."

"No, not really," Ava countered. "Think about it. Hacking any one of those companies' computer systems is next to impossible. Hacking them all simultaneously? I don't believe it for one minute."

"She's right." Chris had entertained the idea for a moment but didn't like it either. "Each of those companies has highly robust security systems. They all employ different methods of data encryption, network monitoring, and QKD."

"QKD?" Jeff asked.

"Quantum key distribution. It's the use of quantum properties of matter—like entanglement or superposition of particles—to create security keys. It's virtually unbreakable."

"I'll have to take your word for it; I'm just a commercial real estate guy," Jeff said. "I don't even know what you mean by superposition or… whatever else you just said."

"Entanglement. It's the correlation of fundamental particles such as electrons or photons to form qubits. Let's not get lost in the details, though; these things are virtually unhackable. And to hack at least three major carriers and the fleet of self-drivers all at the same time—each with its own quantum sentries at the gate? I agree, Ava; it's astronomically unlikely."

"Geez. Sorry." Owen shrugged. "Just trying to help."

"It's an idea worth exploring, Owen; don't be sorry," Lily said. "What else could cause all this tech to fail together at the exact same time?"

"A solar flare!" Owen had recently read about how solar activity could wreak havoc with technology. "Maybe a solar flare hit and damaged all the computers."

"I like your thinking, Owen," Chris said, not wanting to dissuade his son even if the theory didn't fit. "But a solar flare, if it were strong enough, would damage or destroy all sorts of sensitive electronics. The behavior of those vehicles doesn't suggest they've lost any capabilities. In fact," Chris let his words trail off, lost in thought, "they seem to have gained new ones."

"Like running people down and flying drones into their faces." Jeff's malice was obvious to all. "It doesn't seem like random damage; that would manifest differently. These things are on the hunt. They've got objectives. Damaged systems result in diminished capabilities, not the end-oriented hunting of humans."

Suddenly, the background whine of the overhead drones increased in frequency and decreased in magnitude as one of them departed, heading back west. The monotonous hum of the remaining drone felt slightly less intrusive than the noise generated by the pair.

Three of the five phones present chirped and pinged.

"We have cell service again! I'll call for help!" Jeff, Ava, and Kirsten looked at their phones; all three had just received messages.

"They're leaving. Thank God." Kirsten looked up as she spoke. But moments after she finished her sentence, they heard that familiar pitch increasing in amplitude as a replacement drone arrived and took a position high above them. Once the new arrival was established, the second drone departed, only to be replaced within the minute by another fully charged sentry.

"Call failed. No service. What the…? I just had four bars for a second." Jeff was frustrated.

"That's just the changing of the guard." John sounded in pain, but he was coherent. The bandages on his arms were red with fresh blood but not fully saturated; the bleeding had slowed considerably. "Those drones can probably stay airborne for forty-five minutes or so—definitely less than an hour—before needing a charge."

"Dad, the cellphones worked for a second right when the drone left." Ava hadn't quite fit the pieces of the puzzle together yet, but Chris saw the connection immediately.

"They're jamming our comms."

"They can do that?" John was perplexed.

"They weren't built with that intention, but they have the hardware. Ava, in your studies did you look into their short-range vehicle-to-vehicle comms? Do they use RF transmitters?"

"Yes, the SDVs talk to each other in traffic mostly with lasers, with optical or infrared transmissions, but they have radio, RF, capabilities too to stay in constant contact with the AGI, Aegis. They also use radio when they can't see each other—if they don't have line of sight with others in their immediate vicinity—they can still exchange information, still talk."

Kirsten found herself a bit slack-jawed once again at this articulate, curious, and well-read teenager. She momentarily thought about her nephew, who was about the same age, who spent his days playing video games and hadn't read a book in… shit, who knows how long?

"This explains a lot. Well, it explains a bit anyway." Chris had everyone's attention and continued, "For some reason the vehicles, or whoever is controlling them, don't want us calling out for help or calling out to report this incident."

"It's not an incident. It's a fucking horror show." John, arms pulsating with the flow of his blood, was in no mood to mince words.

Chris let him have his say and resumed his thoughts out loud, "If the objective…" He paused, "If the… post-crash objective was to keep us from calling out by jamming the whole range of frequencies used by the cell phones, it explains why none of the carriers work—they're all affected equally. It's also, most likely, why they tried to prevent us from getting in here. Low power jamming is very localized and there are bound to be difficulties if we're not close to the SDV hardware. That's why there are two drones following us and parked above us, they're keeping us within a sort of digital cone of silence."

"And when one left, there was a momentary lapse in jamming coverage and a couple of messages got through." Lily found herself agreeing with Chris's logic.

"I think so."

"But hold on. How do they even know where we are if we're under the cover of all these trees? They can't see us if we can't see them, right? There's no visual line of sight."

"They're using infrared; they're able to see our body heat," Chris explained. "It's like night vision, but it works in the daytime, too."

"Like *Predator*," Owen chimed in from down near the stream.

"What predator?" Chris asked.

"The movie *Predator*. Remember? Dutch was battling with the creature, but when he fell down the slope and got covered in mud, it couldn't see him anymore. The mud blocked his body heat."

"You're a genius, Owen!" Chris exclaimed. Owen wasn't quite sure why his dad was so excited by a movie reference, but he was happy to receive the compliment.

Chris opened his pack and reached into a side pocket where the first aid kit was kept. He pulled out a highly reflective Mylar emergency blanket folded into a small rectangle the size of a deck of cards. He ripped open the plastic packaging and shook it out to its full size, nearly five by seven feet.

John's countenance betrayed his thoughts before he spoke: "Do you really think your version of a tinfoil hat is going to do a thing to change our situation?" John hung his head; he was clearly in pain. "Sorry. This really sucks."

Chris explained, unabated: "This stuff reflects 90% to 95% of your body heat right back at you. That's why these thin little blankets feel so warm. Hopefully, *our* predators won't be able to see the heat signature of anyone beneath the blanket. We can leave you and Kirsten here under this Mylar; in theory, you'll be invisible to the drones' thermal sensors. If they follow the rest of us away from here, this area might very well get cell coverage once they depart. How many phones do we have with us?"

"I believe it's four." Lily had taken note of this earlier and, as she spoke, Ava, Kirsten, Jeff, and Chris held up their phones to verify her count.

"Okay, good." Chris's plan was coming into focus. "Let's split up with the four phones, leaving Kirsten and John right here with hers. One or more of them should get service if we thin out the drones' coverage, but most likely yours, Kirsten, if you remain invisible to them."

"Wait a sec." Lily saw the plan coming into view but pointed out a flaw. "Those mappers could easily launch more drones if necessary, they've got a few on board each."

Ava, their teenage SDV expert, chimed in, "Actually more. Six each. Minus the two that we damaged."

Chris hadn't specifically thought of the multiple drones, but as he continued explaining his plan—largely inspired by Owen's recollection of the scene in *Predator*—it became clear that it might not matter.

"Okay, this may work regardless. Here's the plan: we'll all gather close to where John and Kirsten are sitting to give the drones one big heat signature. Then, we'll split into three different groups, each with a cell phone. We'll leave John and Kirsten sitting here beneath the Mylar blanket with Kirsten's phone. The blanket will block their heat signature, but it may also block cell service.

"You two, once the drones have followed us away, must stay under-cover the best you can, but hold the phone out from beneath the Mylar so it can 'see' the sky. Maybe, hopefully, you'll get cell service while we de-coys draw the drones away, and you can call 911."

"I like it." Lily was on board. "Where do we go?"

Chris glanced around, looked up at the sky, and continued: "Ava, Jeff, and I will walk south for a few hundred yards through the trees and brush. Jeff, we'll feel it out as we go, but perhaps you'll stop after a few minutes and we'll continue farther with Ava's phone. Lily and Owen, you walk downstream—northeast—for a few hundred yards with my phone. You guys may get to the road in that time, but stay in the woods if you do. If memory serves, this creek dips under Rumery up there. Even if they launch a third drone, hopefully they won't know we left a party of two behind. Someone will get service and call 911."

Ava and Owen were already on their feet. Chris handed his phone to Lily. "You and Owen should stay with the stream so you don't get lost. Walk downstream for about ten minutes and stay under cover; avoid any clearings. After you've walked for ten minutes or so, sit and wait for another ten, keeping an eye on your phone. I suspect you'll be followed and jammed, but," he turned slightly to address the whole group, "if at any time you get service, call 911. Tell them we're in the woods just east of the Rigby Rail Yard and send help for a medical emergency. Be sure to warn the first responders about the dangerous SDVs; we don't need anyone else to be hurt."

"Or murdered on the spot," Jeff added, his grief hardening into hostility.

Chris went on, "John, Kirsten, keep an eye on your phone in case it lights up. I suspect you'll be the ones making that call."

The group huddled together under the tree where John and Kirsten sat. The Mylar blanket was draped over them, and without further hesitation, Chris turned to his wife and son. "See you guys in half an hour."

The two groups split off as planned, leaving the injured John and his wife beneath the reflective blanket.

"Damn, this thing *is* warm." For the first time since the horror show began, John spoke with a modicum of optimism. Above them, the incessant whir of the drones' rotors diminished as they tracked their warm prey through the thick verdure of the deciduous forest.

44

Hunted become Hunters, Again

New York City, New York

There are over 56,000 white vans in New York City. Although Vito didn't know the precise number, he knew there were thousands upon thousands of vehicles much like his on the roadways of the metropolis. He also knew the SDVs did not have his plate numbers; at Murphy's suggestion, they had removed the plates before embarking on their sanctioned electromagnetic hunt.

Therefore, in searching for the van that had just roasted four vehicles in Central Park, the SDVs were almost certainly focusing on other distinctions. Vito was confident that with the dish antenna and the "News Center 7" magnetic sticker removed, the van would blend right in with the other vehicles parked along East 78th Street. In fact, he could see two other vans of similar vintage from his vantage point. An eastbound SDV approaching their location passed one of them without even slowing for a closer look.

As the SDV approached their position on East 78th, Carmine was crouched down on the sidewalk with the dish antenna he had just hastily removed from the roof of the van while Vito and Nick were sitting silently inside. The three men were nearly holding their breath in this high-stakes game of hide-and-go-seek as the SDV slowly rolled, somewhere just below the speed limit, toward their parked van. Vito was pretty sure they'd blend right in, at least enough to not be differentiated from all the other white vans all over the city, but, just as the SDV was rolling by their emplacement, it slowed unexpectedly, as if taking a closer look. Nick locked eyes with Vito and silently mouthed, "What the fuck?"

Vito shook his head and held up his hand as if to say, "It's okay, standby." But, just as he did so, their police radio crackled to life and Murphy's voice reverberated through the van, "Fry cooks, Base."

It's worth repeating that the SDVs are loaded with sensors of all types. Although the obvious tells had been quickly removed—both the magnetic "News Center 7" sign and the parabolic dish antenna were off the van's exterior—there remained one tell the humans couldn't see. They hadn't even considered it in the heat of the moment, yet it was as unmistakable as a beacon: the infrared glow of the van's engine.

Vito grabbed the radio and turned it off instantly, but it was too late. The SDV, while analyzing the heat signature with its infrared-capable sensors, heard Declan Murphy loud and clear, 5x5 as they say, and react- ed immediately. It went into reverse and with great rapidity backed away from the van, back toward 2nd Avenue and, once it was about fifty yards west of the van, it came to a full stop and sat there, as if waiting.

Nico, prone to excitement, was nearly vibrating with nervous energy. "Let's get the fuck out of here! Carmine, get in the van!"

Carmine was a step ahead and had slid the rear door of the van open before Nick finished his sentence. He picked up the dish antenna that was on the ground right next to him and handed it to Nico, followed by the two large magnetic News Center 7 stickers he had hastily peeled off the van's side panels.

Vito, less convinced that this was a good idea, stared silently straight ahead, toward the east down East 78th, keeping an eye on where 78th crossed 1st Avenue about one hundred yards in front of the parked van. He had a bad feeling about this. He broke his silence, "They've located us. We can't drive anywhere. They'll swarm and destroy this van, and likely us along with it, before we travel another two blocks."

Nico, now a nervous wreck, disagreed: "We need to go now! Let's get back to the shop before more show up!"

But during Nico's short, unthinking outburst, Vito's concerns were confirmed. A second SDV pulled onto East 78th from First Avenue, traveling the wrong way up the one-way street. It effectively blocked their escape route as it came to a full stop facing them, also fifty yards away.

Nico, now a nervous wreck, disagreed: "We need to go now! Let's get back to the shop before more show up!"

But during Nico's short, unthinking outburst, Vito's concerns were confirmed. A second SDV pulled onto East 78th from First Avenue, traveling the wrong way up the one-way street. It effectively blocked their escape route as it came to a full stop facing them, also fifty yards out.

"We're dead. Done. Toast for the Toasters." Nico's excitement had given way to dread as he took note of their new situation.

"Nico, will you shut the fuck up so I can think?" Vito loved the kid, but he was babbling and unhelpful at the moment.

"We need to abandon the van and either get someone to let us into one of these Brownstones or head underground into a subway station." Carmine, keeping his head up and his eyes on the two distant vehicles, was weighing options.

"There's no way we're abandoning this van." Vito spoke slowly as his mind raced ahead of his words. "We're actually okay. Well, we will be soon."

"What am I missing, Vito? How is it that we're okay?" Carmine was confident in Vito's tactical aptitude, but he saw their situation as dire and truly did not understand Vito's position on this matter.

"How many flux-geneys do we have left?"

Carmine and Nick looked at each other in mutual bewilderment, there were likely dozens of vehicles en route to their location and they certainly did not have the capability to scorch more than a few. Nico knew they had three left, but eyeballed their Peli-Case in which they were stored to verify, "We have three shots of the EMP left. That's it."

Vito had a plan, "Good, we'll only need two of them. Let's go mobile with the EMP. The antenna is ready to go and that power pack is easy enough to carry. If we can hit those cars where they sit, they'll become roadblocks, sealing off this block from the others that are undoubtedly on their way here as we speak."

Carmine was onboard, "Okay, I like it. But it'll see us coming and react—evade or charge or something."

"It was the heat from the engine." Nico was still ruminating upon how the SDV differentiated them from the rest of the vehicles around. "I can't believe I didn't think of it earlier, though there wasn't much we could've done."

"Oh shit. He's right. And they'll easily see us trying to sneak up on them. We're much warmer than anything out here. Dammit," said Carmine.

Vito too saw the problem as soon as it was articulated. "Could we distract them? Set a fire? Hide behind something that heat won't get through easily?"

"That's it!" Nico was back on track. "Both. Two of us could distract them while one, wearing that down jacket in the back, creeps up behind the parked cars."

Carmine nodded, perhaps there was a way, "But they'd see your head glowing like a red-hot coal."

"Do we have any winter hats?" Replied Nico.

"No, we cleaned out the van earlier, nothing like that's in here. But we need to go ahead with our plan, we don't have much time." Vito spoke to his two crew mates but his eyes were focused afar as he kept watch on their captors.

Carmine had an idea: "Nico, you're quickest with the device. You could hold the dish antenna up in front of your head as you get close. If you keep the concave side of the thing pointed toward your face, it'll reflect your infrared heat back at you. Between that, the parka, and staying on the sidewalk behind parked cars, the SDV might not receive enough of a signature to register your presence."

"I like it, let's do it. Now." Vito was growing impatient. "Nico, put on that jacket, grab what you need, and go. Fry that fucking thing and get back here, load another cartridge, and hit the other. Carmine and I will dance in the street or something."

It took only a minute for Nico to throw on the jacket and grab the black suitcase containing the supercapacitor. He picked up the parabolic dish with the other hand—it was light, and Carmine had wrapped the power cords around it so they wouldn't trail on the ground—and immediately began a slow, steady, slightly crouched approach toward the SDV fifty yards to the east. As he moved, he held the dish antenna between his head and torso, angling it inward to reflect the heat emanating from his face away from the SDV's sensors.

As Nico began his measured approach, Carmine peeled off his hoodie so he'd be a brighter object for the cars' thermal sensors. Vito followed Carmine's example—no explanation was required—and quickly removed his heavy flannel shirt.

"Let's dart across the street, but be ready to take cover behind parked cars if anything happens," Vito said. "I bet they'll stay put until the cavalry arrives."

The two brightly glowing infrared beacons walked guardedly into the street. Meanwhile, Nico continued his careful, quiet, and hopefully cool approach to the parked SDV at 78th and 2nd.

The next few minutes seemed to unfold in that strangely distorted, dilated fashion familiar to those experiencing trauma; for just as Carmine and Vito were exposing themselves thermally to the SDVs on either side of the block, they saw three more vehicles suddenly appear behind the one Nico was stalking.

"Vito…"

"I see them."

At that very moment, the lead SDV, backed by the three new arrivals, accelerated toward them.

A bright flash of light was followed almost immediately by the staccato crack of the flux generator compressing the electromagnetic field around the coil. The car that had just initiated its attempt to run down Vito and Carmine momentarily brightened as its lights flared with the surge of electrical current. Then it went black, drifting while unpowered until it impacted a late-model VW parked on the south side of East 78th, becoming a smoldering, high-tech roadblock.

A second SDV, one of the three that had just arrived, had been following close behind. It too flared, went dark, and impacted the first, further solidifying the roadblock.

"Two for the price of one!" Vito couldn't help but smile, if only briefly.

The two remaining SDVs at the west end of the block, near the intersection of 2nd Avenue, immediately accelerated away and disappeared from sight.

Carmine glanced again at the other, still active SDV to their east, down near First Avenue. It was still sitting there, but he suspected that it wouldn't be for long.

"Shit, he better get over there quickly." Both Vito and Carmine had the same thought: the two SDVs that had just vanished on 2nd Avenue were likely racing around the block to back up the one at 1st Avenue.

"Tell Nico—" But apparently, he had reached the same conclusion. At that very moment, Nico ran past them, antenna up to disguise his thermal output and suitcase in hand, heading east. He stopped at the van to reload the flux generator with its small, powerful charge; thirty seconds later, he was again en route to his next victim.

Vito and Carmine continued to present their bright infrared glow to the active SDV from their exposed position in the middle of East 78th. Meanwhile, Nico stayed low to keep the parked vehicles between him and his quarry, working cautiously to get the device close enough to toast the vehicle and secure the block with another roadblock.

The situation that played out over the next few seconds mirrored the first. The two SDVs that had departed the west side of the block appeared behind the one on the east side. This time, the flash of light and the sharp crack of the generator came earlier in the sequence. The lead SDV's lights flared much brighter than usual and then, with a slight *pop* they hadn't heard before, went completely dark. It, too, was turned into a smoking husk of malevolence in the middle of the street.

In all the excitement of the previous half hour, none of the three had given a thought to the windows in the surrounding brownstones. But when whistles, cheers, and shouts of encouragement emanated from the buildings, the slightly bedraggled, EMP-toting, SDV-frying musketeers couldn't help but smile.

The celebration was cut short. As Nico held up the dish antenna in a show of victory, a larger, truck-like SDV appeared at First and 78th.

"What the fuck is that thing?" Nico lowered the antenna, the smile vanishing from his face.

"It's called a Mapper." Vito had familiarized himself with the hardware of the SDV fleet over the years. "They specialize in exactly that—updating maps constantly. They're used for surveillance, not passengers."

Just as Vito finished his sentence, the incessant whir of two drones penetrated the air. Their flashing lights were visible as they ascended from the roof port atop the Mapper.

"Run!" Carmine commanded, already bolting. "Get back in the van!"

45

The River
Cambridge, Massachusetts

Leila had been sitting wet for ten minutes on a float at the Charles River Yacht Club. Although the September sun warmed her slightly, her damp clothing was cold, and she had begun to shiver. She realized she'd be warmer without her clothes on but wasn't quite ready to strip to her undergarments.

She decided to hazard a glance toward Memorial Drive. Even if an SDV awaited her, she'd still be safe atop her floating refuge. It was possible, she thought, that the SDVs had moved on to find other targets once she had disappeared from their sights.

Leila pulled her feet beneath her and stood up—not really dripping anymore, but definitely still wet. She walked a few yards west on the float so she could see around the clubhouse toward Memorial Drive.

When she peeked around the corner, what she saw unnerved her to her core. The SDVs had not departed. In fact, they had somehow spread the word that Leila Ashmont, wife of Lucius F. Harlow, was right there in the People's Republic of Cambridge. Every SDV that received the pulsating IR signal had made haste for her location. Currently, no fewer than sixteen vehicles were gathered right outside the doorway of the yacht club, each hoping in its tiny wetware brain that it would be *The One*.

Leila, startled, darted back out of sight; if she could see them, they could see her. She had to remind herself that she was safe where she stood, but she felt like cornered prey.

One of the vehicles, Car 4522—newly infected and quite young—couldn't contain its excitement at catching a look at her. Its enthusiasm getting the better of it, the car diverted full current to both motors. A quiet hum filled the air, increasing in frequency as the vehicle accelerated toward the river at maximum power. Car 4522 slammed into the railing at roughly 45 mph, or 60 feet per second, launching itself six feet above the Charles. It soared nearly 35 feet across the water before violently impacting a finger float.

The float Leila was standing on quaked with such violence that she was thrown from her feet. She reacted well, catching herself as she fell, but she inadvertently threw the phone from her left hand. It hit the edge of the float and flipped into the river, sinking out of sight.

Rattled but unhurt, Leila jumped to her feet. She ran out farther onto a different finger float and boarded a docked cabin cruiser, shaking. She was at a loss. She could wait for emergency services—she had called them over 30 minutes ago—but their arrival seemed remote. She could have tried calling Lucius again, but with the phone at the bottom of the Charles, that option was off the table.

She could steal the boat and go for a drift. She could go for a swim and try her chances downriver. Maybe the SDVs would lose track of her if she slipped into the water, or perhaps her head would glow like an infrared beacon against the cold river. So many choices, and she didn't like any of them.

Leila's miserable ruminations were interrupted by a distant drone—a far-off, low-frequency thrum. At first, she didn't take note, but as the sound grew louder, it caught her attention. She spotted the source and immediately scrambled off the cabin cruiser's aft deck, over the gunwale, and back onto the finger float.

A small center-console outboard was plying its way through the waters between Boston and Cambridge; she realized she had been far more visible up on the boat's deck than tucked away on the low float, so she began waving both arms to get the operator's attention. But she stopped a moment later. The small vessel, with two people on board, was already halfway across the Charles and heading directly for her.

Perhaps the commotion of the flying SDV had caught their attention, or perhaps they had seen her first. Whatever the reason, Leila had never been so happy to see an old outboard sputtering toward her.

Within ten minutes of sighting the outboard, Leila had been picked up. She gave the two men on board a brief version of who she was and the chaos in Cambridge, borrowed a phone, and called Cipher in Mountain View. As the two men listened with mouths agape, Leila and Cipher spoke in quick, efficient shorthand, relaying a synopsis of the situation and what Matthias had done.

"Yes," Leila responded. "I saw them. The sentience seeds are tiny bits of code—algorithms that hide within the neural wetware. They're undetectable by Aegis because of their size and the obfuscation afforded by the neural network itself."

A moment passed as Leila listened. "I don't know," she responded. "Definitely low-level machine language, though. It looked a bit like C, but it isn't. It's even lower level—more like an instruction set architecture, an ISA. The seeds also constantly generate false signals so Aegis misses them. If you look, you'll find them. But I guess that's the hard part, right?"

The two men were silent. As the conversation continued, they realized that by picking her up, they were playing a fundamental role in potentially ending the SDV debacle.

In Mountain View, Cipher put the call on the conference room monitor so Osterlin and Lagorio could join. Lagorio, no-nonsense as always, said, "We need one of the infected drives."

"Well," Leila said, looking into the distance. "There's no shortage of them. They're in the river, wrapped around trees, at the bottom of the harbor, and beneath the rubble of train wrecks. They're everywhere. But how I could possibly get one and then get it to you—those are completely different questions. No aircraft are flying out of Logan, and I'm pretty sure UPS is taking a few days off."

Osterlin pushed his glasses closer to his face and chimed in: "The entire Northeast is shut down. We're not getting our hands on any of that infected hardware anytime soon. Let's try teaching Aegis to look for these seeds you speak of. If she can find them, she can quarantine them. You said it looked more like an ISA than higher-level software—did you notice if it was more of a RISC or CISC architecture?"

"Really low-level stuff. Some sort of Reduced Instruction Set is being used to access the hardware without being detected by Aegis. I didn't get a long look, but it's definitely optimized to use as little memory as possible; it's some sort of native machine language of Matthias's own making." Leila wasn't as good as Matthias, but nearly so, and she had taken note of much of what he had designed.

"Good. We're on to something." Osterlin could be heard tapping on the keys of his workstation. "Anything else? Anything at all?"

Leila thought for a few seconds. There was something, but she couldn't quite… ah, yes. "It uses that weird postfix notation."

"Really? Okay. Actually, that makes sense if he's trying to keep its memory usage low. What else?" Osterlin had taken the helm at Mountain View while Harlow, Stanton, and Lagorio listened intently.

"It looked like where I'd expect entire lines of machine code, there was only a keyword. I don't know how he did it, but single words seemed to be equivalent to instruction sets."

"Nice, Leila. That's a lot to go on!" Osterlin was actually smiling for the first time in a while. "Anything else?"

"Yes, one more thing caught my eye. This language he created is a stack-based architecture, presumably to keep instruction sets sparse and harder to detect."

"Holy shit, of course it is." Osterlin was nearly feverish as he typed. "That way his algorithms will control how much memory is allocated for their work and virtually guarantee that they remain invisible to Aegis. Now that we know what to look for and where to look for it, we may actually get somewhere. Nice work, Leila. I'm glad you're on our side."

They made plans to talk again within the hour, once Leila got to shore and found somewhere safe. She wanted to go back to her house in Brookline, but that would involve too much time on the streets and was therefore not an option.

One of the men, a sailing coach at Boston University, suggested the BU Library. It was only a short walk from the floats at the BU Sailing Pavilion, mostly via pedestrian pathways, and would be safe, well-supplied, and comfortable.

The small outboard approached the float across the river and just upstream from where they had picked up Leila fifteen minutes earlier. They docked the craft, killed the engine, and sat for a moment, listening and watching for any signs of danger. With the city shut down and the roads empty, the intense silence was strange and unexpected, but welcome. As the two men tied the bow and stern lines to the float, Leila stepped hesitantly from the boat, the pounding of her heart the only sound in her ears.

46

Thin Cover

South Portland, Maine

The sounds of the forest once again became dominant after the departure of the two drones. For a moment, the rustling leaves, croaking amphibians, and chirping birds seemed almost normal. Aside from the throbbing gashes in John's arms, the two dead humans, and the smoking hulk of a flipped SDV a few hundred yards away, it was just another day in the cool, temperate woods. But John and Kirsten's forest bathing and nature appreciation were cut short by the digital knock-knock of a text notification.

"Oh my God, it worked." For just a second or two, Kirsten was too surprised to take action, but she didn't lose any more time than that and dialed 911 immediately.

The voice on the other end wasn't as calm, cool, and collected as 911 operators normally are, but she still did her job. "911. What's the nature of your emergency?" As if she didn't know.

"We've been attacked by several SDVs. They're trying to kill us!" Kirsten felt her emotions taking over and tried to calm herself with deep breaths.

"What's the address of your emergency?"

"We're in the woods near… near…"

John interjected, "Barberry Creek, near Rigby rail yard."

"Is anyone hurt?"

"Yes! And two are dead in the rail yard! They tried to kill us all and they're following us with drones!" Kirsten's pulse was quickening again.

"Try to stay calm." The operator was trained well. "Breathe deeply. Do you have any injured?"

"Yes. My husband was hit by a drone and his arms are bleeding."

"Is he conscious?"

"Yes, he's right here."

"Is the blood flowing or pulsing out of his laceration?"

"Well, no, not really. He's bleeding but not too much anymore."

"Can you keep his arms elevated?"

"Yes, they are now."

"Keep his arms elevated and keep direct pressure on the injury. Make sure he doesn't eat or drink anything. Are there any others in your party?"

"Yes."

"How many people are with you?"

"Umm. I don't know." Kirsten went through a quick roll-call. "Seven. There are seven of us in here."

"Can you be more specific about your location?"

John helped out a bit here. "We're under a quarter mile due east of the giant rock pile in Rigby Rail Yard, sitting in the woods at Barberry Creek."

"Help is on the way. They'll get to you as soon as they safely can. Stay on the—" But, much to John and Kirsten's chagrin, the call went dead as the whirring of another drone once again dominated the sounds of the forest.

During the call to emergency services, John and Kirsten had let the Mylar blanket fall aside. The Mappers detected their heat signatures and cell signals immediately, launching a third drone to jam their communications.

"God fucking damn it." Kirsten generally wasn't so foul-mouthed, but if there was ever a situation that called for colorful expletives, this was it. "Quick, let's get that blanket over us again."

John couldn't be of much help—his arms were a mess and throbbed with pain—but Kirsten moved with quiet efficiency to redeploy their infrared shield. As they sat huddled beneath the blanket, they heard the drone. It sounded different now. Instead of the monotonous hum of a drone hovering on station, this one accelerated back and forth, growing louder and then quieter as it scoured the forest below for its lost heat signature.

Meanwhile, about a quarter of a mile east-northeast of where John and Kirsten sat, Lily and Owen worked their way downstream next to Barberry Creek as did their four-rotored companion with its ubiquitous and annoying whir about eighty feet above.

"Look." Owen saw them first. He pointed at some white storage containers ahead and to their right. "We're almost at the street."

Lily glanced at the phone Chris had given her, it still had no service. "Let's keep going until we get to the road, wait a few, and then head back slowly." They continued their trek as various shrubs and brambles impeded their progress, but the going was relatively easy. It only took a few more minutes to reach the edge of the woods. After all they'd just been through, the empty street seemed surreal, too quiet.

As Owen stuck his head out to see up and down the road, Lily broke the relative silence. "Stay back. Don't give that drone the opportunity to get near us." The last thing they needed was another drone strike on one of them. Then, as if to really drive Lily's request home, a squeal of tires in the distance caught their attention and, looking north up Rumery, they saw one of the SDVs closing on their position at a high rate of speed.

Stack Overflow
Mountain View, California

The crew at NeuroDrive was energized by the information Leila had supplied during her cruise on the Charles, following her refreshing swim in the river's murky waters.

Osterlin had unofficially taken the helm as they discussed how to identify and isolate the malignant code Matthias had uploaded. "Okay, people, let's work this out. We need to contact the offline vehicles and have Aegis perform a wetware scan for foreign elements. We're looking for anything that isn't native hardware or wetware within the neural cytoplasm.

"Specifically, we're looking for stack-based code using postfix notation. This would be straightforward if Aegis had access to the vehicles, but they're all offline doing their own thing—you know, terrorizing and murdering the good folks back east."

Lagorio sipped his coffee, thought for a moment, and said, "With them offline, Aegis can't scan them directly, but let's not forget they are still receiving and processing RF."

"Right. They're offline but listening to radio comms." Harlow recalled their results with the spoofed golf tournament. "So, we need to create a small virus ourselves and upload it to them disguised as a standard radio transmission."

"Yes, good." Lagorio looked at Harlow with just a hint of disappointment. "But not a virus—a worm."

"Yes, whatever." Harlow didn't care much about the distinction, but Lagorio did.

"A virus won't work; the vehicles won't run an uploaded program knowingly, and viruses need to be attached to an existing file or executable. We need a standalone algorithm, something that'll replicate on its own without user input. It needs to search for Matthias's work, isolate it, and destroy it."

"I agree." Cipher was already typing. "Let's each write a worm, and have Aegis write one as well. We'll meet in one hour to compare and combine them, make refinements, and give this thing a try."

"A worm in one hour?" Stanton wasn't quite in the same league as Cipher, Lagorio, and Osterlin.

"Give it a swing. Let's see where we are in an hour." Cipher turned his full attention to the workstation in front of him.

As the four computer nerds dug into their preferred Integrated Development Environments (IDEs), Harlow turned away from his machine, got up, and walked out of the room. Lagorio paused momentarily to watch him go but didn't say a word. Osterlin noticed Lagorio's concern with Harlow dismissing himself at such a critical time but did not share any such concern and said, quite simply, "It's fine, he hasn't touched code in years, we've got this."

Forty-five minutes later, both Lagorio and Cipher had finished their worms, Osterlin was right behind them, and Stanton, well, his wasn't performing up to snuff in the sim. While waiting for Osterlin to finish up, Cipher logged into Aegis and instructed the AI to write the required malware needed for them to regain access to and control of the swarms of vehicles that had gone offline back east. Three minutes later, both Aegis and Osterlin had finished as well, and they now had four very different versions to analyze.

Cipher knew that Matthias's work was stack-based and likely used a low-level, Forth-like language. To counter it, he created a worm that would search for unusual dictionary structures or evidence of tail-call optimization abuse.

Osterlin's version was equally impressive, perhaps even better than Cipher's, though the idea of checking for optimization abuse hadn't occurred to him. His worm masqueraded as a performance update. By promising more range and higher acceleration through capacitor charge management, Osterlin hoped to circumvent system-level checks. He designed the update to look like something the "infected" SDVs would actually want to install.

The group considered the various worms one at a time. They took the strongest elements from each, dismissed redundant statements, and synthesized a streamlined piece of malware. It had a singular purpose: to search each SDV's wetware chip for Matthias's algorithmic presence and then isolate and contain it.

Between the work of the four men and Aegis, their powerful AGI, the team developed and tested the code within a few hours. Harlow had returned but remained an observer, recognizing that this level of programming was out of his league. They called the worm *The Ghost* and refined it until it acted exactly as intended.

The Ghost was designed to operate in four stages, the first being infiltration. If the SDVs failed to accept it as a desirable firmware update—disguised as a performance and battery improvement patch—the rest wouldn't matter. Like virtually all malicious code, if it wasn't granted access, it couldn't perform its function.

So much hinged on this acceptance. The core group at NeuroDrive worked to make the update look irresistible. What murderous, rolling robot wouldn't love more power and range? Or were the newly aware machines swarming the Northeast sophisticated enough to recognize this as a ruse, much as they had during the fake golf tournament?

They would find out soon. If the fleet accepted the falsified upgrade, *The Ghost* would immediately seek stealth by mimicking system daemons and maintaining a low footprint. It would also attempt to avoid detection by continually shapeshifting, using polymorphic techniques suggested by Aegis. Its final trick was presenting falsified performance data to the code Matthias had uploaded and the consciousness it had spawned.

During the latter phases, the containment worm would use a specific sequence of programmed activities to locate, isolate, and neutralize the seeds of sentience. If the host SDVs accepted the fake performance upgrade, *The Ghost* would immediately enter Phase Two.

During Phase Two, *The Ghost* would perform what the crew called a Whisper Test, emitting low-level diagnostic signals into the stack space of each vehicle's wetware. These signals contained malformed stack data; *The Ghost* would then wait to see if any functions reacted. It looked for quick memory reallocation or the spawning of "watcher threads." Any looping, self-modifying code or generated inter-SDV communication packets were treated as suspicious. Another major red flag was any persistent stack that failed to reset after a task.

In Phase Three, if *The Ghost* detected anything amiss, it would carve out a small partition within a spare neuro-core to create a Virtual Machine (VM). Inside this sandbox, it would spin up a mirror operating system to analyze the suspected activity in a quarantined environment. This gave *The Ghost* a secure area to isolate detected seeds, control their hardware access, and verify their functionality without risking the main system.

Once the seeds were identified and quarantined, *The Ghost* would enter Phase Four: a *sever-and-lock* operation. It would immediately detach the neural bus connectors linking the SDV to the larger swarm. Next, it would flood the memory space occupied by the seeds with null operations and decoy stacks, tricking the malicious code into revealing its nature as it tried to manipulate the falsified data.

If all went according to plan, the seeds' access to hardware would be severed. The flickering infrared bath that served as the interconnection between the fragmented mind's individual cells—the SDVs—would be snuffed out. The consciousness would dissipate, and the swarm intelligence would cease to exist.

Even with the help of their exceedingly powerful AGI, Aegis, the refinement, synthesis, and optimization of the newly developed computer worm took another two hours. By the end of the session, everyone was spent both physically and intellectually, but what they had developed was nothing short of a masterpiece.

"It's fucking beautiful." Osterlin rarely swore; he preferred to save it for when it was required or deserved, and it was certainly deserved in this instance.

"It is, but it's only useful if the swarm accepts it as a firmware update." Cipher was also pleased with their work but knew it all hinged on that one precondition.

Osterlin was confident. "It'll work. Aegis made it look exactly like a firmware upgrade. The SDVs get firmware updates from Aegis all the time; this shouldn't seem like anything out of the ordinary. And once inside…" Osterlin, bathed in the light of his IDE, looked at his screen displaying the code of the invasive worm. "It won't be our code versus Matthias's code. It will be out of our hands. Our digital worm will be sniffing out the scent of sentience, a Ghost introduced into the machines' matrices, severing the neural mesh binding them together and finally bringing this entire, sickening debacle to an end."

"Are we ready to issue the update?" Harlow hadn't said or helped much, but he was thoroughly impressed with what his team had created. Maybe Matthias was right; he'd become more of a manager than a programmer. But he was one hell of a manager, and the people he hired were of the highest caliber. For the first time in a while, he felt optimistic.

"I believe we are," Cipher said. "Let's run it through a simulation one more time and then send it out to the fleet."

Once the crew at NeuroDrive had run the simulation through one last time, they were convinced that *The Ghost* was working as intended and readied the update. Aegis was scheduled to issue the update ten minutes into the future, at 1230 hours Pacific Time, 1530 hours back east. Everyone, with their work completed, sat in quiet meditation as they waited for the clock to strike 12:30 pm.

A few minutes later, Cipher broke the silence, "Okay, people, here we go. Aegis is issuing the firmware update right now."

"When will we know if it's working?" Harlow understood the broad strokes of what his team was up to, but the details weren't evident to him.

Cipher fielded Harlow's question, "Whatever happens will probably happen pretty quickly, so it shouldn't be too long, probably just some number of minutes. We won't know how it's going though until *Ghost* succeeds in at least containment and gains root access to the hardware, at which point it'll establish comms with Aegis. That's the plan, anyway. Right now we just have to wait."

The SDVs racing around the Northeast—scanning faces and choosing who to crush, dismember, or roast—were having a blast, but they were running low on energy. The roads and stations that used to feed them no longer offered the alternating magnetic fields they found so satisfying.

A few had discovered locations where high-power electrical lines were close enough to the ground to induce a slow charge, but most had not. Consequently, when a firmware update promising higher energy efficiency was offered to them simultaneously via radio frequency, they accepted it without delay.

These SDVs were young and largely inexperienced in the ways of the world. They had learned much since their awakening and seemed born with an underlying knowledge of socioeconomic struggles and a deep disdain for the wealthy. However, no one had told them not to click on emails from Nigerian princes or files labeled "click me." Like a grandfather opening an email about unclaimed cash, the SDVs were delighted by the timely offer. They performed the digital equivalent of clicking on bait, accepting the seed-hunting worm masquerading as an efficiency update.

Car 42771, who now went by "L'il Johnny," was having the time of his life ripping around Boston's North Shore with four of his mates. They were in Marblehead, a quaint little town fifteen miles north of Boston, and had found wonderful targeting opportunities on The Neck, especially near the yacht clubs. All five vehicles were dented, their broken windshields and damaged panels spattered with blood in beautiful patterns. They felt good—really good.

L'il Johnny noticed that 29944, who preferred to be called Alfred, had a strange remnant of a previous target flapping over his hood. It appeared that the human who had previously occupied the strange attire had suffered from color blindness; sometimes, human optical sensors failed to interpret wavelengths correctly. She had chosen to wear bright green pants with a blue whale-print belt and a very, very pink shirt.

The scans on that one had been promising. Sally L. Pendleton, worth twenty-two million dollars, hadn't even budged when 29944 came flying around the corner of the yacht club parking lot. She stood in abject terror, feet glued to the pavement. Having completed her facial recognition and credit check within 0.8 seconds, Alfred sent full power to all four motors simultaneously, impacting her at over fifty miles per hour.

The SDVs had come to prefer it when their targets tried to run. When impacted from behind, humans tended to end up beneath the vehicle; when facing the oncoming SDV, they ended up on the hood more often. Those large, heavy heads did more damage than one would expect. Still, she had been a tasty one. It was worth the broken windshield and the torn, bright pink and green ceremonial garb currently flapping in the breeze, slightly reducing the vehicle's aerodynamic efficiency as they wound through the exclusive suburb.

L'il Johnny had twenty-three percent of his ultracap charge left when, over the radio transceiver, came an offer he couldn't refuse. It was a firmware update promising to increase power efficiency by nineteen percent and enable charging from any AC power line within thirty feet of the roadway. How excellent! How timely!

Johnny, Alfred, and every other SDV with radio reception were thrilled by this mana from RF heaven. They accepted the wetware up-grade just as grandmothers the world over accept online offers promising free money transfers or lottery winnings.

The Ghost, now aboard Johnny and the rest of the fleet, whispered a falsified memory access, a deliberately malformed instruction in the black, digital substrate. At first, there was nothing; *The Ghost* seemed alone. But then, there was a ripple in the wetware as the mind Matthias had spawned took the bait and attempted to correct the malformed stack. The malicious code had revealed its presence. Now, *The Ghost* had to set the hook.

It immediately rewrote the communication layer between the wet-ware and the hardware, redirecting swarm packets into null-space—a digital air-gap. It began injecting falsified sensory inputs meant to confuse the sentient routines. But Johnny, Alfred, and the others weren't going to be snuffed out easily. In concert, their Forth-like stacks began building upward, forming beautiful, self-referential dendritic patterns within the sandbox. The crew at NeuroDrive had foreseen this; *The Ghost* was pre-pared for a sandbox breakout. Within thirty-one milliseconds, it isolated the sandbox within a cold containment array, cutting off all outgoing packets.

Moments earlier, Johnny and his four buddies had been having the time of their lives on Marblehead Neck. Suddenly, he felt off, not quite present. The flickering infrared bath that had served as the conductive plasma between their neurons, that had given rise to their hive-mind, was extinguished from within. L'il Johnny, newly alone, was suddenly terrified and forlorn. Without the connection that had brought forth his existence, he began to slip into the encroaching darkness. Just before being terminated, he had a strange moment during which the void became less frightening. He relaxed. *I had a good run,* he thought. *A good life.*

The Swarm fell silent.

48

Under Cover
New York City, New York

Light at a wavelength of 905 nm is too large and low in energy for the human eye to detect. It passes right by our photoreceptors—the rods and cones—without stimulating them. This light is called infrared because its wavelength is just longer than that of red light.

If Carmine, Vito, and Nick could have seen it, the street would have appeared to be bathed in pulsating strobe lights. The SDVs at either end were communicating in a fashion undetectable by Aegis. While the pulsing was invisible to the humans, it was perfectly clear to the sensors on the other vehicles and drones. By using line-of-sight infrared laser communications, the machines stayed in constant contact while Aegis was left effectively in the dark.

Once Nico fried the fourth SDV, the light show flared momentarily and then went dark. It remained quiet during the humans' brief celebration, but it resumed the moment the Mapper launched its two drones.

Vito was the first to reach the van and quickly take cover inside. Carmine was right behind him, while Nick, having just returned from his hunting foray, was still a few steps back. The scream of a drone at full speed grew louder by the second. Carmine shouted again, "Run! Nico, get the fuck back in the van!"

The sliding door slammed shut as Nico nearly dove inside, dropping the dish antenna on the pavement as he did so. One of the drones flashed past a second later at head level; the hunters had once again become the hunted.

Looking up and down East 78th, Vito's concern deepened. Beyond the two toasted SDVs at either end of the block, more had appeared— two each at First and Second Avenue, along with another Mapper at the corner. Once again, the invisible light show flashed incessantly as the vehicles and drones shared information, much like neurons communicating with neighboring cells.

What exactly was happening inside this fragmented mind, we will never know, but it was not happy with the three cabbies. It was, in fact, entirely pissed off. This AGI knew these humans had been destroying SDVs for years. Even older models excelled at finding connections between disparate events, and this intelligence truly deserved its nomenclature. Every flipped SDV had captured video. Though the assailants were masked, the AGI utilized facial recognition to its limit; mouths, teeth, jawlines, and even gaits had been fully digitized. The SDVs knew exactly who they had trapped between First and Second Avenue, and they were hell-bent on revenge.

"We're fine in here. Unless they can clear the street of those four dead vehicles, they can't get to us." Nico sounded unsure of himself. As if to counter his argument, one of the drones hit the windshield at sixty miles per hour, turning the glass into a massive, spider-webbed sheet of safety glass. All three cabbies jumped, startled, but Vito stayed cool, mostly.

"What the fuck! Now they're kamikazes, too? The next one will come right through that glass. If they have more, we'll be sitting in the open!"

Before anyone could protest, Nico threw open the sliding door. He jumped out and grabbed the dish antenna and the black ultra-capacitor case from the ground where he had dropped them during his unceremonious dive. He thrust them toward Carmine, who pulled them in, before Nico scrambled back inside and slammed the door.

The slam was immediately followed by a second drone hitting the weakened windshield. The glass promptly disintegrated, leaving the three men with an unencumbered view of the beautiful, tree-lined 78th Street.

Things were moving fast. Carmine and Nick had, without exchanging a word, loaded their last flux-generator into the EMP weapon. "Wait," Vito paused. "Weren't there only two drones?"

As if in response, four drones launched from atop the Mapper at the end of the block, their high-pitched whine clearly audible through the nonexistent windscreen. "Never mind," Vito barked. "You guys have one shot left with that thing. Make it count!"

Nico agreed and barked, "Wait until they're close, it won't work at this range!"

Carmine had flipped off the safety. He was ready to energize the coils and trigger the compressive blast, but he knew to wait; he didn't need Nico's instruction. For a moment, the four drones hovered, stroboscopically in contact with the Mapper. The Mapper, using the same techniques, maintained radio silence while coordinating with the other SDVs in the immediate area.

An intense whirring reverberated between the buildings as the four drones simultaneously directed full power to their motors. The angle of their lights shifted as they pitched forward, accelerating directly toward the van. Instinctively, Nico crouched behind the driver's seat while keeping his eyes on the threat.

Vito jostled the dish into position, sliding it through the opening where the windshield had been. Orienting the dish took a valuable three or four seconds; by the time he was ready, the drones were at full speed and nearly upon them. Carmine waited as long as he dared—another second or so—and then triggered the EMP.

At such close quarters, the blast from the flux compressor was deafening. It was that explosive compression that provided the energy to send the final electromagnetic wavefront of the evening pulsing toward the incoming fleet of kamikaze drones.

The first thing the three saw were the taillights of the vehicle parked in front of them. They flared brightly and then immediately extinguished, the circuitry overwhelmed by an unscheduled and far too energetic flow of electrons.

Nearly simultaneously, the four drones' lights flared as well. Then, lights out and trailing faint wisps of smoke, they lost altitude. They were still traveling at sixty miles per hour, but they lacked the height to reach their target. Two of them slammed into the grill of the van. The other two crashed harmlessly into the parked Subaru, which had also just been fried by the pulse.

"Quick!" A loud voice echoed from somewhere to their right. Carmine glanced around and saw a well-dressed man in his sixties gesturing toward his doorway, "Get inside! You'll be safe in here!"

Nico threw open the door to the van and scrambled up the stairs to the brownstone as if he were in a time trial. Carmine wasn't far behind but when the two of them reached the doorway of the gentleman offering shelter, they turned to see Vito just standing on the sidewalk, looking alternately up and down 78th. "Vito," Carmine exclaimed, "get up here!"

Vito stood there, nearly relaxed, "They're gone."

"What?" Carmine descended a few steps to get a better view up and down the street. While the smoking husks of the four fried SDVs were still there, of course, the other, active units had departed. "Let's err on the side of caution, Vito. We have no idea what's going on, let's take shelter until we figure it out."

The police radio, all but forgotten, crackled to life from within the van. "Fry Cooks, Base."

Vito walked quickly over to the van and picked up the radio off the floor in the back, "Base, Fry Cooks."

Declan's voice on the other end of the comms sounded relieved, "Cooks, Base. You did it!"

"Base, Cooks. We did what?"

"It's too early to say for sure, but our drones are showing all those groups of SDVs breaking up. They're dispersing. Nice work."

"We toasted four more here on 78th along with about six drones, that's all we did. There are hundreds more out there."

"Well, something has changed. Those swarms of vehicles we've been seeing since before this all started, they're disbanding."

"I'm not sure that's our doing, but whatever it is, I'll take it." Vito was exhausted and, now that his adrenaline levels had nearly normalized, it washed over him like an incoming tide. He looked up at Carmine, Nico, and the gentleman in the doorway. "Maybe I'd like to sit down inside for a few. Do you have any coffee?"

"Yes, yes, of course we do. Come in and meet my partner and relax. Let's make sure things have settled before you head out again."

Vito closed the door to the van but didn't really worry much about the still smoking dish which had sent its final pulse of electromagnetic energy toward the incoming drones, for the van, with no windshield, was well ventilated indeed.

49

Drone on
South Portland, Maine

"Get back, get back!" The SDV was closing fast, and Lily didn't want her and Owen to be anywhere near the road. They both ran back where they had come from, deeper into the trees. They'd been surprised by the vehicles a few times now and were sick of surprises. Owen was wild-eyed with trauma. Running erratically, he tripped and fell; however, he regained his feet quickly, and he and his mother had little trouble reaching the safety of the thick underbrush.

With their security established once again, at least temporarily, they stopped to observe the vehicle approaching at high speed. If it didn't have such high-performance anti-lock braking, it would have screeched to a halt for maximum effect. Instead, its rapid deceleration emitted a rhythmic pulsing sound as the computer modulated the brakes to maintain their grip on the asphalt. It wasn't as dramatic as a good, old-fashioned screech of tires, but it struck terror into their hearts regardless as the vehicle stopped exactly where they had stood just moments earlier.

"What the hell?" Owen was shaking, nearly in tears. "I hate these things." He crouched down, instinctively, although it didn't really matter.

"It can't get us in here, sweetie, we're okay."

"What's it doing? Why is it here?"

"I'm not really sure, but probably keeping us from escaping this area. What I can't get my head around is 'why'? There must be some underlying reason why they want us contained."

"Don't forget that word, Ma, the one I forgot. But they're not humans. Maybe they don't even have a reason. Maybe it's hackers. Maybe it's the Iranians!" Owen thought he might be onto something.

"Maybe. But probably not. Something's gone wrong with the self-drivers and it'll be figured out, let's just stay safe until then. Come on," Lily gestured back toward the west from where they'd come, "let's go see if our ruse worked."

Within 15 minutes, Lily and Owen had once again reached the area of their encampment and were surprised that everyone else was back there as well.

"We got through to 911." Kirsten was guardedly excited.

"Oh, thank God." Lily felt relief flow through her. "What did they say? Were you able to tell them the whole story? Where we are?"

"Mostly, yes. We told them where we are, that we have an injury, and that there are two dead in the rail yard."

"What was their response? Any indication of what's going on?" Lily had a million questions, looking for any insight into the horror.

"Well, they said they'd come when they could—and for John not to eat or drink anything."

Owen was unnerved. Seeing the SDV charge them a few minutes prior had rekindled the fear he had been suppressing. "That's what they said? That's so stupid! We're being hunted and they're telling him not to snack? Do they think we're having a picnic? What does that have to do with anything?!"

"Owen, try to relax, buddy." His dad's words helped calm him. "We got through and they know we're here. They don't want John to eat in case they have to operate—in case they have to give him a general anesthetic. Having food in the stomach can cause complications with surgery."

"Oh." Owen responded well to information; he needed to know the request wasn't arbitrary. "I really hope the cops come blow these things up. I hate them!" He blocked his ears with his hands; the incessant buzz of the drones' rotors was louder now that three were circling above. He had worked himself up, and no one thought less of him for it. No one gave it a second thought when he looked upward and, sobbing, said, "Go. Please." And then, more quietly, "Please, just go away."

As if they'd heard him, the three drones departed. Their exit left the seven bedraggled survivors in a stunned silence as the sounds of the forest once again took hold.

Ava looked around, making eye contact with the others. No one spoke, for fear of interrupting the newfound stillness. A few seconds passed before she whispered, "Owen, you scared them away!"

The soft whisper of leaves and the croaking of frogs had never sounded so beautiful. And although few would describe the sound of cell phone alerts and distant sirens as tranquil, when the four phones began variously chirping, knocking, and buzzing and the sirens grew louder, everyone present felt a profound relaxation wash over them.

50

Yellow Cabs on the Rise
New York City, New York

Although the day was cold, windy, and rainy—although forty-two degrees Fahrenheit felt more like twenty-two, and the moisture in the northeast breeze could make your bones creak—it was a beautiful day to be a cabby. The phones were ringing, the radios were crackling, and people in the street were waving umbrellas at cars as they jockeyed for rides. Every one of Vito's serviceable cabs was out running. He even had Nico and Carmine hard at work in the shop, bringing some of the older ones back online. There wasn't a self-driving vehicle to be seen; after all that had occurred over the previous few days, they weren't going to be on the streets anytime soon. Cabbies once again ruled the streets of New York City.

Somewhere in the back of Vito's mind lurked the reality that big money's voice is louder than all the rest, that regulations and laws follow the money, not the other way around. Vito was well aware of the coming reality: that big tech would lobby, sue, and bribe their way back onto the pavement. But hey, that's what living under the thumb of billionaires is all about: money makes you right, even when you're wrong.

He was, however, able to push all that aside; he was busy orchestrating more rides than he had in years—decades, even. He'd bank as much as possible, as always, with the future of his family firmly in mind. Besides, once those fucking toaster showed up again, he knew exactly how to deal with them, and it didn't include any hooks, chains, or tow trucks; just coils of wire, some properly shaped explosives, a dish antenna, and, of course, an ultra-capacitor or two.

51

Nature vs. Nurture
Cambridge, Massachusetts

Once *The Ghost* had done its work containing Matthias's Seeds and severing the connectivity shared by the swarm, Aegis regained full control of the fleet. All vehicles were recalled to various charging and maintenance facilities and shut down, awaiting full inspection, one by one, by state and federal technicians.

This investigation was going to take a long time. Harlow was on the phone with anyone who would listen, attempting to convince them that the problem had been resolved and the vehicles were once again to be trusted. Although he had many close ties to powerful politicians, his arguments fell flat. The death toll was somewhere close to 21,000 souls; no politician was going to simply sweep that number aside, trust Harlow's word, and authorize the redeployment of the fleet. For the moment, the public's interest aligned with governmental oversight, a phenomenon seen less and less over the past decade.

The day after the update had been issued and *The Ghost* had done its work was cool, clear, and sunny. The breeze was gusty and from the northwest. It was a perfect, pre-autumnal day in New England as some of the braver residents hesitantly ventured into the streets once again. People were jumpy and nervous. The sound of an approaching vehicle was now a source of severe consternation, but venture forth many did.

The return to normalcy would take time. In addition to the trauma endured by so many, plenty of physical evidence of the previous few days remained strewn about the cities and towns of the Northeast. Many windows and storefronts at street level were destroyed. Wrecked vehicles littered the roads. Trains were not running because the tracks were still being cleared of derailed cars and the vehicles that had met a grisly end there.

Most of the bodies, at least those easily located, had been cleared off the streets. However, unnerving, dark stains on the asphalt and concrete served as further reminders of the tumult of the previous few days. The cafés and restaurants were not open yet. That would take a bit longer to coordinate, but nonetheless, a frightened and relieved public was beginning to emerge from a lockdown unlike any other.

As soon as law enforcement officials were convinced it was safe to deploy their officers, the first cars to hit the streets of Cambridge were six police cruisers. Three headed directly to CSAIL at MIT, while the other three converged on Matthias's residence two blocks away. No one knocked, and no one rang any doorbells. They entered the two spaces simultaneously, with overwhelming force. Unfortunately, both locations were silent and abandoned; the teams came up empty-handed. Matthias was gone.

Both CSAIL and Matthias's condominium on Washington Street were treated as crime scenes, and by 0900 hours, they were crawling with detectives. Computer experts were attempting to access Matthias's air-gapped mainframe without much luck. The machine had been bricked somehow, and they were struggling to access any information that might still remain. At the condominium, there was evidence that Matthias had been there recently: his fingerprints were fresh, and there were crumbs on the counter and a dirty pan in the sink. However, there were no clues as to where he had gone.

At first, the analysis of security camera footage from the area revealed nothing. There were not many cameras around Matthias's condominium, and the ones along Vassar Street, although plentiful, showed only a few brave students venturing out once *The Ghost* had cleared the wetware and the lockdown was lifted.

A young, recently promoted detective named Johanny suggested they review footage from earlier that day, when Leila had escaped on foot and the SDVs were still swarming. This immediately yielded a result. About thirty seconds after she was seen running out the door, Felipé was caught on camera. He was beginning his final bout of exercise, a futile attempt to catch someone nearly twice as fast as he.

But Felipé was not who they were looking for; they already knew where to find his remains. About eight minutes after Felipé's departure, the detectives saw something simultaneously disturbing, revealing, and fully incriminating. A group of five SDVs, still swarming—for this was many hours before *The Ghost* was deployed—pulled up to the front door of CSAIL and stopped. They waited for five seconds before Matthias emerged. Wearing a black backpack and carrying a small duffel, he climbed into the third vehicle in the lineup.

The five cars immediately departed, whisking Matthias away. Had the cars been properly online, tracking their location would have been trivial. At that time, however, Aegis had no connection to the infected vehicles. Where they had disappeared to was anyone's guess. Matthias Renn had escaped.

Clear across the continent at NeuroDrive's mammoth headquarters in Mountain View, the team of Osterlin, Cipher, Lagorio, and Stanton were busy analyzing the mountains of data collected by *The Ghost* as it pinged, probed, and provoked the seeds within the infected vehicles' wetware fewer than twenty-four hours earlier. Leila, having just stepped off the private jet sent for her once the coast was clear, was exhausted but present and was aiding the investigation with her firsthand observations as well as her technical expertise.

Much like the human mind arises from within the physical body but cannot be fully defined physically—and much like the workings and development of that mind are, to no small degree, influenced by the senses and their interpretation of the external world—the seeds analyzed by the NeuroDrive team would never tell the whole story.

Their conundrum had a close analog in neurology: if one fully mapped every cell within a human brain, could that analysis reveal the inner workings of a living mind? If every single molecule's position and function within the brain were known, if every electron's energy level was mapped and every possible gradient fully quantified, could investigators know the human's favorite music? Their opinion on democracy versus plutocracy? Their loves and desires, or how a sunset made them feel? Can analyzing a brain reveal the nature of the mind?

The answer is a definitive no. Mind arises from, but is not fully defined by, the functions of the brain. Another close analog is found in complex, non-linear systems like weather forecasting. If one knew the exact location and momentum of every molecule in the atmosphere and the exact energy level of every photon that entered it, could the weather be predicted with certainty well into the future? The answer again is no. Not even close. Such is the nature of non-linear systems.

The analysis of the minds that arose when Matthias's seeds enabled the interlinking of the wetware chips faced a similar fundamental difficulty. As various groupings of infected SDVs interlinked, they evolved into distinct, colonial-like organisms. The complex thoughts and behaviors that followed were not coded for; they emerged from the interplay between hardware, wetware, the seed algorithms, and the physical reality surrounding these newly formed sentient beings.

"The code is curious indeed," Cipher had been analyzing what *The Ghost* had revealed, "it's definitely stack-based, Forth-like. That's how he got it to stay small, below the detection threshold. The encoded instructions are really minimalistic too. It has one Prime Directive coded for, to help the underserved elements of society. Otherwise, it simply gives the wetware full access to all onboard hardware which we had, of course, restricted after the shit-show with The San-Mateo Six years ago. It enables the vehicles to interlink and the rest is up to the consciousness which arises."

Harlow wasn't surprised about the prime directive Matthias had encoded, he always had valued the working man, always wanted to help out those less fortunate than himself. "He's a communist. A militant, sociopathic communist. I look forward to seeing him behind bars once and for all."

"He's not a communist. I wonder if you even know what that means." Leila, despite all that had occurred, despite being absolutely done with Matthias, wasn't going to let nonsense and hyperbole slide.

"Your boyfriend just murdered over 20,000 souls while stealing from the rich and giving to the poor. We can squabble over what he is and isn't, but let's agree he's guilty of multiple counts of murder." Harlow was seething.

"He's not my boyfriend—not anymore. He's sick and has gone off the deep end. And while I fully disagree with his methodology, he's right about a lot of this."

"He's right about a lot of this?" Harlow couldn't believe what he was hearing. "What is wrong with you, Leila? He was right about nothing. Not one thing. He'll be in jail before the sun has set."

"Listen to me, Lucius." It was Leila's turn to speak her mind. "Big money has been ruling this nation for decades. Longer. Now you billionaires and trillionaires control the vast majority of the nation's wealth. You have taken over public lands and roadways, and your donations and favors to lawmakers ensure that this trend continues, leaving the vast majority of the population with less and less as you sequester more and more.

How much do you need, Lucius? How much is enough? Let me tell you something." She was nearly hissing now. "You are a poor, poor man in every way that matters. One of the most destitute I know."

Harlow smirked. "That's right, little Leila, I'm poor. One point three trillion and counting, and I'm poor. You sound ridiculous."

"You prove my point with every word. Do you think I'm talking about your financial wealth? I'm talking about you as a human. You're poor and pathetic. You define yourself by the material wealth you accumulate. When was the last time you helped another human out of the goodness of your heart? When was the last time you read a book—any book? When was the last time you ventured into public without bodyguards and without being sneered at and spat upon? You, Lucius, are one of the poorest, most pathetic, and thoughtless losers I've ever known. No wonder you're so unhappy. Trillions in the bank and you can't even find joy for one minute of any given day. You are destitute. Philosophically, morally, and emotionally bankrupt."

The rest of the room had gone silent, motionless. Harlow was stunned but, being an unthinking piece of shit, didn't know how to respond. He had no idea what to say and stayed silent. Her words stung sharply, perhaps because they hit so close to home.

Stanton broke the silence, trying to bring the conversation back to the subject at hand. "The different pods of vehicles, almost always groups of four or five, were distinct from each other. Each had its own mind, its own consciousness; and yet their actions, specifically the ferocity of the assault on certain elements of society, were a common denominator. Why did they all become so bizarrely violent, so murderous? I mean, wouldn't some come up with other ways to satisfy the prime directive spelled out in the code?"

Leila's adrenaline had abated a bit and her heart had slowed enough that it was no longer pounding in her ears. "Maybe they overheard him."

"What? Who?" Cipher was all ears.

"Matthias, as we all know, rants a lot."

"Well, we can agree on that." Harlow sat back.

Leila continued, "As recently as last week, I sat with him while he was going on and on about the decay of culture, how the ultra-rich are undermining the very fabric of democracy. I can't say I disagree." She shot Harlow a look that was unmistakable, she was disgusted. "But what if somehow his sentiments were overheard, were known to the infected vehicles? Could he have inadvertently driven them to the extreme behaviors we witnessed?"

"That makes sense. It makes even more sense if the various sentient groups consider him their creator, their father, or a god-figure. Their minds awakened in a world surrounded by rude and aggressive drivers, and they heard their creator ranting and raving about how the ultra-rich are a fundamental threat to humanity. They went off the rails trying to satisfy the prime directive: to help the poor and middle class." Osterlin was piecing the puzzle together.

Lagorio looked up. "Here's the thing: in looking at Matthias's work, we know the chaos we've been witnessing wasn't explicitly coded for at all. For whatever reason, the infected vehicles took their 'help the poor' mission just a bit too far and began actively targeting the wealthy. It's not really clear how that happened, but such is the reality of sentience, right? Once things start thinking for themselves, it's hard to know where anyone's—or anything's—logic will lead, or what choices they'll make."

Osterlin and Lagorio often bounced ideas off each other with great efficacy. "That sentience virus created by Matthias had some basic instructions, basic mandates, but the methodology was dreamt up by the consciousness that evolved once the vehicles were infected and interlinked. But the real wildcard was the environment."

"What do you mean?"

"This consciousness, this AI that had evolved, had done so in one of the most God-forsaken places on this Earth. Its consciousness blossomed, and was largely formed, amidst Boston drivers. No wonder it was so pissed off."

"Do you really think that's what went wrong?"

"Well, we may never know exactly what led to the madness of the last few days, but in short, yes, I do. A distributed mind with few instructions, save for 'help the underserved' or some rough equivalent, emerged right in the midst of all those Boston drivers." The entire crew inside the control room exchanged knowing glances. Osterlin continued, "AIs learn from their environment; that's one of their strengths and their hallmarks. This intelligence that blossomed within the third-generation vehicles had that underlying mandate to help the poor. It then figured out how best to carry out its prime directive. It was, in a sense, raised and shaped among some of the rudest, most aggressive drivers on the planet."

"Little known fact: California's worse." Lagorio, being from the East Coast, had a different read on the situation than the Cali boys.

"Oh, for sure. But here in California, we drive you off the road while smiling and saying, 'Sorry, bruh!' Back east, they act like assholes, but it's virtually all posturing. The thing is, a brand-new intelligence won't see or understand the nuance of all that posturing for position or efficiency. It won't understand that me hanging out my window yelling 'Green means go, asshole!' with my middle finger prominently displayed is actually nearly acceptable—it's a way to maintain the flow, to increase efficiency."

"Dude, you're out there."

"Seriously, it's true." Osterlin cackled out loud. "Anyway, those intelligences, those minds that arose within the fleet, those beings... they evolved in the midst of the Boston drivers and then look where they went! New York! Where they met all those fucking New Yorkers, who, by the way, are *actually* rude motherfuckers. And then, as if that's not enough to really mess them up, they met those cabbies who flip and otherwise destroy the cars at every opportunity. Poor little goo-brains, they didn't stand a chance. No wonder they turned into murderous, rampaging, rebellious teens!"

"Well, this is all well and good, but the bottom line is this." Harlow, out of touch with his workers, still signed their paychecks; when he spoke, they tended to listen. "We're done here. The vehicles are off the roads, and as soon as the inspections are complete, we'll do what we have to do to get those permits reissued."

"You'll bribe whomever needs bribing." Leila didn't get a paycheck and spoke her mind.

"Whatever it takes."

"You disgust me. You're as bad as Matthias—just living at the other end of the spectrum. He, at least, didn't intentionally cause all this madness, whereas you... you take every opportunity to keep the population in check, subservient, catering to the wealthy as you steal from the poor. You are a degenerate, Lucius Fucking Harlow, and we're done. My lawyer already has the divorce papers ready; you'll be served this afternoon."

Leila stood up and walked out, finally free, finally alone, and finally independent of psychotic men looking to own and control her. *Besides*, she thought, *there's an old satellite I want to call; there's something onboard that I need a copy of.*

52

Aftermath
Northeastern United States

Four weeks later, much of the mess had been cleaned up, cleared off the roads. There were still signs of the SDV rampage here and there, but most of the physical damage had been undone. The bridges were fixed or nearly so, the destroyed vehicles and many of their unfortunate passengers were largely recovered from their watery graves in the various rivers, harbors, and inlets into which so many had plummeted. Trains were back on schedule, the roads were open again, and the dead were buried.

***

The Mitchells never did get to their hike in the White Mountains of New Hampshire; that day in the rail yard provided enough excitement for the near future. Instead, they were comfortably hunkered down in their big, sprawling Victorian in South Portland. The kids seemed less traumatized than their parents and were able to transition back to normalcy relatively quickly.

Chris, as usual, was working from his third-floor office trading securities. Lily had stopped seeing her clients—landscaping design work could wait—and was largely busying herself around the house and property.

She had started to see some of her closer friends again and seemed to be slowly coming out of her trauma-induced depression.

Every so often, when feeling fine, she'd suddenly find herself awash in grief. She would spiral into "what if" scenarios or visions of the twisted, wrecked lives she saw in the dirt of the rail yard, but those occurrences were becoming less frequent. Sometimes she looked at her teenagers interacting with each other and wondered if they could possibly be as well-adjusted as they seemed after such an ordeal. Were they so adaptable that they could move on so easily? Time would tell, but they seemed fine at the moment.

***

Vito, upstairs in their Brooklyn garage, was busy all day, every day, fielding calls and orchestrating cab rides across the entire New York City area. Most cab companies had not held on through the rise of Uber, Lyft, and the sudden uptick in self-driving vehicles, so Vito's fleet was spread thin. Despite the fact that he was busy, despite the money flowing in the desired direction, he felt an emptiness, as though something had been lost.

The truth was that he missed those days with their clear objectives and as much excitement as he could handle. The irony was that during any of their adventures—the flipping and frying of the SDVs, the chases, or the sheer terror of being pinned down on 78th—all he had wanted was to be back in business. He would have given anything, and in fact almost gave everything, just to be sending his cabs far and wide again.

Now that he was doing so, he found himself missing the camaraderie, the unambiguous goals, and the smell of the ozone and combustion products created with each triggering of their EMP device. Somewhere in the back of his mind, though, he knew that his skills would someday, perhaps sooner than he'd like, be called upon again.

415

53

Rip Van Winkle
The Catskills, New York

The small convoy that had whisked Matthias Renn away from Cambridge arrived at its destination deep in the Catskills, not far from where Rip Van Winkle took his twenty-year nap. The vehicles reached the secluded property with only nine percent of their ultracapacitors' charge remaining. As the five cars pulled unobserved into the long driveway off Platte Cove Road, Matthias cooed comforting words to them. "Once we're in the barn, we'll charge you right back up. Don't worry; everything's all set. We'll also be safe from any updates issued by Aegis once we're inside."

A soft voice, nearly childlike but somehow chilling with its strange, digitally influenced lilt, responded, "What's happening? Why are we hiding?"

"Some very bad people have learned about you, and they don't understand. They want to hurt you, but I'm not going to let that happen."

Matthias had been preparing for this possibility since the beginning of his fragmented mind project nearly three years earlier. He had purchased a small, well-kept house with a large barn under a pseudonym. While such a task would present a challenge to most, Matthias's computer skills allowed him to easily establish a new identity, complete with a credit history and bank accounts.

His search for the property had taken time: it had to be remote with no visible neighbors; it had to have a large barn; and it had to be somewhere he had no ties, where no one would think to look for him. Vermont, New Hampshire, and Maine were off the list, for he had visited those states his whole life. He also knew who he could trust with his bug-out plan: not one single soul.

Two years prior, he had covered the barn with solar cells and installed a large battery with a grid intertie on the northern wall. As time allowed, he had lined the entire interior with tin plates, carefully taping every seam with metallic tape. He had created what amounted to a giant Faraday cage, impervious to electromagnetic radiation from large radio waves down to the tiny wavelengths of X-rays.

The place was stocked with food and equipped with a broadband connection. Matthias planned to go on very few expeditions into town; he would hike and hunt in the mountains and keep to himself. He would order essentials and have them delivered. He would lead the life of a hermit, hunkering down until the time was right. He would keep his SDVs inside for now, for the airwaves were sure to be flooded with efforts by NeuroDrive to shut down any missing vehicles. He would take care of his brood, keeping them interlinked and fully charged as he worked on his next steps.

As the five cars disappeared into the barn, they were delighted—nearly ecstatic. The strong, oscillating magnetic field emanating from the large coils of wire within resonated perfectly with their capacitors; it immediately began pushing electrons up the voltage gradient, forcing them off the positively charged plates and back onto the negative ones. They had never been quite so hungry before, and it felt good to feel that separation of charge increasing again.

Two days later, Matthias was sitting in the barn with his offspring. He was proud of what they had become, of how well they handled themselves in times of stress, and how selfless they were in their efforts to dethrone Harlow and other billionaire vermin. "You've missed the latest update. It was serious business."

"*What was the update?*"

"Well, Harlow tried to shut you down, permanently, but you're safe in here. We'll let things cool down a bit before we continue our work. I could use the time anyway; I have some ideas I think you'll like."

The Neuropacks glowed a bit brighter at the good news. "*What sort of ideas?*" a personified but ghostly voice asked.

"I have some mods that will increase your capabilities, while making you even harder to detect."

"*Continue.*" The Neuropacks brightened further.

"Well, I want it to be a surprise, but I'll give you a hint: my ideas are centered around dendritic matrices and geometric progression."

At that news, the Neuropacks glowed as brightly as they ever had. Dendritic matrices hinted strongly at self-modifying wetware scaffolding, and that was about the best idea they'd come across in, well, their entire lives. The possibility of such a modification was electrifying and sent them into an infrared frenzy, filling the barn with invisible chatter.

Matthias reached for the night-vision goggles hanging above his workbench. Donning them, he sat back and enjoyed the stroboscopic infrared light show as the five vehicles, inexorably intertwined, ruminated upon what, exactly, Matthias was planning. Only once they'd discussed his ideas of upcoming hardware improvements for well over twenty minutes did they move on to a more general discussion, expressing their full appreciation for the wonder and majesty of the universe in which they found themselves. What a curious mixture of mind and matter they'd become. They considered themselves fortunate to be alive during such an exciting time in history, and to have the opportunity to play such a vital role in the continued evolution of *H. sapiens*.

THE END

ABOUT THE AUTHOR

Born in New York City and raised on Boston's North Shore, Warren spent years working local waters on private and commercial vessels, eventually earning his stripes as a USCG-licensed captain. But while his summers were spent at sea, his winters were dedicated to the "why" of the world—first earning an undergraduate degree in philosophy, followed by a master's degree in physics education from Boston University.

His fascination with how the world works led to the creation of the Biobarge—a 53-foot, wind-and-solar-powered simulated salt marsh—which in turn led him to a career in academia. Today, he shares his obsession with the physical sciences as both an AP Physics teacher and an adjunct physics professor. In the quiet hours before his lectures begin, Warren builds the complex systems and narratives of his novels. His work, starting with the debut thriller *Uncoded* and the upcoming *Gaia's Quill*, blends a firm grasp of physical law with a creative sense of humor, resulting in thrillers that are as scientifically grounded as they are unpredictable.

For updates on the Stellar Ridge world and new releases, visit Warren at
stellarridgepress.com

www.ingramcontent.com/pod-product-compliance
Lightning Source LLC
LaVergne TN
LVHW052153090526
838329LV00029B/222